Praise for the
Always the Bridesmaid

"A charming, rollicking commentary on weddings in the twenty-first century. I loved the Jane Austen-ish heroine, Cate Padgett, for her untiring fidelity to the whims of her bride-brained buddies."

—*New York Times* bestselling author Jeanne Ray

"[Lyles's] eye for the delightful details . . . makes this the ultimate bridesmaid gift." —*Publishers Weekly*

"The outlandish wedding mishaps and twentysomething angst will appeal to fans of the plucky-single-girl genre." —*Booklist*

"Talented newcomer Lyles has written a compulsively readable novel. Her descriptive gifts transport readers to the single girl's San Diego, with its beaches, bars, and bistros. In fact, reading this book feels deliciously like having a good gossip over lunch with your own best friend." —*Romantic Times*

"This gal has one hilarious fling after the other." —*Cosmopolitan*

"Phenomenally entertaining. The pace of the story is perfect."
—*The Romance Reader's Connection*

"Quite entertaining . . . [an] amusing charmer."
—*Midwest Book Review*

"Written in savvy style . . . displays clever wit and a handful of priceless scenes." —FictionFactor.com

Here Comes the Bride

Whitney Lyles

BERKLEY BOOKS, NEW YORK

THE BERKLEY PUBLISHING GROUP
Published by the Penguin Group
Penguin Group (USA) Inc.
375 Hudson Street, New York, New York 10014, USA
Penguin Group (Canada), 90 Eglinton Avenue East, Suite 700, Toronto, Ontario M4P 2Y3, Canada
(a division of Pearson Penguin Canada Inc.)
Penguin Books Ltd., 80 Strand, London WC2R 0RL, England
Penguin Group Ireland, 25 St. Stephen's Green, Dublin 2, Ireland (a division of Penguin Books Ltd.)
Penguin Group (Australia), 250 Camberwell Road, Camberwell, Victoria 3124, Australia
(a division of Pearson Australia Group Pty. Ltd.)
Penguin Books India Pvt. Ltd., 11 Community Centre, Panchsheel Park, New Delhi—110 017, India
Penguin Group (NZ), Cnr. Airborne and Rosedale Roads, Albany, Auckland 1310, New Zealand
(a division of Pearson New Zealand Ltd.)
Penguin Books (South Africa) (Pty.) Ltd., 24 Sturdee Avenue, Rosebank, Johannesburg 2196,
South Africa

Penguin Books Ltd., Registered Offices: 80 Strand, London WC2R 0RL, England

This is a work of fiction. Names, characters, places, and incidents either are the product of the author's imagination or are used fictitiously, and any resemblance to actual persons, living or dead, business establishments, events, or locales is entirely coincidental. The publisher does not have any control over and does not assume any responsibility for author or third-party websites or their content.

Copyright © 2006 by Whitney Lyles.
Cover design by Annette Fiore.
Cover photo by Nonstock Picture Arts.
Text design by Kristin del Rosario.

PRINTING HISTORY
Berkley trade paperback edition / July 2006

Berkley trade paperback ISBN: 0-425-21130-4

Library of Congress Cataloging-in-Publication Data

Lyles, Whitney.
    Here comes the bride / Whitney Lyles. — Berkley trade pbk. ed.
       p. cm.
    ISBN 0-425-21130-4 (pbk.)
    1. Brides—Fiction. 2. Weddings—Fiction. I. Title.

PS3612.Y45H47 2006
813'.6—dc22

          2006040737

PRINTED IN THE UNITED STATES OF AMERICA

10 9 8 7 6 5 4 3 2 1

For my grandparents,
Annie and Sugar,
who celebrated sixty-one beautiful years
of love in marriage

Acknowledgments

I am forever grateful to Leona Nevler for all her wisdom and guidance in shaping this novel. I feel very blessed to have worked with her to completion on this book as well as my first two books. I always felt that Leona was looking out for me, and I'm sure she continues to do the same for many of us now. She will be greatly missed as an editor and a friend.

Thanks to Tova Sacks for picking up the reins and guiding the book forward. It's been a comfort and strength to work with her.

Many thanks to my agent, Sandy Dijkstra, whom I believe was the first person to suggest writing a sequel way back around the birth of *Always the Bridesmaid*. My appreciation for Sandy runs deep, as does my gratitude to the SDLA team, especially Elise Capron and Taryn Fagerness for all their hard work.

Thanks to my parents, grandparents, family, and friends for all their continuous support.

Endless thanks to my husband, Rob Dodds, for pulling through with many late-night readings and suggestions.

Author's Note

I felt compelled to include this note because of all the questions I always get about my novels. I am continuously surprised when someone laughs and says something to the effect of, "I can't believe what happened to *you* in chapter fifteen! Did that really happen to you?" Me? Honestly, no.

While I often rely on places and landmarks that I'm familiar with for research, my characters are a product of my wild imagination. Truth be known, my heroines lead much more interesting lives than my own.

Due to the convenience of research, I included a few venues from my own wedding in this novel. However, the characters and all the events surrounding Cate Padgett's wedding are a work of pure fiction. I am lucky to be blessed with a wonderful family, great in-laws, and loyal friends.

Part One

Everyone's Gone Mad

·1·
Y-E-S

Cate lifted the top of the small box. Never would she have expected to get engaged in Joe's Crab Shack. She could not recall a happier moment of her life as she looked down at Ethan on one knee. She loved him so much. Before she looked at her engagement ring she scanned the sea of faces that watched them, sharing in their once-in-a-lifetime moment. A tear heavy with mascara trickled down an old woman's cheek.

Inside the box she found a silver ring, one that would probably turn her finger green and looked as if it had been constructed with cheap aluminum and a blowtorch in a parking garage. Cloudy with burn marks, it rested on a bed of cotton.

"So will you?" he asked, as he slipped the ring on her finger. It was a little tight, and she made a mental note not to get it wet, so it wouldn't rust. She looked down at Ethan's face while he waited anxiously for her answer.

Oh my God, we're getting married. He was finally asking. It was *re-*

ally happening. The ring was so . . . ? Different from what she would've picked. But the flamboyantly gay waiter at the restaurant loved it.

"What a beautiful ring!" he said, as he walked past, water slopping over the top of his pitcher.

"Just gorgeous!" The old woman added, sobbing now. When the lady reached for a napkin, Cate noticed that her hands were covered in rings, every single finger decorated with turquoise and onyx.

Cate glanced at the engagement ring again. There was no stone, but the letters Y-E-S had been etched into the metal with something sharp, perhaps the tip of a safety pin. The writing was jagged and rough, like a child's. She pulled the ring to her chest and felt instantly sentimental. "Yes! Y-E-S! Of course I'll marry you!"

The restaurant applauded, and when she looked down at her ring finger, it was green. She tried to lift her arm to show it to her audience, but she realized the sling she had over her shoulder wouldn't allow her to move. Her arm was broken. How did that happen?

She tried hard to lift it again, but ended up opening her eyes instead. Her cat, Grease, slept on her shoulder, curled in a warm, soft ball over her arm. He was becoming more affectionate in adulthood. A year ago he would've never slept anywhere near her.

Though she was still groggy, she laughed out loud at her dream. It was the first one she'd had since she'd found a Ben Bridge Jeweler catalogue wedged in between an Egg McMuffin wrapper and a Styrofoam coffee cup in Ethan's Ford Explorer two weeks earlier. *Ethan proposing at Joe's Crab Shack?* She'd never even been to Joe's Crab Shack, and getting engaged in public didn't really seem like him. Then she remembered that the restaurant was located in the same shopping center as a bridal boutique. Funny how the subconscious works.

She glanced at the clock and realized her alarm would beep in a couple of minutes. It was the first official day of summer vacation, her first morning away from being a kindergarten teacher, but she couldn't afford the luxury of sleeping in. She was heading to Mexico for the weekend with Ethan. Their flight from San Diego left at a disturbing six fifty a.m. Since they were going to Playa del Carmen for only a few days they wanted to get there as early as possible on Friday and leave as late as they could on Monday.

Ironically, they were going for someone else's wedding. A couple of Ethan's friends were getting married. This weekend was one of the only weekends that Ethan didn't have a wedding booked for his catering business for the rest of the summer, so they'd use the time for their own little vacation.

Grease's purr was loud when she petted his white fur. She lay next to him for a moment, thinking about her dream. Even awake, she felt a strange sentimental attachment to the ring. It was like when she'd made out with a random and obscure guy in her dreams, then felt strangely attracted to him the next morning. She felt a similar attachment to her ring and Joe's Crab Shack, and she knew it was the kind of dream that would stick with her all day.

Ever since she'd seen the brochure of engagement rings in his car she'd been fantasizing about proposals. However, she tried not to get her hopes up. There was always the possibility that he'd simply been walking through the mall and had politely taken it from some underpaid and totally bored Ben Bridge employee who'd been passing them out. Ethan was so nice he'd never say no. As much as she racked her brain, she couldn't recall him mentioning a trip to the mall. If he'd gone, it was a secret.

She got out of bed and opened the blinds. It was still dark outside, and she could feel crust in her eyes. The temptation to crawl back into bed was overwhelming, but she still had a few things she needed to pack, and Jill would be stopping by before her early morning jog to pick up the key to her apartment.

She walked to the bathroom and nearly tripped over something next to her dresser. She flicked on the light, then looked down at the headless body of the Parisian doll that had been sitting on her dresser for over a decade. The doll had been a gift from her parents after they'd returned from Paris when she was ten. A little old Parisian woman dressed in a long French country skirt and a bonnet. A wise smile had been painted to her face, and she had held a baguette in one hand and a basket of fruit in the other. Cate picked her up. The baguette had been mercilessly ripped from the doll's fingers and lay near the foot of her bed.

"Grease," she mumbled. "You bad cat." He watched her pick up the baguette and flicked his tail.

She went to the kitchen and found the woman's head resting in a watery grave in Grease's water dish. She fished the head out of the bowl and left it to dry on a paper towel while she showered and finished packing. She took a hot shower and dried her hair. She was just shoving her third pair of sandals into her already stuffed suitcase when the doorbell rang.

Jill wore a pink velour jogging suit with black stripes up the side and tennis shoes that had three-inch soles. Her short purple hair stood on end, and she didn't appear tired, considering the time.

"Thanks for taking care of Grease this weekend," Cate said when she greeted her. "I left the hotel phone number in case anything happens. And twenty dollars if you need to buy him more food." It was impossible not to worry about Grease whenever she left town.

He wasn't the type of cat who lounged around in the sun licking his paws and purring when rubbed behind the ears. She suspected that deep down Grease believed he was really a lion trapped inside Cate's cramped little Pacific Beach apartment.

"No worries at all. I'll check on him twice a day, and I'll grab your mail, too."

Cate led her into her tiny kitchen. "So how was your date last night?"

"Oh my gosh. This guy had the worst breath I have ever smelled in my life, and then he made me pay for dinner."

"A real keeper."

"Never again."

"I love the hair," Cate said.

"Do you?" She touched the top of her spiky purple haircut. A hairdresser, Jill spent more time playing with her own hair than she did with clients'. Every other week she had a different hair color. "I think I might dye it back to black. You know, since there might be a wedding coming up . . ." She winked at Cate.

"I don't know about that." She poured them both glasses of orange juice.

"You don't think he'll propose this weekend?"

She'd wondered the same thing a million times since they'd planned the trip, but didn't want to admit it. "We're going to someone else's wedding, and I don't think he would do it with all his friends there. Ethan's pretty private and sentimental."

"Are you kidding? I think it's the perfect setting. My sister just got engaged in Mexico last year. And just think of how romantic weddings are. It's like everyone gets bitten by a wedding bug when they go to one. You can't help but feel the love in the air."

She had a point. Cate could think of a couple of people she knew who'd gotten engaged right after attending a wedding. While they chatted about the weekend Cate looked through the junk drawer in her kitchen for superglue. She found a tube, and Jill helped hold the French-woman's head in place while Cate added some extra glue to the nape of her neck.

"She's scarred for life," Jill said as they looked at the teeth marks on her small forehead.

She now looked crusty and a little banged up. "She looks like a French homeless woman." Cate held the doll in front of them.

"Her basket of fruit is probably in Grease's appendix," Jill said.

"Or maybe she squandered it on alcohol."

She put the doll on top of her refrigerator so Grease couldn't attack her again.

"Well, I guess you won't be able to call me if you get engaged down there."

"I'm just relieved that I finally get to go to a wedding as a guest. Just a plain old guest. I don't have to do one thing except sit in the audience and watch. My bridesmaid days are over!"

Their glasses clinked together as they toasted. "I'll drink to that."

It was only two years ago that Cate had been a bridesmaid four times in one summer. Since then, she'd stood up for a coworker whom she hardly knew and a distant cousin in Alabama who was already five months pregnant.

"Well, don't get too comfortable because I think you'll be heading down the aisle again soon."

"Why? Are you getting married?"

Jill rolled her eyes. "No. You are. Dummy."

"I'm just kidding." She leaned against the countertop, and Grease rubbed his face against the side of her elbow. He always became overly affectionate whenever she was close to his stash of kitty treats. If she'd been standing anywhere else in the house, he probably would've ignored her. "Just don't hold your breath for me. I know Ethan and I will get married someday, but one little brochure doesn't mean anything."

"Oh yes it does. I have a feeling it's coming soon. Very soon." She took the last sip of her juice. "I should get to my jog. But don't forget to say yes! Y-E-S!"

Cate nearly choked on her OJ. It was just like her dream. She debated telling Jill about the ring with Y-E-S etched into it, but figured this would only add more fuel to the wedding fantasy fire already blazing out of control. Jill's comment was pure coincidence.

"Well, try to call me as soon as he proposes!" Jill said. "And I better be a bridesmaid!"

"Is that even a question? Of course you will be."

Ever since Cate had seen that brochure of diamonds she'd indulged in wedding fantasies. Champagne-colored bridesmaids' dresses were part of the picture. Lucky for Jill any color of hair would look good with champagne. After she closed the door she tried to forget about rings and gowns and proposals. Chances were, he wasn't even asking. She decided her time waiting for his arrival would be better spent Grease-proofing her house.

Twenty minutes later she was wondering how Ethan would do it. It didn't seem safe to tote a ring around Playa del Carmen, through the airport and customs. What if the customs agents searched his stuff and she saw the ring? Would he be forced to ask her in the airport, in front of drug-sniffing dogs and a bunch of Mexican customs agents? She imagined the scenario and thought how they would leave the airport, ecstatic. How they would laugh about his spontaneous proposal twenty years from now with their three genius children. Maybe he'd thought of his luggage being searched too and decided it would be safer to ask before they even left, right here in her apartment.

She picked up a bud vase. Grease was obsessed with water and spent most of his time in the bathtub, pawing at the dripping faucet, staring at each drop of water as it plopped out, occasionally attacking the small puddles. Daily, he knocked bud vases over and watched with delight as the water spilled to the ground. Ethan had once shown up with seven tiny bud vases from Crate and Barrel. "These should last you about a week," he said before presenting her with a dozen Vendela roses.

She searched her apartment, emptying bud vases and double-checking for anything filled with liquid that she'd overlooked. Grease followed her to each spot and watched with interest as she removed any possible mischief.

Ethan let himself in just as she was putting the last little vase away. He was due for a haircut. She liked his dark curly hair a little overgrown. His blue eyes always looked a little darker in the morning, and he smelled like Irish Spring. "I'm sure he'll still find something to destroy," he said as he kissed her. "Are you ready?"

"I can't wait. Let me just grab my camera bag." Photography was one of her favorite hobbies. She definitely wasn't going to leave her camera behind when they were going to a foreign country, especially if there was a chance that she might be getting engaged.

She grabbed her bag, then petted Grease one last time. As she locked her door behind them she wondered whether or not they'd be engaged the next time they returned to her apartment. Everything could change this weekend.

It Came Crawling Back

They made it through customs at the Cancun airport without being searched, and every time she looked at his suitcase she couldn't help but wonder if a ring was tucked somewhere inside. What did it look like? Would he pick the same ring she would've picked if they'd looked together? Before they got in the hotel shuttle she made a silent promise to herself that she would forget about rings and proposals for the rest of the trip. She wanted to enjoy the vacation, soak in the warm sun, and hang out with Ethan's friends—not wonder if he was going to get down on one knee in front of every sunset they faced.

Playa del Carmen was an hour from the Cancun airport, and they had to take a shuttle to get to their resort. Inside the hotel van she snuggled up to Ethan's chest and marveled at how he always felt relaxed and warm. He was the warmest person she had ever felt in her life, and when she didn't spend the night with him she felt herself longing for the feel of her cheek resting against his bare chest. It was hard to believe that she'd known him for most of her life and had waited until just a couple years ago to finally fall in love with him. As children they were next-door neighbors, playing Colored Eggs and Statue Maker with the other kids on her block. In high school, his crush on her had been obvious, but something about him had seemed brotherly.

She went off to USD, and Ethan went to culinary school in San Francisco. It wasn't until a couple years ago when she'd run into him at her friend Sarah's wedding that she'd started to have feelings for him.

The long drive, and the feeling of Ethan's warm chest against her face made her sleepy. She felt him kiss her on the forehead before she drifted off to sleep. It seemed like she had just started dreaming when Ethan's body became rigid. His once relaxed chest felt like a block of wood against her face as he straightened up.

"I don't believe it," he said.

"What? What is it?" Wide awake now, she sat up. She expected to find a Mexican drug cartel holding their van at gunpoint. Dear God, she knew they should've never come to Mexico. Just a few days ago a fellow teacher at school had warned her about kidnapping for ransom.

"It's just . . . It's just that . . . Janet's here," he said stiffly.

It took her a second to remember. Janet? Janet of San Francisco? Janet that he'd met at culinary school and traveled to Australia with? She'd been the first woman he'd ever said the "L word" to. Cate had the horrible disadvantage of knowing all these details because they'd been friends first. She remembered running into him around Christmas time several years ago, looking at his skinny frame and stubbled face and wondering if he'd developed a coke problem. She'd heard later, through the grapevine, that he'd just had his heart broken.

Naturally, Cate had other boyfriends before Ethan. She didn't feel threatened by Janet, just a little stung every time she remembered that he'd grown a beard and locked himself in his room for three days after he and Janet had broken up.

Curious, she looked out the window. "Where is she?" She'd only seen one faded and distant picture of her standing on the Great Barrier Reef in a bikini and had always hoped for a better visual of Ethan's first love.

"Right there." He pointed to a cluster of tourists outside the resort.

"You didn't know she was coming?" she asked, trying to figure out which one she was.

"No. No one told me." He sighed. "But whatever, it doesn't matter. I don't really care that she's here. I just feel bad that you have to be in this situation."

She shrugged. She'd hoped to be surprised with an engagement ring instead of Ethan's ex, but she wasn't going to let this ruin the weekend. "It's no big deal," she said, secretly feeling relieved that she'd gone with the sexy black strapless dress for the wedding as opposed to the flowered V-neck she'd almost packed.

"Thanks for being so understanding," he said. "I wouldn't want to hang out with Paul, or whatever the hell that guy's name was that you dated, all weekend." He always referred to her ex that way.

Their driver slid the door open, and Cate caught a glimpse of herself in the rearview mirror as she climbed out of the van. She had marks from the creases on Ethan's shirt embedded in her cheeks, and her blonde bob looked like a mushroom. Riding on airplanes never did much for her, but today she looked as if she'd just come out of a week in solitary confinement. Dark circles clouded her eyes, and her cheeks were as pale as Mexican hominy. She wasn't even out of the van when Janet ran to him like a golden retriever after a Frisbee.

"Ethan! Oh my God!!" Cate watched as a blur of sun-kissed skin and perfectly sculpted arms quickly folded over her boyfriend.

The awkwardness that followed seemed to last as long as their flight had. Cate stood in the background, grinning like an idiot while she waited to be introduced. When Janet let go of Ethan's neck she caught a better glimpse. She was the type of girl that had been blessed with the God-given gift of wearing absolutely no makeup and still looking gorgeous. Her long, silky hair hung to her waist, and she wore an East Indian inspired skirt and a white tank top that revealed the most delicate collarbones that Cate had ever seen. She imagined her drinking a spirulina milkshake and doing Ashtanga Yoga in her hotel room.

"You look GREAT!" Janet said, as she cupped each of Ethan's cheeks lightly with her hands. She rubbed her fingers through his curls. "I love this hair." Then she looked at Cate. "Doesn't he have the greatest hair?" It was obvious by the way his eyes shifted all over the place that he was uncomfortable.

"Yeah," Cate said. "He sure does." They hadn't even been introduced yet.

"Thanks," Ethan said quietly. "You look nice too." Cate knew he was just saying it to be polite. However, it was hard not to wonder what he must think of Cate's fair skin and flat chest next to her. "Janet, this is my girlfriend, Cate. He was wedged in between Janet and their luggage, so Cate had to wave from over his shoulder.

"Ohhhh, how cute," Janet said it as if he had just shown her his new puppy. "It's so nice to meet you, Cate."

How cute? She wasn't five. "It's nice to meet you too. Are you here for the wedding?"

"Yes, I came with Pat and Greg. They let me tag along." She smiled.

"Where *are* Pat and Greg?" he asked. They were good friends of Ethan's, and Cate wondered why they hadn't mentioned that Janet was coming with them. They both knew what Ethan had gone through after the breakup.

"They're at the beach," she said. "I thought I would explore the hotel. And look! I ran into you guys!" She touched his arm.

"Well, hey, it was nice catching up with you." He reached for the suitcase next to him. "But we should probably check in."

"Oh, of course. I can't wait to hang out with you guys tonight at the wedding! Nice meeting you, Cate," she yelled while they wheeled their luggage away.

"She seemed . . . nice." Cate had to say something because the silence felt so awkward.

"Yeah, she's nice," he said.

"I didn't know she was friends with Pat and Greg."

"They were a long time ago, but I guess she's in touch with them again." His eyes looked vacant, and she couldn't tell if he was just quiet because they'd traveled a long distance and they still needed to check in, or if he'd been shaken by running into his ex-girlfriend.

After they checked in she suggested they drop off their luggage and head straight to the pool bar for a drink. After the encounter with Janet she really needed a margarita, and furthermore, they were staying at an all-inclusive resort. Everything was free, so why not take full advantage?

The hotel was a huge maze of peach and turquoise stucco buildings supported by white pillars. It was set just feet from a never-ending stretch of aqua blue ocean, and each building was shaded with thick patches of palm trees and tropical foliage.

They rode to their room in a golf cart, chauffeured by Sven, a German college student working at the resort for the summer. Every once in a while a strange-looking animal resembling a guinea pig with a pronounced butt emerged from the bushes and foraged for berries on the lawn. Sven stopped the cart a couple of times so she could take pictures of the animals. The second she pointed her camera in their direction they moved, so she didn't know how well the pictures would turn out. They heard monkeys screeching from the palm trees above as they continued to their room.

"This is very nice room you have," Sven said. "Very closs to the vater. Only a few rooms this closs."

The room was beautiful. High ceilings. Big peach Spanish tiles. Dual shower heads and a giant basket of fresh fruit.

They tipped Sven, then quickly changed into their suits before heading to the pool. They walked along the beach to get to the pool bar. Cate and Ethan had grown up near the Mexico border, so they knew that there were strange things that could be found only in Mexico. For instance, only in Mexico could you have your picture taken wearing a sombrero atop a decrepit donkey painted as a zebra. Only in Mexico could you offer a police officer a nice smile and a twenty in exchange for waiving a traffic ticket. So as they neared the pool and the music became louder they weren't shocked when they realized that the DJ spinning the techno music by the bar had sampled his song from a cat food commercial.

"Myow, myow, myow, myow." It was the song from the shrill ad where a pack of cats ran to their dish while a cackling meow repeated over and over again in the background.

Ethan looked at her. "It's that cat food song mixed with Paul Oakenfold."

It was rave meets chicken giblets in gravy. Myow, myow, myow, myow. Myow, myow, myow, myow. BOOM.

They found a couple of lounge chairs and she soon realized there were a couple of other odd things at the pool. A large Mexican man dressed as Santa ho-hoed to all the kids. It was a nice plan to keep the children entertained while their parents tried to sunbathe in peace, but the hotel entertainment coordinator had failed to realize that it was the middle of June. She watched as a puzzled child looked up at Saint Nick then grabbed his mother's leg.

She was about to pull her book from her beach bag when she noticed something even more bizarre. A grown man, wearing red lycra tights, a long-sleeved black leotard, shoes similar to ones she'd worn to jazz class in fourth grade, and a long skinny tail pinned to his butt, tip-toed around the pool, sneaking around people as if he were hungry. He would've appeared harmless if it weren't for his painted face and the pointed ears pinned to his head. Long red stripes covered his cheeks, and the whites of his eyes popped from beneath his black pointed eyebrows. He looked like something Stephen King would've conjured up in one of his novels.

"What is that?" Cate asked.

"I don't know. Maybe he's for the kids."

They watched as he tiptoed to a group of tourists, twenty-somethings sipping on daquiris. One of the girls in their group lay on her back, relaxed, knees loosely bent while she read the latest *People*.

Cate watched as Leotard Man crept toward the unsuspecting woman on all fours. The girls' friends looked up at him, and he held a finger to his lips. What was he going to do? Squirt her with a water gun? Snatch her magazine from her hands and perform the Mexican hat dance? Surprise her with a singing telegram in Spanish? They watched as he moved his head toward her face and then stopped within a couple of inches. He was *Cats* meets Michael Jackson's "Thriller" video. He stayed there, his eyes frozen on the innocent, unsuspecting woman while she flipped though her magazine, comfortably savoring the latest celebrity scandals. It probably took her less than a minute to sense a presence next to the right side of her face. She slowly turned her head to the right before screaming louder than Janet Lee and jumping from her lounge chair as if Freddy Krueger were on the loose. Her friends and Leotard Man got a decent laugh, but the victim looked as if she might have to see the hotel doctor for some heart medication.

"If that thing comes anywhere near me, I'm pushing him in the pool." Cate took a firm sip from her drink. "I'm not kidding."

They watched as he moved to the other side of the pool and found a middle-aged man with a tan like George Hamilton as his next victim. He held a cigarette and sat, relaxed, speaking to an equally bronzed woman who appeared to be his wife. The woman saw Leotard Man but heartlessly allowed her husband to continue puffing on his cigarette in his Speedo while the thing leaned in toward his face. Cate had left her camera in the room and would've killed for a shot of this.

The man put out his cigarette and was just starting to turn around when he sprang from his chaise as if a speeding Amtrack were headed his way, fear torturing his once placid features. His wife burst into laughter, and the man played along, laughing like someone who had just been startled to the point of near cardiac arrest but only laughed because he realized he hadn't dropped dead.

"I can't believe the hotel would let that man roam at his free will, scaring the living daylights out of people while on vacation. Why do they do that?"

"I don't know. It's Mexico. But I think it's for amusement. Just to spice things up a little around the pool."

"If you let that thing come near me I would kill you."

"Don't worry. I won't."

She spent the rest of the time by the pool peeking over the ridge of her book and looking over her shoulder every few minutes. The cocktails made her drowsy, but she feared that if she drifted off the Leotard Man would sneak up on her, or worse, that Janet would come crawling back.

· 3 ·

The Wedding Bug

"So tell me about Lance and Melanie again," she said while she applied lipstick. She was sitting on the bed, Indian-style, getting ready for the wedding. She'd met the couple one other time shortly after she and Ethan had begun dating. But the soon-to-be Kaplans had moved to Dallas, and she didn't know them that well. However, she really wasn't asking to find out about them. She was asking to find out about Janet.

"Well, I met Lance at culinary school, and he's been dating Melanie for about four years. Melanie is from Louisiana, and her father is a Baptist minister, and Lance's family is Jewish. They chose a neutral spot for the wedding because I guess they were getting a lot of heat from both sides of the family, and they figured if they avoided a church or a temple, everything would be fine."

She blotted her lips. "And I bet a lot of people won't come since it's so far."

"I think that's the idea."

"I'm surprised Janet came," she said. "I didn't know they were such good friends."

He shook his head. "They're not. Greg told me when we saw them by the pool that she wasn't invited. She really did just come along with them for fun. I guess her house burned down and she's been having some problems."

She put down her shadow brush. "She crashed their wedding?"

"Well, no. Not exactly. I'm sure Lance and Melanie told Greg and Pat that they could bring dates, so it's not exactly like she crashed it."

"It's kind of weird that Greg didn't tell you he was bringing her."

He shrugged as he looked for a pair of pants in his suitcase. "We broke up . . . what? Over three years ago. I'm sure he knows I'm over it by now." He slipped on his pants. "Look, I don't want to focus so much on Janet for the rest of the weekend. We broke up a long time ago, and I want us to have a good time. Okay?"

She shouldn't have pried. It was childish. She couldn't help it though. Janet had crashed the wedding, then threw herself on Ethan. It all seemed so bizarre.

They finished getting ready, then walked to the wedding. Set on a white balcony overlooking white-crested waves of turquoise, the wedding felt romantic. A chuppah had been placed at the end of the balcony. Bright orange and red tropical flowers dripped from the edges of the wedding canopy. The same fresh flowers had been tied to the chairs at the end of each aisle. The air was warm and dry. She remembered what Jill had said about weddings stirring up romantic feelings in couples. However, if any wedding bugs were flying around, there was also a gigantic frog named Janet who was hungry to devour them.

"Is a rabbi marrying them?" she asked, looking at the chuppah.

Ethan shook his head. "I think Melanie's dad is marrying them. He's a preacher."

Though Ethan was friends with both the bride and the groom, they sat on the groom's side and watched as the guests filed in and took their seats. She loved to people watch and wasn't disappointed by the guests at this wedding. The bride and groom's families could not have been more opposite.

She'd never seen such a mix of people, and it was like someone had drawn a line down the middle of the aisle, and made signs with arrows that read "*If you wear loud hats, speak with a drawl, and have ever made biscuits and gravy, you belong over here. Everyone else sits on the other side.*" Ethan knew almost everyone at the wedding. People either waved to him or stopped to talk.

Melanie's parents' names were Cash and Honey—the mother was Cash and the father was Honey.

"Darlin', you are just as cute as a new piglet in hay." Based on the kind tone in Cash Hail's voice, and the way she touched Cate's chin when she spoke, Cate took this as a compliment. "And a skinny little thing too!" She threw her head back and laughed. "I told Honey when we left for the Cancun airport that I'm on a diet this weekend." She paused. "The *all you can eat* diet. Pack on calories and fat at your own free will. You can join me if you want. There are no losers on this one! This diet leaves everyone with a sense of accomplishment."

Her booming laughter was so contagious that Cate couldn't help but join. "I think I already do that every day anyway."

"I tried to lose weight before the wedding, and I finally just realized that dog ain't gonna hunt."

The music began, a mariachi band. "Well I guess that's my cue," Cash said as the sound of Spanish bugles filled the air. "I gotta head back to go give my baby away." She reached for a handkerchief and began to dab at tears as she waddled away.

Cate remembered Melanie speaking with a slight accent, but she was definitely not as Southern as the rest of her family. She came down the aisle with her parents to "Guantanamera."

The bridesmaids all wore long silver evening gowns with flip-flops. Melanie started crying as soon as she saw Lance, and mascara ran down her cheeks like mud.

Cate sat next to Lance's cousin, Gil, who didn't bother looking up from his cell phone once. He text-messaged people the entire time. The ceremony was going well, but she sort of wished they would speed things up. Every five seconds she could feel something crawling on her calves and up her arms. Skinny hair like little legs tickled the back of her neck. The place was infested with mosquitoes. She should've applied a layer of bug spray all over body instead of the fruity lotion they seemed to love. If they didn't hurry up she'd probably have the West Nile virus by the time the reception was over. She wasn't the only one. Every two seconds she could hear people slapping their own arms or groaning in disgust as they picked insects off their bodies.

Lance had written his own vows, and when he read them there wasn't a dry eye in the audience. "You are the love of my life, and the thing I look forward to the most is waking up to see your dimples every morning," he said. "I know I can get through anything when I have you by my side."

Ethan took Cate's hand from her lap. When she looked at him he whispered, "I love you." Thank God he was being bitten by something other than mosquitoes.

The reception had a Spanish theme. A sombrero and a pair of maracas waited at each guest's place setting and the mariachi band provided all the music. Cate and Ethan found their table, and she felt slightly annoyed when she noticed Janet sitting next to *one* empty seat. They needed two seats—one for Cate and one for Ethan. They were short a seat because of her. She was never supposed to be at the wedding to begin with, and she'd taken one of their seats. Oblivious to her bad manners, she put on the sombrero that was intended for one of them. "Uh-oh," she said. "It looks like they didn't put enough seats at our table." She waved her maracas.

Cate felt like holding up her place card, the one that said *Cate Padgett Table #15*, and asking her if she had one too. Then she realized it was sort of sad and embarrassing to think of how ill-mannered Janet was. Obviously, no one had ever taught her any manners, and her lack of common sense was sort of pitiful.

Ethan squeezed Cate's shoulders. "You stay here. I'll go find us another chair."

It seemed like forever while Cate stood next to the table, waiting for Ethan to return. The first toast started, and she sat in the only empty chair so she wouldn't block anyone's view. Ethan finally returned with a busboy who held a folding chair.

"Would you hurry up? I'm missing the whole damn toast," someone yelled while they squeezed into the crowded setting.

This comment was followed by a loud and irritated, "Shhhh!" from the back of the room.

The new chair was smaller than the rest, and when Ethan sat down he looked as if he were sitting on the ground. For once in her life, Cate felt taller than him. She sat in between Ethan and Janet.

As soon as the toast ended, Janet's head shot in front of Cate and she was forced to lean back so she wouldn't get knocked out by the sombrero Janet had stolen from them. "What have you been up to?" she asked Ethan.

"Really busy with my catering business and . . ." he looked at Cate and smiled, ". . . hanging out with Cate."

"I always knew you would start your own business someday," she said. "I'm so proud of you."

"Thanks. Listen, I'm really sorry about your house."

Cate watched a tear roll down her cheek. "Well, it's been really hard. But I'm doing better. I think I'm going to move to San Diego."

Cate nearly spat her margarita onto the table.

"Nothing is set in stone yet, but I have a few interviews at restaurants next week."

"Great. Let me know if you need any help."

Cate felt sorry for her, but at the same time something about Janet made her uncomfortable. Maybe it was because she hadn't acknowledged Cate once since they'd sat down. Rather, she pretended like Cate didn't even exist, leaning over her and tapping Ethan's arm every time he said something funny.

Luckily the first dance came sooner than expected, and her incessant gabbing was interrupted. They watched as Melanie and Lance took to the dance floor. They looked so in love, never taking their eyes away from each other for one moment. Cate took a bunch of pictures of the happy couple. If they turned out good she would send them to Lance and Melanie. It might save them some money with the photographer.

"Aren't they the cutest thing ever?" Janet looked at Ethan.

Cate had never been to a place where busboys served margaritas from pitchers the same way they gave away water. They dined on enchiladas and salads. There was a brief moment when she wondered if she should eat the lettuce. It was, after all, Mexico, and who knew what kind of water the lettuce had been washed in? But they were at a five-star resort, she reasoned.

The rest of the wedding was a blast. They danced to the mariachis and shook their maracas. It seemed as if every time her gaze stumbled upon Janet, she was watching them with a frosty stare. Several times, Ethan had been twirling Cate on the dance floor and she'd caught Janet's eyes thinly fixed on them.

After the reception they took a long stroll through the hotel grounds, their arms linked. The air was damp and warm, and she could feel her hair frizzing, but she didn't mind. Sure, she'd rather have straight, sleek hair around him, but they were at a comfort level in which he'd seen her with frizzy hair enough times that she was pretty secure he wasn't going to be turned off.

"I had fun tonight," he said. "I'm really happy for Lance and Melanie."

"I know. They seem really happy. That's what happens when you find true love. It's so amazing." He stopped to kiss her. "I love you."

"I love you too." His hands felt warm on her face, and as they kissed again she felt her whole body growing warm all over. They could hardly keep their hands off each other the rest of the way back to the room. As they undressed each other in the dark, she smiled to herself. He'd been bitten by the wedding bug.

·4·

Bitten by Something

Nausea hit her like a tidal wave in the middle of the night. Drowsy, she tried to ignore her need to vomit. Sleep would make it go away. If she could just fall back to sleep she'd be fine. She did everything in her power to force her weak body back to sleep. After she could no longer resist the inevitable, she sprang from the bed, ran to the bathroom, and threw up. She knew she should've never trusted the lettuce, even if they *were* staying at a five-star resort. It was the oldest rule in the book. Never eat uncooked produce in Mexico, and she should've known better. Cold sweat oozed from her pores before she vomited again. Damn. Why did this have to happen? On their vacation?

Her insides constricted like snakes, and her throat burned when she began to dry heave. She was just starting to wonder if she was waking the entire hotel when she heard Ethan's voice behind her.

"You okay, Catie bear?" He crouched down behind her and rubbed her back the same way her mother had when she was a child. She hadn't bothered to dress after the sex they'd had earlier, and she sat in the nude next to the toilet.

She shook her head, and when she glanced at him she noticed that he wasn't dressed either. She was afraid if she opened her mouth to speak she might start crying tears of frustration. She wasn't supposed to get sick on their vacation. This was supposed to happen during the school year when she could miss work.

He gave her a hand towel.

"What time is it?" she asked.

"Four thirty."

"You can go back to bed." She didn't expect him to sit on the bathroom floor with her while she barfed in the buff all night. Close as they were, she didn't really want him to see her vomiting stomach bile like a bald eagle regurgitating food for its young.

"Do you think you can drink some water?" he asked.

"Maybe just to rinse my mouth with." The sour taste of acid intensified her nausea. Worse, her entire body itched. She was covered from head to toe in mosquito bites.

"Do you have any bites?" she asked.

He held out his arm. "Just this one." It was the size of a sunflower seed. "Geez!" he shouted when he looked at her arms and legs. "You're covered!"

"I know. I think they liked the sweet taste of my lotion."

"As soon as the shops open I'll walk to town and get you something at the pharmacy."

He filled a glass with water then helped her to her feet.

She swished the water in her mouth before spitting in the sink. "I actually feel a little better."

He helped her back to bed.

She struggled with sleep for a couple hours before falling into a light doze. She dreamt that Ethan had proposed. The ring was adjustable, similar to those found in gumball machines. Instead of a diamond, a tiny plastic golf ball rested in the setting.

When she woke she felt overcome with nausea, and again ran to the bathroom. Her body racked as she vomited nothing but stomach acid.

When she returned to the bedroom Ethan was pulling a T-shirt over his head. "It's ten," he said. "The pharmacy has gotta be open by now. I'm going to town to see if I can get you something."

It seemed like he was gone forever, and she felt too sick to read. Three of the five channels they got were news. The other two stations were in Spanish, so she watched CNN. The bites on her ankles itched the most, and she scratched them with her toenails. She knew she shouldn't indulge in scratching them, but the temporary relief was too satisfying to resist.

She looked at her camera bag sitting on the dresser. As she thought about all the unused film and time she was wasting in the hotel room she felt totally helpless. They should be out exploring, bargaining with the vendors in town, or taking the ferry to Cozumel, not wasting away in the hotel. There was nothing she could do to make herself feel better, and she hoped that Ethan found some potent drugs at the pharmacy.

He finally returned carrying a huge bottle of Gatorade and a plastic bag. "Feeling better?" he asked.

She shook her head.

She noticed a billowy white fabric sticking from the bag. "What'd you get?"

"Well, I passed a few vendors on the way to the pharmacy and I thought since we're in Mexico you need a Mexican shirt." He unfolded the fabric and held up a loose white blouse with orange and red flowers embroidered over the chest. It was beautiful.

"I love it," she said. "It's adorable."

"They didn't have any men's, but next time we go into town we'll have to look for something Spanish for me. I went to the pharmacy and the guy told me that he could give you pills, but you'll probably just throw them up. He said what you need is a shot. He asked me if I could give it to you . . ." He laughed. "Of course I said no. So he told me to either bring you back to the pharmacy so he could give it to you or get the hotel doctor. I didn't really want this guy giving you a shot, so the hotel doctor is coming in ten minutes."

"Do you think it's safe to get a shot in Mexico?"

He reminded her that they were at a five-start resort, and it wasn't like they were going to some shaman in the middle of the jungle.

While they waited for the doctor he rubbed anti-itch ointment over every single one of her bites. Sure enough, ten minutes later the doctor arrived. He carried a small case and wore crisp khakis, a golf shirt, and a Rolex watch.

"Tell me your symptoms," he said in perfect English.

She explained what had happened. "I have to give you a shot. You will just throw up the pills."

"Okay." She sat on the bed.

There was an awkward pause, and the doctor frowned. "So, uh, turn over."

"Oh," she said, suddenly realizing where he was going to stick his needle. She rolled onto her stomach and pulled her shorts just beneath her butt.

She never thought it would be possible to feel closer to Ethan, but as she lay there with her bare white butt smiling at the ceiling and Dr. Carlos standing over her with his syringe she felt as if she had just moved to a new level of intimacy with her boyfriend. If he'd planned to propose on this trip she hoped he wasn't changing his mind.

The doctor advised her to stay out of the sun for the rest of the day and drink a lot of fluids. "You can return to the beach tomorrow. I'm sure you'll be feeling much better by then."

Ethan paid the doctor, and she hoped that whatever he'd given her would work wonders and bring back her appetite and craving for booze so she could take full advantage of the free drinks and food they were supposed to be stuffing themselves with.

"You can go to the beach," Cate said as soon as the doctor was gone. "I don't expect you to sit here all day and rot in this room with me."

"No. I'll stay."

He stayed with her all day. The only time he left was to go on a quest for plain white rice and bananas for her to eat. It took all her willpower to eat, and she knew she had to take a few bites if she wanted to get her strength back. They lay around all day, recapping parts of the wedding from the night before and playing cards. She taught him to play dice, and by sunset he was a pro. By the time they went to bed she felt a little better, and she snuggled into his warm body. As she drifted off to sleep she didn't feel like the day had been wasted at all.

·5·

The Invasion

The following morning she felt much better. Her appetite hadn't returned, and she still felt weak, but she was definitely ready to soak up some sun. They walked to two empty lounge chairs by the pool and set up camp. "So," Ethan said. "This is what I propose."

Her ears perked at the word *propose*. "I propose that we lounge around all day today and maybe if you're feeling up to it we can do something mellow like snorkeling tomorrow. We'll have a few hours before we catch our flight."

"That sounds good." She was still thinking of how he'd used the word *propose*. Then she realized that it wasn't going to happen this weekend. Food poisoning. Ethan's ex-girlfriend watching them like a hawk. It wasn't exactly a setting for *The Perfect Proposal*. The truth was, she had no idea when he would ask. Just because she'd found a brochure and he'd been bitten by the wedding bug, she really had no clue. It could be months—years, even. She knew he wanted to be with her. They'd talked about how many kids they wanted and where they'd build their dream home, but they'd never been specific about when their relationship might become permanent.

"I think I'm going to head to the bar," Ethan said. "You want anything?"

"Just water." She'd listened to all her friends rave about the benefits of staying at an all-inclusive resort. Descriptions of a constant flow of margaritas and a steady supply of nachos had given her something to look forward to. Of course, her stomach felt like a hurricane while she had her opportunity to indulge.

Instead of getting drunk with Ethan she decided to take pictures of the view from the pool. She could see the ocean, dotted with parasailers and Jet Skis. She snapped pictures of the Mexican vendors that set up their jewelry and pottery around the bar. There were tropical birds, an iguana, and several interesting Europeans that she caught on film.

After using up a roll of film she went back to her chair and spread sunblock on her arms. Ethan had gone to the bar again, so she'd have to wait until he returned to apply a second round of lotion to her back. While she rubbed sunscreen on her body it was hard to resist the urge to scratch her bites. Some of her bites were so swollen they made her skinny arms look fat in places.

"Oh my God! What happened to you?" Janet's perfectly smooth long legs greeted her. Cate was pretty thin, but she'd never felt comfortable prancing around in public in her bikini. If she got up to use the bathroom or get a drink she always put her shorts or a T-shirt back on. Janet wore only her bikini and a pair of high-heeled flip-flops.

"I was attacked at the wedding," Cate said. "Weren't you bitten by any of the mosquitoes?"

"Me? No. Not one."

Figures.

"Is anyone sitting here?" She pointed to the empty chair next to Cate.

Maybe she should lie and tell her it was taken. "No. I don't think anyone is sitting there."

She watched while Janet spread her towel over the lounge chair. Her tiny butt had obviously never seen the wrath of cellulite. "I heard about your food poisoning," Janet said. "We saw Ethan in the lobby yesterday when he was coming back from the pharmacy."

Funny, Ethan had never mentioned running into them.

"Yeah, I'm feeling much better today."

Janet rubbed an SPF 2 oil over her legs. "That's the worst. Vomiting and having diarrhea in front of your boyfriend," she said. "Really not a flattering way to look."

"We're pretty comfortable around each other. I had to bathe him once when he had too much to drink."

Frustration flashed quickly over Janet's eyes. If Cate would've blinked she would've missed her sour expression. "Well, and you know Ethan. He is the best. I mean, the guy is such a catch. Really skilled in the . . ." She giggled. "Oh, what am I thinking? You don't want to hear about that."

No, she definitely didn't want to hear how skilled in the bedroom Janet thought he was. What an idiot. After that remark, she decided to take a nap. Maybe if she closed her eyes Janet would go away.

She dreamt that they returned to San Diego. Grease was happy to see them, and she had new blue curtains. When she opened her suitcase Janet popped out. "Hi guys. I decided to come back with you," she said.

Cate was thinking about stuffing her back inside and shipping the suitcase to Serbia when she was awakened by a bloodcurdling scream. As she opened her eyes a dark shadow lunged over her. Ethan hurtled over her lounge chair. She turned to see what he was running toward. There was Janet, screaming as if an ax murderer were after her. Cate watched as she decked the Leotard Man hard, knocking his ears from his head and sending him on all fours.

On the ground, he didn't look as menacing. In fact, he looked rather scrawny. He sat there for a moment, trying to figure out what had hit him. His face was drenched in what appeared to be beer, and his makeup had been removed where her fist had hit him. He grabbed his ears and ran.

"Are you okay?" Ethan asked.

Hysterical, tears spilled from Janet's eyes. "No, I'm not okay. That scared me to death." She fell into his chest.

He paused for a moment before he put his arms around her. "It's okay," he said. "He's gone now."

She cried harder, resting her head on his shoulder. "Oh Ethan, that scared me to death. I've never seen anything like it."

It wasn't that scary. Cate had seen scarier things at Disneyland.

He stroked the back of her head, "Shhhh. It's okay now. He's gone."

"Oh Ethan, you're the greatest." Then she kissed him on the cheek.

"She kissed you," Cate said, throwing her clothes into her suitcase.

"Oh c'mon. It was on the cheek." He folded a pair of his shorts.

"Ethan, you are so naïve if you think it was harmless."

"Seriously, she's just a really affectionate person. I'm sure she didn't mean any harm by it."

The image of Janet's long fingers cupped over his face as she kissed him, the way she'd closed her eyes when her lips made contact with his skin, was impossible to forget. It hadn't been an innocent kiss. It had looked sensual, and it drove her mad thinking of Janet's nerve. Obviously, she had no respect for Cate. The more Cate thought about Janet's audacity, the more she fumed.

She was about to tell him that she hadn't seen her kissing anyone else all weekend when she realized that Janet was probably off somewhere having a celebratory cocktail. She was probably scheming up her next plan to play the damsel in distress in front of him, and if she knew they were arguing she'd be thrilled. They had one night left, and she promised herself she wouldn't let Janet ruin their weekend.

·6·
Now You See It, Now You Don't

She'd gotten used to their oceanside bungalow and the sound of waves crashing outside every night. Returning to San Diego was like stepping into harsh lighting after a good movie. Just as it took time for eyes to adjust to the lighting, it would probably take a couple of days to adjust to normal, daily life again.

Her apartment was dark and smelled like cat litter when they entered. "Grease," she called. He usually waited for her by the front door. She flicked on a light switch and found him sitting on the back of the couch. He yawned, then looked at her through slitted eyes.

"Greasy," she called. "Come here, little kitty. I'm home." Instead of running toward her as he did whenever she returned, he flicked his white tail in the air, jumped from the couch, and walked in the opposite direction.

"He's mad at me," she said. "Because I left him."

"He'll get over it." Ethan followed him. "Come here, Grease."

Grease trotted away. "As soon as I get my own place I'd like to get a dog," he said.

Get his own place? He made it sound like he was leaving his current apartment and moving away from his roommate so he could live alone. She couldn't help but succumb to analyzing comments like these. Obviously, he wasn't thinking about getting a place with her any time soon if he was getting his *own* place. His remark was minor, and she was probably thinking about it much more than he was. Sometimes she felt like he was hard to figure out. Just when she thought he'd been bitten by the wedding bug, he was talking about living alone. She was too tired to get into a "where is this really headed" discussion and decided to check her messages.

"Call me the minute you get in." It was Jill. "Did he do it?"

She pressed Delete.

The next message was from Beth. "Dun dun ta da!" She sang a very off-key "Here Comes the Bride." "So? Did he do it? Just wondering. Call me. Bye." She must've talked to Jill.

They were both going to be sorely disappointed when she told them the only thing she'd gotten on her vacation was a shot it in the butt. She made a mental note not to ever ask unengaged friends if they were engaged yet. She decided to call them tomorrow after he left. Feeling like she'd just spent ten days on a plane, she headed to the bathroom for a hot shower.

"Holy shit!" she said when she looked at her shower curtain.

"I know," Ethan called. "I saw."

A hole the size of a beach towel resided in the middle of the curtain, and claw marks covered the remaining pieces. She'd have to take baths until she replaced it. Otherwise, her little bathroom would be flooded. She washed her face in the sink, and when she returned to the bedroom she found Ethan sitting on the edge of the bed, still fully clothed. Odd that he wasn't undressed, resting beneath her comforter with the remote control in his hand. She'd expected to find him absorbed in an episode of *The Iron Chef* or *Monster House*. Grease sat at Ethan's feet, scratching his neck with his hind leg.

"What are you doing?" Cate asked.

"Nothing. Just waiting for you."

She looked at his feet. He was still wearing his shoes. "Okay. Are you sleeping here tonight?"

"Yeah."

"Are you going to get ready for bed?"

"Yeah, I will." She was too tired to try to figure out why he was acting so weird. She was about to head for her pajamas when she noticed Grease scratching his neck again. She went away for one week and he had fleas? The she remembered that guy Jill had been sleeping with on and off, and his Doberman. It didn't seem like something she'd do, but maybe she brought the dog over here. She did take him jogging sometimes.

"Come here, Grease." She bent down and picked him up. She combed through the fur on the back of his neck with her fingers. He squirmed in her arms then sprang from her hands and ran from the room.

"I'm exhausted," she said. She had a zit as bright as a traffic light on her forehead, but wasn't in the mood to put toner on it. She slipped into a pair of her coziest pants and an oversized T-shirt and decided to look at Grease's fleas tomorrow.

"I'm hungry," Ethan said. He sat on the edge of her bed.

"I am too, but there is nothing in the house, and I don't know of anywhere we can order takeout at this hour."

He still sat there.

"You could walk to 7-Eleven," she suggested.

"You want to rent a movie? Order one from pay per view? That Brad Pitt movie you've been wanting to see is on there."

What was wrong with him? One, he never wanted to watch anything with Brad Pitt, and two, they'd been traveling for nearly twelve hours. Maybe he was just feeling sad that their vacation was coming to an end, and he was trying to prolong every last second of it.

Grease returned and jumped on the bed. He sniffed the corner of her comforter, then began to scratch the back of his neck, with his hind leg this time. Maybe his collar was too tight. Something was wrong. Ripping the daylights out of his red collar, wasn't fleas. A white tuft of fur floated in the air as he scratched harder.

"Ethan, have you noticed Grease scratching like this since we got home? I think his collar is too tight."

He shook his head.

Grease's eyes narrowed, and his ears shifted back on his head when she lifted him. He looked absolutely miserable, and she wondered if a piece of the shower curtain had gotten lodged beneath his collar. He squirmed and struggled to free himself from her arms. She could feel his claws digging into her arms as she hung onto him. His body felt rigid and tense as if he were going to shoot from the bed and run into hiding at any moment.

"Grease, just hold still, baby. I'm going to make you all better." He tried to bolt, but she managed to keep him pinned. She touched his collar, twisting so she could unbuckle it. She gasped when her fingertips ran over something hard, something that didn't feel like a buckle. It felt like . . . a ring. Oh holy . . . oh mother . . . oh God, it was a ring! A diamond ring! On her cat's collar. It was . . . she was . . . they were . . . When her eyes grew wide, she noticed Ethan moving, going down. He was getting on one knee, and this time she was wide-awake.

Words slipped from his mouth like bubbles, and she only caught bits and pieces. "The love of my life . . . I want to be with you forever . . . will you . . . marry me?"

Marry me? Marry me!!! MARRY ME! The words pounded in her head. He was asking her to marry him. Proposing. The lighting in her room was dim, but she could still see his blue eyes, wide and sincere— and a little nervous.

"Of course!"

He stood up, and they fell into one another's arms, kissing and laughing.

"I wanted to do it in Mexico," he said. "But I got worried that the ring would be stolen, so I chickened out at the last second and hid the ring in a jar of vitamins in your fridge."

"You mean the ring has been sitting in with my vitamin E this whole time?"

"Yeah." He chuckled.

"I was wondering why you were acting so weird."

"I've never been that nervous in my life. Could you hear my heart pounding? My heart has never pounded like that before. I honestly thought you had to hear it."

She shook her head. "No."

"I mean, I knew you were going to say yes. But I had no idea that actually getting on one knee and asking you to marry me would be so intense. Now I understand why it's so emotional. I have *never* been that nervous in my life."

"I just thought you were being very unhelpful with the cat."

He looked toward her bedroom door. "Where *is* Grease?"

The cat had bolted somewhere in the excitement. "I don't know," she said as she followed him into the living room. They found him on the couch, licking his paw. Fear swam through her veins when she looked on the ground next to the couch. Lying like a withered eel was his collar. The ring was nowhere in sight.

· 7 ·

Spreading the Word

"I'm going to kill that cat," Ethan mumbled as they dismantled the couch.

It was the following morning, and the first time since they'd started their search to recover her engagement ring that he'd blamed Grease. Up until now, they'd both been so happy that they'd searched for the missing gems with a positive attitude. An attitude that promised a safe return of the diamonds.

Any signs of optimism had faded after the sun rose, and now he was placing blame everywhere. "I'm not gonna kill him," he retracted sadly. "It's my own dumb fault. I should've known it would get lost if I set it anywhere near that cat."

They had taken apart everything. The bed. The couch. They had moved furniture and looked inside shoes. They'd gone over every inch of the house with both sets of eyes. Behind the TV and the stereo. Beneath rugs and dust ruffles. Ethan had even sifted through the litter box and didn't find anything pretty in there. She didn't want to tell him this, but she'd been thinking about Grease's obsession with water ever since the ring had vanished. Countless times, he'd taken his fake mice and drowned them in the toilet or batted a shampoo cap down the shower drain. She looked in his water dish, hoping to find it resting there, but the only thing she found was her Parisian woman's head, which she'd have to superglue back on again.

Everything had happened so fast, and she'd only glimpsed the ring for an instant. She'd made him describe it to her at least a dozen times while they searched. At first, she'd loved listening to his descriptions. White gold. A trio of diamonds. The center diamond, a round cut and the largest at .5 carats stood a tad higher than its two neighbors weighing in at .25 each. She was starting to worry, and listening to descriptions only made her ache for the ring. If she let him see how concerned she was he'd probably have a nervous breakdown.

"It's going to turn up," she said optimistically. "It's probably where we least expect it."

"We've looked everywhere." He slumped onto the cushionless couch.

"Why don't we take a break? Call some of our friends and tell them the news? We've hardly called anyone. And then as soon as we stop looking I'm sure the ring will turn up somewhere."

"How could I have been such an idiot!" He slammed his fist onto the edge of the couch, and she knew he hadn't heard a word of what she'd just said.

A knock at the door startled them. He looked at her. "Who's that?"

"I don't know," she whispered and wasn't really sure why she was whispering. "Maybe Jill? Maybe she heard us."

Ethan crept over to the door on his tiptoes and looked out the peephole in his boxers. He jumped back from the door as if a Mafia hit man stood on the other side with a machine gun. "It's your mother!" he whispered loudly.

"Are you kidding?"

"No. She's standing out there. Right out there." He pointed vigorously at the front door. Then he ran into her bedroom and threw his clothes on as if he were committing adultery and his lover's spouse was heading through the front door. Cate quickly slipped into jeans and a T-shirt as well.

When she opened the door she found not only her mother, but her father lurking in the hallway too.

"Good morning." Connie grinned as if she already knew the good news.

"You know, don't you?" Cate said as she let her parents in.

"We think we know," her father said.

"We're engaged!"

"I knew it! Congratulations. I got your message this morning and I knew that's what it was!" She threw her arms around Cate.

Her father shook hands with Ethan. "Congratulations!"

"We were just in the area, and we thought we'd stop by," Connie said. "What's wrong with your phone, anyway? It's been busy for over an hour."

The phone had been propelled from the couch when they'd stripped it. It now lay off the hook in a corner of her living room. Ethan went to fix it.

"So how did he do it?" Her father asked.

She was relieved that Ethan hadn't proposed in Mexico. Her mother had not approved of them traveling together and had reminded Cate that she was spending the honeymoon with him before the wedding at least a dozen times before she'd left. She told them all about Grease scratching himself and how she'd felt the ring and how Ethan got on one knee.

"Let's see the ring." Her mother reached for Cate's hand.

"Well, uh, that's the thing. The ring has disappeared."

They told them how Grease had run off and they found his limp collar and no ring, and how they'd stayed up all night looking for it. She had a feeling she'd be repeating the story a thousand more times throughout the day.

"You need to pray to Saint Anthony."

She'd always been instructed to do this whenever anything had gotten lost.

"Pray to him right now, and I'll say some prayers too. He always finds everything. He does. *Always.*"

Cate wanted to mention the time in junior high when she'd lost her report on the Mayan Indians and Saint Anthony had never led her to it, despite prayer chains she had going throughout the neighborhood.

"So have you thought about where you guys want to get married?" her father asked.

"Well, we talked about it a little bit last night, and I think we want to get married in Founders Chapel at USD."

"You better book it soon. I heard it's booked years in advance, and you'll need to ask Father Al to marry you, and sign up for Pre-Cana classes."

Father Al was her cousin, and she couldn't imagine anyone else marrying them. However, this was all too much to think about, and she looked at her dad. "You knew it was coming, didn't you?"

"I sure did. A real good one, Cate. I'm so proud of you two."

"Thanks, Dad."

Her parents visited for a few more minutes before inviting them to breakfast.

"No, that's okay," she said. "We really need to find this ring, and we have tons of people to call."

She walked them to the parking lot in her slippers.

"Don't worry about the ring," her father said. "I'm sure it will turn up."

"I accidentally lost my ring in the trash once, and we found it. I searched in every crevice of our house for days."

That made her feel better. "I'm moving soon anyway, so it's bound to pop up when I start packing."

They looked shocked. "You are?"

"Well, yeah. Ethan and I are going to buy a house."

"You mean, after you're married. Right?" The tone of her mother's voice suggested there was only one right answer.

"Um, actually. No. We were thinking about moving soon while interest rates are still low."

Why, oh why, had she ever mentioned this? *Change the subject,* she thought. She looked to her dad with a *help me* look in her eyes, but for the first time in ages he looked just as puzzled as her mother.

"You can't move in until you're married," he said.

"Well, nothing is set in stone yet," she said. "We only got engaged yesterday." As far as she was concerned everything was set in stone, cemented actually. She was moving in with Ethan.

When she returned to her apartment her sister was on the phone. "Congratulations!" Emily said.

"Mom already told you?"

"Well, I knew that Ethan had asked dad a few weeks back, and then mom called me this morning, saying you'd left a message, sounding absolutely ecstatic, so we knew it could only mean one thing. So how'd he do it? What does the ring look like?"

Cate repeated all the details to her sister. "Well, I'm sure it will turn up somewhere. It's not like the cat could swallow something that big. I mean, think how small his throat its. He would've choked."

"The thing is," Cate whispered so Ethan wouldn't hear. "I'm worried sick that Grease dumped it in the toilet or down the sink. He's obsessed with anything water-related."

"Noooo. Grease didn't do that. You would've seen it in the toilet before you flushed it."

She thought hard about who was the last to flush the toilet. It was her, right after they'd had sex. Had she flipped on the light before she'd gone? She tried to remember. She had. Had she looked inside the bowl before she'd sat down? Probably, but she couldn't remember. It wasn't like she expected to find things in her toilet. "What about the sink, though?"

"Go get one of those snake things from Home Depot and shove it down there. Maybe it will bring it back up. Or better yet, call a plumber."

"All right." She was about to say good-bye when she remembered one of the main reasons she'd called. "So, are you going to be my maid of honor?"

"Of course! I already have plenty ideas for the shower. Who else are you asking to be in the wedding?"

"Jill and Beth of course. Leslie."

"Leslie Bridezilla Lyons? The one who had the horse in her wedding?"

"Uh-huh." Cate continued. "Cousin Val and Sarah, and I'm debating asking Ethan's cousin, Denise. I'm not that close with her, but she is close with Ethan. After her mom died she moved out here and lived with them her last two years of high school."

"You should ask her. It's the right thing to do."

After Cate hung up she found Ethan digging like an animal through her dirty laundry basket. "It's not in there. I already looked," Cate said. She noticed a five o'clock shadow forming around his jaw, and his eyes were bloodshot.

"Ethan, it's going to turn up. Okay? It didn't get up and walk away. Let's take a break. You haven't even called your parents to tell them we got engaged."

He flopped back and lay down on the floor, spreading his arms out beside him. "Is there *any* way Grease could've gone outside?"

"No. But please call your parents. I think you'll cheer up if you just relax for a little while."

It took a lot of convincing, but he finally sat up and reached for his cell phone. Talking to his parents seemed to cheer him up a bit. They'd already seen the ring and luckily hadn't even asked about it. After he spoke with them he passed the phone off to Cate.

"Oh Cate! I've always wanted a daughter," Rita Blakely said. "He told me he wanted to marry you shortly after you started dating, and I just couldn't be happier."

"He did?" Cate's heart melted. Once they had started dating she knew they were meant to be together, but she'd had no idea he'd been confiding this to his parents.

"Oh yes," Rita said. "But listen, Charles and I would like to throw an engagement party for you guys. We'll have it here at the house. It will be wonderful. You can invite whoever you want."

"That would be great!" Cate thought of what it was going to be like to merge their two families together. Several years ago the Blakelys and the Padgetts had been neighbors. Cate and Ethan had been friends since they were children, but that didn't mean that their parents had been the type of neighbors who shared barbecues together on Sunday afternoons and sipped wine on lawn chairs in the driveway. In fact, it had always seemed that their parents had very little in common. Ethan's parents were both doctors, and if they weren't at the hospital, their hands were dirty from growing all their own produce in their garden in the backyard.

Cate's mother had never worked, would've never dreamt of leaving her kids with a nanny, and hired a gardener to handle their landscape. Connie had taught catechism and organized food drives for the homeless at church while Rita had kept her maiden name and split the responsibilities of child rearing with her husband and a baby-sitter.

The Blakelys camped in the mountains and considered Christmas a family holiday with no religious meaning, whereas Cate's parents considered camping staying at a Holiday Inn, and there was only one reason for Christmas as far as they were concerned: God. It made her a little nervous to think of their parents uniting.

For the first time since she'd thought about being engaged, it occurred to her how strange it was to merge two families. Two vastly different families that had no say in the matter. Outside of Cate and Ethan, they would never be friends. Now suddenly they'd all be related for the rest of their lives.

"An engagement party would be great." Cate said, hiding her worry.

Ethan went home, and Cate called a plumber. She waited anxiously behind the plumber, keeping her fingers crossed the whole time. He looked as if he'd dropped out of high school a week earlier, and he wasn't fazed in the least that she'd lost her engagement ring or that she'd even gotten engaged.

She waited while he unscrewed the pipes beneath the sink. "There is a lot of hair in here," he mumbled. Her stomach turned when he pulled out what looked like a large blond rat. Then he dumped the pipe. "But no. I don't see your ring."

He checked the bathtub next, and his search produced the same disappointing results. Two hundred dollars later she started to wonder if it was really gone for good. She spent the rest of the afternoon praying to Saint Anthony as phone calls from friends and relatives flooded in. She explained the story again and again.

· 8 ·

Choices vs. Obligations

Fantasizing about her dress had probably begun the summer of Princess Di's wedding, and thankfully she hadn't married at seven. She'd woken at the crack of dawn and watched with her sister while Lady Di headed down the cathedral wearing a train longer than an aisle at Vons. After watching this, some pretty creative wedding gown fantasies had emerged. She'd pictured herself in poofy sleeves, a satin V-neck with lace filling in her bare chest, and a skirt that the cast of *North and South* would've appreciated.

In college, her fantasy gown was something almost as hideous. A full satin skirt with long, sheer sleeves, like white nylons. After that her tastes had turned more classic, and the dress she wanted now was very different.

Over the past few years she'd stolen many glances at bridal magazines while hanging out with her engaged girlfriends. While they thought she was scouting out ideas for them she was actually planning what she would wear down the aisle. Now she had her own stack of bridal magazines to tackle, and buying them had been a wonderful feeling. This time, as she stood in line at the grocery store, she didn't feel like she had to provide excuses to the checker, explaining that she was actually buying them for someone else—that she wasn't some desperate nut who wasn't engaged but collected wedding magazines because she was dying to get married. Now engaged, she'd carried them to the counter and felt confident when the cashier had given her a congratulatory smile.

However, she looked at the stack of magazines and felt a tad overwhelmed. Some of them were as thick as phone books, and she had no idea where to begin.

She was just starting to flip through one of the thickest ones when her cousin Val called. They'd been playing phone tag ever since Connie had sent Cate's engagement over the family wire.

"Ohmigod!" Val shouted. "Are you so excited? You must be dying."

"Yeah, I am really excited." She dog eared a page in her magazine and set it on the coffee table.

"So tell me everything. Where are you having it? What's the date? Have you started looking for a dress?"

"Well, it's going to be in November and, no, we haven't figured out where yet. But it will definitely be here in San Diego." She was relieved Val hadn't immediately asked what the ring looked like as everyone else had.

"I can help you with anything you need help with. Don't forget it wasn't that long ago that I got married, and I can give you all my vendors and tell you who sucks and who's great. So, what have you done? Have you done anything yet? Started looking for anything?"

"A little bit. I really want to look for my dress first."

"Searching for a dress is *absolutely* draining," she said.

Draining? She'd always imagined that shopping for a dress was going to be one of the best parts of the wedding planning.

She had a willowy frame. She worried about lugging forty pounds of tulle and crinoline down the aisle. Rather, she imagined herself in an elegant, form-fitting sheath dress. She wanted simplicity and planned to avoid beads and lace and anything sparkly at all costs. Very Carolyn Bessette. She described all this to Val.

"Oh, everyone wants that kind of dress."

Cate didn't know anyone who had worn a sheath dress. All the brides she had ever known had worn strapless gowns with a huge full skirt and a veil that dropped just below their shoulders. That was the other thing; she was ditching the whole veil thing completely. She didn't want a veil.

"Well, I'm glad you called because I want to ask you to be a bridesmaid in the wedding."

Val screamed so loud that Cate had to pull the phone away from her ear.

"Of course! Ohmigod, I think I'm going to start crying. Seriously, I have a tear in my eye. I would be honored, Cate."

They chatted for several more minutes before Val had to go to her spray-tanning appointment.

That afternoon she found her dress on the Internet. She instantly fell in love with the low-cut back and slender V-neck, the way the silk flowed smoothly over the model. It was perfect.

"Find out where it is, and we'll go try it on," her mother said into the phone. "You never know until you try something on."

Oh, she knew. "I'll figure out which salons carry it, and we'll go tomorrow," she said.

"You know, Cate," Connie's voice was heavy with pessimism, "it seems to me I remember the same thing happening with Emily's dress. She found this tiny picture in a magazine, and we carried that little picture around *everywhere* looking for something similar, and she ended up getting something completely different. So keep an open mind."

"It will be fine. It's a really popular designer, so I'm sure we can find the dress."

Feeling relieved and excited that she'd found her gown, she decided to take a break and call Ethan. If he wasn't busy finishing up the menu for the graduation party he was catering this weekend, maybe they could go see Founders Chapel. He still hadn't been there, and she wanted to make sure he liked it before she went ahead and set the date.

"Did you find the ring yet?" he said when he picked up the phone. This was becoming a standard greeting every time she called.

"No," she said, her voice low. More than anything, she wished she could tell him it was sitting on her finger. It had been five days, and there was still no sign. Every time it came up she wanted to cry for him. He'd put so much time into shopping for the ring that he could probably teach a small course in the color and clarity of diamonds. Worse, she was afraid to think of how much he had spent. She didn't want to know.

She thought she heard a groan and quickly changed the subject. "I was thinking that we could go look at Founders Chapel and then grab a bite to eat."

He hesitated. "Yeah, um, okay. That should work. I was actually going to see if you wanted to go meet with Denise. I talked to her today, and she said she would be our real-estate agent and waive her fees for us as a wedding gift."

"That's nice of her!" Now she really felt obligated to ask Denise to be a bridesmaid.

"Yeah, it's gonna save us about five grand. So we really have to appreciate that."

"Of course." She propped her feet on the coffee table. "I might ask Denise to be a bridesmaid. What do you think?"

"I'm sure she'd love to."

They made plans to buzz by Founders Chapel and then meet Denise at Filippi's in Little Italy afterward.

He arrived at her place twenty minutes later, wearing jeans and his favorite T-shirt. It was a vintage baseball tee with Waylon Jennings on the front. Cate was never really sure where he'd found it, but he would probably wear it every day if he could. He kissed her on the forehead.

He reached into his pocket. "Look, this whole thing with the ring is really driving me crazy. I mean I can't even think about it anymore, and I decided earlier today that I just want to move on." He pulled out a jewelry box. Her heart began to race. Had he purchased another ring? A replica of the old one?

She almost hoped he hadn't. It was too much money for him to spend, especially when they were talking about buying a house. She watched as he popped open the box. "So I decided you needed to have a ring. We're engaged, and you need *something*. My mom gave me this ring. I know it's not really great. But it's just temporary until we can get you one like the other one. It was actually my mom's original wedding band. My dad gave it to her when they were in the peace corps over in Asia, and then he got her a new one a few years ago."

Cate looked at the ring. Was that a diamond? She held it up to her face and saw three diamonds the size of pepper specks set on a gold band. The prongs on the setting had seen better days and were pressed at awkward angles over the tops of the stones. However, the ring was sweet and deeply sentimental and the first one she'd be slipping on her finger since they'd been engaged. She liked it, and if this was the ring she wore for the rest of her life, that would be fine.

She glanced at the ring on her finger at least a dozen times on the way to USD. Something about wearing it made her feel different. She was really engaged. *Married woman* sounded so different than *single girl*, but she didn't feel like she'd changed. She didn't plan to cut her hair short like half her friends had or make casseroles anytime soon. She still felt like the same old Cate.

Memories of the last wedding she'd been to at Founders Chapel surfaced when they pulled up to campus. She was the maid of honor and the bride's ex-boyfriend had shown up drunk. Cate was the one who had to get rid of him, and the whole thing had snowballed into near-disaster. Maybe they shouldn't get married here. What if it was bad luck? Mary Star of the Sea was disaster-free. She wondered if they should just get married there.

She dipped her finger into a gigantic vat of holy water before proceeding into the church. She still became breathless every time she entered. However, she was not interested in looking up at the ornate Spanish Renaissance ceiling and the colorful stained glass. She wanted to see Ethan's reaction. His eyes wandered over the marble floors, down the dark wooden pews, and onto the magnificent gold altar. He was quiet, and she wondered if the scene of Jesus hanging on the cross with several apostles at his feet was too religious for his family. His gaze took a path to the ceiling and without taking them away from the stained glass Stations of the Cross he whispered, "This is awesome."

She clasped his hand.

"Really, it's unbelievable," he said. "Yes, let's get married here."

"Really? Do you want to see Mary Star of the Sea?"

He shook his head.

"No. I love this."

Denise was already waiting in a booth when they arrived, sipping on a Coke. On Ethan's birthday last year, Cate had flipped through some Blakely family albums and had spotted several pictures of Denise from over a decade ago. Except for the addition of twenty pounds she hadn't changed much. She'd worn her brown hair in the same shoulder-length cut since she was a child. She still used a curling iron to curl the ends and a comb to tease and hair-spray her bangs. Her clothes consisted of tapered slacks, basic flats, and plain, simple short-sleeved sweaters that came in safe, neutral colors. She wasn't unattractive, but with a little effort she might look really pretty, and Cate wondered why she was so attached to her outdated hairdo.

"Let's see the ring," Denise said, as they sat down. "Rita told me she was going to give this to Ethan after you guys lost the other one." She looked at Cate's hand. "I remember this ring so well when Aunt Rita used to wear it." She turned to Ethan. "Remember how every time she used to make meat loaf she would take it off and let me try it on? But only if I washed my hands."

Ethan laughed. "That's right. I do remember that."

"And remember the time when Chuck had a girlfriend over and she wanted to try it on too and Rita said no?"

"Oh yeah. What was that girl's name?"

"Sally Woods." She turned to Cate. "Rita and I used to think that Sally's name sounded like a porn star, some kind of pseudonym. She was so skinny and weird with her black eye makeup. We called her The Sassy Sally Woods. We had names for all of Ethan's and Chuck's girlfriends." She still held Cate's ring. "There was that one girl that we called Dandy Mandy." Cate remembered her because Ethan had dated her while they were in high school. "Rita and I would say she'd probably stolen Cyndi Lauper's wardrobe." Denise laughed as if remembering something. "Yep, we do. We have names for all . . ." Her voice trailed off, and she glanced at Cate. "Except you, of course."

Something about Denise bothered Cate. She'd tried to ignore it. Perhaps it was the fact that Cate had suddenly realized they were going to be related. Or perhaps it was just that she was tired of Denise constantly taking long exclusive trips down memory lane.

Cate didn't really want to hear about Denise wearing her engagement ring. It sort of ruined the sentimental value of the ring between Ethan and her. Now she had an image of little meat loaf hands running around in the ring Ethan had given her. Couldn't she just say, *Hey congratulations, you guys. I'm really happy for you*—like a normal person?

It had always bothered Cate a little bit that Denise insisted on sharing stories that Cate had never been a part of, talking about people that she'd never met. She tried to rationalize that Denise really liked to reminisce, and so she'd politely listened to Ethan and her while they shared all kinds of memories.

Denise looked at Cate and said something about how she had known they were going to get married the whole time they were in Playa del

Carmen, how Ethan had shown her the ring before he left, and blah blah blah.

Cate wasn't listening to her. She was thinking about step aerobics. It had actually been Denise who had made the first move in their friendship and invited Cate to join her. "I can get you a free pass at my gym anytime you want to come with me," she'd said.

Cate hadn't done step aerobics since her freshman year of college and would've preferred a walk around the bay for exercise, but she wanted to be friends with Denise so she'd gone to the class.

The whole car ride to the gym Denise had done nothing but tell her how difficult and intense the class was going to be. Cate wasn't worried because she had been a pro back in college and had even practiced some of the moves the night before.

The class was great, and sure enough, it had all come back to her, just like skiing or riding a bike. She had done some turns in the wrong directions a few times, but so had most of their classmates. She'd had a great time and felt happy that she'd finally found something in common with Denise. She heard from Denise the following morning.

"Hi," Denise had said sweetly. "I was just calling to see how you were doing. I told Rita this morning, 'She is going to be so sore today.' And I called Ethan and told him he needs to give you a massage."

"Oh thanks," Cate said. "That's so nice of you!" Every part of her body had ached—places she didn't even know she had muscles. "Yeah, it was a rough day at school. I couldn't wait to get home and soak in the tub."

"Hopefully after you heal we can go again."

"I'd love to!" She hung up, glad that they were finally friends.

The strange thing was, Denise never called again. Never invited Cate to join her again, and every time Cate mentioned step aerobics after that, Denise changed the subject. She'd asked Ethan about it, and he'd said that he doubted she went anymore. She was too busy with her job, and she wasn't really in that great of shape anyway. The funny thing was, Cate had overheard Denise talking about step aerobics at family events. Even though the results weren't obvious, she made it sound like she went all the time.

Cate couldn't help but take it personally, wondering what she could've done to drive Denise away. She'd worn deodorant, but maybe she'd had vicious BO that had scared Denise out of inviting her again. Maybe she looked like a jackass when she did right basic, left basic, and Denise was embarrassed to be seen with her.

Cate remembered the way she had eyed her while they were stepping away to Britney Spears. She recalled catching glimpses of Denise's eyes narrowly watching her in the mirror in front of them. The more she thought about it, the "check in to see if you're okay" call had been tinged with a slight tone of pleasure when Denise had found out how sore she was. She hated to make assumptions, especially negative ones, but maybe Denise just couldn't stand it that Cate was good at something. It was a horrible thought and probably why she'd pushed the whole memory from her thoughts, but it really ate at her nerves that Denise had discussed how sore Cate was with Rita. Had they come up with a name for her too? Muscle Ache Cate?

"Cate?" Ethan said.

They were both staring at her when she looked at them. "Cate, don't you have something you want to ask Denise?"

"Huh?"

"Yeah, I thought you had something you wanted to talk to Denise about."

She shot him a look but quickly recovered and smiled.

"Really?" Denise said. "What is it?"

They both waited for her to say something.

"Well, uh . . ." She'd changed her mind. She didn't want to ask her. But what was she going to say now? Ethan had already cornered her, and it would look awkward if she asked her something else. Besides, she was so shocked that he'd put her on the spot that she couldn't even think of something else to ask. They waited, Ethan smiling, Denise fingering the beads on a necklace she wore.

"Well, I wanted to ask you to be a bridesmaid in our wedding."

"Oh. Sure, of course. I've never been a bridesmaid before."

There it was. Denise would be in the wedding. As she sat there sipping on her wine, she wondered what she had just gotten herself into.

·9·

Dream Dress . . . or Not

The following morning she called all the local vendors listed on the bridesmaid dress designer's Web site. A discouragement unlike anything she had ever felt kicked in when, one after the other, each San Diego wedding boutique informed her that they didn't carry a sample of her dress. Even though her stomach growled and her ear began to ache from pressing the phone against it for over an hour, she dialed Los Angeles. *They have everything in L.A.*, she told herself. Someone will definitely have it.

She listened while the saleslady in Los Angeles flipped the pages of a catalogue. Then she delivered words that made her feel as if she had just won the California Lotto. "Yes, we have it."

She asked her to repeat the style number. She wanted to double-check before she schlepped her mom through the worst traffic in California for her wedding gown. When she read the style number back to Cate she felt her throat tighten. She was looking at the wrong dress.

Again, she repeated the style number, which she knew as well as her ATM PIN code at this point.

"Ohhh," she muttered. Cate could hear her flip a page in the catalogue. "*That* is a *gorgeous* dress. But no, I'm sorry, we don't have that style in yet."

She began to hate the designer. Who puts something on her Web site if it isn't available to the general public? Only someone who was seriously sick would want to torment brides-to-be. She politely e-mailed the designer's customer service, asking for help. Several hours later they replied. The dress wasn't available anywhere in the state of California, but she could try Chicago.

"We're not going to Chicago," Connie said, looking over her shoulder at the computer screen. She stopped by to look at the picture of the dress and go over a list of things they needed to do for the wedding. "And how do you know if you even like it? You haven't even tried it on!" Connie suggested they try the most popular bridal boutique in San Diego. "Let's see if we can get an appointment for this afternoon."

She printed a picture of her beloved style #045323, and later that day they drove to the bridal salon with the picture neatly folded and tucked into Cate's purse. They arrived at the boutique, and she felt slightly nervous when she noticed racks overflowing with full skirts.

"Hello, you must be uh . . ." She flipped through an appointment book. "Cate?"

"Yes." She smiled at the chipper young girl in a suit.

"Welcome to Bridal Couture! And congratulations on your upcoming wedding!"

"Thanks!"

Her eyes wandered to Cate's ring finger, and the smile wilted from her face. For a moment Cate thought the girl was going to say something. Instead, she returned her pert little smile to Connie.

"And you must be the proud mother of the bride!"

"Yes." Connie's smile was flat, and Cate knew her mother had seen the grim look on the girl's face when she'd glanced at the ring. The receptionist's snobbishness didn't bother Cate. For years now, she'd silently listened to some of her more shallow friends compare rings and flaunt their gigantic gems like they were designer labels. Stuff like that never mattered to her, because she knew they all had problems with their husbands anyway, and she'd often thought bigger rings had only compensated for a lack of commitment.

However, Connie was a force of nature. She didn't have the same kind of patience for people. She was the kind of person you wanted with you when you got bad service at a restaurant, because she'd make sure not only the manager knew but the owner and everyone else who happened to be nearby. Cate was willing to bet the woman had never been ripped off once in her life. She was even worse when it came to her children.

Cate would never forget the time when she was six years old and she was having a hard time doing step ball change in her tap dance class. Rather than making Cate feel comfortable, her idiotic teacher had singled her out and made her do the step ball change over and over again in front of the entire class, and a few parents who had stayed to watch. Humiliated beyond words, she'd told her mother what had happened on the car ride home. She could still hear the wheels of Connie's Volvo screeching when she turned around. With Cate in tow, Connie had marched back to the class and interrupted the teacher. Cate couldn't remember the words Connie had chosen, but by the time they'd left she had the teacher doing the step ball change in front of everyone, humility covering her face.

"Fantastic that you both could come," the girl said. "Let me get Edith. She's going to be working with you guys today."

"You do that," Connie said, watching her go.

While they waited in the lobby for Edith, she noticed another bride-to-be with her mother, laughing and strolling around the boutique with a perky and fashionable little sales consultant.

Her view was suddenly blocked by an obese woman in her late fifties, wearing turquoise slacks and a green and white striped T-shirt. A

banana clip held back her graying hair, and a mole the size of a maca-
damia nut stuck from her chin. She was going to be helping them.

"Great!" Cate said. She handed her the picture while explaining
what she had in mind.

"Hmmm." Edith handed the picture back. "Okay, let's take a look
around."

She led them to a rack of dresses that looked nothing like the picture
Cate had shown her. "What do you think of this dress?" She pulled a
strapless gown with beading on the bodice and a full skirt from the
rack. It looked like it had been tried on a million times by women who
never bathed. The edges were brown, especially around the armpits, and
some of the seed beads had come loose. "Do you want to try this on?"

No. But she also didn't want to hurt her feelings. "Um. Okay. But
I'm looking for something that has a V-neck and thin material. A sheath
dress." Hadn't she just explained this?

She spotted the other bride-to-be and watched with envy as her
salesgirl pulled out dozens of V-necks made of flowing silk and thin
straps while she happily nodded approval. Her heart sank as she
watched them leave with the pile.

"I want to look at those dresses," Cate said, following their trail
with her eyes.

Edith told her to look around while she searched for another dress
she had in mind.

"I don't like our saleslady," Connie whispered as soon as she was
gone.

They began to frantically comb the rack where the other bride had
been looking. They spotted a few gowns that resembled what she was
looking for and held onto them as if they just stumbled upon potatoes in
a famine.

When Edith returned, she held more of the same strapless style with
full skirts. Cate debated asking for a manager. Feeling completely discouraged, she followed Edith to a dressing room that was larger than a
studio apartment she had once lived in. She waited for her to leave.

However, Edith didn't budge. Instead, she began pulling sharp little silver pins from a pincushion. All Cate could think about was how grateful she was that she'd worn underwear.

She tried on her favorite sheath dress first. It was ten sizes too big, and she stood patiently while Edith pinned and tucked the gown. After Edith was finished pinning, she reached for a long veil hanging in the dressing room. Cate wanted to tell her not to bother with the veil because she didn't want to wear one. She'd envisioned her hair in a loose knot near the nape of her neck, a couple Vendela roses tucked into the bun for decoration. But Edith had already started tucking the veil on the crown of her head, and Cate figured she might as well experiment while she had the opportunity. After Edith crookedly attached the veil, she quickly reached for another accessory. "Here you go," she said. She handed Cate a fake bouquet of flowers.

Stiffly, she turned toward her mother. She was afraid if she made one false move she would trip over the dragging gown or cathedral-length veil that dug into her scalp.

"It looks like a nightgown," Connie said instead of getting tears in her eyes, as Cate always imagined her mother would the first time her youngest daughter stepped into a wedding gown.

Fashion had never been a common interest among them. Cate remembered the time in high school when she'd bought leopard skin creepers and Connie said she couldn't understand why anyone would purposely want to wear orthopedic shoes. However, this time Cate agreed with her. The dress did look like a nightgown, and she could see every unflattering crevice and bulge in her body beneath the silk. She imagined all of their friends and relatives seated in Founders Chapel, looking at her butt cheeks clenching as she took each step down the aisle.

The most flattering part of the whole ensemble was the veil. Though crooked, and giving her a headache, she actually liked it. Something about its long cathedral length was elegant yet dramatic and very flattering to her silhouette.

The other two sheath dresses were the same story, and it was then that she understood why her dream dress had been so hard to find. Only Gwyneth Paltrow and Uma Thurman would look good in it.

At this point she was open to anything. She tried on the first dress Edith had selected—the strapless one with dirt around the edges. As Edith began to pin the dress to fit her figure, she felt that same surge of adrenaline she felt when she spotted her dream dress online.

She turned to Connie. She was dabbing at her eyes with a Kleenex. "I told you that you have to try them on," she said. "You look beautiful."

"Twenty five years' experience," Edith said. "I always know what looks best."

After that she listened to Edith. In fact, she hung on her every word. Eventually, she found her dress. Pure satin, it was strapless with beads that sent prisms of rainbow lights from the mirrors. It had a mermaid style skirt, and there was no tulle or crinoline to create any poof. She also selected a cathedral-length veil with white piping around the edges.

She was in a wonderful mood when they left the bridal salon. Her mother threw her arm around Cate's shoulders. "Isn't this exciting?" Connie said. "You're going to look beautiful! I can't wait for everyone to see you in that dress. Ethan's gonna die."

"Thanks, Mom. Thanks for coming with me. I had a really good time today." She was about to put her arm over her mother's shoulders when her cell phone rang. "It's Ethan."

"Don't tell him what it looks like," her mom chided as Cate answered the phone.

"Hey, pretty," he said. "How's it going? Did you find a dress?"

"I sure did."

Her mother's car made a beeping noise when she opened her door. She climbed into the passenger side of the car. "What's going on?"

"There is a house I'm really interested in looking at. I drove past it, and it looks pretty good. When are you coming back? Denise said she can get us in there around six."

"We're on our way now. So if we don't hit traffic we should be right on time."

She agreed to pick him up at five, and they would drive up to Escondido together. She hung up and slipped her cell phone back into her purse.

"How's Ethan?" her mother asked.

"Great. He found a place he wants to look at." She was going to have to tell her sooner or later, so she may as well get it out in the open now, especially when her mother was in a good mood.

"Already?" Her tone suggested that she was taking it well.

"Yes." Cate smiled.

"Can he afford the mortgage on his own?"

"No." She decided to make it sound as harmless and natural as she possibly could. "Remember? I told you and Dad before, I'll be living there too."

Her mother took her eyes off the freeway and looked at Cate as if she'd just said she was applying for a sex change. "You? Are moving in with him? Before the wedding?"

She sensed the mother-daughter bond they'd formed that afternoon in the dressing room breaking like a tree branch hit by lightning.

Even though Connie's voice had risen, Cate kept hers calm. "Mom. We're engaged."

"You can't move in with him before the wedding!"

"We're getting *married*. I think it's okay for us to live together. I don't know why you're getting upset. I told you guys this already."

"Oh no you're not. Not in the Catholic church you're not getting married. No priest will marry you if you live with each other."

If this were true then all of her married Catholic friends would've never made it down the aisle. Furthermore, her cousin Al would probably marry them. She hadn't asked him yet, but she knew that he'd married her cousin, Toby, and he'd lived with his fiancée before they were even engaged. She pointed this all out to her mother, trying to sound calm the whole time. She noticed a vein bulging from Connie's neck and knew this was a bad sign. The vein always appeared whenever she was angry.

"Well, who is paying for your wedding, Cate?"

A cheap shot. Her parents were paying, of course. It's not like Cate could afford to pay for the wedding on her teacher's salary, and it wasn't like her parents couldn't afford it.

"Well, if you think I'm going to pay for this wedding or one of those dresses, you're crazy! If you move in with him, you're on your own!"

Technically, Connie wouldn't be paying. She hadn't held a job since before Cate's older sister Emily was born, but Cate decided not to point this out. However, her mother did have a huge influence over her father, and they couldn't hold Cate at her mercy, force her to live alone, throwing away rent when the cost of homes in San Diego rose another sixty thousand dollars by the time they were married.

"Mom, you're being unfair. Do you realize how the market is in San Diego right now? Homes are going up ten thousand dollars a month. We can hardly afford City Heights. If we wait a year we won't even be able to afford the ghetto. Where will we live? We have to strike while the iron is hot. And besides, I'm twenty-eight!"

"Do what you want. But I won't come to the wedding if you move in with Ethan. And I won't pay for it, either."

She felt like she'd just had vodka thrown in her face. Two minutes earlier they'd been strolling arm in arm from the bridal shop, and now her mother was boycotting the wedding?

She tried to imagine a wedding without her mother. Not only would she feel empty and alone, but there probably wouldn't even be a wedding. On a teacher's salary they could invite a little over a dozen people, and Ethan could make his famous Greek lasagna and lime rice. She could pick up flowers in bulk from Costco, and buy her dress from Overstock.com. What did it matter anyway? She didn't even want a big wedding to begin with. After all her bridesmaid duties she felt as if she were weddinged out.

However, the thought of her mother boycotting the wedding made her miserable.

They didn't speak for the rest of the ride, and every time Cate bravely glanced in her mother's direction, the vein still bulged from her neck. When they arrived at Cate's complex she actually thought she was going to have to jump from Connie's Volvo as though she were being dropped off by a bookie that she owed money to. Her mother barely slowed down to let her out then sped off before she could close her door.

She decided to call her sister. She'd never really confided in her friends about her mother's over-the-top religious convictions. Val, Beth, and Sarah were all Catholics. They had all lived with their fiancés before marriage, and as far as she knew none of their mothers had threatened to boycott their weddings. She was also pretty certain none of their mothers had visited Rome six times with the sole purpose of viewing the pope, or told their children that hardly anyone went to heaven. Rather, their first stop in the afterlife would be purgatory, a desolate and foggy place where you had no friends and were constantly lost. The only person she felt would understand would be someone who'd been exposed to the same kind of upbringing.

"Hi Cate," Emily said. Cate could hear her niece cooing in the background. "I just got off the phone with Mom."

"You did?"

"Yes. She told me what happened."

"I'm twenty-eight, Emily. They haven't supported me since I left college, and even in college they were only half supporting me. She can't control my decisions. She can't do this to me."

"Well, Cate." Her voice was flat. "I really don't know what to tell you."

"What do you mean?"

"Frankly, I think she's right. I didn't live with Bradley until I was married. I thought it was disrespectful to Mom. And besides, what are you really saving for marriage? I always wanted something to look forward to."

Emily. Always the angel. Always Mom's favorite. She and Connie were cut from the same mold and had played on the same team since Cate had been alive. Unless, that was, Connie had done something to piss off Emily, and then she'd come running to Cate. How could Cate have forgotten this?

She gave her sister the same argument about the cost of living she'd given to her mother.

"So buy the house now and have Ethan get a roommate."

"I can't do that to him."

"Why not?"

"Oh here is the plan, Ethan. We're going to buy a house, but a stranger will be moving in to cover my half of the mortgage because my mom won't come to the wedding if I live with you. That's crazy."

"He's a big boy. He can handle it."

The cost of homes was really only half her argument. The truth was, she wanted to move in with Ethan. Plain and simple. They were getting married, and this was the step she was ready to take. Maybe Emily would've let Bradley fend for himself, but Ethan and she were partners. They were going in on this together, and she wasn't going to leave him high and dry.

"I can't do that to him." Grease rubbed against her calves, but she was too annoyed to notice. "It's just not fair. He's my best friend. It's not as if this is some kind of arranged marriage by our parents and I'm indebted to them until the moment Dad presents me and my dowry to this strange guy at the altar."

"Look at *My Big Fat Greek Wedding*. She made that guy do all kinds of stuff for her, and he went along with it because he loved her, and she wore that hideous dress and all that makeup just to make her parents happy. He even converted to Greek Orthodox for her."

She didn't want Ethan to convert to anything religious for her or anyone else. As far as she was concerned, spirituality was a personal decision. You followed a religion because you felt it in your heart, not because you wanted to make your girlfriend's parents happy. She said good-bye to her sister, and for some reason while she thought of Connie and Emily, Denise's face popped into her head too. She was starting to realize that the only thing that had changed since she'd gotten engaged was everyone else.

·10·

A Cottage for Two

Ethan was watching HGTV when she arrived. "See. This is what I want to do to our place. He pointed to the television set with the remote. "When we get a place," he added quietly.

She watched a man nail-gun a piece of crown molding to the ceiling. "Do you know how to do that?" she asked.

"No. But I'm going to learn."

Normally the thought of him renovating their house would've excited her. But she was still feeling deflated from her fight with her mother. Maybe Emily was right. Maybe moving in with Ethan was disrespectful to her parents. They had, after all, raised her, given her their Volvo when she was sixteen, paid for her college tuition. Maybe she should just wait and move in with him after the wedding. But where would they be able to live? If the cost of homes kept increasing, they wouldn't be able to afford a house, and Ethan had been fantasizing about having his own garage and a yard for a dog for as long as they'd been dating. This was supposed to be "the happiest time of their lives," and telling him about her mother would only drag him down too. It wouldn't be fair to impose her parents' beliefs on him.

"I can't wait to check this place out," Ethan said. "It's the best I've seen yet."

It must be good because he hadn't even bothered doing a walk through any of the other houses he'd scouted out with Denise. This had been the first acceptable one. "I drove by it earlier, and it looks really good. It's historical. Built in the twenties, and located in a historical part of Escondido. It has a porch and a little picket fence."

The twinkle in his eyes faded. "What's wrong?" he asked.

"Nothing. I'm just tired."

As they drove to Escondido, she thought of ways she could appease her mother. It wasn't going to be easy, but she figured if she could get some kind of influential figure on her side, someone her mother couldn't argue with, she'd have to go along with it. She'd talk to her cousin Al. That is, if her mother hadn't already gotten ahold of him and talked him out of performing the ceremony if Cate went into escrow.

"This is it," Ethan said, slowing down in front of a tiny white bungalow with lace curtains and a darling little porch. Some of the paint was chipping, but it was nothing that a new paint job couldn't fix. "Now just remember to keep an open mind," he said as he pulled the parking brake up. "You have to look at the big picture. What we can fix."

"I know," she said, wondering what lay inside.

Denise pulled up in front of them. Her apple-shaped body emerged from the car, and she held a manilla envelope. "The owners aren't home," she said. She looked Cate up and down, and Cate noticed her eyes pause on her green beaded shoes. She looked back up at Cate's face. "So Ethan told me you found a dress." Cate thought of her gown and then of her mother speeding off, and felt her heart sink.

"I think I did."

"Great." She smiled, and her eyes swept over Cate's body again. "You're so thin I imagine you can probably wear anything."

"Oh thanks," Cate said. "That's really sweet of you."

She led them to a lock box. They waited while she fiddled with a giant-sized lock.

The house was tiny. Two small bedrooms, a minute bathroom with enough room for one person to comfortably stand, a small kitchen, and an adjoining family room and dining room made up the nine-hundred-and-eighty-square-foot floor plan. Most of the walls were covered in peeling gold paint, and the bathroom floor looked as if a lawn mower had peeled out over the linoleum. The kitchen countertops were as marked as an old cutting board. However, there were built-in shelves, chair rails, bay windows, and French doors in the master bedroom. She could see the potential in it. She could see them taking out the linoleum and sifting through paint samples and kitchen countertop choices. She loved it.

"What do you think?" Ethan asked.

"I think it's great. What about you?"

"Love it."

Several minutes later they were en route to Denise's office to write an offer.

Denise faxed their offer to the agent representing the seller and told them she would call as soon as she heard anything. As they walked back to their cars she asked how the wedding plans were going, and Cate lied and said everything was fine. Then Denise turned to Ethan. "You'll never believe who I'm going to be representing."

"Who?" he asked.

"Janet Griffin."

Cate almost stopped dead in her tracks, but Ethan's hand gently rested on her back, and she kept walking.

"Really," he said.

Denise nodded. "She saw my name on a bench at a bus stop and contacted me. She's looking for a condo. Her place burned down in San Francisco, and I guess she got a good insurance—"

"I know."

"She's really down in the dumps and needs a lot of help, so I told her I would represent her."

"That was nice of you." He unlocked the door for Cate.

"Well, you know. That's what friends are for. Also, she needs help finding a job, and I figured with all your connections you might be able to help her. I gave her your number. I hope you don't mind."

"No. Not at all."

This would all seem perfectly normal if Cate could forget the way Janet had eyed him that day at the pool, the way she'd kissed him on the cheek when Leotard Man had scared her. Something about the whole thing was weird. Why was she moving back to San Diego, contacting people she knew that Ethan was close to?

"Anyway," Denise said. "I'll call you as soon as I hear back from the selling agent." She smiled at them. "Keep your fingers crossed."

Approved but Not Settled

The following morning they woke up to the sound of Ethan's cell phone ringing. It was Denise. Cate had been fantasizing about drinking cold sodas on the porch in the summer and making homemade soup in the winter in their little cottage ever since they'd left Escondido. She also thought she might feel a tiny bit relieved if they didn't get the place. It would buy her a little more time to mend the fences with her mother.

"We got the place!" Ethan said excitedly as he pulled the phone away from his ear. "They accepted our offer. We're in escrow!"

She gave him a thumbs up as he continued to gather all the details from Denise. "Aren't you excited?" he asked after he hung up the phone.

"Yeah! Of course."

"What's wrong? I can tell something's wrong."

She told him about her mother, only she watered down the story so he didn't think he was marrying into total religious insanity. When she was finished, he squeezed her knee. "I'll do whatever makes *you* happy."

"I want to move in with you. I want to get our house."

"She's not going to boycott the wedding."

She hugged her knees into her chest. "I don't know. She seemed pretty serious, and I haven't spoken with her since she dropped me off yesterday."

"Why don't you talk to your dad?"

"I don't know." She shook her head. "I get the feeling he's not going to support me on this one."

"You can't let them make all our decisions."

"I know."

"I have to get some work done today," he said. "But let's do something fun tonight. Celebrate our new house." He kissed her on the forehead. "Don't worry about your mom. Everything will be fine. Let her be angry for a few days and she'll get over it."

She spent the rest of the day at the beach. She had a million wedding things she wanted to do, but without her mother or maid of honor on her side it seemed pointless. Even if she could afford to put deposits down on flowers and a photographer, it wouldn't be as fun or fulfilling without them. She wanted her mother's opinion and expertise. Connie was a master party planner and hostess. If any anyone knew how to create ambiance and atmosphere it was her. Cate recalled years of holiday parties and feasts that had been made special because of her mother's eye for detail and great taste in food. Cate was clueless when it came to napkin rings and centerpieces, and she'd often wondered if she'd ever be able to take after her mother. Putting a party together, in Cate's mind, usually involved chips and salsa and some Pinot Grigio in whatever glasses were clean. Planning a wedding was always something a mother and a daughter shared, and now she felt alone.

Despite the gorgeous day, the beach was pretty desolate. Empty stretches of sand were typical on the weekdays, and this was how she liked it. Weekends, on the other hand, were packed, and if you didn't make it there by eleven, you'd be lucky to find a seaweed-free section of sand to set your towel down. Radios competed over one another, and after a while the various types of music sounded like one big buzz. Trash cans overflowed with aluminum, and there was always a line for the bathroom.

Today, there were a few small clumps of families, undoubtedly tourists, and several surfers in the water. She noticed the occasional girl like herself sunning and reading a book or flipping through a fashion magazine. She spotted one girl thumbing through an issue of *Modern Bride*, and she felt her heart sink when she realized she might not be looking through any more magazines if they had to elope.

She loved summers because they gave her so much time to read. During the school year it was too hard to work all day, spend time with Ethan and friends, and really sink into a good book. She had a long list of summer reading. At least she'd have time to read with the wedding plans on hold.

She rolled onto her stomach and tried to read her book but found herself just thinking about the type of wedding she and Ethan would have without her parents. She was just starting to think Las Vegas might be fun when something cold and wet sprayed over her shoulders. Her first thought was that a seagull had shit on her. Afraid of what she might find, she flipped over.

"Oh sorry, man, I didn't mean to get you. I just broke my board, and I'm a little bit ticked. Sorry, I wasn't even paying attention to where I was going or what I was doing, and I was shaking the water from my hair and I completely nailed you."

If Brad Pitt was missing a twin, she'd just found him. It was hard for her to be irritated that he'd shaken his head over her like a wet German shepherd when his stomach looked as hard as the battered surfboard he held. She looked at the broken board, wax covering it like bacon drippings, then at his perfectly white, straight teeth.

"That's okay. It's no problem. Really."

"I didn't get your book wet, did I?" She could see droplets of water sliding down the tip of his nose, dangling from his long eyelashes like raindrops on palm fronds.

"No, it's fine," she said, even though she noticed the first few pages of the novel shriveling like wilted lettuce.

"Well, hey, you have a great day. And again, I'm sorry."

"You too." She watched him walk away, his orange and red swim trunks dangling on his perfectly sculpted hips, revealing one of the sexiest tan lines she'd ever seen in her life. She felt a little guilty for checking him out and wished Jill was with her. She could introduce her only remaining single friend to the hottest guy she'd seen in San Diego in ages.

For the second time since she'd arrived at the beach she applied sunscreen. Being as fair as she was, she never really came to the beach for a tan. It was more just to relax and listen to the waves. People watch. After her encounter with hot surfer guy, she couldn't complain about the people watching. It was always easy to spot the tourists, because when they got up to leave they always left someone with a mouthful of sand. They never paid attention to what direction the wind was blowing when they shook out their towels.

Something about the sound of the waves and the heat always made her sleepy. She found it hard to take naps during the day, but give her a half hour at the beach, and she'd be dozing off in no time. She had just started to dream that she and Ethan had decided to get married wearing only their bathing suits when her phone rang.

It was Ethan. Groggily, she answered.

"Hey, you sleeping?"

"Sort of," she said.

"Well, I just talked to my brother. He's in town for the weekend. I guess he has a new girlfriend, and he invited us to go a belly dancing festival in Balboa Park tonight."

The invitation would've sounded odd coming from anyone else, but it was Chuck they were talking about. The same person who'd once belonged to a band called The Land of Pot and Death. Belly dancing seemed tame in comparison.

"He has a new girlfreind?"

"Yeah, she's from Czechoslovakia."

"Really? Is she a belly dancer?" She brushed sand from her legs.

"I think so."

It sounded intriguing. The last time she'd seen belly dancers had been at Papadakis, a mouthwatering Greek restaurant in Los Angeles, and they'd been wonderful. "Yeah, okay. Let's go."

After they said good-bye she shook the sand from her towel and collected the rest of her belongings.

One new message waited for her, and she hoped it was from her mother. Connie and Cate had faced their share of arguments in the past. Usually the resolution came a day or two later when her mother called, acting like nothing had happened. Cate hoped that her mother would be the same in this situation. That she would simply accept that Cate was moving in with her future husband, pretend as if they had never argued, and move on. She pressed the Play button on her machine.

"Hello Cate. This is Peg Migillicuddy." It was the wedding coordinator Cate had contacted, and she sounded just like Mrs. Doubtfire. Her voice was low and calm and seasoned with a hint of Ireland. "I'm just returning your call, dear, and would love to sit down with you to discuss your very special day." Cate wrote down her phone number. If anyone could sway her mother it might be this woman. However, Cate couldn't call her back when she didn't even know if there would be a wedding to coordinate.

·12·

A New Minister

She took a shower, then blow-dried her hair. As she was finishing, Ethan arrived.

"Did you talk to your mom?" he asked.

"Not yet. It's so embarrassing. What will your parents think of my family if my mom boycotts the wedding and we have to elope?" She wrapped the cord around the hair dryer.

"I feel like Tori Spelling."

"What?"

"The whole situation is something that would happen on a made-for-TV movie." He laughed at her observation, but it was true. The situation with her mother was something she would've gobbled up with a bag of popcorn, soaking in the juicy details of someone else's drama. This wasn't supposed to happen to her.

"She's not going to ditch the wedding. Just give her some time to get over it. Or talk to your dad. Why don't you talk to him?"

"He's not back yet."

She pulled a pair of jeans from her dresser. She imagined the festival outside, sitting Indian-style on the grass while women dressed like Aladdin danced in the middle of a circle. She put on her most comfy white tank top and grabbed a hoodie with a Hawaiian flower on the front of it.

They rode in Cate's Volvo to the park, and Ethan parked in front of a building shaped like a circle and covered in bright murals.

"It's indoors?" Cate asked.

"Yeah, this is where Chuck said to go." They headed inside and bypassed a small cluster of people. Cate swiped up a program from a card table, and Ethan paused to throw five bucks in a glass vase labeled Donations.

"That was generous of you," Cate said, looking at the coins that were piled inside.

"It was all I had."

They were heading through the double doors of the auditorium when they heard a voice behind them. "Um, did you guys pay?"

They spun around and faced a woman with a baby in a sack on the front of her chest, no makeup, long straw-colored hair that looked as if it hadn't been trimmed since birth.

"We just did." Ethan pointed to the vase.

The woman smiled. "That's just for donations for the staff. Tickets are on sale for the show. It's fifteen dollars each," she said matter-of-factly. Typical Chuck. He always left out important details, and if they had known the event was going to cost thirty dollars, they would've stopped at an ATM on the way.

He turned to her. "Do you have any money?"

She was already fishing through her purse. She pulled out a tiny wad of cash. "Uhh . . . Oh, here is a five." She gave it to Ethan. "And. One . . . two . . . three. I have three more dollars. Eight dollars." She could feel her cheeks growing warm as the woman watched her hand the crumpled bills to Ethan.

He immediately turned on his soft negotiating voice. The "meet me somewhere in the middle because I'm so sweet and reasonable" voice.

She'd heard him use it a million times with clients when they were start-ing to freak out over their five-hundred-person retirement party or whether to have shiittake egg rolls or ginger-crusted salmon bites for a graduation party. He'd gotten his wonderful people skills from dealing with so many frantic party planners on a regular basis.

He looked at her, right in the eye, an innocent expression on his face. "My brother invited us to this, and he told me tickets wouldn't be more than a few bucks. Then when I saw your donation vase I figured it was free, so I just threw my last five in." He leaned over and plucked the bill from inside the donation vase. Cate's cheeks were as warm as a crockpot as he added it to their stash. He shook his head. "I swear to you, I just threw my last five in there. Is there any way we can just do a two-for-one special? I mean, this is all we have, and we really just came here to meet up with my brother."

Cate wanted the ground to open up and suck her inside. He'd ac-tually revoked their donation and then asked for a two-for-one special when in reality they wouldn't even be paying for one with their thir-teen dollars.

"I guess," she whispered as she grabbed a stamp. "But don't tell anyone." She stamped their hands.

Once inside, they spotted Chuck, sitting in a folding chair in the front row. His face unfolded in a giant smile when he noticed them. He was wearing black leather pants and a blazer with no shirt beneath it. She could see his chest hair and belly button. His hair was slicked back, and both his hoop earrings shined beneath the overhead lights. "Hey! Here's the happy engaged couple!"

He gave Ethan a quick hug then turned to Cate. His hug felt tight and his kiss firm on her cheek. "You guys have to meet Tatiana."

The figure next to his empty chair greeted them with pursed lips. Cate wasn't sure what she noticed first. The jewel placed on her fore-head, or the gigantic crack of cleavage that split through the center of the blazer she wore. There was no sign of a shirt or even tank top from beneath her blazer. Just her gigantic boobs. What do these people have against layering? Long blonde hair spilled over her jacket, and she had pouty, glossy lips, narrow eyes, and a tiny turned-up nose.

"Tatiana, this is my brother Ethan and his fiancée, Cate." His eyes flashed over them. "I've told her so much about you guys."

"It's nice to meet you," Cate said, offering her hand. The gesture was returned with Tatiana's left cheek. Cate was slightly offended, but then remembered she was from Czechoslovakia and probably didn't speak English. Maybe she'd misunderstood her.

"Sorry, it was packed when we got here, but you guys can sit in the seats behind us." Chuck pointed.

They slid into two empty seats behind Chuck and Tatiana, and Cate couldn't see over Tatiana'a head. She peered through a small wedge in between their shoulders. A couple minutes later a woman wearing a flowing skirt and a suede vest walked to a microphone. She spoke for nearly fifteen minutes about what a wonderful night they had in store. Cate thought she heard Ethan groan somewhere in the middle of it, and she sort of understood his fear. They thought they were attending a free festival where they could mingle amongst other attendees and leave at their own free will. What they had gotten themselves into was a full-fledged evening of performing arts, and as she thumbed through the program she knew they were in deep trouble. It could be hours before they escaped.

"And now I would like to introduce to you one of the finest performances we have tonight. They are a magical band. A blend of spirituality, diversity, and understanding. Ladies and gentlemen, I give you Unite."

Seconds later a trail of musicians quietly entered the dance floor like ants. The most conservative one was the violin player, a twenty-something Asian girl with a shaved head and pierced eyebrows. In her company was a variety of dreadlocked characters, a guy with a pink Mohawk, a middle-aged woman holding a bongo drum who looked as if she taught anthropology at the local university and wrote occasional articles on saving the seals in La Jolla Cove. A toddler, no older than two, clung to the woman's dripping beige skirt.

The woman sat on the floor, crossed her legs, and placed her drum in front of her. The blonde child, dressed in a cute pink sweater set and white pants, took a seat next to her, popped a pacifier in her mouth, and remained still as if she were used to being part of a New-Age band, rather than singing nursery rhymes in front of *Sesame Street*.

The music was the type that quickened her pulse and made her imagine people dancing around incense while a cobra emerged from a basket. Only seconds into their first song a barefoot guy with thick, heavy dreadlocks and tribal tattoos covering his arms skipped from backstage. He wore heavy eye makeup and beaded genie-style pants. Feathers dangled from his hair. The most interesting part of his outfit was the deer tail that dangled from his butt. He had a face like Jared Leto, and a demeanor that suggested a decade worth of hallucinogenics.

Pulling the microphone from its post, he began to chant in a foreign language. One minute he was hopping from foot to foot, and the next minute he was twirling across the stage like Baryshnikov, doing the air splits and pirouetting like he was part of *The Nutcracker*.

Cate glanced at Ethan. He was slouched in his chair, but his eyes were glued to the performance. He didn't even sense her watching him.

The singer set his microphone back on the post, threw himself on the ground, and began to roll around. On all fours he popped his tongue from his mouth twice before crawling toward the audience.

Don't let him come near me. Don't let him come near me. Don't let him come near me. Do not let him near me.

He was headed her way and crawling quickly. She moved her feet into her aisle, praying he would crawl right past her. She began to sweat when she noticed him crawling straight toward her, flicking his tongue the whole way. He crept to her, paused at her feet then flicked his tongue within a millimeter of her leg. She began to relax when it appeared he would find his next victim. However, he grabbed her calf like it was a microphone, and began to sing into her foot—something about finding the light, and a better source of peace. Maybe what he really meant was that she needed a pedicure. She looked to Ethan for help, but he was too busy staring in shock.

"We are oooonnne! Bring us to the liiiiiight!" When he wasn't singing in tongues he sounded like he belonged in the lead role of *Phantom of the Opera*. "Give us liiiiight!"

She could feel his thumb pressed into the ball of her foot, and she wondered if he ever worried about athlete's foot when he performed. He began singing in tongues again. Possessed—he had to be.

He sprang up to his legs. Startled, she flinched. For a split second she feared he might throw her over his shoulder and use her butt for a bongo drum. She'd never felt more relieved when he twirled back to the dance floor. As she watched him go, she caught a glimpse of Chuck's delighted face.

The first song lasted fifteen minutes.

Loud applause followed, and Ethan leaned toward Cate. "We're getting the hell out of here the first chance we have," he said through clenched teeth.

"We can't leave," she whispered back, still clapping. Even though she felt like her foot had been molested, all she could think about was the woman holding the baby who'd let them in for free. What kind of people weaseled their way in, then rudely snuck out in the middle of the show?

"*Yes* we *can* leave. There is *no* way I'm sitting through three hours of this." He pointed to his program. "This is only the first band!"

The next song started, and she crossed her legs and aimed her knees toward Ethan. The music was slower this time but true to the same mystical tune. She heard the light sound of little bells, and when she turned to see where they were coming from she saw the belly dancers. Apparently, belly dancing wasn't much of a calorie-burning activity because both women had fleshy, curvy bodies, their pudgy tummies hanging over their low pants as if they hadn't done a single sit-up in their sensual lives. They danced all over the place with Foot Sniffer, moving their hips and shaking their bells above their heads. One of them never removed the thin veil that covered her face.

The most intriguing part of the whole show wasn't Mr. Foot Fetish hovering on all fours over a Bible or the two belly dancers balancing swords on their foreheads. It was the little blonde toddler in her pink outfit sitting next to the bongo drum as if she were an adult waiting for a bus to arrive. There was no fascination in her eyes or excitement in her gaze. She hardly even moved. She just sucked on her pacifer as if she'd seen these freaks perform a million times before, as if the novelty had worn off in her infant days. Cate wondered what the child must think of *Teletubbies*. If the Foot Sniffer and his deer tail didn't amuse her, the *Teletubbies* must be like reading *War and Peace*.

The song ended, and Ethan turned to her. "Okay, go," he whispered. "I'll meet you outside."

"What about Chuck? You're just going to ditch him?"

"We'll catch up with him later. There is no way I'm sitting through the rest of this," he hissed.

"Ethan, they basically let us in for free. We can't be rude. That's sooo rude."

"I don't care. I'm dying *and* starving." He looked to the right corner of the building before gently pushing her from the chair.

Cate staggered from his shove, but once she regained her balance she quickly scurried from the building, praying her departure wasn't completely obvious.

The air was chilly outside. Guilt washed over her when she thought about the woman letting them in for free. A couple seconds later Ethan came through the double doors, walking a mile a minute.

"Sorry," he said when he saw her. "There was no way I was going to sit through the rest of that. How's your foot?"

She cracked up. "Fine. I just thought I might never get it back."

She was just starting to feel like they'd made a clean getaway when she heard footsteps behind her.

"Hey! Wait up, you guys!" Chuck.

They spun around. "Oh hey," Ethan said. "Sorry. I didn't mean to leave like that, but we're starving, and I thought the show would be much shorter."

"No problem. We weren't planning on staying for the whole show."

Cate had always felt pretty average in size but she felt minute next to Tatiana.

Each boob alone was the size of her head.

She sensed what was coming next, and if there had been a polite way to stop Ethan from speaking, she would've done it. "You guys are more than welcome to join us for dinner," he said.

"You want to go eat, baby?" Chuck squeezed Tatiana's butt.

She turned her pouty smile to him. Cate was hoping she'd say she was stuffed and that she wanted to go to Mexico, but something told her it took a lot to feed those boobs. "Yes, baby. I need to eat." Her accent was thick, and it was the first full sentence Cate had heard from her mouth.

She was glad they'd made plans to drive separately to The Red Fox.

"Are you out of your mind?" she asked when they got in the car.

"What? I had to invite them. It would've been totally weird."

"Did you see how that girl looks at me?"

She expected him to act totally oblivious, so he wouldn't be responsible for making them attached to Chuck and his scary date for the rest of the night, but to her surprise he admitted that he'd noticed how rude she was. "But you're so nice, Cate. Maybe you can just kill her with kindness. I'm sure you'll win her over by the end of the night."

Tatiana and Chuck were already waiting in a circular booth when they arrived. She was chewing delicately on the end of a cherry stem, wearing a bored expression. Chuck's arm was draped over her shoulders. Even in the booth she was a good three inches above him.

Cate slid into the booth next to her. If she did have a conversation with her, she'd be talking mostly to her cleavage.

"So that was neat," Cate said, opening her menu. "Unite."

"Aren't they great?" Chuck boomed. "Tatiana dances with them sometimes, but she's still learning, so sometimes we just go and watch.

And let me tell ya, I don't mind watching." He winked at Ethan then downed the cocktail in front of him.

"So, um," Cate continued. "What religion are they? I mean, I thought they were probably something from an Eastern tradition, but then they were singing about Christianity and stuff."

"Totally Fucking Confused," Ethan chimed in. "That's their religion."

Chuck laughed at the sarcasm, but Cate sensed that he was only being polite and didn't find Ethan's remark that amusing. "Actually, they embrace all religions, but Ezekiel, the lead singer, is Christian."

"Really?"

"Oh yes. A while back he had this *amazing* revelation." The way he spoke of Ezekiel reminded her of Stone Phillips on *Dateline*, explaining the tale of a heroic child who pulled his parent from a flood, or an eighty-year-old man who still competed in triathlons. "He didn't sleep or eat for seven days, and in that time he realized he might be the reincarnated soul of one of Jesus's apostles. He believes he is here to spread the message."

Cate nodded politely, thinking of what her mother would probably call Ezekiel. Nuts. The Antichrist. Possessed by the devil. "How intriguing."

"Chuck," Ethan said. "He was probably on drugs. No sleeping. No eating. Having visions. It's a freaking week of LSD."

Chuck shook his head. "He wasn't on acid. It's really quite fascinating. He actually saw Jesus, and Jesus told him that his name is Ezekiel now."

"What was his name before?" Cate wanted to know.

"Bill."

Ethan looked at him as if he were crazy, and Cate thought it was best to just change the subject. "So Tatiana, how long have you been in the U.S.?" she asked.

"Six years."

And remarkably, you speak horrible English. "Oh, great."

"Uh . . . my parents, they bring me over ven I vas still in grade scul, and then they leave, but I legally emancipate myself from them because I vant to stay."

Vait a minute, Cate wanted to say. If she had only been here for six years and she had moved here in grade school, then she couldn't be out of her teens. "How old are you?"

"Eighteen."

If she'd had a drink in front of her she would've chugged the whole thing, just so she could have something to do with her mouth. She was at a loss of words. "Well, eighteen! That's uh . . . young!" What in the world could this eighteen-year-old possibly see in thirty-five-year-old Chuck? When Cate was eighteen, twenty-three seemed over the hill.

As if reading her mind, Ethan flagged down the waitress. "What do you want to drink?" he asked as their server headed toward them.

"Vodka. With a splash of tonic" Cate said.

"Tatiana's great." Chuck snuggled up to her. "She's going to be an actress. I got her an audition for Pam Anderson's latest pilot. A friend of mine has the connection."

"Yes," Tatiana said. "I'm trying out for show. How do you say? Keep your hands folded for me."

Chuck threw his head back and laughed as if she were his two-year-old who had just done something adorable. "It's 'keep your fingers crossed for me!' "

She giggled. "Oh. Fingers crossed. I do not know all these things you speak."

"Isn't she perfect for television?" Chuck pointed to her, and whether he realized it or not, his finger was aimed directly at her tits. "I mean, look at her. She's perfect."

He kissed her again, this time tickling her cleavage. *He tickled her cleavage. In public.*

"She looks great." Cate smiled at her. "I'm sure you'll do great."

"Yeah, good luck." Ethan lifted his glass before taking a gigantic swig. "Let us know how it goes."

When it came time to order dinner, Tatiana ordered a Caesar salad. "You want anchovies with that?" The waitress asked.

She looked puzzled but began to nod her head anyway. Cate thought it was gross, but Czechoslovakians ate differently than they did here.

"Whoa, whoa, whoa. Wait a minute," Chuck interrupted. He set down his menu. "What did you just ask her?"

"Does she want anchovies?" The waitress looked like she had better things to do.

He looked at Tatiana. "Do you know what an anchovy is?"

She shook her head. He turned back to the waitress and sliced his hand over the table before chuckling. "No. She doesn't want anchovies."

"I vould like pineapple and vodka."

"Okay." Chuck said. "She'll have a pineapple and vodka with dinner."

"ID please?" The waitress held out her hand and waited while Tatiana produced a license. Cate almost asked to see it too, but decided she better wait until the waitress left. She watched as the waitress looked at the ID then back at Tatiana, then back at the ID. "All right," she mumbled before she returned the license.

Cate and Ethan both ordered burgers with fries. As soon as the waitress left they asked to see Tatiana's fake ID. "It is my friend, Anya. She return to Czechoslovakia for a vile and let me use. She is twenty-two."

The girl in the picture did look very similar.

"Yes, she is my roommate. I live with her for three years. After my parents leave ve stay together."

"Ver—I mean where do you live now?"

"I stay vith Chuck for a vile."

She asked them what an anchovy was, and they spent ten minutes trying to describe the salty, wormy little fish. She kept asking if it was like tuna, and they kept telling her it was more similar to a sardine, only she had no idea what a sardine was either.

"Anyway, so how are all the wedding plans going? You guys! Getting married!"

Cate and Ethan exchanged glances. "They're going good," Ethan answered.

"Yeah, we're running into a little bit of a glitch with my mom. It's nothing though." *She might not attend the wedding, which means we'll be marrying in our backyard with a weenie cookout to follow. Hope you guys can come!*

Ethan nodded. "Yeah, Connie's having a hard time with the fact that we might move in together before the big day."

Tatiana looked utterly puzzled. At eighteen, living with a man nearly twice her age, this made absolutely no sense.

"Old-fashioned, is she?" Chuck asked.

"She doesn't want to come to the wedding if we move in together, which means she definitely won't be paying for it and will probably tell my cousin not to marry us and I don't know what we'll do. Probably elope." Every time Cate thought of her mother she felt a sense of sadness creep up on her. The sadness was always there, like a bad sore that she'd forget about until she noticed the Band-Aid.

"Well, I have an idea," Chuck said. The look on his face told her it was going to be something good, a diplomatic way to achieve peace during the wedding planning. "It's simple. You guys can have Ezekiel marry you. Did I mention that he's an ordained minister?"

Ethan signaled the waitress for their check. "Uh, yeah. We'll figure it out," he said as he turned back to the table. "I'm sure Connie will come around, but thanks for the offer."

"Well, just let me know. I'm sure he'll do it."

Ethan paid the bill. Outside Tatiana opened her arms to hug Cate. The gesture surprised Cate, as only two hours ago the girl looked as if she wanted to squash Cate beneath her stiletto. When she hugged her, Cate's feet actually came off the ground, and she could feel her cheeks pressed into the side of Tatiana's boobs.

"I hope you have vonderful vedding. And do not vorry about mother. I don't even speak to my mother now. Be happy you have one who didn't let boyfriend beat you."

"Oh thanks. Yeah, I'm sure it will be fine. And good luck with the pilot. You're just beautiful. I'm sure you'll get it." She looked at Chuck. "Let us know what happens."

"Of course, doll." He kissed Cate on both cheeks.

As they walked back to the car they laughed about the evening and talked about how crazy Chuck was. "Did you see how he had to order for her?" Ethan asked.

"I know. The poor thing. She's clueless."

He pulled his phone from his pocket. "I think I have a message."

She let him listen to his voice mail, figuring all messages probably had something to do with work. He was always flooded with a million messages. In fact, half the time when she pictured Ethan in her mind it was with a cell phone pressed against his ear. When he hung up he slipped his phone back into his pocket then stared off in front of them as if he were preoccupied.

"Is everything okay?" she asked.

"Yeah, everything's fine. It's uh. Fine."

"Who was it?"

"Well, actually I wanted to tell you, but I didn't want you to freak out so I was just kind of waiting for the right moment."

No one should ever start a sentence like that. She stopped walking. "What do you mean?"

"Well, uh, that was actually Janet."

"She calls you?" Her voice remained low. She wanted him to know that she wouldn't "freak out," but really she was dying to rip his phone from his hand, demand to hear the message, and tell Janet to go find someone who wasn't engaged to call.

"Denise gave her my number. She called me yesterday—"

"She called you yesterday?" Her voice wasn't as low.

"Yeah, she did. But it was just to say hi and congratulate me on getting engaged to you." He took her hand. "She said she was very happy for us."

"Why didn't you tell me this?"

"Honestly, I forgot. You know, she just moved back here and she said she was looking for a job and I knew that Ryan was hiring at his restaurant and I thought I would help her out. Ryan's short-staffed, so I'm helping him too."

Ryan was one of Ethan's closest friends and a groomsman in their wedding. "You're going to let her work for Ryan?"

"Yeah, I mean look. I don't care about her. But I don't hate her, either. I can still be friends with her, and she's been through a lot. Her house just burned down. Her parents are divorced, and she doesn't speak to her mom. She has no siblings. She basically has no one. I feel bad for her."

She reminded herself that this was one of the reasons that she loved him so much. He had the best heart. However, she knew that women didn't just randomly move to cities where the only person they knew was their ex-boyfriend. Women didn't just conveniently decide to use their exes for job resources, or any favors, unless they still had feelings for them. In fact, there was no way in hell she would call Paul for *any* reason. She was over him, and if she heard he was getting married she would wish him the best, privately. She wouldn't call to congratulate him.

She'd never been the type of girl to break up with someone and then show up at parties and bars where she knew they hung out. She never called "just to be friends." When it was over, it was over. Moving on had always seemed like the healthiest thing for everyone. She knew Ethan was over Janet, but was Janet over him? Plain and simple, Cate didn't trust her.

·13·

Hallelujah

The following morning the phone woke them at seven thirty. It could only be one of two people. Her mother or her sister. Ever since Emily had given birth to her first child and become a stay-at-home mom she rose with the chickens, and seemed to believe everyone else did too. Her mother, also an early riser, was the only person who had enough time on her hands to call someone first-thing in the morning. Everyone else she knew was sitting in a commute, waiting in line at Starbucks, or taking a hot shower.

"It's got to be my mother or my sister," Cate said, rolling over.

"Are you going to answer it?"

"Yes." She held a finger to her lips. "Hello."

"Hey Cate!"

The voice was male, and she felt as if she should recognize it immediately.

"It's Al!" he said.

"Al! Oh my God, I mean gosh. Oh my gosh." She had just taken the

Lord's name in vain to a priest. One whom she really needed on her side, on top of it. "It's so great to hear from you." She really wasn't prepared for this. She hadn't resolved anything with her mother. He was returning her phone call that she'd placed several days ago when the wedding was still on. He'd married all her eligible cousins and now she was engaged. She only had one choice—she had to be open with him about everything. If her mother was going to boycott the wedding, she might be taking him with her, and she decided that Al might as well hear her version.

"Sorry for not getting back to you sooner. I was just in Rome for two weeks." Praise be. This meant that her mother may not have gotten ahold of him yet.

"Rome! Wow. That's great. What were you doing over there?"

"I went on vacation with some of my friends from seminary. It was kind of a reunion thing for us. Great to be back there. I really miss Italy. And hey, congratulations!" On second thought, if he knew about the engagement, Connie must've told him. "My mom just told me."

Phew! Aunt Agnes had told him. "Well, that's actually why I was calling. Um, I, well, I was hoping you would marry us."

"Absolutely. I would be honored. As long as we can work out a date."

She told him it was November eighteenth and waited while he flipped through his calendar. "That should work out just fine for me. I'm putting the weekend on my calendar."

Even though Al was one of the most reasonable people she'd ever known, she still felt nervous about coming clean. She'd expected her mother to freak out about moving in with Ethan, or missing church on a Sunday. It would feel worse if he scorned her too.

"Well, I'm running into some real roadblocks here, Al. Ethan and I are, well we're buying a house. Um, now. We're in escrow and uh . . . we're going to live together. My mom has boycotted the wedding. We got in a huge fight, and she's not coming." She ended up pouring out the whole story to him while Ethan made pancakes in the kitchen.

As she finished she prepared to listen to a lengthy yet kind lecture on exactly why the Church doesn't approve of living together before marriage and how as a priest he couldn't find it within himself to marry them. He wouldn't be as hysterical and angry as her mother, which would almost be worse, because everything that came from his mouth would probably make sense. He would sound diplomatic and calm, and he'd only be reinforcing everything she was raised to believe. There was no way she'd be able to argue with him. She'd have to accept one of three options: One, Ethan getting a roommate so her cousin could marry them in the church. Two, Ethan and Cate taking out a loan for their wedding while Cate frantically searched San Diego for a liberal Jesuit who would marry them in Founders. Three, they skip the loan and elope.

"Well, listen," Al said. "Of course the Church doesn't approve, but let me handle your mother."

"What?"

"I'll talk to your mom."

"Really? Uh, so you'll marry us? I mean, you're not going to tell us we can't marry in the church?"

"Cate, do you know why the Church doesn't approve?"

"Um, well, yes."

"Well then. It's your decision. I deal with this stuff all the time. I'll tell you the same thing I tell everyone who is in the same boat. Part of getting married is breaking away from your parents." He paused. "I don't mean severing ties with them or anything like that. But it's important to know that you and Ethan are going to be your own family now. You still have your parents and your sister. But your main family, the one that is most central and important to you, is going to be Ethan. Your parents and Ethan's parents shouldn't get involved in the decisions that you two make. I'm not saying that living together is the answer, and you know the Church doesn't approve, but that is a whole other issue. I want you two to start developing your own bond through your *own* decisions. If you start letting family members interfere now, just wait till later. I'll be seeing you guys in marriage counseling. You have to set barriers, Cate."

"But my mom . . . be careful of her. She might change your mind."

He laughed. "She's just like my mom."

"Well, be careful," she said again.

"Don't worry. But listen. There is one thing you guys have to do. I want you to attend the Pre-Cana marriage prep class."

She'd practically forgotten. She knew they'd have to do this. Every Catholic did, and she'd already heard the horrific tales of a sixth grade camp experience with religious extremists who discussed natural birth control all weekend. Nonetheless, she was up for it. She remembered Sarah saying that she and Miles actually felt much closer after their retreat. Maybe it would be a real bonding experience. "All right. No problem," she said happily. "Make sure you tell my mother we're doing that. It will help."

"I will. Oh, and hey, I made you a CD. I'll put it in the mail."

"Thanks!"

"Yeah, it has all those old songs we used to listen to."

Al lived in Arizona, but he'd often stayed with them during summers when they were kids. He was several years older than Cate and had always seemed like a big brother as opposed to a cousin. He was the first person who'd taken her to see a movie in the theater when she was a child. It was *E.T.*, and she'd bawled her head off when the extraterrestrial turned the color of bad steak and almost died at the hands of scientists. To this day it was one of her favorite movies.

She recalled days by the pool listening to Men At Work, or Hall and Oates. He used to buy her CDs and send her letters with music that he suggested. She thought he would've changed when he entered the priesthood. But he was the same old Al.

Speaking with him made her feel much better, but she still didn't want to get her hopes up. She'd had fights with her mother, but none as serious as this. Boycotting your daughter's wedding was something she'd always associated with the type of drama that would be on *Lifetime*. It wasn't something she'd ever expected to happen to her.

She told Ethan about Al over breakfast. After they ate Ethan's banana pancakes she debated calling her mother but quickly decided against it.

She'd wait until her mom made the first move. Connie needed time to cool down, and if anyone could put out her fire it was a priest. She decided to relax the day away at the beach again. She was reading her book when she noticed a shadow cross over the pages. For a moment she thought a cloud had passed over but when she felt sand on her back she knew someone had walked past. Someone very rude. Someone who paid no attention to others and didn't find the need to watch where they were going so they wouldn't senselessly kick sand on others' backs. She quickly flipped over, and as she did so she heard a familiar voice. "Sorry, man. Did I get you?"

It was the hot surfer who had dripped water all over her back the other day. The Brad Pitt look-alike. "Oh it's okay. I didn't even really notice." Why was she lying?

"It's you!" he said. "Man, you must think I'm such an idiot. Didn't I nail you the other day with water from my board?"

She nodded, trying to hide her surprise. He'd remembered her. Her? Flat-chested, flabby butt, slightly pale and sunburned easily—her? Someone who looked more like Cindy Crawford seemed like the kind of woman who'd be worthy of him.

"I'm on my second strike here I guess." He leaned forward, and she caught a whiff of floral shampoo. She'd expected to smell sunscreen, but then she realized he probably wasn't the type of person who bothered with sunscreen. "Nate," he said, offering his hand. "It's nice to meet you."

"I'm Cate." Even when she unfolded her hands to shake his hand, he didn't notice the ring. Something told her he didn't think much about marriage or wedding rings, and he probably didn't even know which hand engagement rings were worn on.

"Nate and Cate," he said, the corners of his mouth turning up just slightly. "We rhyme." When he smiled she noticed that his straight teeth were perfect. "Well, hey, Cate. I'll let you get back to your book, but again, sorry for the sand."

"Don't worry about it. It's fine, really. Enjoy those waves!" *Enjoy those waves?* Enjoy those waves! The minute the words left her lips she felt like the biggest cornball to ever set her towel on Pacific Beach. She may as well have said, "Have a swell time. I hope it's not too crummy out there for you!" She set her head down on her towel. What did she care anyway? She didn't need to impress this guy.

She read for twenty more minutes before deciding she was too restless to lie there. She collected her stuff and walked back to her apartment. She hoped to have a message from her mother, but there was nothing.

She decided that Al was right, and her mother was bound to call, mend the fences, and move on. Perhaps it was premature, but she decided to pick up where she'd left off with the wedding planning. She sat down in front of Yahoo and typed "bridesmaids dresses" in the search bar.

Even though this was Cate's first marriage, she was a veteran of weddings. She was well acquainted with the perils of being a bridesmaid. The bank-breaking cost of bridesmaid attire, sacrificing many weekends to watch friends open packages filled with forks, and preparing for toasts that still made her stomach turn were just a few things that were permanently etched in her subconscious when it came to weddings.

As she sat in front of the computer she thought of how Leslie had made them all starve the day of her wedding so they wouldn't get food on their hideous and overpriced bridesmaids suits before pictures. Then there was the time when Beth had forced everyone to dress in costume for her Halloween wedding. The list of bridesmaid torture she'd been subjected to, all in the name of her friends' "special days," was long and painful. There was a fleeting moment when she considered putting each one of them through the torment she'd endured during their weddings.

She deserved a bachelorette weekend with spa treatment in Santa Barbara or an extended stay at Mandalay Bay in Vegas, didn't she? If she could afford airfare and three nights at swanky hotels while falling into the lowest tax bracket in the country, they could too. She'd made quiche and chicken salads and sat through hours of gift-opening for all of them. They should have to plan a theme shower for her with an international twist and entrées that represented each country.

Then she realized that wasn't the way she felt at all. Even if she felt a need for bridal revenge she simply didn't care about shower themes and wild bachelorette weekends. She was getting married to her best friend in the world, and she cared more about her life with Ethan. She would be the coolest bride ever. Those lucky bastards would never know what they'd escaped.

While she clicked away on Web sites she decided she might even be cool enough to let them pick their own dresses. She would pick the color and a cheap bridesmaid dress designer, and they could choose the style they wanted. Some of the more voluptuous girls like Denise and Jill might want something a little less revealing so they could choose styles that provided more coverage. Cousin Val and Beth would definitely want the trendiest looking ones while Sarah and Leslie would most definitely opt for a classic halter or strapless.

She still got chills when she recalled the credit-card debt she racked up while paying for dresses costing well over three hundred dollars or the spine tingling e-mails she received from Leslie surrounding her duties as a bridesmaid. Instead of hunting down just the right bridesmaid dress she sent the following e-mail.

Hey Ladies,
I was just thinking about bridesmaid dresses, and I think I might just pick a designer and a color and let you guys have at it. You can pick whatever style dress you want, so you might be able to get some use out of the dresses again. I'll let you guys know when I find the designer, and the color will most likely be champagne. Hope you are all having a great day.

Love, Bridezilla ☺

Shortly after sending the e-mail she realized it might have been a mistake. She'd had her heart set on champagne dresses, and all the attractive champagne dresses started at two fifty. She just didn't have the nerve to ask her friends to spend that much when most of them were still working in entry-level positions. All the low-budget designers had horrible, baby-shit shades of champagne. After three hours, she stumbled upon an inexpensive designer that was in her price range and made dresses in exactly the shade of champagne she wanted. She sent out a friendly e-mail with a link to the designer's Web site. She wanted their approval before making up her mind.

Shortly after she fired off the e-mail, her phone rang. She felt a little edgy when she noticed her mother's number. Nervous, she let it ring twice before picking up.

"Hello." Connie's voice was normal. No anger, but no apologies either. Just normal, as if nothing had happened. "What are you doing?"

"I was sear—" She didn't really want her mother to think she was still researching wedding events in light of everything. "I was just, um, getting back from the beach."

"Oh. Have you registered yet?"

Cate's heart skipped a beat. It could be a loaded question. She might be asking so she could then tell Cate not to bother registering because the wedding was off. "No, we haven't. Why?"

"Because everyone has been asking me where you're registered. They want to send engagement gifts. You and Ethan better do that soon."

"Okay." For the first time in days she felt like she could take a deep breath, relax a little.

She should've known it would turn out this way. This was always how her mother operated. She'd pretend like nothing had happened, as if she'd never threatened to boycott the entire wedding only a few days before. Just like that, the storm was gone.

Cate debated saying something about their fight, apologizing, and restoring their friendship. But she decided it wasn't worth the risk. Whatever Al had said had plopped her mom right back on the wedding bandwagon. Discussing their previous argument could wreck all his hard work.

"And we need to work out a budget," Connie said. "I've been thinking long and hard about this, and I really don't think we need to have any alcohol at the wedding."

The clouds had cleared, and apparently they were only making room for a bomb to drop. No alcohol? No alcohol! What was a wedding without alcohol? There would be no wedding drunk dominating the dance floor and entertaining all the guests all night. She could feel her back stiffening again and tried to remain calm.

"Mom, why would we do that?"

"I just don't understand why people think they need to drink to have a good time. People can still have fun without drinking. We'll have good food, and no one will even notice that there is no alcohol."

Clearly, it had been a long time since her mother had been to a wedding. The first thing ninety percent of wedding guests did when they entered the reception was head to the bar. It was perfectly fine if Connie didn't want to loosen up a little, but it wasn't fair to inflict her Elliott Ness beliefs on everyone else. To think her biggest obstacle with alcohol was going to be whether they should have an open bar or not.

How on earth was she going to resolve this? Something told her Uncle Al wouldn't be able to smooth this one over. Then she remembered the wonderful, kind sound of Peg Migillicuddy's voice.

"So I heard from a wedding coordinator. The one that Sarah recommended. Peg Migillicuddy. I think we should meet with her."

"How much does she cost?"

"She's really reasonable."

"Set something up for later this week."

As she hung up she prayed this woman would be able to handle her mother. Visions of all their guests standing around, glancing at their watches while they sipped on sodas was worse than a weenie cookout in their backyard.

Advice from the Wedding Wise

Three days later they had a meeting with Peg Migillicuddy. Cate had some time to kill before they met with her so she decided to call Bridal Couture to see if they carried the champagne bridesmaid dresses she'd found on the Internet.

"I want my girls to be able to pick their own dresses. I'm just going to pick the color." She explained to Edith that her bridesmaids came in a variety of shapes and sizes, and she wanted to make sure they were comfortable.

"Hmmmm," Edith said slowly. "I wouldn't suggest doing that."

She was puzzled. It was like saying, "I wouldn't suggest giving people easy directions to get to your house. Tell them to take the most confusing route."

"A lot of people come in with that idea," Edith explained. "The problem is, when we order the dresses from the designer, they cut the pattern from the same bolt of fabric, so if you order a bunch of different styles, they might have to use different bolts, and not all the bolts are exactly the same. You might get a few dresses that are a little darker or lighter. And trust me, it's just a mess when you do it that way. I really suggest just finding a style you like and sticking it to it. Unless you want black or white bridesmaid dresses."

She felt discouraged and worried that the e-mail she'd sent out had been premature. She should've waited to tell everyone they could pick their own dresses. After she hung up she returned to the Web site and selected a strapless, drop-waist dress. She e-mailed everyone and included the link to the dress.

Hey Girls,
I think I found the perfect dress. It's under one seventy and it's champagne. Hope you guys like it. Let me know what you think!

Love, Cate

They'd planned to meet with Peg Migillicuddy at the Rancho Bernardo Inn. Connie had to baby-sit Emily's daughter, Cassidy, at two thirty, and Emily and Bradley lived near the hotel. Furthermore, they were considering the Inn as a possible site for the reception, so it would give Cate an opportunity to explore it.

Peg and her mother were waiting in the lobby when she arrived. She could tell by the softness in her mother's smile that she liked Peg already.

"This must be the lovely bride," Peg said when she noticed Cate. She was a small woman with a gray flip that looked as if it had been hot rolled on the ends.

"Hi, it's so nice to meet you." She took both Cate's hands in her own when they shook. "Oh, I do love working with pretty brides. You're going to make such a lovely bride."

They found a table in the dining hall and ordered iced tea and rolls. "They have the freshest bread in the world here," Peg said. "I've done quite a few weddings at the Inn."

"How long have you been a coordinator?" Connie asked

"Thirty-five years." She took a butter knife and was about to reach for the bowl of butter, but pointed instead. "Now you see, I don't like this." Cate looked at the small dish, wondering what there wasn't to like in a bowl of butter. "This is pat butter," Peg said. "Pat butter is not acceptable when you're planning a wedding." Even when she disapproved of something her voice remained cordial and low. "When you go to spread pat butter on your bread, it rips the bread, and who wants ripped bread?" She smiled at Connie. "The butter should spread smoothly, right onto the bread. We'll ask for nice rolls of butter. The rolled butter just spreads on in a nice smooth layer, and that's how butter should be served."

Cate would never think of things like butter. They needed this woman. They talked for a while about the type of wedding they were thinking of having. Two hundred people, a band, seven bridesmaids. When they told her they'd set the date at Founders, she smiled. "Oh, I just love it there. I know the coordinator over there well. She's very busy, and if you have a hard time getting ahold of her, let me know. I can handle any questions you have about the church."

She recommended florists, a photographer, a videographer, a hairstylist. It was like she had come in and taken the weight of the entire wedding onto her shoulders. "Are you thinking about having a buffet or a sit-down dinner, dear?"

"Sit-down dinner," Connie answered. "I don't like it when everyone is walking back and forth to the buffet all night. Tell me what you think about this, Peg." Cate sensed what was coming next. It was the "See, I told you" voice that Connie often used when she disagreed with Cate and was about to add someone else to her army. "I really don't think we need to have liquor at the wedding. I just don't understand why everyone feels like they need to get drunk these days." She said all these things as if they were from the same old-fashioned generation, and she expected Peg to vigorously nod her head the whole time. "I think everyone can still have a wonderful time *without* alcohol. But Cate seems to think that everyone needs to get drunk to have fun."

"That's not what I said, Mom."

"Well, you're absolutely set on having open bar and letting everyone get plastered." She flashed Peg a knowing smile.

Cate was a little worried. Peg was old, and maybe a little too old-fashioned. What if she *did* agree with Connie? "Well, Mrs. Padgett," she said in a very soft voice. "I think that most people will want to drink at the wedding. It's part of the celebration, and no one will get terribly drunk, dear." She shook her head. "And if they do, well, it's easy, I just give the bartender one of these when I see that person heading to the bar." She sliced her hand over her neck. "That's the signal for they've had enough. And then the bartender will fill their glasses with water. They'll be so drunk they won't know the difference."

For once her mother was speechless.

"Now, if you're worried about the cost," Peg said, "there are many ways to be economical with the bar. You could just have beer and wine. You see, when people drink a glass of wine or a beer, why, it takes them quite a while. However, those mixed drinks only take a couple gulps. Some places may even let you bring in your own wine."

"All right," Connie said. "I guess we can figure out something for the alcohol."

'All right'? Is she agreeing? It's that simple? Cate loved Peg! Wanted to adopt her, have her be her grandmother. Cate wondered if she could come along to every wedding errand and even family holidays, for that matter.

As planned, Connie left early to go baby-sit. Cate and Peg took a quick stroll through the Rancho Bernardo Inn grounds. Peg showed her the different ballrooms that were available for weddings. She pointed out the ones with the best sound for the band and showed her where cocktail hour would be held. The Inn was gorgeous, but she'd need a final opinion from Ethan before she booked it. It would be beautiful for a late-autumn wedding because it had a warm feeling to it.

She walked with Peg to the parking lot, and they chatted about how Ethan had proposed. Peg seemed like the only person who wasn't completely horrified or worried that Cate's ring was missing. They discussed the type of flowers Cate liked. She could've spent the rest of the day with Peg, discussing wedding plans.

"Now, listen, dear. Remember that everything that is important to you for this wedding is important to me. I just stayed up until two in the morning, talking with one of my brides. She called me at midnight crying, and she said, 'Peg, the tablecloths and the napkins aren't in the correct shade of periwinkle blue, and no one will listen to me. Everyone thinks I'm just being crazy.' And I told her I know how important it is to her, and not to worry, I will take care of everything." She touched Cate's arm. "If there are things that are important to you, just let me know."

This woman was a gift from God. "Now, you have a lovely day, and let me know if you need me for anything." The wedding was starting to seem like fun.

·15·
What a Dip

The following morning Cate checked her e-mail. The responses she got from some of her bridesmaids made the color drain from her face.

"I feel very uncomfortable wearing anything strapless. And could you pick something with more of an A-line? My butt will never fit into that dress." From Denise.

"I thought we were picking our own." This from Beth, who was usually so easygoing. "Strapless dresses are so unflattering on me." And to think of what Beth had put her through for her Halloween wedding.

This one, the best of all, came from Jill, her dear friend, who she loved and admired. "Can I make mine? I'll get the same color of fabric and design my own." She had no background in sewing whatsoever.

She was about to have a nervous breakdown in front of her computer screen when the phone rang. She glanced at the caller ID. It was Leslie "Bridezilla" Lyons, one of her dearest friends and the most anal person she'd ever known. She was the bride who'd sent out itineraries that weighed more than most novels. The phone rang like a throbbing time bomb. Cate stood over it, biting her nails and debating if it was worth the risk to answer. Who knew what kind of dress Leslie wanted? On the final ring she picked up and weakly said hello into the receiver.

"Cate? Are you there?"

"Yes. Hi, Leslie." She waited for Leslie to give her an earful about her choice in dresses, but she sweetly offered this: "I was just calling to see how everything is going and if there is anything I can do to help you. I know how stressful these times can be."

"Oh. Thank you." She sat down on the couch. "Did you get the e-mail?"

"No. What e-mail? I haven't checked my e-mail today."

Cate told her about the dress selection and the surly responses she'd received from the girls. "I mean, I expected something like this from Denise. But Jill and Beth? I don't know. . . ."

"Listen, Denise . . . what a dip. Only someone who has never been in a wedding would behave that way. Beth made everyone wear Halloween costumes to her wedding. Jill is not married, and frankly, people who have never been married just don't get it. They have no idea what it's like. Only married people know what it's like to plan a wedding, and I think this is why you need to just do what I decided to do. You just have to make the decision that information will be given on a need to know basis only. For everyone. And I mean *everyone*."

Cate thought about her bridesmaid days and how she was never given a forum to voice her concerns over the attire. She was never given a link to check out the dress. She was given the following instructions: Please take all measurements and return them with credit-card info by the designated date. She never even saw the dresses she'd spent a small fortune on until they arrived, grossly oversized, on her doorstep. Now she knew why.

"You just pick a dress," Leslie said. "And you tell everyone to take their measurements and pay for it. The end."

"You're right." In all her life, she never thought she would be agreeing with the person who'd caused her so much bridesmaid anguish that she still woke in a cold sweat thinking about losing her dyed to match shoes. Was she becoming Bridezilla? The last thing she wanted to be.

She hung up the phone and decided to let the girls cool down for a few days. Then she would e-mail them back, telling them all where to send their measurements and credit-card info. That was all the information they needed. She'd let them off the hook with shoes. They could wear whatever they wanted as long as they were black.

Ethan had been tremendously overwhelmed with work all day, and she decided to surprise him with E-Z Jay's. She picked up his favorite turkey with ranch on toasted bread, and she got a ham for herself. She found him on the phone when she arrived. His hair was a mess, and he was still wearing the boxer shorts he'd slept in the night before. "I will be so happy when this weekend is over," he said after he hung up. "A wedding tonight and a bar mitzvah tomorrow." His eyes lit up when he saw the bag of sandwiches. "You're the greatest." They ate at his coffee table.

"Well, let me know if there is anything I can do to help," she said.

"Actually, there is. I meant to mention this to you yesterday. I'm short-staffed for a couple weekends this summer, and I was thinking if you want to make some extra money you can come along with me to the weddings, help out. Maybe you'll get some ideas for ours. Meet some vendors we might want to use. I'll pay you."

"Okay, but I've never catered before, so I don't want to bug everyone with questions all night."

"You won't. It's easy. All you have to do it walk around with appetizers on trays, and then serve dinner. That's all. I think we have a shirt and vest in your size, and you need black pants and black shoes, which I know you have a million pairs of." He took a bite from his sandwich, and a huge glob of mustard dropped onto the table.

"All right. Sure, when do you need me?"

"Tonight."

* * *

A couple hours later she was riding in the Good Time Catering van with Ethan. She wore her gray vest and tie and had pulled her hair back into a ponytail. He owned the company with his best friend, Sean. Their company had done so well that they had two vans, a huge kitchen, and several prep cooks who prepared all the food. Sean and Ethan double-booked weekends so each one of them could oversee an event. The only time she'd really seen Ethan in work mode was when she'd run into him two years ago at Sarah's wedding. He was wearing baggy white chef's clothes then too. But she hadn't remembered him being so serious. It's not that he was uptight or nervous, he was so thorough, such a perfectionist, and she sensed there would be absolutely no slacking off allowed. She felt a little nervous.

The wedding was at an enormous house in Rancho, Santa Fe. His staff had already been there all day, setting up and getting ready for the big outdoor event. An enormous white tent covered the backyard. White lights dripped like diamonds from the satin-covered poles. She looked at the flowers, huge centerpieces of purple and pink roses, orchids that were bigger than her face, and the sweet scent of gardenias filled the air. Each centerpiece must've cost well into the hundreds.

Only minutes after arriving, Ethan disappeared. He was pulled in fifty million different directions by the wedding coordinator, the bride's mother, employees with questions. He never seemed to lose his cool, and watching him solve problems one after another really gave her more respect for what he did.

They couldn't have picked a hotter day for the wedding, and the ceremony started forty-five minutes late. The bride apparently needed "more time" to get ready, so she'd left her guests burning to death in the blazing afternoon heat. The reception was tented, but the white folding chairs for the ceremony were right out in the open. She watched from a distance while men sweated their asses off in suits, and women fanned themselves with wedding programs while trying to block off UV rays. All she could think about was the BO that must be accumulating out there.

Instead of looking with heartfelt interest when the bride finally did come down the aisle, they all looked relieved. Cate didn't see a single tear. Worse, the ceremony seemed never ending. The minister wouldn't stop talking about what a great couple Hillary and Jason were, and he stopped every two minutes to listen so some folksinger could perform cheesy love songs.

Helping Ethan had been a good idea. She'd already gotten a few ideas for their wedding. Not only would everything be indoors, but she would be on time.

To say the guests were starving was an understatement. The bride and groom had barely left the aisle when Cate was practically stampeded by sweaty people who were after bacon-wrapped shrimp and olive crostini. The guests took two, sometimes three appetizers at a time, and she found herself running back to the kitchen every five minutes to restock her tray. The kitchen was a frenzied whirlwind of servers brushing past one another to replenish their stock. She hardly even saw Ethan. Things simmered down after cocktail hour. Everyone took their seats, and the toasts began. Cate delivered salads and poured wine.

She stole a brief moment to relax and watched from the back of the reception while the bride and groom took to the dance floor for their first dance. The band played Frank Sinatra's "The Way You Look Tonight."

It was a popular wedding song, and she realized that they still hadn't discussed their first dance. She had no idea what their song would be. She could see the bride and groom's lips moving, and their bodies looked as stiff as blow up dolls as they assumed ballroom dancing positions. At first she thought they were talking to each other, but then she realized that they were counting.

"One. Two. Three. Four," the bride whispered as they did the box step around the stage.

There were a few timed twirls, and his arms looked as rigid as pencils when she spun beneath them. The groom stuck a firm arm out, as if he were setting up the pose to dip the bride. A split second passed when they both exchanged confused glances, as if he'd skipped a step. At the exact moment when he took his arm away, the bride dramatically leaned back for the dip. Unfortunately, there was nothing there to catch her, and she went down like a tree struck by lightning.

Her dress came up over her waist, and everyone on the west side of the dance floor got a pretty revealing view of her butt.

Cate heard a loud cackle from an elderly man wearing a horrible toupee. He was seated at the table with the groom's parents. He had a raspy yet high-pitched Jersey accent, and a cigar dangled from his mouth. "Ya, ha, ha, ha! What a dip. Ya, ha, ha, ha! What a dip."

Cate could only imagine how mortified the bride must've felt, and if it had happened to her, she probably would've curtsied and run from the dance floor. However, this bride jumped up and did the air splits before pouncing onto her new husband and wrapping her legs around his waist. Startled, the groom stood for a moment. She whispered something in his ear, and he began to spin around with her still attached to his waist. It was like a bad pairs-skating competition, and Cate wondered if they would ever get dizzy. But he kept going. Cate figured this wasn't a move they practiced when rehearsing the box step.

"What the hell is this?" the old man groaned. "If I had wanted to see Patrick Swayze I would've rented *Dirty Dancing*." He cackled again. "Unbelievable."

The groom spun his bride until the climax of the song, when they finally went for the dip. This time he didn't move his arm, even after she landed on it. They stayed in the pose for several seconds. A moment of silence passed before the applause started. Even the band looked a little shocked by the whole performance.

The wedding went until midnight, and Ethan had to stay until every last crumb was cleaned up.

"Did you see the bride and groom's dance?" she asked on the way home.

"Yeah, I did actually. I've never seen anything like that before."

"I thought for sure they would've died of embarrassment after the fall, but instead she tried to cover it up with some weird *Dancing with the Stars* moves." She propped her feet on the dashboard and realized how bad they ached. It had been hours since she'd sat down.

"Please tell me we don't have to do that," he said.

"Dance like that? No way."

"No, I mean dance in front of people."

She loosened her tie. "Well, yeah. We have to have a first dance."

"We do?"

"It's our wedding."

"I'm a horrible dancer."

"It's okay. We'll be up there together, and it's just going to be our friends watching us. It's not like we'll be performing in front of a million people."

"All right." Even though he agreed, she sensed he was only saying it to make her happy.

Stuck in the Middle

Hello Girls,
I'm sorry to be such a pain, but I just wanted to let you all
know that I'm going to Bridal Couture to look at the dress I
picked out. If it's as cute as it looks online I'll send everyone
instructions on where to send their measurements and pay for
the dress. Thanks guys, and sorry to be a pain!
Love, Bridezilla ☺

Within minutes Denise Blakely's name popped into her e-mail account.

Cate,
Do you think I could come with you to try the dress on? It's
just that I'm really worried about my butt and I just want to
see what it looks like.
Sincerely, Denise

It was pretty nervy of her, but then again everything Denise did was beginning to make Cate wonder if the girl had actually grown balls since they'd gotten engaged. What was she supposed to say? *No. You can't come. I expect you to drop over a hundred dollars on this dress that you'll never wear again, but we don't want you along.* She thought for a moment before replying. Did she want her bridesmaids to wear the dress she liked? Or did she want them to look good? What if Denise did look like a champagne-colored potato?

She e-mailed her back and told her to meet them at five o'clock outside Bridal Couture. Prior to Denise inviting herself to the bridal salon, Connie had offered to come along too. At first Cate felt a little reluctant to add yet another opinion to the bridesmaid dresses, but her mother was actually a neutral party, so she'd included her in the plans.

She spent the rest of the day packing. Escrow closed in two weeks. She'd been living in her Pacific Beach apartment for nearly four years, and she'd thought she'd be sad about leaving it. Jill was just an elevator ride upstairs, and they saw each other almost every day. The beach was a stroll away, and her favorite bar, The West End, was a drunken stumble down the block. However, she was too preoccupied to be sad.

Lord only knew what lay in store for her at Bridal Couture. She tried to remain positive. Denise would look great in the dress, and if she didn't, they'd try others on. The last thing she wanted to do was be selfish, so she would pick something else if it made her more comfortable.

She spent the afternoon cleaning out her bathroom cupboards and stumbled upon things she'd forgotten that she'd even owned. Fake eyelashes that she'd purchased for her Marilyn Monroe costume in Beth's wedding. There was a box full of beaded necklaces and bracelets she'd made at Beth's beading shop. Hot rollers that she'd used once. A bag full of mini shampoos and conditioners that her ex-boyfriend used to bring her back from all his trips. She tossed the entire bag. Moving felt like taking a trip down memory lane rather than breaking a sweat as she stuffed boxes full of heavy stuff.

She got so wrapped up in trying on all her old jewelry that she was almost late to her meeting at Bridal Couture. She wore one of her old bracelets. It was made of red and black seed beads, and she spent ten minutes just looking for a red top to match it.

Denise was waiting for them at the salon. Inside, they found Edith. She pulled the champagne bridesmaid dress from the rack and led Denise to a dressing room.

Several minutes elapsed before Denise returned, and Cate started to worry about her. She and Connie exchanged a couple of concerned glances. The look on Denise's face when she pulled back the curtain wasn't one of fashion satisfaction.

"I love the color," Connie immediately said. "That's going to look good on all the girls." She was glad she'd brought her mother. She needed some backup.

Denise was quiet.

Cate looked at her butt and thought that if Denise were in an avo-cado look-alike contest she'd be the runaway champ. She didn't want to be mean, but she was beginning to wonder if any dresses would be flat-tering on her. An A-line might look a little more flattering, but how was she supposed to please everyone? If she ordered an A-line dress, then lit-tle people like Val and Sarah would be swimming in it. "How do you feel?" Cate asked, already well aware of the answer.

Denise shrugged. "I just think my butt would look better in an A-line."

"You do?"

"I just don't think I'll feel very comfortable if I'm in this dress all night."

If this was *Survivor*, Denise would be the first person voted off. Hang-ing out with her was like being beaten. Really, Cate had to wear a three-hundred-dollar royal blue polyester suit in Leslie's wedding. The only people it would've looked good on were Janet and Chrissy in *Three's Com-pany* decades earlier. However, she'd slipped into the dreadful outfit, bad wedding hair included, and headed down the aisle without a single protest.

"I think it looks fine, Denise," Connie said. Then Connie cocked her head to the side. "But you know, I do think something with sleeves would be more appropriate for church. What about this dress?" She pulled a champagne A-line with short sleeves and a covered chest from the rack.

Next time Cate came anywhere near the bridal salon it would be alone. She looked at the gown, then noticed that Denise looked the happiest she had since her arrival.

"That looks great," Denise said. "And I agree with you about church. This one is more appropriate."

She wanted to make a voodoo doll of Denise out of a ring bearer's pillow and the seamstresses' pins. She remembered her conversation with Leslie, and how she'd advised her to exclude the wedding party from all decisions. She didn't really want to be Bridezilla though.

"I really wanted something strapless, and I know some of the other girls did too, so no. Sorry, that dress is not going to work. Let's ask if we can get the strapless one that Denise has on in A-line cut," she said, compromising. "I want Denise to feel comfortable, but I'm sure strapless will be fine for church."

They waited while Denise tried on a similar dress with a fuller skirt to cover up her tush. "I like Denise," Connie said.

"That's nice," Cate said.

The dress didn't look that different, but if it made Denise feel comfortable, it was fine. She just wanted to get out of there before Denise and Connie made plans to attend Bible study together.

Cate gave Edith all her bridesmaids' names and addresses so she could send them a packet to fill out for their measurements and credit-card information. Cate couldn't help but wonder what Leslie would say if she knew that she had changed the skirt style for Denise. It didn't matter, because something about ordering the bridesmaid dresses made her feel guilty anyway. The dress was reasonably priced, but she couldn't forget how it felt to buy a dress she would only wear once.

It was late when they left, and Edith walked with them to the parking lot. "I guess I'll see you at the engagement party next weekend," Denise said.

"Yes. I'm looking forward to it."

"How do you have time for all this stuff with all the packing you have to do?" Denise asked.

She didn't want to discuss the move in front of her mother. Connie was aware of its upcoming date, but it would be best if she wasn't reminded.

"You're moving?" Edith said as she fished for her keys inside her purse.

"At some point. Wow! Isn't it a chilly night for summer?" She tried to change the subject.

"Where are you moving to?"

"Escondido. With my fiancé." Her voice was almost inaudible.

"Wonderful," Edith said. "We're thinking about putting our house on the market next month."

Denise immediately pulled a card from her wallet. "Please let me know if you'd like to talk."

Connie had driven, and once in the car she screeched from the parking space like she was wanted by the law.

"Geez, Mom. Take it easy there. What's your problem?"

"You just had to tell Edith you were moving in with Ethan."

"Oh c'mon, mom. Edith doesn't care."

"I'm so embarrassed." Her knuckles were white on the steering wheel. "In my time you just didn't go around announcing stuff like that. It was really taboo, something to be ashamed of. You just didn't go around announcing it to anyone who would listen."

She wanted to argue back, but the whole conversation was so ridiculous.

She was saved by her cell phone. "Hey, Ethan."

The buzz of voices and music blasted into her ear. "Cate! Can you hear me?" He yelled, and she had to pull the phone away from her face.

"Where are you?"

"I'm at Longboards!"

"Oh. Who are you with?"

"Ryan and I were supposed to meet, but Janet had her interview with him today, so they're both here!"

Just what she needed.

"Come meet us!" he yelled. His voice was so loud that her mother glanced at the phone. She could hear Ethan too.

A stiff drink was tempting, but a stiff drink with Janet might just drive her over the edge. She needed to burn off some steam, and the best way to do this was to pack. "No! I think I'll pass!"

"I'll stop by later! I'll spend the night tonight!"

Connie gunned the gas pedal as she sped onto the freeway. If she was pissed before, Cate could only imagine what kind of volcano was about to erupt.

Why hadn't they gone to Vegas again? Ever since they'd gotten engaged everyone around her had gone mad—except her. Most of her bridesmaids were acting a little weird. There was Denise, and Connie. Now there was Ethan's ex-girlfriend to contend with too. Everyone had gone mad.

She'd never felt happier to see her apartment complex. She was just making a clean getaway from the car when her mother shouted, "Just remember it's your soul that will pay in eternity!"

"Thanks for coming with me!" She yelled as Connie sped away. She headed into her apartment and felt the happiest she'd felt all day when she noticed Grease waiting by the front door for her.

"C'mere Grease," she said, as she set down her purse. His purr was as loud as a Jet Ski and the best thing she'd heard in a while. She loved it when he got in one of his affectionate moods. He rubbed the side of his nose against her face. She carried him to her bedroom and decided she wouldn't answer the phone for the rest of the night. Empty boxes already occupied half her apartment, and filling them seemed like the best way to relieve her tension. She set Grease down, and he jumped inside a box.

She decided to clear off her bookshelf first. She made three different piles of books. Shitty ones—ones that she wouldn't have the heart to lend to anyone but planned to donate to the used book store. Fantastic ones—these she would feature on her shelves for the rest of her life, and included the work of Jack London, David Sedaris, and Flannery O'Connor. And juicy ones that she'd breezed through in a day and would be passed along to Jill and Beth, who were always hungry for something to read.

She picked up a blue and white vase that she'd purchased at a garage sale down the street several years ago. It had never matched anything in her apartment, but she had always left it sitting out simply because she liked the style of it.

She was carrying it to a box in the kitchen when she tripped over a stack of books. She went down fast, and the vase almost slipped from her hands. She managed to hang on to it, but right before hitting the floor something small popped from the inside and made a light ping on the tile of her kitchen floor. She couldn't imagine what could be stuck inside there. She wondered if a rose stem had broken off and become trapped inside. Her chin stung from where she'd hit it, and her knees felt weak when she stood up. She brushed her clothes off and examined her knees and elbows for cuts before heading into the kitchen. She shook the vase, and whatever was rattling around in there couldn't fit through its neck. Then it occurred to her—her engagement ring. That's what it had to be. She'd remembered Grease's obsession with water and vases. She'd shaken the vase the day the ring had gone missing. The vase's neck was so skinny it was possible that it had been stuck in there, and her fall had dislodged it.

Excited, her eyes scanned the kitchen tile, but what she found was not so exciting. It was the basket of fruit that Grease had stolen from the French woman. Well, at least she didn't have to worry about his appendix rupturing. She went back to packing and picked up the vase. Her heart skipped a beat when she heard something rattle inside. She shook it again and heard the same sound. There was definitely something in there. She tried to empty it, but whatever was inside only made a clinking sound. She shoved a wire hanger inside and tried to pry it out, but the object wouldn't budge. In a moment of sheer excitement she threw the vase on the kitchen floor. She watched as bits and pieces of clay crumbled into a million pieces. There, in the midst of the chalky clay lay her engagement ring. She could see the diamonds sending prisms off the kitchen walls.

· 17 ·

It Has a Nice Ring

"I have another wedding I'll need help with in a few weeks. Do you think you'll be available? It's the last weekend of July."

The only sound that followed Ethan's question was the squeaky wheels of the grocery cart she was pushing through Vons.

"Cate? Are you even listening to me? Cate! Oh my . . . Jesus! Cate watch where you're—"

She snapped her gaze away from her ring right before she crashed full speed into a produce display. They watched helplessly as Granny Smith apples and a mountain of pears toppled from the table like an avalanche. "Oh, my . . ." She threw her body against the tumbling mountain of fruit, but it all came at once, and her hands were only capable of catching one apple at a time. The nectarines went next, which snowballed into the peaches. Lemons fell to the ground like hail, and it sounded like an earthquake when the cantaloupes on the other side of the display flew from the table like molten lava.

"Maybe we should just run," Ethan breathed.

She felt like a trapped rabbit. Every single person in the produce department was watching them. A couple picking out their salad ingredients paused to look at the idiot who'd turned Vons into a disaster. Two small children looked absolutely fascinated by the mess she'd created. A not-so-fascinated elderly woman scowled at her. However, it was the gentleman wearing a Vons-issued visor and apron who looked the most peeved.

"Sorry." Her voice cracked when she spoke.

Ever since she'd found her ring, she'd escaped nearly five car accidents, had missed her turn at Communion at Sunday Mass, and had accidentally knocked a Chihuahua over on the boardwalk when she was jogging with Jill. She still shuddered when she thought of the little dog peering from beneath her running shoes.

"Were you staring at your ring again?" Ethan mumbled under his breath.

She was afraid to answer. Instead, she began picking up apples.

"Cleanup! In Produce!" The man wearing the apron yelled. "I'm gonna need a few people!"

A voice crackled over the loudspeaker in Vons. "Calling all employees, Code red in Produce. Code red. Bring boxes."

She'd caused a code red. She didn't even know what a Code red was, but judging from the mound of fruit that covered the floor, she knew it was bad.

They were supposed to be on the way to the engagement party and had stopped at Vons for limes and ice. Rita had called shortly after they'd left her apartment and said she'd forgotten to pick up the party essentials when she'd gone to the store earlier that day. Happy to help, they'd agreed to stop. Now she wished she'd just waited in the car.

They helped half the disgruntled staff at Vons pick up fruit. They were asked to quit helping when Cate set a handful of lemons back on the display and they rolled off again. Dying of embarrassment, she paid for Rita's stuff and left.

"I'm glad you like your ring," Ethan said, and they both started laughing so hard she thought Ethan would lose his breath.

Cate wiped a tear from her eyes. "I didn't mean to. I swear."

"You better be careful. You're going to really hurt someone."

"I love my ring."

"Good." He reached over the console for her hand.

A large bunch of tuberose rested in her lap. She'd picked up the flowers for Rita at the farmers' market, a token of her appreciation for hosting the party. She felt excited when they turned down the Blakelys' street. The celebrating was officially beginning. All her bridesmaids were coming. Ethan's groomsmen would be there. Their families would be together. Mostly everyone they loved was coming to their engagement party.

Cate wanted to get there early so they could help Rita and Charles before any guests arrived. She noticed Denise's car in the driveway and wondered what had possessed her to arrive early as well.

She could smell something delicious cooking from the driveway, and tiki lights lit the long path to the front door. Chuck stood by the door when they entered. "They're here!" he called to the rest of the family in the kitchen. He kissed Cate on the cheek, and she could feel his nose ring press against her cheekbone. "You look stunning as always!" he said.

"Thanks!" For all his crazy ways, he really was a nice guy. She noticed Tatiana standing alone in the corner of the Blakelys' living room. Cate was about to say hello when she was blinded by Denise.

"Hi, you guys," she said. "Oh Cate, I can take those for you. I'll put them in water. I know where Rita's vases are." Cate felt slightly annoyed when Denise pulled the flowers from her hands. She wanted to give them to Rita herself. It was a small gesture to show how grateful she was for the party.

They chatted with Chuck and Tatiana for a moment. "So, did you have your audition yet?" Cate asked.

"No. It is next veek."

"That's exciting. I'm sure you'll do fine."

She heard Denise walk into the kitchen with her flowers, then Rita's voice. "Wow, those are pretty!"

"Aren't they?" Denise said. "Ethan brought them. I'll put them in a vase for you."

Ethan brought them? Ethan? Well, technically they had arrived together. She didn't mind sharing credit, but Denise had taken them from *her* hands. Cate was the one who had walked to the farmers' market in eighty-five degree heat and picked out just the right bunch.

"I love tuberose. That's so Ethan. Isn't it?" she heard a familiar yet unidentifiable voice. Had Denise brought a friend? As far as Cate knew, she didn't have any girlfriends. If she did, this person definitely didn't know what the hell she was talking about, because while Ethan was very thoughtful, he hadn't even known what tuberose was until he'd seen the long stems and white buds resting in Cate's lap on the drive to the party.

"Well, why don't we head into the kitchen?" Ethan suggested. He put his hand on her back. She could hear Rita laughing wildly at something the stranger had said.

When they entered the kitchen, Cate realized this person was no stranger at all. It was Janet. She leaned against the Blakelys' countertop as if it had only been yesterday since she'd broken up with Ethan.

"There you guys are!" she exclaimed. "The adorable lovebirds! Let me see your ring!" She ran to Cate and roughly yanked her hand. "I was with Ethan the night you found it. We were at Longboards, and you should've seen the relief that came over him. He was soooo cute."

She studied the ring, and Cate saw a flicker of something sinister pass over her eyes. "Hope you guys don't mind that I came. Denise invited me. It's been hard since I've moved from San Francisco." She actually wiped a tear from her eyes. "Denise thought it might be nice for me to go out and be around some old friends."

"Uh, yeah. Great," Ethan said.

Cate could see Denise from the corner of her eye, a narrow smile turning the corner of her thin lips. The girl truly was a friend of the devil.

She nodded. "Thanks." Then she bit her lip. "I knew you would understand. It's been so hard."

"Thanks for the flowers, Ethan," Rita said.

"Don't thank me. Thank Cate."

Denise's eyes narrowed when Rita hugged Cate. "That was so thoughtful of you."

Cate said hello to the rest of Ethan's family wearing one of the fakest smiles she'd worn since the last time she had taken bridesmaid photos. At this point she wasn't sure why Denise's behavior rattled her so much. She should've expected some kind of stunt from her, but never would she have imagined her to stoop this low. It was their engagement party. Not some backyard burgers and dogs barbecue. What was she going to do next? Loan Janet a bridesmaid dress and have her be a part of the wedding party?

Seeing Beth's husband, Ike, walk through the front door brought some relief. Behind him were Beth and Jill. Apparently, they'd arrived at the same time as her mother and father. She needed her comrades. She needed them to talk her out of grabbing Denise by the back of her neck and dragging her to the punch bowl where she fantasized about dunking her head in its small, fruity pond, the same way Pony Boy and Johnny had been tortured in *The Outsiders*.

"What's wrong?" Connie asked suspiciously as Cate approached them.

"Yeah, what happened?" Beth whispered.

"You look so pale," Jill said.

Their smiles grimly faded from their faces as they all leaned toward Cate.

"Don't make it obvious that we're talking about anything serious. Just pretend like you're smiling and laughing."

"Okay." They all leaned back and slapped smiles on their faces.

"I fucking hate Denise," she said between gritted teeth.

"Cate," Connie snapped.

"What did she do?" Jill asked, still wearing her phony smile.

"Let's pretend to get drinks on the wine table outside, and I'll tell you there."

"Okay."

They all followed her, and Cate even managed to toss a smile in Denise's direction on the way out.

Outside, she told them everything. She tried to keep her body language and voice under control. She started with the tuberose and then with the giant bomb of Janet crashing their party.

"You mean that girl we passed on the way out here?" Jill said. "The one whose hair is as thin and brittle as a hula skirt at the ends? I should give her a card."

"Yes." It was nice of Jill to try to make her feel better, but really, the the girl looked like Heidi Klum.

Beth looked over Cate's shoulder. "I wasn't paying that close attention. Where is she?"

Connie looked across her shoulders too. "Her? Oh please, Cate. Forget about her. Ethan loves you."

"That's not the point. It's not the point that I feel threatened by her. It's just that I get the feeling that Denise is trying to get under my skin, like she wants me to be jealous. She wants to ruin our party, and make me look bad in front of Ethan's parents. She took the flowers from my hand and then told everyone Ethan brought them."

"She's so jealous of you," Jill said.

"But why? What have I ever done?"

"Who knows?" Connie said. "Just ignore her. She's miserable."

"Because look at you, Cate," Beth said. "Denise is like a cracker. A dry, boring, plain, white cracker you would dip in soup for some flavor. There is not much to her. There is nothing interesting or appealing about her. She is just a cracker. And you, you're like a . . . a honey-glazed rib. Full of flavor and taste." This was why Beth was her oldest and dearest friend. She always had a way of making her feel better.

"Thanks," Cate said, taking such a strange compliment. She'd never been compared to food, let alone ribs.

Beth looked over Cate's shoulder. "I still can't find her though."

"You want to know what I think?" Connie said.

"What?"

"I think you need to forget about all this. Don't let it bother you. Just go on with your night as if they don't even exist."

"How can I not let this bother me?"

"Because you're getting married to Ethan," Jill said. "He loves you. Not her. And if you let this bother you, you're letting Denise win."

"It's your engagement party," Connie said. "Rita and Charles have gone to a lot of trouble. So just ignore Denise and that girl and enjoy the night. Just forget that those two are even here. Pay no attention to them, and watch your language while you're at it."

"You're right," Cate said. She felt like she was being dragged into eighth grade against her will. No one had treated her this way since she'd bought a pair of coveted topaz-colored jelly shoes and some matching bracelets. She wasn't going to let Denise drag her down and decided it was best not to waste another minute feeding the situation and standing around like they were in some kind of junior-high clique.

It was time to mingle. She said hello to Leslie and her husband, Russ. He always looked like he had been dragged along behind Leslie like a banged-up wagon on wheels. His expression suggested he'd rather be anywhere than standing behind her unscuffed stilettos and tight French twist.

Leslie had been one of Cate's closest friends in college. She was a good, reliable friend, the type of person who would treat you to happy hour when you'd had a rough day at work. Once she'd been browsing Bath and Body Works and had noticed Cate's favorite lotion on clearance. There were only five bottles left, and she bought them all for her. She cut out articles of interest for her friends and would be the first to stick up for you if you'd embarrassed yourself.

However, she was also the type of person who demanded a ton of attention. Her house was plastered in stunning photos of herself, and in more than half of them at least two other people in the picture had their eyes closed. She'd made all her bridesmaids wear hideous pantsuits on her wedding day while she looked stunning and came down the aisle on a horse, and she worried about things like which table linens to use for her hors d'oeuvres table on Super Bowl Sunday. Who even *used* table-cloths for the Super Bowl?

"So have you decided what you'll give as favors?" Leslie asked.

"No. Not yet." *Favors?* The wedding seemed so far away, and picking out favors was a minute issue in light of dealing with your mother boycotting the wedding, losing your ring, and having your fiancé's ex crash your engagement party.

"Are you having linen or polyester napkins?"

Only Leslie would think of these things, and really Cate could care less what kind of napkins they had. She had a feeling if she said this, Leslie would think something was wrong with her. In her sheltered world, napkins were as important as breathing.

"I'm not sure yet," she said, acting as though she were mulling over the idea.

"Oh!" Her pashmina shifted on her shoulders when she reached for Cate's hand. "Let me see your ring!"

Cate proferred her hand, but instead of taking her hand as everyone else had, Leslie asked if Cate would take the ring off. She shrugged. "Sure." No sooner had she handed Leslie the ring than someone came up behind her.

"Cate, how are you?" It was Sarah. Her husband, Miles, was with her. She hugged them both.

"How are the plans going?" Miles asked.

"Good. A little stressful, but good."

"Just enjoy it," Sarah said. "I wish I had taken more in throughout the whole wedding process, really enjoyed being a bride. As opposed to racing around worrying about all the details. Where is your ring?" she asked.

"Oh, Leslie has it. Hold on. Let me grab it."

When Cate turned around, Leslie was gone. She knew Leslie would never leave with her ring, but in light of everything that had happened, she felt slightly insecure that her ring was floating around the party. She found Leslie beneath a patio light. She'd removed her engagement ring as well and was now examining both of them beneath the glow. Her expression was pinched as she turned the rings, watching the prisms that Cate's ring sent off the walls. Cate watched as Leslie scrunched up her eyes then searched through her handbag for something. She pulled a magnifying glass from her large purse. She hunched over the lens while she looked at both rings in the palm of her hand.

"Leslie, what are you doing?" Cate asked.

She sighed as she handed Cate her ring. "It's really true. The round stones are just so much brighter. Mine just doesn't have as many cuts in it. It's just not as sparkly."

"Leslie, your ring is gorgeous." Cate glanced at her princess cut stone.

She shrugged. "Yeah, it is. But it's not as bright."

Poor Leslie, not because anything was wrong with her ring, but because she was constantly bound by the shackles of comparing herself to everyone else. She lived in a world where nothing would ever be good enough.

By the time Cate had taken her ring back, the party was in full effect. She knew the Blakelys had a ton of friends, but she'd never known they'd had so many. The backyard was packed full of people, and she moved from group to group with Ethan. They soaked in showers of congratulations, repeatedly telling the story of how he'd proposed, then how they'd lost the ring.

Ethan was pouring them each another glass of wine when Rita came over. She threw her arm over Cate's shoulders. "Ethan, you have such a beautiful fiancée."

"I know." He handed Cate her wine.

"There is a surprise for you two tonight."

He lifted his eyebrows. "Really?"

"Yes, it was Chuck's idea. Something he said you guys love!"

"Great, I can't wait." She was already surprised. She had no idea that Chuck knew what they liked. He really could be thoughtful sometimes.

"What do you think it is?" she asked after Rita left.

"No idea. Maybe a bottle of champagne or something?"

He was interrupted by a couple of his friends and turned to chat with them.

"Caaaate!" she heard a screech from behind and instantly recognized her cousin Val. "I'm soooo excited for you." Val threw her arms around Cate's neck and lifted her feet from the ground. Her hard little body felt light in Cate's arms.

"I just saw your mom," Val said as Cate set her down. "And she told me about that wicked witch of a cousin Ethan has."

"Shhhh." Cate glanced over her shoulder. "She might hear you."

"Oh who cares? I hate her already. She is no friend of mine, and I can tell you right now that if she does one thing to ruin your day, and I mean one, you just let me know and I'll deal with her. You deserve the best wedding ever!"

Despite Val's tiny size and the fact that Denise could probably cover Val's body with one thigh, Cate believed her. She could ruin Denise. "Thanks Val, but I think we should probably just try to ignore her."

They were talking about wedding plans when she heard the light sound of bells. They came closer, and it wasn't until a hush had fallen over the crowd that she noticed the belly dancer—one she recognized from the concert Chuck had taken them to. Veiled, the woman balanced a giant sword on top her head. She moved through the party, softly shaking her hips, and leading an entourage of the same cast of characters from the concert.

"What's this?" Val asked.

"A . . . uh, surprise." In a million years, she would've never guessed that Unite was the surprise, and all she could think about was her mother. She was probably clutching rosary beads while Ezekiel figured out whose feet he was going to latch on to.

It was the whole crew from Balboa Park, minus the electrical instruments. It was all acoustic and bongos. All the guests at the party cleared a space for them to perform. Ezekiel held a Bible over his head, and she wondered why he had chosen such a prop. She could see Sarah and

Leslie exchange glances and was certain neither one of them had belly dancers or a band inspired by an acid trip at their engagement parties. She watched as Rita clapped her hands and moved her hips to the beat of the music, and Cate wondered if she was drunk, or if her mother was watching her.

Ezekiel was like a dog—and not because he was crawling around on the ground. In her experience, she'd found that dogs always chose to shower the people who liked them the least with attention. Those who were either afraid or allergic were usually the ones who got the most slobber on their faces.

Ezekiel had passed his Bible off to one of the belly dancers and hounded Connie the whole time, pirouetting and singing in front of her as if she were the only person in the room. The look on her mother's face was confusion and a little humor. At least she was trying to be a good sport. Cate became really worried when he took her mother's hand and led her to the middle of the circle. Couldn't he grab Tatiana? Someone who would appreciate the attention? Her mother looked like she might bolt at any moment when Ezekiel knelt in front of her. Cate wanted to jump in the circle and sacrifice herself. Something like this could send Connie over the edge.

Things took a turn for the worse when he lifted Connie over his shoulders. It occurred to her that the only reason he'd picked Connie from the crowd was because she was the only person from the party who didn't have a cocktail in her hand. Otherwise, alcohol would've spilled all over his head while he held her on his shoulders as if they were at a Van Halen concert.

Perched on his shoulders, Connie clung to him for dear life. Cate watched as her glasses bobbed on her nose while Ezekiel danced around. She shouted something, but the words were inaudible, and Cate thought it best that no one could hear her.

After the song was over he set her down, grabbed her mother by the waist and formed a conga line. Startled, Connie moved forward and led the group. Jill and Beth latched on, and Rita and Charles joined. The line came full circle, and Connie looked over her shoulder when she trotted past Cate. "This is a Satanic cult," she yelled.

Ethan hopped in behind her mother. "It's not so bad, is it?"

"How do you know *these* people?"

Cate tried to wipe the smile from her face. It was sort of funny watching her mother being hounded by the antithesis of her entire existence. However, she didn't have to wipe the smile off her face. It left on its own when Janet hopped in line and wrapped her fingers around Ethan's waist. *It's not a big deal,* she told herself. *It's a conga line.* Maybe she should just hop in too.

She couldn't chase after it though. She had to wait for it to come full circle. From where she stood, she could see Janet tickling him. He laughed hard.

She whispered something in his ear, and she thought she saw Ethan mouth the words, *Thank you.* It wasn't just Denise. It was both of them. They both wanted her out of the picture. When the song ended, Janet hugged Ethan.

Ezekiel, clueless, turned to them. "Congratulations, you two! I hope you enjoy your party!"

Puzzled, Ethan looked as if he were about to correct him, but Janet threw her arms around Ezekiel. "Thanks! That was so much fun!"

She was just going to let him believe that she was actually Ethan's fiancée? The girl was sick. The next thing Cate knew she'd probably be stealing her clothes and cutting her hair to look like Cate's.

She was psycho, and Cate felt like marching over there and introducing herself as Ethan's fiancée to Ezekiel, but she was interrupted by her drunk sister. "Did you see Mom?" Emily slurred. "That was too much. I wish I'd had a video camera for that!"

Emily and Bradley had gotten a sitter for Cassidy, and since it was rare that Emily ever went out for a drink, she was completely buzzed off the two glasses of wine she'd consumed.

Ethan made his way toward them. "This has been really fun," he said. "When I first saw the band, I thought, 'Oh shit, what has Chuck done now?' But I think they actually added quite a bit of spice to the party."

"Ethan," she whispered. "I think Janet is after a little more than a job interview and some friends."

"What do you mean?"

"If you can't tell . . . she's all over you." Her whisper sounded harsh.

He shook his head. He was completely oblivious. "No she's not. She's been hooking up with Ryan. Ever since she started working for him."

"Are you sure?"

"I'm positive."

Cate looked at her standing over by the cheese buffet with Ryan. She laughed loudly at something he said then French-kissed him. As soon as she was finished she looked at Ethan. "She's trying to make you jealous," Cate said. "I just know it. Ethan, she didn't even correct Ezekiel when he congratulated *you two*."

"She's drunk."

"Hey you guys," Denise said, cocking her head to a side. "Listen, I just want you to know that I hope it's okay that Janet came. I was showing her a condo this afternoon, and I felt so bad for her. She seemed soooo low and it's been hard for her to get back in the loop again after the move and everything and I just thought it was the right thing to do."

Her apology brought some comfort, and Cate wondered if she was overreacting. Maybe Denise's intentions weren't entirely evil, and maybe Ethan was right about Ryan and Janet. "So it's okay? I knew if anybody would understand you it would be you guys."

Ethan shrugged. "Yeah, it's fine."

"No worries. It was nice of you," Cate said.

Ethan excused himself to use the restroom.

She looked at Denise beneath the porch light. Her forehead looked damp and clammy, and there was a gray cast to her complexion. "I hope you're not mad," Denise said. "I didn't want to make you feel awkward or anything." Maybe she was truly an idiot and had no idea that inviting his ex to the party was obnoxious. At any rate, Cate didn't want her to know that it had bothered her. She'd probably run to Rita and Charles and tell them how insecure and catty Cate was. Then Denise would be the sweet, thoughtful person who had helped poor Janet, and Cate would be the selfish and uncompassionate wench.

"No, it's fine, Denise. Janet seems like a really nice person. I like her."

"Oh good. I knew you wouldn't mind, and I knew Rita wouldn't mind. She *loves* Janet. Always has. She was like family all those years they were together. It's hard to believe she's . . . well . . . never mind."

One last stab.

Cate wanted to get away from her as soon as possible and was glad when her family interrupted to say their good-byes. She offered to walk them to the car just so she could get rid of Denise.

Emily was quiet, and her gait a little staggered. Cate felt sorry for her. Hungover with a toddler running around all day sounded like torture.

"Are Ethan's parents in a cult?" Emily asked as soon as they reached the driveway.

"Don't be ridiculous. It's just some band Chuck likes."

Emily looked at Chuck and Tatiana making out near a trash can in the driveway. "Figures."

Their footsteps were loud in the quiet neighborhood.

"That was some strange music," Bradley added. Anything that wasn't played on the local top-forty station was strange to Bradley. He was a complete dork, and she'd often wondered if he'd ever done anything exciting in his entire life.

"I thought the music had a nice ring to it," her father said. He squeezed Cate's shoulder, and she was so glad that he was there. "It reminds me a little of some music your mother and I heard when we went to Greece before you were born." Her mother was awfully quiet, which was interesting. She figured if anyone would have something to say about the evening, it would've been Connie.

"Do Ethan's parents know you're getting married in the Catholic church?" Emily asked.

"Yes."

"And they're okay with it?"

"Yes." Cate pulled her sweater around her shoulders.

"Ethan's family seems like the type of people who would want you to sign a prenup."

"Emily!" She nearly tripped over the curb.

"I don't think they'd do that to Cate," Connie said. "And you shouldn't drink, Emily."

"This is how people get contracts put out on their heads," Bradley said, eager to add his opinion.

"What?" Cate asked, wondering what the hell he was talking about and how far they were parked so she could figure out how much more of this conversation she was going to have to take.

"When people sign prenups, most of the time, it says that the cheating party gets nothing," Bradley said. "So when someone goes out and cheats, and then they decide they want a divorce, they realize they'll get nothing if it comes out during divorce court that they cheated. It's just like an episode of *American Justice*," Bradley explained. " 'Cheating spouse kills wife so she won't discover lover.' And it all comes down to money."

"Okay, enough." She couldn't believe they were having this conversation. Ethan would never want a prenup, let alone hire a hit man to kill her because she was cheating. "Ethan is not going to hire a hit man to kill me, all right?" *But don't be surprised if you disappear,* she wanted to add. What the hell was the matter with him?

As she said good-bye to them she realized that she wasn't the only one who was gaining some unique family members. Ethan was getting Bradley.

·18·

A Taste of Dirt

By coincidence escrow closed on the same day as their cake-tasting appointment. Let Them Have Cake was in between Escondido and Pacific Beach, and there wouldn't be enough time to schlepp all their belongings to Escondido, unload them, and return to the bakery in time for their appointment. The plan was to leave Grease with Ethan's parents for the day, pack up all their belongings, and park close to the bakery so they could keep an eye on all their stuff while they tasted cake.

All of the Good Time Catering vans were full of equipment, so they borrowed Ethan's father's dilapidated Toyota truck from 1980 that he'd been saving for over two decades just so he could pick up firewood. It had been shaded beneath a fig tree in front of the Blakelys' house for over a decade now. Tiny and low to the ground, it probably hadn't seen a hose in the twenty-some years that Charles Blakely had owned it. Ethan's king-sized mattress stuck over the edges like a gigantic waffle.

"Are you sure that it's not going to fly off on the freeway?" Cate asked as they finished wrapping bungee cords across its corners.

"Nah, it'll be fine," Ethan said.

Just climbing into the truck made her feel as if she needed to wash her hair. She was wearing denim shorts, and the fabric seats felt scratchy and damp across the back of her thighs when she sat down.

"You don't think we should put some plastic over the mattress?" she asked as she looked at the sky. It was one of the rare July days when thunder erupted, and everyone thought they needed to pull out sweaters and make soup. Rarely did San Diego see rain in the summer, and even when they did, it was warm.

Ethan revved the gas, and the truck died. "Nah," he said. "It's not going to rain. It's just humid."

He revved the engine again, and this time the little truck came jolting to life. Wasting no time, he screeched from the driveway of her Pacific Beach apartment.

"Does the AC work?" she asked, reaching for the knob.

"I don't know. Try it."

She turned the knob and felt a moment of joy when she heard the rush of air coming from beneath the dashboard. It was a miracle. Her happiness came and went quickly. Air came pouring from the vents bringing ten years' worth of dust and twigs along with it.

"Holy shit!" Ethan batted small leaves away from his face.

She wanted to say something, but her mouth was full of dirt. She quickly switched the AC off, but not before they were covered in grime. She attempted to manually roll down her window, but the crank was so old and rusty she had to use all her might just to crack it. They were going to cook inside the grime mobile.

The wind that forced itself through the crack was deafening and rattled the cab. The truck only went fifty on the freeway, so they drove in the slow lane the whole time, cars whizzing past—some occasionally laying on the horn. She screamed the directions to Let Them Have Cake over the howling wind. She held her hair down with her fingers so the wind wouldn't whip it into her eyes. "Turn here!" she screamed.

He accidentally drove over the curb when they pulled into the shopping center, and the mattress shifted like a pancake sliding from a spatula. "There it is."

"Oh yeah, I see it." As he drove to a parking space in front of the bakery, she heard an awkward thud and glanced in her rearview mirror. The mattress had accidentally sideswiped a parked car, and its rearview mirror had popped into the car.

"Ethan!"

"Crap, I hope there isn't damage."

She looked at the silver Buick and wondered if the owner was standing somewhere in the parking lot watching them. Chances were it belonged to an elderly person. Most of Rancho Bernardo was a retirement community, and the way most of the people drove around here she figured banged-up side mirrors were probably a daily occurrence. The driver would probably feel lucky that it wasn't a dent in his bumper. However, she couldn't help but think that this was the way road rage started. She imagined Ethan, filthy and fixing the mirror. A Robert De Niro type coming after him with a club.

"Maybe you should just leave the mirror. Let them pull it out themselves," she said. "We're late anyway."

She caught a glimpse of herself in her own side mirror. *Rat's nest* was what came to mind. She noticed trace amounts of dust on her cheeks, and when she lifted her hands to pull the twigs from her hair she saw dirt beneath her fingernails. Her placid and sharp bob had been blown to resemble the tangled mess of junk that had come from the AC.

Ethan looked as if he had just returned from forty days of filming *Survivor*. They pulled the twigs out of each other's hair, and when they were finished, she tried to comb her hair with her fingers, but it was too tangled. The humidity had served as some kind of styling gel, locking the twists and waves into shape, as if she had dreadlocks.

She waited in the car while Ethan darted over to the Buick. She could tell by the expression on his face that something was wrong. There was a Taco Bell nearby, and she figured whoever the car belonged to was probably sitting inside munching on a Gordita and had no idea that his window had almost been removed by a Sleep Therapy mattress. She watched as he pulled the mirror back out then ran back to the truck. "The door's scratched," he said. "It's pretty minor, but still."

"Great," she said sarcastically. "We better leave a note." She fished through a million recepits and gum wrappers inside her purse for a pen. She found a pen and a receipt from the grocery store. "How bad is it?" she asked.

"Nothing a little touch-up paint won't fix, but I still feel like we should leave a note."

She waited while he trotted back to the car and slipped the note under a windshield wiper.

The bakery was crowded. Retired folks munching on pastries and sipping coffee occupied the tables. There was a young father with two kids who devoured a stack of sugar cookies. Except for the children, who were too engrossed with their cookies to care, everyone seemed to pause from their treats to glance at the two frazzled-looking weirdos who came through the front door.

"You must be Cate and Ethan," a woman from behind the counter said. She was petite and middle-aged, and Cate wondered how she managed to stay so cute and trim working at a bakery. If Cate worked here, she'd get acne and never be able to fit into her favorite jeans again.

"Yes. We are!" Cate smiled warmly, but the woman's smile was thin in return. "All right."

"Sorry we're a few minutes late," Ethan said. "We're in the process of moving, and we ran into a few problems."

"Yes, I know. That was my husband's Buick you hit."

Cate wanted to shrink.

Luckily, Ethan spoke up, because she was so embarrassed she didn't know if her tongue was capable of forming words. "Was it?" Ethan said. "I'm *so* sorry." He looked at her name tag. "Myrtle, I went over there to look at it, and there is one *tiny* scratch." The situation would've been much easier if the entire bakery wasn't listening to their conversation. "I left a note, and I promised to pay for any and all damages."

For the first time the woman's smile was sincere, and she lowered her voice. "It's okay. My husband has actually done the same sort of thing before—to someone else. I'm sure it will be fine."

Thanks to Ethan, they'd started over. She felt as if they'd turned over a new leaf as Myrtle led them to a table. Cate tried to follow, but her foot stuck to the carpet. Myrtle and most of the bakery watched as Cate lifted her foot and brought up a stretchy rope of hot pink gum. It stretched from her shoe like soft, sticky rubber cement, and she held her foot in midair, as if she'd just stepped in dog shit. Running from the store and changing her name seemed like the only way to redeem herself at this point. First, they hit the manager's husband's car. Now she had tracked strawberry gum into the bakery.

Myrtle sighed. "I'll get a paper towel."

Cate wanted to track down the slob who'd thrown his gum on the sidewalk and pave his driveway in Bubble Yum. She went outside and scraped her foot against the edge of the sidewalk as hard as she could, rubbing it back and forth until she was certain the gum was not only gone, but the sole of her shoe had probably melted from the friction as well.

When she returned, Ethan was picking the remains of the gum from the floor. After he was finished, Myrtle led them to a table.

They sat down, and Myrtle placed a book bigger than the King James Bible in front of them. "Here is the first book," she said.

The first book? There are others?

"And here is the second." Cate watched as Myrtle's biceps flexed, and a groan escaped her throat while she heaved the second book toward the table. It landed with a thud.

Myrtle explained that there were four popular cake flavors: strawberry, chocolate, Bavarian cream, and raspberry. There was so much information about frosting and cake sizes, and servings, and sheet cakes that it was hard to keep up with all the information. They listened to a brief course on a frosting called rolled fondant, which according to Myrtle was extremely expensive, created perfect corners and edges, but tasted like tar.

"Most of guests will simply peel it off and place it on to the side of their plate." She shrugged. "A lot of couples want it because it looks so nice, but no one ever really eats it." She lowered her voice. "I think it's a real waste of money, if you asked me. Whipped frosting is much cheaper, and we can still make the corners sharp. Well," She glanced at the door. "Another couple just arrived for a cake-tasting appointment too, and I need to help them, so you guys browse through the books. Pick out what you want while I let them do the tasting, and then we'll pass the books to them and you guys can do your tasting."

Cate glanced at the other couple. Freshly groomed, they were both a tad on the chubby side and looked as if they'd just graduated from college. The bride's mother was with them. The groom had a severe part in his hair, and the look on his face suggested that he'd been dragged to the bakery against his will. The bride's khaki pants were freshly ironed, and the pointy collar on her powder blue blouse was sharp. She and the mother both carried large Dooney and Bourke handbags. The bride gave Cate and Ethan a once-over before turning her gaze to the books.

"I definitely don't want rolled fondant," Ethan said. He was so engrossed in the book he didn't even look up when he spoke. "I want our cake to taste good. What's the point in having that kind of frosting if no one is going to eat it? A cake is meant to be eaten."

"I couldn't agree more."

He eagerly flipped through the first book, and she was glad he had taken charge, because if it were up to her, she probably would've told Myrtle to point out the top ten styles, and they would've taken it from there. She never knew that cakes came in so many styles. Did guests really care about the cake? Maybe a few wistful single girls who were fantasizing about their own wedding actually took time between the electric slide and the bouquet toss to admire the cake. In her wedding experiences, people just wanted to get smashed and dance.

Some of the styles were exceptionally outdated. Straight from the early eighties, they had small plastic beams separating each tier, with a plastic bride and groom perched on top. Bright yellow and brown flowers made of thick, heavy frosting covered the edges. She actually kind of liked those, and thought it might add something interesting. Then people would really stop and look at the cake.

"What do you think of this one?" Ethan asked. He pointed to three tiers, one resting right on top of the other. Little beads of frosting outlined the edges of each tier, and a cascade of Vendela roses fell over the edges.

"It's great, but isn't that rolled fondant?"

"Yes. But she said if we saw something with rolled fondant in the book, we could substitute it for whipped frosting and it would look very similar. Weren't you listening?"

"Oh." The other group sat down at the small table next to them. Cate could feel their eyes boring onto them, and it made her uncomfortable to know they were being watched.

"What are we doing? What are we waiting for?" the groom groaned.

"The other couple," the bride said loudly. "*They* have *the books*."

"I'm missing the tournament for this?" he mumbled. "I thought you said we had to be here at ten sharp."

"Like you don't watch enough golf as it is."

"I can't believe they don't have more copies of those books," the mother said. Cate could see them out of the corner of her eye. They were staring at Ethan while he flipped the pages, and the bride still hadn't removed her purse from her shoulder.

Totally oblivious to the Bridezillas, Ethan kept right on turning.

She watched as Myrtle delivered their tasting samples, and even the sight of food didn't wipe the scowls from their faces. She knew it was evil, but she sort of hoped Ethan took forever with the books. Assholes. Couldn't they just taste their cake and be happy with what they had for the time being? Then she realized how childish she was being and felt an overwhelming sense of pressure to hurry. She could feel the weight of their stares hovering over them like they were vultures waiting to attack. Long, frustrated sighs and groans came from their corner until finally Cate couldn't take it anymore.

She turned toward their table. "So when is your big day?"

The mother only shot her a look, and the groom's face remained placid. He hadn't even touched the sample. "June seventeenth. Next summer," the bride said politely before she tasted something with pink filling.

"Are you stressing?" Cate kindly asked, even though the answer was obvious.

"Yes. She is," the groom answered.

"No I'm not," she snapped. *Okay, wrong question.*

"I love your bag," she said, lying through her teeth.

With this, Bridezilla's eyes lit up. "Oh! Thanks. I just got it last weekend."

"Wonderful. Sorry about this whole thing with the books. We're going as fast as we can."

After that they seemed to lighten up a little bit.

Eventually, Cate and Ethan had narrowed it down to three styles. In the end, they chose the first cake Ethan had suggested, the one decorated with Vendela roses. She decided that she would probably have all the bouquets and centerpieces made in Vendela roses as well. They were the color of cream and so smooth and satiny they almost looked edible. They would look beautiful with champagne dresses.

When it was time for the cake tasting, she let him pick too. There were so many details of the wedding that he wasn't going to have a say in, and the cake could be all his. He chose the chocolate filling, and before they left they bought a small birthday cake with the same filling and frosting. It wasn't anyone's birthday, but they wanted it to celebrate their new home.

As they paid, she felt a sense of accomplishment. There was one less wedding task to worry about, and she'd figured out what kind of flowers she wanted too. When they stepped outside, she almost dropped their birthday cake on the gum she'd scraped off her shoe. It was raining all over their mattress.

·19·

In the Zone

*T*he *Texas Chainsaw Massacre* had found her house. The buzz of power tools brought snow with it. *Strange,* she thought. *For San Diego.* Her eyes flicked open, and she tried to remember where she was. Oh yeah, her new house. She was on the kitchen floor, lying in a bed made of sleeping bags. It had been two weeks since they'd arrived, and despite fans aimed on the mattress twenty-four hours a day, the humidity had kept the king-sized bed from drying.

She brushed something away from her face and heard the sound again, a grating sound like a hedge trimmer rubbing against an oak tree. She sat up and found a Mexican man on stilts in their living room, grating away at the wall, while drywall and paint came down like a blizzard. Thick black construction paper covered the hardwood floors, and their furniture was wrapped in cellophane.

"Hello," the man said from nearly ten feet above.

She wiped drywall from her face and waved. Ethan came from the dining room, holding the same kind of power tool, the cord trailing behind his filthy clothes. He'd been wearing the same jeans and T-shirt for five days. Two inches of white powder covered his hair. A surgical mask and goggles protected his face.

"Oh good. You're up." He pulled his mask away. "We need to move the bed into the back room, because Enrique is going to sand and put drywall in here too." When he said *bed*, he didn't mean the mattress drying in the bedroom. He meant the campground formerly known as their kitchen.

"I had no idea he was coming," she whispered.

"I forgot to tell you. I thought he was coming on Thursday, but he called today and said he had a cancellation." He smiled as he pulled the sleeping bag from beneath her. Dust from his hair spilled all over the bed, like flour from a sifter. "Trust me, you're going to love this. The walls are going to look so much better."

She still thought they looked fine just the way they were, but Ethan Pennington over here had other things in mind.

"How are we supposed to live like this?" she whispered. "All our furniture is covered in Saran Wrap." She watched as the man sanded away. "It's like Lake Tahoe in December in our living room."

"Well, it won't be this way for long. I promise. Why don't you go to the beach today?"

"All right. Fine."

She quickly changed into her suit and a sundress and headed out the door without breakfast. She had just stepped onto the porch when she heard the neighbors from across the street.

"Deb, wait! Please let me explain!" She watched as a woman with a mullet and Reebok high tops bolted from the front door and dodged the primered El Camino that rested on bricks in the driveway.

A man chased after her. "Please! Don't!" He pleaded as he tried to catch up. Cate had seen him before, and he'd never looked so desperate. Usually he sported loose-fitting fluorescent tank tops and had a cigarette dangling from his lips. Today he was topless, wearing only acid-washed jeans and slip-on Vans. He looked tortured. "I swear, I don't know any-one named Pamela!" He tried to catch up.

The woman, clearly not interested in his story, pulled herself into the driver's side of a lifted truck as if she were climbing into a tree house. Over the engine, Skid Row's "Eighteen and Life" blasted through the neighborhood. The motorcycle and four wheeler in the bed of the truck jolted when she put the car in reverse.

"Stop! Please!" Desperate, he began to sprint.

"Go cry to Pamela, you son of a bitch!"

The tires turned, and she left him in a thick cloud of dust.

"No! Nooooooo!" His howl was full of heartbreak. For a moment his knees looked weak, and she thought he would actually fall to the ground, but instead he kicked the mailbox. "Godammit! My bike! And my quad! How could she?" He stormed back inside.

She suddenly had second thoughts about heading over to their place with Ethan and introducing themselves. They really didn't seem like the type of people who would ever need to borrow an egg or have an extra cup of sugar sitting around.

At least the neighborhood wasn't crawling with gang members. So far she hadn't heard any gunshots or gangster rap, but she'd heard a lot of Kenny Rogers.

They lived in the type of neighborhood where people didn't get their animals neutered and almost everyone traveled on bicycles be-cause they'd lost their licenses to DUIs. However, she felt safe. Com-pared to the other neighborhoods in their price range, this place seemed like paradise.

She slipped into her car and realized the only thing that bothered her a little about the move was getting used to sharing everything with Ethan. For the past two years they'd spent nearly every night together. However, it wasn't the same as actually living under the same roof. She'd never seen his dirty shoes resting on their kitchen table, or the way he made the mirror on the medicine cabinet wet and spotted after he shaved. She felt like every time she got finished cleaning the kitchen or picking up the living room, he'd come ripping through like a hurricane and mess everything up again.

They'd always been comfortable around each other. He'd seen her without makeup on a daily basis. She'd listened to the steady sound of his urine every morning since they'd begun dating. Moving in together had brought them to a new level of intimacy. She noticed his used floss sticking from the wastebasket, and he'd almost walked in on her plucking a dark hair from above her upper lip.

The beach was a little muggy when she arrived, and the water was dark, olive green, almost black. She expected the Loch Ness monster to emerge, but instead her hottie surfer came sauntering toward her. He was wet, and she noticed thick patches of sand covering his tan feet.

"Hey," he said when he spotted her. "I haven't seen you lately."

"Yeah." She was about to tell him that she'd moved to Escondido but changed the subject. "How was the water?" she asked.

"Not bad. Red tide. Everyone gets freaked out and doesn't want to go in when it's like this, but I don't mind. Less competition for waves out there."

"What exactly is red tide anyway?"

He sat down next to her. "I think it has to do with the seaweed or something. Water gets really thick with it." He shrugged. "It doesn't bother me much." She figured there probably wasn't much that bothered him. He'd just sat down in a wet suit on the sand.

"Why don't you get out there?" He nodded toward the ocean.

She shook her head. "I just like to sit and read in the sun." She sounded like such a dork, but what bothered her the most was that she cared so much about impressing him.

"You don't surf?"

She laughed. "No. I don't think I could ever get up on the board."

"There's not much to it. I bet you'd be up in a day."

"Doubtful." He was sitting so close to her, and she was afraid she had sour breath, so she tried to keep her sentences short.

"Well, get a board, and I'll teach you. You know I'm pretty much here every day. I don't mind takin' you out."

"Yeah, we'll see. I don't know." She tried to talk between clenched teeth and wondered how he could feel so comfortable being so close to someone he hardly knew, let alone offering surf lessons. Bringing up Ethan would be the right thing to do, somehow subtly mentioning that her *fiancé* had already offered to teach her to surf. But she didn't. She'd always thought she knew herself pretty well, but now she was beginning to wonder.

He stood up and brushed some sand from his knees. "Just find a board, and I'll show you."

Something about watching him walk away made her heart sink. There would never be surf lessons. Not that she would've taken surf lessons from him prior to being engaged. She'd always been devoted to Ethan. It was just that knowing that surf lessons from hot men were now officially completely banned made her feel a little sad. She remembered graduating from college, and looking at the apartment she'd shared with Sarah and Leslie. There would be no more sleeping in on weekdays and eating in the USD deli together. The party had ended, and she felt her heart sink a little when she'd handed over the keys to their landlord. She felt the same way now.

A brand-new 750 BMW was parked in front of their mailbox. Black and sleek, the windows were tinted, and she wondered which of their neighbors had a BMW. Her parking brake squeaked loud when she pulled it up.

They wouldn't get their mail today. Their mail woman was a Nazi. Ever since they'd moved to Escondido they'd learned that one had to be parked at least three feet in front of the mailbox, or mail would not be delivered. If a car was blocking the box, postal workers were not responsible for delivering mail. The mail woman was shaped like a penguin, and if she had to waddle her way out of the truck to put the mail in the box, then she wouldn't stop. There had been several occasions when Cate's Volvo had questionably been in "The Zone." Ethan had been so ticked he'd taken some chalk he'd used for God only knows what task around the house and had drawn a line, writing *three feet* with five exclamation points in bold.

For most people, missing a day or two of mail wouldn't be a big deal, but for Ethan it was a problem. With his catering business he received lots of deposits and checks in the mail.

Living with a mail Nazi had given her a new awareness about parking in front of people's mailboxes, and she had now made a solid pact with herself that she would never, under any circumstances, block someone else's mailbox. So who was the jackass that had parked in front of theirs? Probably Pamela.

To say their house was in shambles was an understatement. Their little cottage resembled nothing of the clean, airy little place she'd briefly known. She'd expected Enrique and everything that came with him to be gone. Construction paper still covered the floor. It looked as though someone had *tried* to sweep all the dust from the papers, and the furniture was still covered in plastic. Her feet crunched over the paper as she stepped inside, and when she closed the door behind her, a dustbowl of powdery drywall sprinkled over her head. She touched her hair, and when she pulled her hand away, it looked as if she'd dipped it into a sack of powdered sugar.

She heard Ethan's voice. "I think we should tear this wall down right here and expand the walkway into the kitchen."

Who was he talking to? The idea of "tearing" anything down in their brand-new house made her a little nervous.

"Oh! That will look great!" Denise.

Did she get a new car?

"I just think it would open up the room more, make it look bigger. Otherwise, each of these rooms looks like a box. You see, bigger walkways create more open space, which gives the illusion of a much bigger house." It was a notion he'd probably gotten from HGTV, which he'd been watching, frankly, too much of these days. Lately, the things that had been coming from his mouth seemed to be in direct correlation with Bob Vila. Picturing him with a sledgehammer and pair of work gloves was unsettling.

"You're just so smart and creative, Ethan! Everything is going to look gorgeous!" It was that damn Janet.

"Oh, hey, Cate!" Ethan noticed her.

"Hi. Enrique's gone?"

"He left a while ago. I told him not to clean up though."

Why the hell would you do a thing like that?

"I'm gonna paint this weekend, so it will save me a lot of time if everything is wrapped and covered."

"Oh." She nodded. His plan made sense, but she wasn't thrilled about the idea of several more days without furniture and floors covered in paper.

"I was just telling Janet and Denise how I want to tear down this walkway so we can open up the room up more. What do you think?"

"I think the walkway is fine," she said. "The house has so much charm, I hate to tamper with everything." Not to mention that he'd been blowing off work ever since they'd moved in to fulfill all his remodeling dreams. If he kept this up, not only would expensive changes be out of the question, but they wouldn't have a house to make changes in.

He looked annoyed. "Sure, it's fine. But it could be *so* much better."

"I think a simple paint job could make all the difference. Why don't we just paint?" She suggested, hoping one big task might wear him out. "Why don't we wait till after the wedding to make any other major changes? We have enough going on with all that, and besides it's the heart of wedding season, and you're so busy with work, how are you going to find the time to do all of this?"

They all looked at her as if Ethan's fantasies had just been crunched beneath her shoe.

"I think you should definitely knock that walkway out," Janet said. "You really have such a vision."

He looked at her and smiled. "Thank you. Let me show you what else I want to do." Janet followed him to the bathroom.

Were they teaming up together? Obviously, he felt like Janet was supportive of his dreams, and where did that leave her? She was the grouchy dream squasher that he was marrying. She stood there for a moment until she noticed Denise was staring at her.

"What's in your hair?" Denise asked.

Cate remembered the plaster that had fallen over her head when she'd closed the door behind her. "It's just some drywall." She set down her beach bag. "What have you guys been doing all day?" she asked, when what she really wanted to know was what the hell they were doing in her house.

"I've been showing Janet a bunch of places, and we just looked at one right down the street."

God help them. Janet—moving in down the street? "What happened?" she asked, her heart racing. "Did she like it?"

"We went to make an offer, but it was already in escrow."

"Darn."

They came back out of the bathroom. Needless to say, Janet was supportive of ripping out the tub and shower that already existed and putting in an old-fashioned claw-foot tub, complete with a pedestal sink and a new plumbing system. Cate wished someone would remind him that he was a caterer, not a construction worker.

"Ha! Ha! Ha!" Janet cackled when she looked at Cate. "Look at your hair! You look like the one who has been sanding all day." Her laughter came out in squeals.

"I have to take a shower anyway because I have sand all over my body."

"I love your new car!" Ethan said as he walked them to the door.

"Isn't it great?" Janet said. "I guess everything happens for a reason, you know. I thought having my house burn down would be the worst thing that ever happened to me, but then I got a great insurance settlement. Even better, I'm in San Diego with such wonderful friends." She looked at Ethan and Denise.

If she thought that her house burning down was going to bring her back to Ethan she was even crazier than Cate had thought. She was absolutely puzzled as to why Ethan couldn't see through her.

He went outside with them to see Janet's new car, and for the first time since Janet had come back into their lives Cate felt like she had won.

Part Two

Goin' to
the Chapel

20

Up in Flames

A month later their floors were still covered in the same dusty construction paper, and most of their furniture was still stacked in the middle of the rooms—covered in cellophane. Thanks to the massive heat wave that hit the inland valleys of San Diego, their bed had dried. Every night when she went to bed she tracked dusty bits of plaster and drywall into their sheets. When she woke in the morning she set her feet on the same crusty paper she'd come to recognize as their floors.

Furthermore, their bed had become an island in The Construction Ocean once known as their house. They'd taken the plastic off the TV and dresser in their bedroom, and watched all their favorite TV shows in bed. They ate meals and paid bills sitting on the edge of the mattress. If Grease wasn't eating or using his litter box, he was sitting on top of the bed too. Even he hated getting his paws dirty.

With weddings booked solid until mid-September, Ethan never got around to painting as planned. Due to the amount of stress he was under, she didn't want to be a nag, so she got used to living in squalor and had actually forgotten what their hardwood floors and couches looked like.

The last month of summer went by fast, and she spent most of it taking care of wedding plans. They decided on the Rancho Bernardo Inn as their reception site, and she had Peg Migillicuddy and her mother polish up a lot of details such as tablecloths and seat covers. It was wonderful to have their help. She'd be lost without them.

Once school started it would be hard to interview photographers and florists, so she picked out her flowers and the right person to take all the pictures while she had a chance. She chose centerpieces, invitations, and favors, and hired a videographer and a band.

They registered, a task she'd always anticipated being the ultimate shopping experience. Picking out everything you wanted and not paying for it sounded like a dream, but when they finally got their hands on a registry gun in Macy's she found it to be one of the most draining tasks of all. She'd never felt so overwhelmed. She'd spent hours looking at china, her vision blurring just studying the endless brands and patterns. She eventually decided to make it easy on herself and skip fine china completely. She realized they'd probably only use it once a year, and that was a generous assumption. It would only clutter up their limited closet space or collect dust in the attic. By the time they had a house to host a major holiday in she could probably afford to buy a set for herself. They ended up registering for a set of Villeroy and Boch everyday china that they could mix and match to dress up or dress down.

"It's the little black dress of china," the woman helping them had said. "You can use it every day, and register for accents to dress it up."

They picked out their menu and a song for their first dance, "Ain't No Mountain High Enough," by Marvin Gaye. They ordered Ethan's tux and discussed honeymoon ideas. To say they were busy was an understatement. Due to their hectic schedules there wasn't much time for Janet or Denise to weasel their way into their lives. They'd stopped by twice after they were "looking at condos in Escondido" and both times Ethan had been on his way out the door to cater an event.

Cate tried to help with his catering as often as she could. She was getting used to riding in the catering truck, inhaling the scent of the pine air freshener that hung from his rearview mirror.

The last weekend of August they catered a wedding on a thirty-acre ranch in Jamul. She helped prepare the appetizers in the kitchen with the rest of the staff. It had been fun getting to know all the people that Ethan worked with. She'd listened to him tell so many stories about his employees, and now she understood all his descriptions. When it seemed like everything was under control in the kitchen she sneaked away to watch the wedding from a distance. She always liked to watch the weddings so she could get ideas for her own.

The entire event was outdoors, but there were a few massive old oak trees that provided a decent amount of shade. The August heat felt like a heavy blanket and made her crave a nap. She hid under a shady oak behind the guests. Some of the guests looked as if they'd been hosed in sweat, and Cate noticed that many held lavender and sea green pom-poms. In lieu of programs, poms-poms had been placed on each seat, and most of the guests examined them as if they were wondering what exactly they were supposed to do with a pair of pom-poms at a wedding.

She watched as the wedding party came down the aisle. The bridesmaids' dresses came in the same shades as the pom-poms. A rare arrangement, the bridesmaids and groomsmen came down the aisle in pairs. Most of her trips down the aisle had been alone. The return trip had always been with a groomsman. After watching the first couple come down the aisle she realized why they might have chosen to pair them up. Some people in the wedding party needed help. They all seemed like they'd been pounding shots of tequila while they'd been doing hair and taking photos. One of the bridesmaids waved to everyone the entire way down the aisle. An aura of meathead accompanied all the groomsmen, and she watched while, one after the other, they high-fived the groom when they reached the end of the aisle. Sweat dripped from the groom's bangs like raindrops falling off a storm drain.

Lucky for everyone, the bride was on time. If she'd been any later,

Cate worried that not only would the groom have a heat stroke, but the waving bridesmaid would pass out. She struggled to keep her balance and a couple times had almost nodded off standing at the altar.

For a moment she thought she recognized "Here Comes the Bride." The high, quick notes that came from the brass band seemed similar to the classic song, but then she realized it was the fight song played at college football games. All the guests shook the poms-poms with the music and cheered as if the bride had just scored a touchdown.

Luckily the ceremony went by quickly.

"I now pronounce you man and wife," the preacher said.

"Yes!" The groom shouted. He made a fist and jerked his elbow back. "I'm fuckin' married!" The bride didn't seem startled when he picked her up and carried her away.

Cate went back for her appetizer tray and expected to be bombarded as soon as the guests hit the reception tent. However, it was obvious by the line that wrapped around the ranch that the guests were less interested in her seared steak kabobs than in doing shots of Jägermeister. Though her catering experience was limited, it was the easiest wedding she'd ever catered. The grandparents seemed like the only people who were interested in eating. Everyone else was drunk and dominating the dance floor. She'd always been able to pinpoint one wedding drunk at each wedding she'd attended. She could always count on some obnoxious little character who'd had too much to drink and took over the entertainment. There were so many drunks at this wedding that it was impossible to keep track. She actually had to hunt out people to take some of her food.

"Can I interest you in some spring rolls and steak kabobs?" she asked a dozen times.

At most of the weddings she'd catered she'd usually said things like, "I'll be back as fast as I can with refills."

Some drunk had the genius idea of passing out sparklers. They were probably smuggled across the Mexican border and had always made her nervous. She remembered her uncle Jack showing up to her parents' house one New Year's Eve when she was a small child. He'd bought enough firecrackers and exploding party favors to blow up a small town. He'd passed out sparkly little wands to all his nieces and nephews, and Cate had watched as sparks flew off the sticks like tiny grenades. Even though the flames died the second they hit the asphalt, she'd been afraid that a large spark would fly into her eye or burn her hand off. So while all her cousins ran around the yard, waving their sparklers like they were in a Hawaiian luau she stood stone-still, holding the very end of the wand away from her body with the tips of her fingers.

She watched all the guests wave their sparklers around as the bride and groom made their grand entrance. All she could think about was what a bad combination alcohol and fire were. The whole situation worried her, and while she carried around her tray she did her best to avoid anyone holding a sparkler.

She watched from a distance as the happy couple took to the dance floor for their first dance, "Shameless" by Garth Brooks. Their dancing reminded Cate of the same way she'd danced in eighth grade. The bride's arms were wrapped around the groom's neck, their bodies sandwiched together as they moved around in circles. The only difference from junior high was that the groom's hands were cupped over each of her butt cheeks. That would've been forbidden at her middle school.

She was starting to get a little bored watching them and was just about to head back to the kitchen when she noticed the bridesmaid who'd waved the whole way down the aisle. Her eyes were closed, and she swayed around to the music, while her sparkler dangled between her fingertips. It wasn't the cocktail spilled down the front of her dress or the mascara running down her cheeks that had caught Cate's attention. It was the way she held onto her wand that had made Cate stop dead in her tracks. The bridesmaid stood behind the bride's grandmother, who was no bigger than Smurfette and oblivious to the drunk jackass waving flames dangerously close to her wig. Too large for the old woman's head, the white wig had the same kind of points and peaks as a lemon meringue pie and settled in a straight line across the middle of her fore-head. Each time Drunk Bridesmaid moved, Cate held her breath.

Should she say something? If she didn't act fast, Grandma was going to ignite like a Duraflame log. She set her tray down and tried to get the attention of some of the guests in front of her, but they were too drunk to notice her, and she was afraid to get close to their sparklers. Franti-cally, she waved her arms at the grandmother, but the old lady couldn't see. Really, no one was paying attention to her.

She was just about to run to the other side of the room when Grandma's wig lit up like the Olympic torch. Neither Grandma nor Drunk Bridesmaid noticed. Just as Cate darted across the dance floor, one of the groomsman ripped through the crowd from the other direc-tion and threw an ice bucket over the old woman's head. Frigid water splashed over Cate's face and chest. She felt as if she'd just sat in the front row of the Shamu show and was fairly certain that most of the ice bucket landed on her. She watched through drenched eyelashes as the groomsman pulled the hairpiece from Grandma's head like a hot piece of meat from a barbecue. He threw her hair on the ground and began stomping on it. Several other groomsman decided to help out and began stomping on the wig with all their might. Bald as Bruce Willis, the grandmother looked startled as she witnessed her wig become roadkill. It resembled the corpse of a burned raccoon, and the smell that followed was not one that created an atmosphere for romance.

She touched her bare head, then looked at the ground. "My wig!" She hollered. She looked as if she might push her way through the groomsmen to retrieve her hair, then paused. She stood with both hands on her head and watched as the wig dangled from the tip of one of the groomsmen's black loafers. He tried to kick it off, but it was stuck, so he karate-kicked his leg. They all watched as the woman's white wig soared over the crowd and landed on an ice sculpture of a swan near the head table.

Someone handed Cate a napkin, and she wiped her face. The fire was well under control, and several kids had raced to capture the wig as if it had been the bride's bouquet. She decided it was best if she went back to the kitchen where she was supposed to be to begin with.

"What the hell happened to you?" Ethan asked as soon as she returned. "Did someone spill a drink on you?"

"Long story. I'll tell you later. But I know one thing for certain. We're not having anything with flames at our wedding."

He shrugged. "All right." Then he handed her a tray full of salads. "Time to serve the first course."

She felt damp and clammy while she served dinner. She could feel her hair drying in a strange style and couldn't recall feeling more uncomfortable and self-conscious. However, when she looked at the bald grandmother buttering a dinner roll, she realized she had nothing to complain about.

"Can I take your plate?" she asked, trying to not to stare at her bald head.

"Actually, could I just have some napkins, dear?" she asked. "I'm just drenched."

Cate had never given away so many napkins. It seemed like every five seconds someone had spilled their drink or dropped a forkful or steak in someone's lap.

The best man was too drunk to give the toast, so the groom ended up rising to the occasion. His head was still sweaty, and his bow tie, jacket, and vest were long gone. The white tux shirt he'd worn was unbuttoned mid-chest, and someone had spilled red wine down the front of it. He held a cocktail in one hand when he took the microphone. He was quiet for a moment, and he actually looked a little wistful when he looked at his bride. "I love you so much," he said. Loud applause followed. Savoring the attention, he quickly snapped out of his sentimental moment, straightened up, and chuckled. He took a gulp of his drink then continued. "You know, it's a miracle that Shannon even married me."

"No shit!" A beastly voice shouted from the back of the tent. "You wanker!"

The groom held the mic loosely in his hands. "The first night I met

Shannon I puked in her driveway." Loud laughter and a siren of catcalls followed. "She wouldn't even let me inside her house. She threw me in a cab and sent me home. I woke up the next morning with the worst hangover I've ever had in my life, and I couldn't even remember her name. All I could remember was this hot chick I had met at Moose's Taco Tuesday night. Man, I thought . . . I'll never see her again. I couldn't get her face out of my mind. I kept thinking Sharon, or Susan, or whatever her name was. I went back to Moose's for two nights in a row and hoped I'd see that blonde hair and those blue eyes again, but nothing." Some oohs and aahs followed. He took another gulp of his drink then held up his glass, signaling a refill to the bartender. "Then, luckily, she called me three days later. I had given her my phone number, and I didn't even remember. Thank God she called. I thought, after everything that happened, there was no way she'd go out with me again." A groomsman carried a new vodka cocktail to him, and he paused to take a swig. "Thanks, JJ," he said under his breath. "Anyway, I thought for sure she would never go out with me, but she said she would. I thought, *Boy, do I really have to make an impression this time.* So I went and picked her up, and we went out to a football game, and let me tell you, she got absolutely plastered. This time she was the one barfin', and all over my car." He paused to bask in the applause. "To this day, I haven't been able to get the smell out of my Bronco. But as we sat on the side of the freeway, me holding back her hair, I realized, this is the girl for me. This is going to be my wife! And let me tell you, it was the best realization I ever made. I never looked back, and I love her just as much as I did the day she puked all over my car." He raised his glass. "So you can all drink to that one! Whew hew!" Some of his drink spilled onto his chin and neck when he gulped it down.

In its own weird way, his toast was kind of touching. Love was the same, no matter how one chose to look at it. Everyone just had different reasons for falling in love.

It was midnight when they finally got into the van. Her shirt had dried, and she was exhausted. She slumped into her seat and kicked off her shoes.

"Happy birthday to me," Ethan sang as he glanced at the clock on the dashboard.

She bolted up. "Yes! It's your birthday! Happy birthday!" Technically, it was his birthday—since it was midnight. She'd known it was coming. It's not like she'd forgotten. She'd just been so busy that it had snuck up on her. In the back of her mind she'd kept thinking that it was farther away. She thought she had another week. It scared her to think that she'd gotten so wrapped up in wedding plans that she'd almost forgotten his birthday. If he hadn't said something she probably would've completely forgotten. "What do you want to do tomorrow? Well actually today?" she asked.

He turned the dial on the air conditioner. "Nothing. Really, don't go to any trouble for me. We're both so busy. I have to meet with some clients during the day, and then I just want to relax."

"Well, I have gift for you." She lied.

He smiled. "Thanks, Catie bear."

He talked about the groom's toast and the grandmother's baldness the rest of the way home, but she wasn't listening. She was trying to figure out what the hell she was going to get him for his birthday.

21

Parents for the First Time

$\mathcal{M}$en were always difficult to shop for. Most women would be thrilled to get a vanilla-scented Henri Bendel candle or a set of lavender bubble bath, but there weren't many easy selections with men. He had all the CDs and clothes he needed. He loved cooking but he had more than enough utensils and gadgets for any gourmet chef. She thought about getting him something he could use on their honeymoon in Kauai, but he already had most of what he needed.

Luckily, he'd woken early to go over a menu with a client, and she had the morning to herself. She needed some time alone to shop and wrap his gift without him knowing what she was up to. She looked around the house. Tools would probably make his day. However, she had no idea what kind of tools he needed or wanted. She could always take the safe and convenient gift-certificate route. Then he could get whatever he wanted from the Home Depot.

Then she thought about what he'd given her for her last birthday. The month before her last birthday rain had pounded San Diego, and they'd spent several weekends behind closed doors. They'd curled up with blankets and hot cocoa and fantasized about going to Kauai. Since they couldn't afford to go to Kauai, a place they both dreamed of visiting, they decided to rent *South Pacific* instead. The music from the movie had stuck with her for weeks after. She'd hummed "Bali Ha'i" while folding laundry or sitting in traffic, and found herself singing "There Ain't Nothing Like a Dame" while making her bed.

For her birthday, he'd given her a jewelry box with little palm trees and a hula dancer on the top of it that played "Bali Ha'i" every time she opened it. It had been such a thoughtful gift, and he'd combed the Internet for days looking for it. She couldn't give him a gift certificate.

She looked online to see if there were any concerts coming up soon. A pair of Rolling Stones tickets would probably put a smile on his face for a few days. A quick visit to the Stones Web site killed that idea. They weren't on tour, and all the other bands she looked up had concerts that landed on days that were too close to the wedding.

She was just about to log off the Internet when a pop-up invaded the screen. She almost closed the advertisement until she noticed the precious face of a tiny Maltese puppy staring back at her. It was the perfect gift. A puppy. He'd wanted one for as long as she'd known him, and now that they had their house he could have one.

She was tempted to go to the pound and adopt one, but she knew that he'd had his heart set on a boxer. He'd always talked about his old dog, Rocky, that he'd had growing up. "He was the best dog ever," she'd heard a million times. She wondered how Grease would adjust and felt slightly guilty about bringing another animal into the house. What if Grease thought she didn't love him anymore? She'd just have to shower him with affection until he got used to their new pet.

She walked to the convenient mart down the street and picked up a newspaper, so she could comb the classifieds. As she strolled along she thought about how wonderful it would be to have a dog to walk.

When she returned home her phone was ringing. She ran to the phone and saw Jill's name flash across the caller ID. "Hey! What's up?"

"I have the day off today and I just wanted to see what you were up to. I miss my old neighbor. It's so sad without you around here."

Cate was surprised by the sudden and strong sense of nostalgia that she felt. She'd always thought that once she was engaged to the love of her life and moved into their first home together she'd never look back. Wasn't this what she'd always wanted? Hearing Jill's voice didn't make her living situation seem like a dream come true.

She thought of her old apartment, all the mornings Jill had come over with Krispy Kremes and the way they used to venture off to happy hour whenever they felt like it. She suddenly felt as if she wanted to run to Pacific Beach and go barhopping. The days of spontaneous happy hours were over. She now looked forward to evenings filled with redundant dinners for two. "I miss you too," she said sadly. "How's the new neighbor?"

"I haven't met her yet, but she doesn't put my mail on my doorstep if it ends up in her box. She just crams it into the crack in between our two boxes."

"She does?" Cate said, feeling very possessive of her old apartment.

"And she listens to Jessica Simpson. Blasts it all day."

"In *my* apartment?"

"Uh-huh. I swear if I hear that damn 'Take My Breath Away' cover one more time . . . I don't know what I'll do."

"Tell her to stop!"

"I will. Anyway, what are you up to for the day?"

"I'm trying to find a puppy. I'm getting Ethan one for his birthday."

"Ohhhhh!" she crooned. "Are you serious? That's so cute."

"Yeah, do you want to come with me?"

"Of course."

They made plans to meet at Cate's house before saying good-bye. After she hung up she looked around her house. What would Jill think of the construction dungeon they lived in? Then she realized it was Jill—the same person who took furniture from Dumpsters. She probably wouldn't even notice the mess.

She was excited to see Jill, and while she waited for her she made a few phone calls. The first breeder she called was selling boxer puppies for a thousand dollars. "The father was a champion in Eukanuba," she said.

Cate didn't care what kind of champion lines the puppies came from, she wasn't spending a grand on a puppy. The second breeder she called was unavailable, and the third sounded the most promising.

"I have one fawn one with white paws and two white ones left," he said in a friendly voice. "The white ones don't have papers because you can't register a white boxer. I'm selling those for one-fifty, and the fawn is three hundred."

"What does the fawn look like?" she asked.

"It's your very stereotypical color for a boxer. Tan with some white. This pup has white on his paws, chest, and just a little on his face."

It sounded adorable, and she made plans to meet him in an hour.

"I also breed Persian cats, Hotot rabbits, and quail. Are you interested in those?"

What kind of a place did this man live in? "I think I'll start with a puppy," she said politely. Grease was plenty cat for the time being, and the last thing they needed was a rabbit and some wild birds.

"Well, keep it in mind for the future. I show my rabbits at the fair. They're champions."

She wasn't surprised to learn that he lived in the middle of nowhere. Where else could one raise a small zoo without driving their neighbors crazy? She wrote down the directions and said good-bye.

After she hung up she was glad Jill was coming with her. Her imagination was always slightly overactive, but she realized the afternoon could unfold like the plot of a Mary Higgins Clark novel. Young woman answers ad from "dog breeder." Drives to the middle of nowhere without telling anyone because the puppy is a surprise for her fiancé and is never seen again after she comes face-to-face with a psychotic serial killer who lures his victims in by placing ads for animals in the paper.

She told Jill her idea when she got there. "You really should be a writer."

"What do you mean?"

"Because these ideas you come up with are so creative. Listen to yourself. He's not a serial killer. He breeds dogs! I'm sure he's a weirdo, no doubt. But he's not going to kill us. I lived in Ramona. Everyone breeds something. It's like a law. My mom bred chinchillas."

They drove forty-five minutes to the breeder's house. The last part of their journey took them down a desolate dirt road dotted with home-made NO TRESPISSING and SLOW! QUAIL CROSSING! signs. It appeared that some clever little soul had scraped off the *a* in *trespassing* and re-placed it with an *i*.

A full-grown boxer similar to the one he'd described ran alongside a chain link fence with barbed wire along the edge. Nipples hung from the dog's belly.

The house looked as if it were eroding on the bottom. Stucco crum-bled onto the ground, and rust-colored streaks ran up the walls. Several Jimmy Buffet stickers were plastered to the front window, and she'd never seen so many rusty car parts. Tattered hubcaps and a couple of steering wheels covered the dead lawn. Two cars, whose make and model were unidentifiable and looked as if they had once caught fire, rotted near the driveway.

Three small children ran toward Cate's Volvo. They were barefoot and topless and obviously not concerned with stepping on foxtails and rocks. One of them held a rabbit in his grimy hands. "Are you here for a puppy?" he asked.

"Yes, I am," she said as she climbed out of her car.

"Okay, follow us." Melted chocolate covered the entire circumfer-ence of his mouth.

The smallest child pointed to Jill. "Why is your hair blue?"

"I don't know . . . because I like it this way."

"My daddy sometimes passes out by the toilet, and I always wonder if he passed out with his head inside if his hair would turn blue from the water."

Cate and Jill exchanged glances.

"Well, if it did, I think it would wash out," Cate said.

"That's what my aunt says too."

They followed the kids to a barn around the back of the house. "Dad," the oldest boy called. "They're here."

A man with blond graying hair down to his shoulders emerged. He wore moccasins and had feathers pinned to his hair. Turquoise rings covered almost every finger. "Hello there, I'm Dan," he said.

"Cate." She extended her hand.

"I put the pups in the barn because I didn't want the mother to bug you."

"Is she mean?" Cate asked.

"No. She's just really playful. She'd probably be jumping all over you the whole time you were here." He opened a door in the barn and two white puppies came running out. They jumped up on Cate's calves, and when Jill reached down to pet them they licked her face. She looked in the stall of the barn and noticed a little fawn one with a black nose and white paws watching them. He looked a little frightened, as if he were wondering where his mother was. Cate immediately went to him. She picked him up, and the look in his eyes made her want to melt.

"Oh my gosh, Jill. Look at him."

She gasped. "He is so cute. And he seems really mellow. Quiet, calm pups are always the best. You don't want one that's going to be too out of control."

"I have papers for that one," Dan said. "And he's three hundred." The white pups were cute and cheaper. As she watched them wrestle she wondered if spending one hundred dollars on a pup was a better idea. She was against dog breeding anyway. However, she couldn't resist the little fawn one. His round, droopy eyes and his soft ears were too precious to pass up. Furthermore, Jill was right. The last thing they needed was an out of control dog. Spending an extra two hundred dollars was worth it if the dog had a soft personality.

She paid Dan, and he gave her a huge Ziploc bag of food, the papers, and a record of all the dog's vaccinations. Jill held the pup in the car, and he whimpered when they pulled away. Eventually, he set his little head on Jill's lap and went to sleep.

"Ethan is going to die when he sees this!" Cate said as soon as they were on the freeway.

"This is the cutest pup ever!"

When they arrived he still wasn't home yet. "I'll let you surprise him by yourself," Jill said. "Let me know how it goes."

She wondered if the pup was hungry, and while she went to get an old cereal bowl for his food, he peed on the kitchen floor. "Oops," she said as she scooped him up and ran to the backyard. "My fault. I should've let you pee the second we got out of the car. We'll work on that one."

When she returned inside she found Grease suspiciously sniffing the area where the pup had gone to the bathroom. He looked startled when he noticed Cate, and his eyes quickly narrowed on the pup. She figured now was as good a time as any to introduce the two animals, so she set the pup on the floor a good five feet from Grease. She didn't know what Grease was capable of.

She thought Grease would've instantly stood on his tiptoes while all the hair on his back pricked up like a cactus. Instead, he walked directly over to the pup, crouching down on all fours as if he were hunting. When he came close to the puppy, he hissed directly in his face. The pup did nothing but release nervous little whimpers while Grease sniffed his body. So he probably wouldn't be the type of dog that fought off burglars or barked at the mailman, but that was okay. She didn't want a dog that barked all the time. Grease hissed at him again before running off and jumping on top of the kitchen counter where he proceeded to clean his paws.

The puppy wasn't interested in running around or checking out his new surroundings. He just sat there, looking miserable.

While she waited for Ethan to return she checked their messages. "Happy birthday, Ethan. It's Denise, and Janet's with me too."

"Happy birthday Ethan!!" Janet's voice popped from the background.

"We've been trying to call you, but you're not answering. Anyway, we're in the area again and thought we'd stop by. I left a message on your cell phone too, so call us when you get in."

Too bad. He's meeting with a client. She deleted the message and debated whether or not she even wanted to tell him that they'd called. She didn't really want them intruding, especially when she was surprising him with the puppy. She figured he probably got the messages they'd left on his cell phone.

She was about to pour some food into the pup's bowl when she heard the front door open. She grabbed the pup and scrambled to her feet.

Ethan dropped his briefcase on the ground when he noticed them. "What?" He pointed to the dog and laughed. "What's this?"

"I found him outside, wandering around all by himself."

"No you didn't. Did you?"

She shook her head. "Happy birthday," she said, handing him over.

Ethan took him into his arms. "He looks just like Rocky! Tan with white paws." He held the pup in front of him. "He's so cute!"

"Doesn't he seem so sad?" They looked at the pup's droopy eyes as he dangled in Ethan's hands.

"A little," Ethan said. "He just needs to get used to us." He put him on the ground then kissed Cate. "This is the best birthday *ever*!"

"What are we going to name him?" Cate asked.

"He has to be named after a famous boxer." He crouched down to pet the pup.

"As long as it's not Mike Tyson, I don't care." She looked at the pup's long face. He didn't seem like a fighter, but he was Ethan's birthday gift, and she wanted him to pick out the name.

"Maybe he's hungry," Ethan said. They placed the bowl of food in front of him, but he wasn't interested. Instead, he crawled beneath their bed and went to sleep.

"I think something's wrong with him. Why is he so sad and lethargic?"

"He's fine," Ethan said. While the puppy slept, they thought of every single famous boxer they could think of. Sugar Ray. Evander Holyfield. Muhammad Ali. More than once, the dog was close to being called Sugar or Ray. They considered calling him Sly after Sylvester Stallone, but Ethan's old dog had been named Rocky, and it was too similar. They finally settled on Oscar, after Oscar De La Hoya.

By dinnertime she was concerned about Oscar. He didn't play. He didn't whimper. He didn't bark. He just sat there, with the same sad look in his eyes. "Seriously, do you think something is wrong with him?" she asked.

"Nah, he's just nervous. Probably a little scared."

"You're probably right," she said, reassuring herself that the dog was fine.

Grease followed the pup's every move but kept a safe distance—sometimes perching himself atop ladders that went with all Ethan's unfinished projects.

Later that evening she made a quick trip to the bookstore to purchase some puppy training books. When she returned, Janet's black BMW was blocking their mailbox. She wished they'd come to say that Janet was moving to Iraq and that she needed to say a final farewell to Ethan before she disappeared from their lives forever. However, she knew they'd probably come to say happy birthday.

Helium balloons blocked the doorway when she entered. She pushed her way through and found Janet holding Oscar up to her face. Cate suddenly felt very maternal toward the dog. She wanted to take Oscar from her.

"Oh my God," Janet whined. "This is the cutest thing I've *ever* seen in my life."

Shreds of wrapping paper covered the floor. "Look what they got me," Ethan said. He lifted a large box. "It's a nail gun." She was no expert on tools, but she had a feeling it cost a small fortune.

"We figured since he's becoming such a good carpenter he needs his own nail gun," Janet said.

"We spent the entire afternoon at the Home Depot picking out just the right one," Denise said.

From her recollection, Denise had always had provided a nice card and an occasional gift certificate to Starbucks or Blockbuster for his birthday. Never had she bought him such an expensive gift, and she wondered how Ethan felt about taking something so nice. If he didn't think it was weird that his ex-girlfriend still bought him expensive gifts he was blind, truly blind.

They stayed for nearly two hours, and she never thought they would leave. Janet walked around their house discussing places Ethan could put up crown molding with his new nail gun.

At one point during their visit Cate snuck away and secretly Googled the exact brand and model of the nail gun. Her jaw nearly hit the keyboard when she learned that it was three hundred dollars. They'd each spent one hundred and fifty dollars on him? She didn't even spend that kind of money on her closest friends.

They finally left, and she'd never felt happier to close the door behind them. "That's an expensive gift they gave you," she said. "Doesn't Denise usually just get you a card?"

"Sometimes she gets me gifts." He sat on the couch and ran his hand over the sleeping puppy.

"Gifts that cost three hundred dollars? And ones that she goes in on with your ex-girlfriend?"

"Well, you know, I think they're just trying to be helpful, and they know we just moved into a new place and have a lot of work."

"Ethan, it's weird. I mean . . . if you don't think that's weird, I don't even know what to say. Think if I was going around buying my exes expensive gifts and showing up at their house whenever I pleased."

"Well, you wouldn't do that. It was probably Denise's idea anyway. She knows how much I want to put crown in and she was with Janet all day and Janet probably just went along with it to be nice."

She was shocked by his naïveté. She'd always considered him an intelligent person, and it infuriated her that he couldn't see through Janet and Denise. She tried to sound calm and reasonable when she spoke, but her frustration was starting to melt away her patience. "It doesn't make you uncomfortable that they got you that?"

"Oh, c'mon!" He was yelling now, and it woke up Oscar. "It's my freaking birthday, Cate! They got me a gift—big fucking deal! I'm getting married to you! You! Not Janet! You! You don't have to analyze everything they do!"

He was turning it around on her? Once again she sensed that those two thorns were probably off somewhere celebrating. This fight was exactly what they wanted. They wanted her to look bad. He must've sensed her anger, because his face softened and he walked toward her. He pulled her into his arms, and she didn't hug him back.

"I'm sorry," he said. "I didn't mean to snap at you. I understand why you're upset. I wouldn't like it either if your ex-boyfriend gave you gifts." He kissed her on the forehead, and she didn't budge—didn't even look at him. "But you have to understand that Janet's just trying to be nice, and she's dating Ryan. I think things are going really good with them."

"Well, why doesn't she go spend her money on him?"

"I told you—it was probably Denise's idea. She knows how important the house is to me."

It occurred to her that Ryan was a groomsman in their wedding. Did this mean that Janet would be coming as his date? She remembered how she'd crashed the wedding in Playa del Carmen. She'd probably just come with Ryan even if he wasn't invited to bring a guest.

"I don't want Janet at our wedding," Cate said. Maybe it sounded insecure and ridiculous, but she didn't care.

She expected him to protest and tell her how irrational she was since Janet was dating one of his closest friends. However, he nodded. "I understand. We'll figure out a way to tell Ryan she's not invited."

"I don't want them coming over here anymore either."

He was silent for a moment. "Look, we've had such a great day." He looked at Oscar. "I don't want to fight with you. Let's not spoil the day."

"All right. You're right. I don't want to argue on your birthday." Maybe she was jumping to conclusions. Perhaps he was right, and the gift was just a kind gesture to help them get settled in their house. Either way, she still couldn't stand either one of them. She may as well get used to Denise, because she wasn't going anywhere. The idea of being related to her was unsettling, but she needed to get used to it.

The makeup sex that followed was unbelievable. They spent the rest of the evening reading the books and discussing ways to train the dog. In many ways, it felt as if they were becoming parents for the first time.

Oscar slept most of the time, and when he was awake the expression on his face looked as if he'd been kidnapped. He whimpered twice during the night. They both took turns taking him outside, watching while he peed, then praising him as the books had said to do. After her trip outside with Oscar she found it hard to fall back to sleep. All she could think about was the flicker of something she'd seen in Ethan's eyes when she told him she didn't want Janet at the wedding. She wasn't sure if it was sadness, or maybe it was just dread that he was feeling. Dread that he'd have to tell Ryan she couldn't come. Either way, it bothered her.

22

A Monster Is Born

The following morning they were awakened by howling. It sounded nothing like the soft little whimpers of the night before. This was high-pitched, desperate howling. She bolted from her bed, walked to Grease's cage, which served as Oscar's crate for the time being, and immediately set him loose. He charged out and began frantically licking her face. He wagged his stubby little tail, and his small paws pressed into her chest as she knelt in front of him. His tongue tickled her face, and she felt relieved to see a spark in the dog's personality.

She glanced at the clock. Six a.m. Rising with the sun wasn't exactly how she wanted to spend the last days of her summer vacation, and she prayed the pup would go back to sleep after she took him out to use the bathroom. She carried him to the backyard and waited in a daze for fifteen minutes until he finally lifted his small leg and peed on their barbecue. She scooped him back up and went inside. Ethan was asleep, and she envied him. She tried to put Oscar back in his cage, but he struggled in her arms. When she closed and locked the little gate be-hind him, he cocked his head to the side and looked at her as if he were confused.

"Go back to sleep," she whispered.

She climbed into bed and enjoyed one minute of silence before the howling started. Ethan rolled over. "I don't think he's going back to sleep," he grumbled.

She couldn't remember what the puppy books had said to do. Should she let him cry so he learned to sleep in, or did she take him out of the crate? After just a few minutes of listening to his frantic howls, the answer was easy. She had to take him out. He sounded as if he were being tortured, and she couldn't believe that such a loud noise could come from such a small body.

Maybe he would just curl up in bed with them. Thrilled to be free, he ran in circles. She put him on the bed, and he immediately covered Ethan's face with rapid licks. When he was finished, he grabbed the edge of his pillow with his teeth and tugged on it. He bit so hard that feathers floated out, and he tore the pillowcase.

"No," Ethan said firmly as he pulled his mouth away. "We can't let him chew on things like that," he said.

As soon as Ethan set him down, he ran to Cate's pillow and did the same thing.

By noon it became obvious that Oscar's previous personality, the one of the mellow, frightened little pup, was all an act. The puppy that tore through their house that morning resembled nothing of the shy dog she'd brought home. He was out of control. If they took their eyes off him for one second, he chewed on electric cords or table legs. He tugged at trash bags and peed on the floors. Just as soon as she finished mop-ping up one puddle, she'd turn around to find him making another one.

It only took one swipe from Grease's paw for Oscar to figure out that the cat wasn't interested in making friends. Unfortunately, it seemed as though it was the only thing Oscar was capable of learning.

He wanted to play with everything he wasn't supposed to play with and had no interest in any of the toys she'd purchased for him.

Ethan had a client meeting, and she had to go to Tierra Bonita Elementary School to set up her classroom. Leaving him in Grease's cage until they returned that evening was out of the question. Until they bought a large crate, he'd have to stay locked in the bathroom. She couldn't trust him in the house alone.

She distracted him with a toy then slipped out of bathroom and closed the door behind her. She was gathering her car keys and a couple boxes of school supplies when she heard him howling like a wounded coyote. Listening to his cries broke her heart, but she had to go to work. She had fifty million things to do before school started. She debated taking him with her, but he'd probably pee all over her classroom like he'd done to their house. His cries were so loud that she could hear him all the way to her car. It took all her willpower to drive away.

She spent the afternoon sorting through her autumn ceiling borders and figuring out which one would look best for the first day of school. She wanted the room to look bright and cheerful. She was standing on top of a ladder when her new teaching assistant stopped by to introduce herself.

Simone was in her early twenties and had shoulder-length curly auburn hair.

"It's nice to meet you." Her French accent was light and barely noticeable at times, but her voice strong. She had a spunky personality, and Cate knew the kids would love her. "And congratulations! I heard about your engagement!"

"Thank you," Cate said. "I guess word travels fast around here." She climbed down from the ladder.

"So you won't be Miss Padgett for long. What will your new last name be?"

Cate was quiet for a moment. She hadn't really thought much about changing her name. She'd always known a name change was inevitable, but it was the first time since she'd gotten engaged that she really realized she would no longer be Cate Padgett. "Blakely. I guess I'll be Miss Blakely, I mean Mrs. Blakely now." It sounded so old, and who was Cate Blakely anyway?

"Let's see your ring!"

Cate held out her hand, but she wasn't paying attention to all Simone's compliments. She was still thinking about her new name.

She remembered secretly signing Cate Blakely on pieces of paper that promptly went to a shredder, in the days when she'd fantasized about becoming engaged. During her marriage fantasies she'd never considered how strange it would be to actually change her name. *Cate Blakely*. The name repeated itself over and over again in her head, and the more she thought about it the more she wanted to cling to Padgett for dear life. She thought about dropping her middle name and being Cate Padgett Blakely. Agnes wasn't the most appealing name anyway. Would her mother freak out if she lost her middle name? It was, after all, her aunt's name too. Maybe she'd never really change her name. She could go by Blakely when she was with Ethan and be Ms. Padgett at work, instead of Miss Padgett. That seemed so confusing.

"So, I know you must be having some stress about the wedding, so I'll be happy to do as much as I can around the class to help out."

"Thanks," Cate said, snapping out of her thoughts. "Let me show you what I'm thinking about doing for the first day." They went over some of her lesson plans, and Cate discussed ideas for the following week.

She thought about the name change the entire way home. Maybe she'd just conveniently never get around to going through with it. Ethan would be devastated if she didn't change her name. Then she thought about her kids. Did she really want to have a different last name than them? No. Being a Blakely would probably take some getting used to. She'd just gradually start going by his name, and then eventually she'd have to drop Padgett for good.

When she returned home, Oscar was still howling. She could hear him from the street while she grabbed the mail. A champagne-colored envelope stood out from the junk mail. She saw her sister's return address, and she knew it had to be her shower invitation. She quickly looked at it while heading to the bathroom. The invitation was everything it should be for a shower—cute and bridal and flowery. She already knew most of the details surrounding the event. Emily's townhouse wasn't very big, so it would be hosted at their parents'.

Oscar's howls were so loud that she quickly abandoned the invitation to let him out. She was positive that he'd be in the same exact spot until she opened the door. Shambles was what she found. Their bathroom had been toilet-papered, literally. As he jumped all over her calves in excitement she looked at the empty cardboard roll resting on the toilet paper dispenser. He'd apparently gotten in his teeth on a dangling strand of paper and had unraveled the entire roll of toilet tissue. It wasn't the only thing he'd ripped to shreds. All the towels that had been hanging from the walls had been pulled down as well, and shreds of cream-colored cloth were scattered all over the floor like old rags.

His tongue hung from his mouth when she looked down at him, and he was out of breath. As she expected, he'd peed all over the linoleum, but it didn't take much to clean it up, as most of it had soaked into the paper and towels that already covered the floor. It took an entire garbage bag to collect the mess he'd made. Grease watched through skinny eyes while she picked up the mess. She almost expected the cat to clear his throat to tell her what an idiot she was for getting a dog.

She was starting to wonder if she'd done the right thing. Perhaps a gift certificate from Home Depot would've been the best bet. She looked down at Oscar's face watching her. His good looks were his only saving grace.

The rest of the week went by quickly. She juggled her time between keeping Oscar out of trouble and preparing for school. In between staff meetings and setting up her classroom she took him to the vet for shots and spent time *trying* to train him. Ethan spent a lot of time working out of the house, so they traded off dog responsibilities. She wondered if they would ever get a full night of sleep again, or if their lives would ever be the same. The dog was like the Duracell bunny. He *never* ran out of energy.

He ate Grease's poop straight from the litter box. Other favorite snacks included rotten vegetables, paper towels, and week-old lunch meat from full garbage bags that he tore apart. Naturally, after filling up on all these treats, he never had room for his expensive puppy food. Rather, he filled the house with the foulest-smelling gas Cate had ever caught wind of in her entire life.

For as much of a nuisance as Grease had been, she was beginning to think that cats were the only way to go. She'd only had to show Grease once where his litter box was, and he hadn't gone to the bathroom any-where else. Except for the occasional bud vase and his animosity toward the French doll, he really didn't destroy much. Oscar, on the other hand, destroyed anything that came near his teeth. Ethan's sandals had be-come rubber mincemeat. She'd seen three pairs of sunglasses turn to plastic confetti. Trash had to be placed on countertops, and table legs were covered in little teeth marks. For as monstrous as he was, he was still adorable, and Cate couldn't deny her maternal feelings for him. When she was busy at school she worried about Ethan taking his eyes off him and Oscar chewing through an electrical cord and shocking himself to death. It made her sad when they both had to leave, and he howled like they were wounding him.

The Sunday before school began she had some free time and decided to go to the beach. She hadn't been in a while, and her chances of seeing the ocean again would be nonexistent once she went back to work. Ethan had to cater a birthday party, and she felt terrible about leaving Oscar. Dogs weren't allowed on most beaches in San Diego, so she de-cided to settle on a walk down the Pacific Beach boardwalk. She made plans to meet Jill.

"Is that the same dog?" Jill asked as soon as she saw them. "He's grown so much!"

"I know. I think he's going to be huge," Cate said, tugging on the leash. Ever since she'd buckled the leash onto his collar, he'd struggled to get loose. He pulled so hard that he choked himself.

Walking down the boardwalk was impossible. Oscar pulled so hard that he dragged Cate behind him, and she found herself breathlessly chasing after him. Furthermore, they stopped every five seconds for someone to pet him.

"Look at that!" A voice would screech every ten steps. "He's so cute! Can I pet him?" It was usually women, and the occasional child, and Cate always felt horrifically sorry for them as they knelt in front of Oscar and laughed happily while he covered their faces in trashy, cat poop–laced licks.

They weren't even ten minutes into the walk when a small crowd had formed around him.

"He's just the most adorable thing I've ever seen!" a woman Rollerblading in her bikini said.

"Can we get one?" a little boy asked his mother.

"I want a puppy," another child whined.

"Where did you get that dog?" A girl riding a bike asked.

She was about to answer when she noticed a pair of familiar sandy feet standing next to Oscar. "So you got a puppy?" Nate said, leaning down to pet the dog.

"Yes." She wanted to tell him it had been a gift for her fiancé, but for reasons she didn't understand, the words wouldn't form in her mouth. "This is Oscar."

"He's a good-looking pup," he said but wasn't looking at the dog. His eyes were focused on her. "I've missed you," he said, revealing a sly smile.

He missed her? She felt her heart race with excitement, and butterflies flocked to her stomach. She hadn't felt the excitement of a hot guy flirting with her in years. It was wonderful. "You er . . . uh, you did?"

He nodded. "I kept wondering where my friend from the beach was, but I haven't seen you around for a while."

"Well, I've been busy with . . ." *Say it. Say it, you cheating bitch!*

Say you're getting married! "I've been busy with Oscar, and going back to work." It was all true. It just wasn't all of the truth.

"The offer's still open for surf lessons." She almost wished the offer wouldn't be open. Knowing that the offer even existed made her heart ache for some reason. It would just be easier if he moved to Tahiti, so he could surf there. That way she'd never have to see him again nor be constantly reminded of what she was missing.

"Thanks. That's really sweet of you."

"You know where to find me." His dimples were almost impossible to resist. He nodded before he walked away holding his surfboard. She watched water trickle down the muscles on his tan back.

"Who the hell was that?" Jill asked as soon as he was gone.

Cate looked at her and realized that she'd been in a world of her own since she'd started talking to him. Someone could've kidnapped Oscar, and she wouldn't have noticed.

"No one," Cate said, weakly.

"That was not *no one*. That was the hottest guy I've ever seen in my life."

"Yeah, he is pretty cute." She watched as Oscar tugged on a woman's towel.

"He was flirting with you," Jill said. "He offered you surf lessons."

She debated telling Jill how she'd seen him every time she'd come to the beach, and how she thought he was gorgeous and her heart sank a little every time she realized that her days of making out with hot guys she met on the beach were over. However, feeling this way scared the hell out of her. She felt like an evil, horrible person. She couldn't imagine what *Jill* would think if she told her that she wished she could experience the excitement of discovering someone new while her wedding was only weeks away.

"He's just some guy that I happen to run in to every time I come to the beach. I could care less about him. Really, I forgot he even existed." After she said the words she sensed that Jill knew she was full of it.

23

Back to School

She woke up early the first week of school. Wide awake at five a.m. It was the first week of school jitters, and they plagued her every year. She knew within a couple of weeks she'd be fighting off the alarm clock and desperately wishing for a few more minutes of sleep. Until she fell into the swing of things her body would be on overdrive.

Despite her anxiety she was also a little happy to get away from their house all day. Each day that she came home from school she'd hoped that, by some miracle, Ethan would've worked as if he were on a *Trading Spaces* episode. She had visions of walking in and seeing hardwood, having a couch to lie on and a kitchen table to even just look at. But each day she came home and found him sitting on their bed, Oscar chewing on something expensive at his feet, while he chatted on the phone with a client. She was tempted to hire a team of contractors to come in and finish the work for them. But then she remembered she lived on a teacher's salary, and they'd be lucky to afford a teenager to come help.

The first couple weeks of classes were mostly just orientation for the kids. A way to put the kids at ease and get to know them. She gave them a tour of the school and told them about her summer. She showed them pictures of her puppy and Ethan and explained that she would be getting married. They asked if she could bring the puppy to class one day for show-and-tell. She had visions of Oscar tearing through the school, knocking over everything in his path, digging a trench the size of a swimming pool in the playground sandbox, and eating her kids' lunches while they weren't paying attention.

"No, I don't think Oscar will be able to come visit. But if anybody has a hamster they'd like to bring in, maybe we can arrange for that."

She figured out early on who her most interesting child for the year would be. His name was George Franklin, and he was the only boy who'd come to class with his lunch in a pink and black Lancôme makeup bag. It was one of those gift-with-purchase giveaways. Cate recognized it from a summer sale. His mother, a large woman with meaty hands and a poofy shag haircut, sent him through the front door of the classroom then bolted before he could notice her leaving.

"That's a neat lunch bag," Cate said.

He nodded. "I locked my lunch pail in my parents' new safe this morning, and they don't know the combination." His chubby cheeks looked like they were stuffed with cotton balls when he grinned at her. "My mom just recycled all the grocery bags, so she said I had to take this." He held it up.

"Oh. Well, you get the best fashion award for the day. Would you like to draw a picture or read a book?" Every day on the first day of school the kids came in, and she gave them the option of a book or a drawing. It was a good way to distract them from having a complete meltdown when they said good-bye to their parents, plus she needed the time to introduce herself to all the parents and kids.

"Read a book." He was the only child who had chosen to read a book. She sent him to the rug to pick out a book and read quietly until class began. His chubby thighs connected to his knees, and she watched him waddle away.

Several days later they went to recess, and when they were finished playing, she asked all the kids to line up so they could head back to the classroom. Everyone got in line except George. He sat against the wall, his knees against his chest and his arms wrapped around his ankles.

"George," she called. "It's time to line up." He looked away.

"George, please get in line," she asked again.

He turned his head even farther away from her.

She walked over to him. Her voice was soft and kind when she spoke. "George, why aren't you getting in line?"

He was quiet for a moment. "I can't."

"George, of course you can. You've been doing such a great job all week. Setting a good example for all the other kids. I know you can get in line."

"No I can't."

"Did you hurt yourself?"

He shook his head. The other kids waited in line, and Simone was doing a nice job of keeping them preoccupied by singing "The Wheels on the Bus." Cate knew it wouldn't be too long before they became antsy and Simone ran out of ways to entertain them. It was going to be a long year if George required this much attention. She stooped down to his level and touched his arm. "George, tell me why you don't want to get in line."

"Because I can't."

Perhaps he'd wet his pants and was embarrassed to stand up. There was always one child who left school holding soiled underwear in a Ziploc bag the first week of class. "George, is there something you want to tell me?"

"I can't get in the line."

"Did you have an accident?"

He shook his head, and she wondered if this was all a cry for attention.

"No, I really can't get in line." Then he lifted his hands and revealed his shoes. The graying laces of his sneakers had been tied together in a million tiny knots. She watched as he attempted to pull his feet apart. While the other kids had been playing handball and pushing each other on the swings, George had been sitting against the wall tying his shoes together.

"I see." She tried to undo the first knot, but it was too tight. She realized she was going to have to stick something sharp in there to loosen them.

"Okay," she said. "You're going to take your shoes off and walk back to the class in your socks." It was the only alternative. There was no way she could hold up the rest of the class while she untied his shoes. They'd be singing all afternoon. It was required that all the children have a spare set of pants in the classroom in case of accidents, but no one brought a second set of shoes. A difficult task, she yanked his shoes off. He'd made the knots so tight that the laces were as tight as one of Scarlett O'Hara's corsets. He'd practically cut off his circulation.

The rest of the day, he sat in his socks, singing songs and finger painting. She sent him home with his shoes in a grocery bag.

On the way home from school she listened to a CD by the string quartet who would be performing during their ceremony. The disc had arrived in the mail a few days earlier with a note asking her to select all the music she wanted for the event.

She'd always wanted to head down the aisle to Canon in D, but just hearing the first low notes of the song made tears fill her eyes. She'd never felt a similar emotion and couldn't describe exactly how she felt. They weren't tears of sadness, but they weren't tears of joy either. It was a bittersweet feeling, similar to visiting relatives and feeling sad when it was time to say good-bye. She felt as if she were saying good-bye to something, but she couldn't exactly pinpoint what. She was thrilled to be marrying Ethan. She loved him more than anything in the world, but she still felt like she was saying good-bye. Maybe it was her name and the fact that flirting with hot surfers would be forbidden once she was married. Or perhaps it was the fact that her father would be giving her away, and she'd never be his little girl again. It was so many things.

In all her wedding dreams and fantasies she'd never realized that she'd be so emotional. She was bawling by the time she reached the freeway, and she wondered if she should pick a song she didn't like. Maybe something that annoyed her would keep her from blubbering like a fool the entire way down the aisle.

Again, she was shocked by herself. It was hard to believe that she was even worrying about being the kind of bride that cried. She'd never been one to even shed a tear during movies.

She'd managed to control her emotions by the time she arrived in Escondido. Any sadness she felt vanished the moment she saw Ethan standing on a ladder with a paint roller. He was painting! Their walls would no longer look like white cardboard, and after nearly two months of living in shambles they could have their floors back. The chorus of one of the classical songs she'd just listened to in the car ran through her head. *Hallelujah! Hallelujah! Hallelujah!*

"Wanna help?" he asked. She noticed a dried ecru streak of paint across his cheek.

"Sure," she said, smiling.

"Why don't you go into the bedroom and change into some paint clothes."

"Okay." She carried her schoolbag and purse into their room. She almost screamed for joy when she opened the door. He'd painted the entire master bedroom. The construction paper was gone, and he'd even painted the chair rail white. She wanted to lie down and touch their honey-colored wood floors. Grease was asleep on their down comforter and cracked his eyes when she gasped. In the corner, stood a beautiful antique Louis XIV chair. Rose-colored velvet upholstery covered the oval back and square seat. Ornate details were carved into the amber-colored wooden arms and legs.

"It's our first piece of antique furniture," he said from over her shoulder. "You like it?"

"I love it!" She quickly went to the chair and ran her fingers over the soft fabric. "Where did you find it?"

"I walked to the antique store on Grand this morning and saw it there. I thought it could replace your old wicker one."

"Oh my gosh. This is the best replacement ever. It must have cost a fortune though."

"Don't worry about that. I figured we could gradually start collecting antiques for the house."

"This is wonderful." She'd have to douse the legs with bitter apple spray so Oscar didn't sink his teeth into them. "Where's Oscar?" she asked.

"Playing in the backyard."

"You mean, digging holes in the lawn."

They spent the rest of the evening painting, and for the first time since they'd moved in she realized that it finally felt like home.

·24·

Grandma, the Great

The morning of Cate's shower she received a phone call from her mother. "I forgot to tell you that Nana is coming."

"Really?"

"Yes. Greta asked for the weekend off a long time ago, so we have to take Nana this weekend. Bradley is picking her up right now."

"You're letting Bradley pick her up?"

"I had to. Emily and I are too busy getting ready, and we sent your father to Palm Springs for the weekend so he wouldn't be in the way."

"Isn't she going to freak out? She thinks every man besides Dad is out to get her."

"She'll be fine with him. I'm just more worried that it's going to bother you to have her there."

"No. It's fine. It will probably do her some good to get out of her house and spend some time with other people." Her grandmother on her father's side of the family had fallen into the murky abyss of Alzheimer's nearly seven years earlier and lived in a constant state of something similar to an acid trip. Her daily life consisted of conversations with people who didn't exist, and searching for objects that went missing that no one ever recalled existing except Nana. For the most part, she was actually pretty interesting to be around, and Cate didn't mind her. Nana usually made no sense, but every once in a while she'd blurt out something honest and hysterical. For example, the first time she met Ethan she asked him when he was going to take her for a drive in his convertible so she could show him her legs. When they'd pointed out that Ethan had never owned a convertible she'd insisted he did—a yellow one with white seats. Ten minutes later, she was acting as if she'd never seen him before, asking who he was, and what he wanted with her.

Cate was glad her family could laugh about some of Nana's delusions. Otherwise, it would've been completely heartbreaking to see her grandmother deteriorate. The vulnerable, haunted woman resembled nothing of the classy and sophisticated grandmother she'd grown up with.

Cate sort of wondered what interesting things she would say at the shower, and she felt bad for her mother. Nana was a handful. She was paranoid about everything, always uncomfortable, and extremely needy. She wondered if her mother would be able to enjoy the day, or would she have to constantly baby-sit Nana?

Most women Cate knew looked forward to their showers as much as Cate had looked forward to turning twenty-one and retiring her fake ID for the rest of her life. Most of her married friends had viewed their showers as "their very special day"—one of the rare chances they'd have to totally bask in the spotlight.

Cate felt a slight sense of dread when thinking about her shower. Not that she didn't want a shower or wouldn't enjoy seeing all her friends. It's just that everyone was there for *her*. Honestly, it scared her. She hated being in the spotlight, especially when everyone was giving her a gift. What if she didn't seem grateful enough? Or failed to say hello to someone? There were a million opportunities to insult someone, and the last thing she wanted to do was hurt someone else's feelings all in the name of some measuring cups. While she got ready she tried to keep herself from getting nervous.

On the way to her mother's house she stopped at the farmers' market in Poway and picked up several bunches of sunflowers. She'd heard many of the teachers at work talk about the two-dollar bunches of sunflowers they grabbed on Saturdays, and she didn't want to arrive empty-handed when she faced her hosts. She knew they'd gone to a lot of work.

Her mother's house was immaculate when she entered. Not a speck of dust or a sign of clutter anywhere. The wood shined and the carpet looked untouched. Beth and Leslie had already arrived and were helping tie tiny ribbons around champagne-colored napkins. Again, she felt a pang of guilt. She'd never been one of those girls who'd been waiting her whole life to be the center of attention. She was the center of attention every day when she went to work and twenty kindergartners hung on her every word.

Being a bridesmaid so many times had made her witness to many undesirable behaviors from wedding obsessed friends. It seemed as if so many girls felt entitled to all the wedding fuss, as if it had been something they'd deserved since they were old enough to fantasize about their own weddings. She'd never felt like she deserved to have her friends tying ribbons around napkins for her all morning, and it felt a little strange to see them going to so much trouble for her.

"Thanks so much, you guys," she said as she handed them each a bunch of flowers. "You really didn't have to do all this."

She picked up some of the ribbon and began to snip and tie. "Stop!" Leslie said. "You shouldn't be doing any of this. Just go make yourself comfortable. You don't have to worry about *anything* today."

"Go have a mimosa!" Beth said, taking the scissors from Cate's hand.

With that suggestion the shower seemed much better. She headed into the kitchen and found Emily arranging mini-quiche on a platter. "Thanks so much for the flowers," she said. "You really shouldn't have done that."

Cate grabbed a bottle of champagne from a bucket and began to pour some into a plastic flute. There were dozens of flutes, and each stem had been decorated with the same ribbons the girls were tying around the napkins.

Her mother's black slip-ons came tapping into the kitchen. "Cate," she said disapprovingly. "You shouldn't drink alcohol."

"Why not?" she asked, mixing in the orange juice.

"Because it's bad for you, and not an attractive thing for the bride to do."

"Well, why'd you buy it then?"

"I didn't. The girls did."

She was about to double up the champagne when Bradley walked in, Nana in tow. Ever since Nana's mental illness had begun her body had wasted away as well. Her skinny frame was as thin and flimsy as a wilted carrot stick and she looked as tall as a hobbit. Her eyes were wide, and she wore a velour pantsuit with stripes up the legs and heels that looked as if they were straight from a Dr. Scholl's store in 1972.

"Nana, how are you?" Cate hugged her.

"Oh thank God," she said. "Finally, someone who can help me." Her voice was low and brittle, and she looked genuinely relieved when she made eye contact with Cate.

"Of course I'll help you. What do you need?"

"I need you to find the papers. They're in an envelope, and I lost them in the fountain outside."

Last time Cate had checked there was no fountain in her parents' front yard. "This man here . . ." Her eyes moved to Bradley then she lowered her voice. ". . . told me that I don't have any papers with me, but I think he's just trying to steal them."

"Nana. What papers? Why don't you come play with Emily's baby? You remember Emily? Right? And that man is Emily's husband. He's a nice man. He wouldn't try to steal anything from you."

"Oh?"

Connie intervened, taking Nana gently by the elbow. "C'mon Be-atrice. We'll get you all settled in the living room. How would you like to listen to some music?"

Nana looked at Cate. "Who is this?"

"It's Connie, your son's wife."

"Whose wife?"

"Your son."

"Do I know him?"

Cate and her mother exchanged looks as Connie led her to the other room.

After they were gone Cate glanced at the clock. It was time for guests to start arriving. She wondered if Denise would dare bring Janet to this event. There was no way. Denise was clueless and definitely had balls of steel, but she must have enough sense not to bring Janet to the shower.

She greeted Cousin Val, and Emily swooped in to take her gift. For a half hour, the front door remained open, and she spent the entire time greeting guests—teachers she worked with, Simone, family friends, a couple of her aunts from her mother's side of the family. Her grand-mother on Connie's side couldn't make it because she lived out of state, but she would definitely be there for the wedding.

Toward the end of the arrival she saw Rita heading up the Padgetts' driveway. She was in typical Rita attire, wearing a long, flowing skirt, loose bracelets, and a billowy top. Behind her was Denise. She'd defi-nitely brought someone. But it wasn't Janet. It was Ethan's grandmother, Oma. Though she was born and raised in America by American parents, she chose to go by Oma, the Dutch word for grandmother.

As Cate watched Oma hobble up the driveway she couldn't help but think of her own grandmothers. Prior to the Alzheimer's, Nana had been a charming, sweet old soul who loved to tend to her roses and al-ways smelled of gardenia. She had naturally rosy cheeks and sang wholeheartedly in the church choir. She liked to bake, share recipes, and talk about the past. This frail, confused old woman bore no resemblance the grandmother Cate had grown up with. And, Gran, her maternal grandmother, was still sharp as a tack and had never lost a trace of her sweet personality. Cate could always count on Gran to watch an old Alfred Hitchcock flick with her or sing every tune from *South Pacific*. She liked to ballroom dance and play gin and always had a genuine interest in other people. So Cate had formed her impression of grandmotherly types based on her own sweet, soft grandmothers. People who liked to laugh and comfort and say bedtime prayers. Ethan's grandmother was cut from an entirely different cloth.

Oma shared the same profile as women who delivered poisoned apples. She was the largest elderly person Cate knew. Not just chubby, she was tall and looming and had the biggest wrists Cate had ever seen on a woman, or a man for that matter. Her voice sounded beastly and was as rough as eggshells going down the garbage disposal. Her eyes were permanently bloodshot, and if she ever laughed it was usually at someone else's expense. Despite all this, Ethan really liked her, and Cate wondered if it was because this was the only grandmother he ever knew. He didn't know what he was missing.

"My God," the woman rasped when she saw Cate. "Where the hell do you live?"

Escondido, she was about to say. *About thirty miles from here.* But there was no time for words as Oma continued. "I mean, who makes driveways this long? It's so damn long you can hardly see the house. It's taken us half the day just to walk up this damn driveway. What kind of a house is this anyway?"

Denise laughed then turned a serious eye toward Cate. "This is a really long walk for Oma. It's hard on her knees. There really should be more accommodating parking for her."

Cate suddenly felt terrible, as if they should've prepared for the elderly, marked handicapped spaces with stones or chalk in her parents' driveway. However, the drievway wasn't *that* long. It wasn't the typical tract home driveway. But her parents didn't live in a tract home, and it's not as if walking to their front door would break a sweat.

Rita looked embarrassed when she handed Cate her gift. "You look beautiful! And I just love this house. We have so many wonderful memories of this neighborhood!" She turned to Oma. "Remember when we lived just right next door, Virginia?"

"Oh, yes. That damn house—" She was about to continue her rant when Cate interrupted.

"All right! Well, why don't you guys come in and I'll introduce to everyone and you get you some drinks!"

"That's sounds like a great idea!" Rita said. Poor woman. She'd had to ride in the car with them.

"What can I get you, Virginia?" Cate asked.

"Do you have any bourbon?"

Please let my mother have bourbon.

"So are you excited?" Denise whispered as they walked to the kitchen. Her breath smelled like an old tennis shoe.

"Yes," Cate said, picking up her pace so she wouldn't be assaulted by another surge of toe breath.

She got their drinks then introduced them to a few other guests at the shower.

Just as Cate was about to go say hello to some of the new arrivals, she was cornered by Emily and Beth. "So we have some games planned. Are you ready?"

Of course she was ready. The best part of showers were the games. Who wanted to sit around watching gift-opening while politely dabbing at finger foods? Bring on some spiked punch and a little competition, and the ice would surely break. Maybe if she was teamed up with Denise and Oma they could forge a common bond through teamwork. Her hosts began to herd everyone into the living room, and she followed the group, wondering what creative idea the girls had come up with for a game.

"All right, Cate," Jill announced. "You're going to sit here. In the throne." *Even better,* she thought. She headed over to a large chair that was normally reserved for the head of her parents' dining room table. It was decorated with champagne ribbons and flowers. She took a seat and for some reason instantly felt nervous. Maybe it was because of the sly grin on her sister's face or the mischievous flicker she caught in Leslie's eye. Emily stepped forward. "So this is the game. We're all going to pretend like Cate is going on her honeymoon. Imagine that she is with Ethan in their hotel room . . ."

Oh dear God, what are they going to do? Her eyes felt like the lens of a camcorder as she scanned the room. The guests' faces reminded her of her kindergartners when she explained a fun song they were going to learn or a new game they would play. They looked delighted as Emily explained what the game entailed. As she listened, she realized it was actually a game made for one person, and one person only—Cate.

The thrill in Emily's voice was obvious as she continued. "The lights have gone out in her hotel room, and she has to find her clothes. So I went through her old closet and found some of her clothes. We're going to blindfold her, and she is going to go through this old backpack in the dark and dress herself. She has to guess what she puts on, and she'll get a prize if she guesses at least three items of clothing correctly."

Her old closet? She wanted to run. Not only could she not remember what was in there, but she knew it all had to be hideous. She hadn't set foot in there since high school. How had Emily even found clothes? She thought her mother had cleaned the closet out ages ago. She should jump from the throne and take off. She'd pick up the gifts later.

"This is going to be great!" Cousin Val shouted from the back of the room.

"Okay, so here we go," Emily said. "Leslie." She nodded.

The look of pleasure in Leslie's eyes was the last thing Cate noticed before she strapped a pair of American Airlines goggles over her head. Then, "just to be safe," they tied something scarflike over the goggles.

"Okay, here is your bag," Emily said, shoving her old backpack into her hands.

She reached inside and pulled what felt like a dress from the bag. "Does this go over my head?" she asked. For some reason the simple question made the whole room burst into laughter. Then she realized they weren't laughing at her question. They were laughing at whatever it was she had to wear.

"It sure does!" Emily said. "I'll help you."

Cate lifted her arms and felt Emily pull the garment over her torso. More laughter.

She had no idea which dress it was, but it felt like it was one of those baby-doll dresses that were so popular in the early nineties. She'd had dozens of them. She reached in the bag and recognized boots. "Oh, these are definitely boots. Wait a minute! These are cute. I left these here a few months ago. I still wear these!"

They laughed, and she hoped it was because of her comment and not at her black stiletto boots. She liked the boots and had been meaning to grab them every time she'd stopped by her parents' house. The next item felt like a ski hat. She quickly figured out that it was no beanie, but rather a bonnet she'd worn when she'd been an extra in O Pioneers at La Jolla High nearly fifteen years ago. Going along with their "game," she acted like a good sport and tried to focus on the prize she would get for guessing everything correctly.

She blindly reached into the bag again and heard several cameras clicking. For crying out loud, these people were merciless. It was bad enough that she couldn't see herself while she became the biggest laughingstock in bridal shower history, but they had to have it all on film too? She pulled the next item from the bag.

It was jewelry, something large with rows of beads. "It's the pearl choker I wore to prom my junior year," she said as she fumbled to wrap it around her neck.

When all was said and done she had turquoise gloves on, leg warmers over her pants, and ski goggles that she'd only worn once. She hated skiing and wasn't sure why her mother had kept them. An oversized red and blue baby-doll dress fell to her knees. She stood in several poses so everyone could capture the moment and keep her new look on film for eternity. After today, she was taking everything but the boots and burning the rest.

They finally took the blindfold off, and it was no surprise that she looked ridiculous. Nonetheless, she got a good laugh out of looking at herself in the mirror, and a free set of vanilla-scented bath and shower gel.

The goal of gift-opening was to get through them as fast as she possibly could. She'd never been superstitious. For the sake of everyone's sanity, she decided to hell with the old wives' tale that for every ribbon the bride cut with the scissors a child would result. She knew what it felt like to be a spectator. She could think of fifty million better things to do than watch someone open boxes that held wooden spoons and cutting boards. Everyone would be dying of sheer boredom, and she kept a very sharp pair of scissors next to her chair.

She breezed through a few cookie pans, some muffin tins, and her dish towels. She was glad to see that some of the guests were chatting amongst themselves and not paying any attention to her. She didn't blame them.

"Rita, don't you love that she's using the scissors?" Connie asked.

"Yes! We're going to have lots of grandchildren!" As of right now, it looked like they would get seven.

About four gifts in, she opened a gift from Beth and Jill. They'd gone in on it together. It was three of her place settings, and she held them up for all to see. "We registered for stuff we could dress up and dress down. It could be everyday stuff or—" She was just about to repeat exactly what the woman at Macy's had told them when she was interrupted by Nana. "Stop! Stop that talking. Your incessant squwaking is driving me crazy. We're trying to have a conversation over here. And you! You're so loud! All you ever do is talk!"

Cate felt her cheeks grow warm as the room erupted in laughter. Nana looked around to see what was so funny. She had no idea that everyone was laughing at her. No one had spoken to her since they'd sat down to open gifts, so if Cate had interrupted her, it had been a conversation with herself.

"Sorry, Nana. I'll try to keep my voice down." She moved on to the next gift.

She plowed through beer mugs, a chip and dip platter, a wine bucket, and a cheese plate. Jill passed her the gifts while Emily recorded them on a pad of paper.

After she handed Leslie her trash, Jill passed her the next gift. It was from Denise—their towels. Only they weren't in the olive green they'd registered for. They were periwinkle blue. Was there a mistake on the registry? She'd have to secretly exchange them. But what would she do when Denise came over and noticed the towels were green? Would her feelings be hurt?

"Thank you!" Cate said. How does one really rave about towels, especially when they're in the wrong color? Pointing out the mistake might embarrass Denise, and she didn't want to make it obvious that something was wrong, so she began to pour it on thick. "I love them. They're so soft, and cuddly." She pressed a hand towel to her cheek just like a fabric softener commercial. "And, oh, they smell good too! I love towels!"

Denise smiled. "I know you registered for them in green."

"You do?" She tried to conceal her astonishment.

"Yeah, but I just liked this color better. I thought it would go better with your house."

The girl was truly insane. Ethan's grandmother laughed. "Spoken like a true Blakely. One with style and class. When you see something good, you just have to take matters into your hands. I mean, olive green! That sounds awful. Who decorates anything except a marine base and prison barracks in olive green?"

Oma was against her too? Cate hoped her mouth hadn't dropped as far as Emily's and Jill's had. It was Leslie who spoke first.

"I love olive green," she said, poking a pointy toed olive green Stella McCartney pump in front of her. "It's the color of the season. But I suppose if you're still living in 1984 you wouldn't know that." She lifted the garbage bag she'd been collecting all the trash with and reached her long fingers toward Cate. "Why don't you hand me all that trash, sweetie."

Cate closed her mouth as she gave her the wrapping paper. "Here," she said blindly handing her everything.

Denise spoke up. "Didn't Ethan mention he wanted to paint the bathroom cream? I thought blue might go better."

No, he'd never mentioned anything about cream, and he hated pastels, so he definitely wouldn't want these towels. Before Cate could respond, Nana interrupted.

"You!" She turned to Denise. Her voice was so loud that everyone stared, even the few stragglers who hadn't been paying attention stopped their chatting and watched Nana. She stared at Denise as if she'd just shot someone. Her eyes were wide, and even from where Cate sat she could see that Nana's lips were as sharp as the steak knives she'd opened a few minutes earlier. Oh dear Lord, what was she going to do? She aimed a bony finger at Denise's face. "Your breath! I mean, God help us! It's like a dragon. And your nonstop squawking. Please just stop. Stop! Stop spraying me with that dragon breath!"

It was impossible not to laugh. Everyone did, except Oma and Denise, who both looked mortified. Denise immediately reached for a pillow mint from the coffee table. Cate tried hard to hide her smile and covered her lips with her fingers. Even Connie, who never laughed when someone was insulted, had to remove her glasses to wipe away tears that had collected on her eyelids.

"Oh Nana," Cate said as soon as the laughter had died a little. She tried to think of something to remedy the situation. She wanted to wrap Denise up and put her in a UPS truck headed for Egypt, but she also didn't want World War III erupting between the Blakelys and the Padgetts. Bad breath or not, she had to live with these people—for the rest of her life. "Nana, why don't you come sit over here next to me?"

"That's a great idea," Connie said, jumping into action. "Let's move Nana. She can sit by me."

Cate looked at the crowd. "Nana says things sometimes that she doesn't mean. I did notice a funny odor over in that part of the room earlier today when I was looking out the window. I think maybe it was that gouda cheese that was sitting on the coffee table. That's probably what she smelled." Where this had come from, she had no idea.

She mouthed *sorry* to Denise, who was actually doing a pretty good job of hiding her embarrassment. Her cheeks were a little pink, and she seemed less confident. If the tables had been turned and she were in Denise's shoes she probably would've grabbed the bowl of pillow mints, run from the room, and moved to another country so she would never have to see any of these people again.

·25·
Dancing Away

Waking up in the middle of the night had become routine in her world, and it wasn't because of Oscar or school anxiety. It usually involved some kind of wedding nightmare. She'd wake up sweaty and haunted with visions of Denise holding a pitchfork designed like the flatware they had registered for, or Janet dressed in solid white, crashing their wedding. Going back to sleep after these kinds of dreams was difficult. Her mind would reel out of control with all kinds of wedding disasters that kept her tossing and turning. Tripping down the aisle. Spilling something dark and ugly on her dress minutes before the ceremony, or having a hairdo similar to a poodle on crack were all things that often made her restless. So when she was startled from a dream by Ethan's tossing and turning, she felt an immediate surge of irritation. Sleep had become a precious commodity, and any interruptions could send her spiraling into insomnia.

Upon opening her eyes, she was immediately assaulted with the most toxic Oscar gas she'd ever been exposed to. He slept in his crate on a bed made of Denise's towels. At least they'd gotten some use out of the gift. It was dim in their room, but she could see the tower of shower gifts that stood on her Louis XIV chair. She still hadn't found places for everything in their tiny house. As of right now the waffle maker was in their bedroom closet.

"Ethan, quit moving around," she snapped despite her fatigue. "Just lie still and say the 'Our Father' over and over." Someone help her, she sounded like her mother. Grease jumped from the bed and ran to the other room.

"Sorry," he said.

She glanced at the clock. It was four thirty, and her alarm would go off in a little over an hour. She'd never fall asleep now. The day would be spent dragging her feet, struggling through story time and recess to keep her eyes open.

"Something has really been bothering me." His voice was thick with worry.

Had something happened with one his clients? Did he feel guilty about taking the nail gun from Denise and Janet? And for a fleeting moment, she felt a flicker of guilt over the hottie from the beach. Had he found out that she'd been flirting? That she'd found someone else attractive? She immediately dismissed it. There was no way he could possibly know about him, and anyway, she hadn't done anything wrong. She'd just been nice to someone—personable and friendly to a stranger on the beach. Anyone would have done the same thing.

"What's wrong?" she asked, rolling over to face him. She could see his long eyelashes resting on his cheek in the dark. Knowing he was worried made her anxious too.

"It's just that . . . well . . . I really . . ."

The way he was talking reminded her of the way her ex-boyfriend sounded when he'd dumped her. For a moment she wondered if there was something he wasn't telling her. Did he want to postpone? Had Janet finally had an impact on him? She'd never heard him sound so tormented. Her heart pounded in her chest. "What is it?" she asked, sitting up now.

"It's just that I hate dancing."

"Huh?"

"It's the first dance," he said. "I'm really nervous."

"The first dance? At our wedding?"

"Yes, all these weddings I've been catering . . . I never realized what a big deal the first dance is. I'm dreading it more than anything." He was talking rapidly now, and she'd never heard him sound more worried, as if he were being forced to apply for a job that he hated. "I can't ballroom dance. And everyone's going to be watching us, and I just don't want to look like an idiot. Can we please . . . I don't know. Practice or something?"

"Of course. But listen to me, it's not a big deal at all. No one cares or remembers the first dance." She rubbed his arm. "I don't know how to dance either, and it's not like a bunch of strangers are going to be watching us. It's going to be all of our closest friends."

"I know. But I still don't want everyone watching us."

"What if we take dance lessons? From a professional? Do you think that will make you feel better?"

He sighed. "I guess."

"Okay. I'll call this afternoon and sign us up for lessons."

"Do it as soon as possible. I really need to practice."

She kissed him on the cheek. "Don't worry. It will be fine." She spooned into his warm body and managed to catch another hour of sleep.

At lunchtime, she borrowed the phone book from the office. She realized after just a few conversations that most of the dance studios had skilled salesman who lured people into signing up for dance packages that would result in so many lessons they could qualify for *Dancing with the Stars*. She didn't have five hundred dollars to blow on dance lessons, and with the wedding only a month and a half away there wouldn't be time to master the fox trot and Viennese waltz. She just wanted a few lessons that would provide them a simple routine to get through their first song.

She finally stumbled upon a woman who agreed to give them one lesson for the bargain price of fifty dollars. They'd see how it went from there. If they liked it they could sign up for more.

The following Saturday they headed to the dance studio. It was raining, and when they arrived their shoes were soaked and the bottoms of Ethan's jeans were heavy with water.

The studio, a garage in a residential neighborhood, stood behind several puddles. A woman who appeared to be in her sixties answered the door. Her eyes immediately wandered to their feet and lingered there for a moment. Her dark hair was pulled into a French twist, and a solid inch of gray roots sprouted from her scalp. It was hard not to wonder how someone who taught dance lessons every single day could be shaped like a Butterball turkey. When Cate had spoken to her on the phone she could tell that Madeline was older than the other instructors she'd called. Cate had expected a svelte Shirley MacLaine type of instructor. Someone with leg warmers, high-heeled tap shoes, and snazzy tights. Not this rotund little grandmother wearing sweatpants and jazz shoes.

"You have to wipe your shoes off before you come in," she said. The remark was followed with a terse smile.

They wiped their feet off as best they could, then Cate extended her hand. "You must be Madeline. I'm Cate, and this is Ethan."

She nodded. "Yes, it's nice to meet both of you." When Cate shook her hand it felt fleshy and cold. She immediately noticed a wall covered in pictures of happy-looking couples dressed in wedding clothes. Some were doing dips while others waltzed. There were even a few letters and notes that accompanied the photos. "Thank you, Madeline!" wrote Jenny and Steve. "You really taught us to trot!" declared a beaming and obese Melody and George. "Madeline is the best thing that ever happened to us!!" swore Karen and Todd who had the brightest and most bleached teeth Cate had ever seen in her life. She made a mental note not to overdo it with the Crest whitening strips before the wedding.

Seeing all the testimonials brought some relief. The woman must be skilled, and knowing that she'd saved many other couples made Cate a little excited for dance lessons. All these couples looked truly delighted, thanks to the wonderful lessons they'd received from this dance genius. She was glad that they were receiving lessons from an older woman, a real expert. Madeline would be better than any young instructor out there. It was just like *Rocky*. Burgess Meredith was their coach. They didn't need some young buck.

"We have a CD," Cate said, handing her the disc.

"Good. That's good. I'll definitely need to hear the music."

She watched as Madeline pushed aside several cassette tapes so she could clear the way to the CD player. It was hard not to stare at Madeline as the CD played. Her lips became tight again, only there was no smile. Rather her brows furrowed as she did a few little dance moves by herself. A few seconds into the music she turned it off. "Do you have to have this song?"

"Well, um." How was she supposed to answer this? It was "their song," and the woman was basically telling them to pick something else. She didn't want to dance to their second or third choice at their wedding. She bet Karen and Todd didn't have to pick a new song. "I mean, I guess—"

"It's just a really hard song. It's fast, and since the two of you have had no experience, I'm wondering if you have your heart set on this song."

"Well, we hadn't really considered any other songs. I mean, can't you just teach us something simple and basic to get us through it?"

Ethan had been quiet ever since they'd arrived, and she wondered what he was thinking.

She tilted her head. "Let me hear the song again." She tapped her foot this time, but her lips were still pursed as she listened to the music. "Ah yes. East Coast Swing. Or maybe a fox trot." She did a quick little jig by herself to the music. "Definitely an East Coast Swing."

"Great." Cate said. She had no idea why she was saying "great" when she didn't even know what either dance entailed, let alone the difference between the two. She caught a glimpse of Ethan. The terrified expression on his face reminded her of a cat let out of its cage in the vet's office, searching for the nearest route of escape.

"Okay, let's get started," Madeline said, leading them to the middle of the dance floor. Mirrors surrounded them, and Cate noticed that her hair was frizzy and damp, and she had this weird wavy style going on around her face. She looked like a man from the Civil War era.

"Okay, first I'm going to teach you how to lead." She looked at Ethan. "The man always leads, so you'll be doing most of the work. Are you good at math?"

He didn't answer right away. "Yeah. Sure."

"Good. Because you're going to do all the counting. It's easy for the woman. She just follows your lead. Okay?"

He nodded. His silence made Cate feel as if she had to be smiling and bubbly so she could maintain a good mood.

"The first thing you both need to know is how to position your arms and hands. "Eric, I want you to put your hand like so." Neither one of them corrected the mistake. Instead they watched while she lifted her arms and demonstrated how they were supposed to stand. She looked as if she were dancing with a ghost. "I call it the loaded-pistol position. Your hand sort of looks like an upside-down gun, with your thumb being the handle and your hand being the barrel." She reached for Cate's hand. "Now you, Cate, are going to have the same loaded pistol, but you're just going to slide your hand into his, flat. Okay?"

Cate moved her hand into Ethan's. "Good, Cate. Your arms are perfect. Not too high, but very firm and nice and smooth. Eric, you, however, need to move your arms." She demonstrated the first step Ethan would do, then she looked at Cate.

"Now give me your hand. I'm going to use you to demonstrate what I want Eric to do."

"It's Ethan," Cate said. "His name is Ethan."

She looked puzzled. "Oh? What did I say?"

"You were calling him Eric."

"Sorry. All right, moving on." Madeline's hands were still cold when Cate slipped hers in. "Okay, now while I'm leading Cate, watch my feet, Eri—I mean, what is it? Ethan?"

They nodded.

When she said *lead*, she wasn't kidding. Cate felt as if she were being whisked around like a blow-up doll while Madeline did all the work. After they were finished dancing she instructed Ethan and Cate to assume the same position.

She taught them several steps, one at a time. Cate couldn't believe how complicated one turn could be. It was all a bit confusing, but Cate felt confident that it would come together eventually. They weren't going to become Fred and Ginger overnight. She was teaching them how to turn when she paused. "Now Cate, you're doing great. Ethan, you on the other hand, need some work."

"I do?" He looked nervous.

"Yes." She touched his arms, which were still in dance position. "Your arms are as stiff as boards. You look like you're sleepwalking." She held up her arms to demonstrate. "The arms should look natural and relaxed, and a little bit more like you're in control. Remember, you're leading her. Now start over again."

Not two seconds into practice he almost tripped over Cate's feet. "Sorry, he said. I'm such a mess."

"You're doing fine," Cate said. She squeezed his hand, but her encouragement didn't seem to make him relax. She figured once they could get through one song with all the moves he'd feel much better. Then they could go home and practice until the wedding.

"Start again," Madeline said.

They hadn't even reached the first turn when Madeline interrupted again, which caused Ethan to stumble over Cate's feet. Based on the way Madeline's critical gaze was aimed at him, Cate figured she was probably about to tell him all that he was doing wrong. She was glad when Ethan spoke up first.

He pulled his loaded pistols away. "I'm not doing this!" He snapped. "I just don't get it. I can't do this step, or swing or whatever it is. Isn't there something else . . . something really basic you can teach us? I hate this! Seriously, I don't want to do this anymore."

A moment of silence passed, and Cate's cheeks felt like they were on fire. Of course, she'd seen him irritated, but she'd never seen him like this.

She figured that Madeline had seen her share of men who weren't exactly ready to get in touch with their inner Patrick Swayze, and had been dragged to dance lessons by overachieving brides. Madeline must have crisis intervention skills to smooth over disgruntled grooms, as she probably faced people like Ethan on a regular basis. Cate expected her to tell Ethan how wonderful he was doing, and how it was natural for him to feel like this—that most men felt the same way. However, Madeline looked just as startled as Cate.

Cate was about to tell him he was doing a great job when Madeline giggled. She sounded much younger than her years, very girlish actually, as if it were the fifties and one of her girlfriends had accidentally farted at the drive-in. "Really?" she said to Ethan.

"Yes really," he said.

She thought for a moment. "Well, I don't know what to say. This is one of the easiest steps I teach."

Cate wasn't tired of the dancing, but she was getting a little tired of Madeline. If she didn't have the skills to encourage people, how were they ever going to get better? Maybe if she could've made the situation a little more fun, a little more lighthearted, rather than picking on him, he probably would've felt more comfortable.

"Ethan, I think you're doing great," Cate said. "I know it's hard, but I think you'll be wonderful if you give it a chance. You're not doing any worse than I am. I'm learning too." Then she thought about how annoying Madeline was. "But if you want to stop—"

He nodded. "C'mon, Cate." He walked to the stereo and pulled the CD from the player. She felt a little relieved.

Madeline looked stunned when Cate turned around to say good-bye. "We'll pay you for the hour," she said. "I'll put the check in the mail."

They were dance-class dropouts.

·26·

Camp Get Us the Hell out of Here

The days that followed flew by, and it was impossible to find time to practice dancing at the wedding. She figured if they could dance to the song a few times in the privacy of their own home he might feel comfortable about getting up in front of everyone. However, there weren't enough hours in the day to dance, and she wondered how the whole first dance was going to unfold, and if they would even have a first dance.

She did manage to squeeze in some time to schedule an appointment for Oscar to get neutered. For now, neutering the dog was more important than dancing. He was humping everything that crossed his path, including poor Grease. She could only imagine what would happen if her two-year-old niece were over. The dog had to be stopped.

She scheduled an appointment to have him fixed the day before their Pre-Cana weekend. She dropped him off early in the morning before work. When she returned to pick him up, she expected him to rip through the double doors of the operating room, knock over a few people and a couple armchairs, before jumping on her, coating her face with fish breath, then eating something expensive and important in the office.

Instead, he limped out of the back room wearing a gigantic plastic cone over his drooping head. Misery hung from his jowls, and he looked as if he'd just consumed a liter of Smirnoff. He stared blankly at the wall for a moment before bumping into a chair and standing immobile, as if he were crippled.

"He's under a lot of anesthesia," the vet tech said. She was a motherly woman with frosted hair and scrubs decorated with little puppies. "He's very tired and weak."

"How long will he be this way?" she asked, doing a horrible job of concealing her joy.

"He'll probably be very tired all night. You might want to get pain medication too. He might be in some pain tomorrow, but it will knock him out again."

"I'll take two bottles of that."

For once there would be a moment of peace. To think that Rita and Charles got him with drugs seemed unfair yet comforting. At least, he wouldn't destroy their entire house. The Blakelys' dog had died earlier that year, and ever since his departure they had missed having a canine friend around the house. Despite excessive warnings about Oscar they'd graciously offered to take him and Grease for the weekend while Cate and Ethan went to their marriage retreat.

That night she packed for their weekend in peace, and the only disturbance they had had from Oscar was his gas.

The following day they put Grease in his carrier and dragged a droopy Oscar to the car. Grease's meows sounded as if he were a tortured jungle cat, and each time they stopped at a light she was certain that pedestrians could hear him. A car ride with Grease guaranteed nonstop deafening meows. One would think they were torturing him to death. They dropped them off at Rita and Charles's along with a bottle of pain medication and a weekend's supply of food.

"We'll bring them back on Sunday," Charles said.

"You sure?" Ethan said.

Charles nodded. "Of course. We'll be up in that area anyway."

They turned Grease loose, and the moment he came out of the cage he quit crying.

"Where is your weekend of marriage counseling?" Rita asked.

Ethan laughed. "It's not counseling. It's preparation. It's supposed to prepare you for marriage."

Cate was glad to hear that Ethan actually sounded a little enthusiastic about the whole thing. "It's downtown at an old convent," she said.

"Oh." Rita seemed intrigued. "That should be neat. You guys will be near the Gaslamp, and that part of San Diego is so beautiful now. Maybe if the rain lets up you can walk around downtown."

With this in mind, the weekend didn't sound so bad. Cate had gotten such mixed reviews about the Pre-Cana weekend from her friends. She didn't know what to expect. Furthermore, she felt totally responsible for the whole situation. Being a Catholic, she'd always known she'd have to attend the Engagement Encounter Weekend. However, Ethan wasn't Catholic, and if the retreat was horrible, he'd have her to blame.

"*It's utter hell,*" had been Val's words before they left.

"*I loved our instructor. He was a former fireman who became a priest,*" Sarah had said. Better.

"*I loved it! It was really beneficial for both of us, and we learned so much about each other.*" This from her sister.

Rain came down in buckets as they drove around looking for the convent. It wasn't completely unusual for San Diego to get a little rain in October. However, this weather was more typical of an El Niño season in January.

It only took a few turns before she realized that they were nowhere near the Gaslamp. She thought she heard gunshots as Ethan parked his Explorer in front of the graffiti-covered convent walls. They were soaking when they entered.

A small group waited inside. It was easy to spot the engaged couples amidst the chaperones. The engaged couples looked just as worried as

Cate and Ethan. Everyone was quiet, except for the older couple in the front, holding clipboards.

The woman with the clipboard looked at Cate. A smile the size of a gutter spread across her face, as if a buzzer had prompted it. She had the type of hair that had probably been silky about a decade ago. It was way too long for her age group, which hovered somewhere around forty-five, and the brittle ends were thin.

"And you are?" She turned her head to the side. Something about the way she looked at them reminded Cate of the way she would greet her kids on the first day of school.

"Cate Padgett and Ethan Blakely," Ethan said.

"Wonderful!" It was also the way Cate might greet a group of deaf kindergartners. Her voice was loud and precise, and she enunciated every word as if they were hard of hearing. "I'm Ava, and this is my husband, Stu. Father Flannagan will also be joining us later this weekend. We'll tell you all about ourselves in the getting-to-know-each-other session that will be starting in just a few minutes." She turned to her husband. "Stu, why don't you give them their room assignments?" Stu looked as if he weighed less than Cate and had struggled for months to grow the sparse mustache above his upper lip. Something about his sweater vest and shifty gaze insinuated closet homosexual.

He smiled at them, revealing a set of crooked teeth. "Cate, you're in room twenty-nine, and Ethan, you're in room thirty-seven. Boys on one floor. Girls on the other, and absolutely no sneaking around." He waved a finger at them. "We'll be watching." She imagined that Liberace sounded the same way when he'd laughed.

"I think your roommates have already checked in," said Ava.

Growing up she'd had several bizarre catechism teachers, and she would've been shocked if the couple leading the retreat had been young, cool, and hip. However, Ethan wasn't used to these types. His experience with religious teachers had been limited to Al, who was a great person. Al's personality was so magnetic that everyone always just wanted to be around him.

"I'm sorry," she whispered as they dragged their suitcases to their rooms.

"Ah, no. Don't be sorry. I'm fine."

"Are you sure?"

"Yeah. I'll be okay." He really was a champ and an okay liar. Despite his positive attitude she knew he was probably dying.

A wonderful set for a horror movie, the convent smelled of mothballs and mildew and looked as if it hadn't been renovated since it was built in 1941. She expected to hear howling at night.

On the bright side, maybe her roommate was cool. She'd make a new friend for the weekend, and they could stay up late, giggling and commiserating over the situation. She opened the door to her room and wondered if there had been some kind of mistake. She double-checked her number assignment. It was definitely the right room. Maybe there was a youth retreat going on this weekend and they'd run out of rooms? The pimply, overweight girl sitting on the bed couldn't be older than seventeen. She had braces and wore an oversized blue sweater with cream-colored leggings and Keds. "Are you my roommate?" she asked.

"I think I am," Cate said. "Are you here for the, um, Pre-Cana?"

She nodded. "Yeah, my fiancé is up in room thirty seven."

"Oh, that's where my fiancé is too! They must've put couples with each other. I'm Cate." She stepped inside and shook the girl's hand.

A split second of surprise flashed over the girl's eyes before she offered hers. "Summer." Her hand was limp and weak.

Cate looked around the room. As of yet, she'd never stayed in a mental institution. However, she'd seen enough movies to know what they looked like. If it weren't for the peeling flowered wallpaper she would've imagined that the cast of *Girl Interrupted* had occupied the squeaky metal beds while filming on location. To say they had twin beds would've been generous. The beds fit more into the size group of military cots. A prisonlike sink and mirror occupied the front right corner, and a banged-up nightstand with a black Bible resting on top of it separated the two beds. The knitted afghans that covered the beds definitely weren't what she would've found at the W, but at least the sheets looked clean. They'd been starched and bleached so much that the corners looked like envelopes.

She set her suitcase down, then peeled her jacket from her body. "Is it just me or is it roasting in here?"

"Yeah, it's pretty hot," Summer said. "They only have heat on this floor. The guys don't even have it upstairs. But they really crank it up down here. And according to the rules you can't open your window past nine p.m."

"How long have you been here?"

"Just an hour." She handed Cate a yellowed piece of paper. Created on a typewriter, the list of rules inspired rebellion.

Lights out at nine thirty.
Absolutely no boys allowed in girls' rooms, and vice versa.
No gum.
No smoking.
Absolutely no alcohol.

It went on and on. She hadn't seen anything like it since sixth-grade camp. Even then, she remembered better accommodations. She sighed and sat down on the end of her bed. She glanced at the powder-green clock nailed to the wall. They still had a half hour until their first activity. She wondered how Ethan was doing, if he was ready to jump from the second-story window and decide this wasn't worth getting married.

She decided she might as well kill the time by getting to know Summer. She was getting tired of talking about her own wedding. It would be refreshing to hear about someone else's plans for a change.

She soon learned that Summer worked at Hollywood Video, still lived with her parents, and was getting married at the Marine Corps base. Her fiancé, Dawson, a marine, had three groomsmen. They were having a buffet of fettuccine alfredo and Salisbury steak with sourdough. Her mother was making her dress, as well as the bridesmaids'.

She had five bridesmaids, and they'd be wearing purple. Cate pictured them all in barrel curls and dyed-to-match purple pumps.

"How old are you?" Cate asked.

"Eighteen. Dawson's twenty-four."

"How long have you guys been together?"

"Four months."

"Oh—er well, you know, some people just know right away I guess." She could feel her body growing hotter by the second.

"He's getting deployed. Six months to Japan, so we figured we may as well do it now. We really didn't want to wait till he got back."

"No time like the present." She folded her pillow in half, then placed it against the wall so she would have a cushion to lean on. It really was interesting to listen to someone who was so different from Ethan and her. "How did you guys meet?"

"TJ."

She hadn't heard anyone refer to Tijuana by its abbreviated initials since she'd gone down there to drink in high school.

"Yeah, I'd seen him before when I'd been dancing down there with my girlfriends, but I'd never talked to him until he bought me two tequila poppers. He gave me a ride home on his motorcycle that night, and we snuck through the window at my parents' house and had sex on my bedroom floor."

Cate had only known her for five minutes. "Oh. Um, that must've been uh . . ." she searched for the right word. "Nerve-racking. Weren't you worried about your parents?"

"A little. He snuck in my bedroom window every night for three months. We couldn't do it at the base because he had a roommate, and they don't allow women in the barracks anyway. My dad walked in on us one night." What Cate found most odd was that Summer laughed at the memory. Cate would've never been the same if anyone in her family had walked in on her having sex at eighteen. She hadn't even lost her virginity until college, and it was in the safe confines of her long-term boyfriend's apartment at college. "What happened?" she asked, trying to conceal her astonishment.

"My dad kicked his ass. Gave him a black eye and fractured his jaw. You can still see the bruises if you look close enough."

She should've known that she would end up with someone who wanted to share the most intimate details of her life. This always happened to her, and she often wondered why people felt so comfortable around her. Just the other day, an old lady in the grocery store told her all about her hemorrhoids. All Cate had done before listening to the gory details was smile at her.

"My dad was in the military too, so Dawson didn't even fight back. He wanted to show respect. Just kept apologizing while my mom and I tried to calm my dad down."

She couldn't imagine. Really, she'd be scarred for life if anything like this had happened to her. She felt so old and boring around Summer. Suddenly all her problems with her mother seemed petty. "Was he naked while your father was beating him?"

"Yeah, he was, and I was too. My dad just ripped him right off me and started whaling into him. I jumped on my dad's back at one point and choked him."

"Oh my God," was all Cate was capable of saying. She wondered what kind of conversation Ethan and Dawson were having upstairs. She prayed he wasn't ready to kill her for dragging him into this.

"So how did you and Ethan meet?" Summer asked, leaning back on her pillow.

"Oh we were friends for a long time, since we were kids, and then I finally realized he was the right guy for me. We sort of drifted over the years but caught up a couple years ago at a friend's wedding. After that I fell in love with him."

Summer yawned.

Sorry my dad didn't attack him while we were both naked, Cate wanted to say.

"Do your parents like him?" she asked.

"My parents love Ethan."

"That's good. I think it's always good when your parents like your boyfriend. My parents hate Dawson. My dad threatened to cut his balls off, and he wasn't allowed into our house up until a few weeks ago when we got engaged. It was really horrible, and we almost just ran away on his motorcycle, but then he got deployed, so we decided we better just get married."

Cate tried to think of something positive to say. "Well, *his* parents must like *you*."

She shrugged. "I guess." She tugged on a piece of yarn from the afghan on her bed with the tips of her acrylic nails. The nails looked too mature for her chubby hands, like a little girl wearing high heels and lipstick. "I've only talked to them over the phone. His mother is morbidly obese so she can't afford to come to the wedding because she'd have to get two plane tickets, and I guess the airfare from Fresno is really expensive. His father might come though. He's up for parole next week, so we'll see if it works out."

Denise suddenly seemed like a minor problem. A fly buzzing around a picnic compared to Summer's in-laws. Cate glanced at the clock. "Well, we better head down. I think the first activity is about to start."

Ethan was waiting for her by the entrance to the activity room. He looked tired but put his arm around her shoulders. He kissed her on the forehead. She was afraid to ask him how he was for fear he might tell her that she would pay dearly for this. She envisioned giving him free massages and serving him wine and cheese on a platter for the next five years since she was responsible for taking him to the Pre-Cana weekend. She could hear someone singing from the activity room and recognized a church song she'd spent most of her childhood believing was the national anthem for Canada.

As a kid she'd always thought the choir was singing in soft melody,

"Ohhh Canaaaada! You take away the sins of the world," when really they were singing, "Ohhh lamb of God. You take away the sins of the world."

At ten, she was absolutely shocked to learn the real words to the song. Emily had to prove it to her by producing a songbook with the lyrics. To this day, Cate still sang the wrong words when the song was stuck in her head.

"How's your roommate?" he asked.

"Interesting," Cate said as she walked into the dimly lit room. "And she's your roommate's fiancée."

"No shit?"

"Ethan, the language. We're in a religious setting."

He smiled. "Sorry."

The room was tiny and full of people, so she lowered her voice. "Is your roommate's name Dawson?"

"Sure is. Man, you have to point her out. I'm trying to picture the type of chick he'd be with."

"Is he a total weirdo?"

"Let me put it this way," he whispered. "The guy has a rattlesnake tattooed to his calf, is wearing shorts in the middle of a rainstorm, and spent the past twenty minutes showing me Polaroids of all his guns he trains with at the marine base."

"Are you kidding me?"

He shook his head.

"Ethan, that's scary," she hissed. "My cousin Mary's husband is a marine, and I bet you he doesn't keep pictures of any of his guns." She saw Stu perched on a stool with his sleeves rolled up. An acoustic guitar rested in his lap as he belted out the Canadian anthem.

Ethan chuckled. "Dawson's wacky. I think it's funny though. And he brought a flask of Goldschlager." He smiled slyly. "So things aren't looking that bad after all."

"Did you already take a shot?"

"Three." He grinned from ear to ear.

"Everyone. Everyone!" It was Ava, and she was waving her arms around like she was taping *Lost* and a helicopter had just flown over the island. "Everyone take a seat! We're going to start now!"

Cate and Ethan followed the rest of the group to several rows of rusty fold-out chairs. Ethan stopped at the back row and pointed to two seats closest to the exit. The back rows filled up quickly.

Ava began by welcoming everyone to the Pre-Cana weekend; then she explained how wonderful the weekend was going to be. She passed out schedules for everyone, and it reminded Cate a little of college, getting her syllabus. A portion of her was filled with dread over the amount of work ahead, and a portion of her was excited to learn new things.

After Ava passed out the schedules they all went around the room and said their names and what they hoped to get out of the Pre-Cana weekend. She'd expected something like this. They were the very last people to go, and she hoped Ethan didn't smell like alcohol when he spoke.

"Ethan Blakely," he said. "I hope to learn more about Cate's religious background." Fair enough answer, and he didn't smell.

"Cate Padgett. I hope to be more prepared for marriage." It was a forced answer, and something she would've never said if she hadn't been put on the spot.

"Okay. Now let Stu and me tell you a little bit about ourselves." Stu sat on his barstool looking smug while Ava spoke. A smile returned to her face as if someone were pressing a buzzer in her back. "Stu and I got married four years ago. We were older, thirty-nine when we got married for the first time, and we were both virgins." The smile again. "We decided to wait until our marriage night to make love, and this weekend we're going to teach you why sex is so holy."

As long as it didn't involve listening to the details of Stu and Ava's sex life she didn't mind.

"Anyway, Stu and I got married, and Stu is really in touch with his feminine side, so he wore a kilt to the wedding instead of regular tux pants. Didn't you, Stu?"

He smirked.

"And then," Ava continued, "we wanted to make love the night of our wedding, but we were just too tired. And I want you all to know that it's okay if you feel this way. So we went on our honeymoon, and the first night of the honeymoon Stu couldn't perform. He was so nervous."

The same smirk returned to his face.

"Anyway, we'll talk more about that later. But it's okay to be nervous going into marriage. We all have fears, and that's what this whole weekend is for. To talk about our fears, and to talk about what life will be like in a Christian marriage. So tonight I want you all to think about your fears. Anything you might have in mind that you want to discuss with your partner." She reached for an ugly straw hat with a lopsided pink flower pinned to it, and Cate wondered why on earth she was going to put this on.

"We're going to pass around a hat. We call this the secret question hat. I want each and every one of you to write down a question you wouldn't feel comfortable asking in front of the group. Something you would like to ask a priest, but you might be embarrassed, and then Father Flannagan will open these up when he's here and answer the questions for the group. It's completely anonymous, so don't be shy. And everyone must ask a question. Chances are, if you're confused about something, someone else is too."

Many people looked just as stumped as she felt, but some people scribbled vigorously. She wondered what they were coming up with. She couldn't think of any secret question she wanted to ask. She'd been raised Catholic and pretty much already knew all the answers. She was further surprised when she noticed Ethan writing away, as if he'd already had a question in mind before they even got there. He had an embarrassing question? That she didn't know about? If he'd been having some concerns, she wished he would come to her.

"What are you writing?" she whispered.

"It's private." She knew by his tone he was joking.

"Let me see."

"Okay. Hold on." He finished writing, then held out the piece of paper for her to read. The twinkle in his eye should've been her first clue. As she read the words she covered her mouth.

"Is it still considered wife-beating if you're not married yet?" He'd even disguised his writing.

Her eyes were so wide she could feel them popping from her head. He was grinning when she looked at him. "You can't put that in," she hissed between clenched teeth.

"Why not?" He managed to keep his laughter quiet.

"Give me that." She tried to grab the paper from his hands, but he was too quick and snatched it back. Just as he did so, the hat came by. He dumped his question inside. There was a brief moment when they tugged back and forth on the hat, but when Ava and Stu turned in their direction, she surrendered. With the hat in his possession, Ethan stood up and returned the hat to Ava.

·27·

In the Dark

The following morning they were awakened by a quick rap on their door. "Time to rise, sleepyheads," Ava called through the decaying walls.

Cate would've rather been awakened by a horny feral cat, and she could've easily slept for another four hours. The previous nights' sleep had been some of the worst she'd ever experienced. She looked over and noticed Summer sprawled over her cot, wearing only her underwear and bra. Cate had always thought of herself as extremely pale, but around Summer she actually felt kind of tan. She couldn't blame her for stripping to the bare minimum. Their room had been hotter than hell, and Cate had also kicked her afghan and flannel pajama bottoms off sometime in the night. She'd felt too self-conscious to lie over the covers in her underwear. She'd stayed beneath the top sheet, and her legs had never gotten used to the scratchy feeling of the bleached sheets.

She sat up and looked at herself in the mirror. Sweat had soaked her bangs, and they'd dried standing away from her forehead, like a picket fence. She'd indulged in another fifteen minutes of sleep, and there wasn't time to shower. She spent most of her time getting ready trying to fix her stubborn bangs, which seemed to have grown a mind of their own overnight. She wet them and tried to slick them back down with her comb, but they just popped back out again. She pressed on them for nearly five minutes with her hand. When she removed her palm, they stayed against her head for about ten seconds before slowly popping off her forehead again.

She borrowed Summer's blow dryer and just as she was about to plug it in, the lights went out. It was pouring rain outside, so she wouldn't be surprised if the storm had caused the blackout. However, the building was so ancient the electricity probably couldn't handle twenty people attempting to get ready at once.

Amidst the darkness, she saw a bright ray of hope. Without power, how could they continue? Perhaps they'd all be sent home and excused from this whole bizarre camp experience! Her prayers may have been answered.

She was ten minutes late to breakfast, and the power still hadn't come back on. This was fine with her because her bangs stood from her scalp like horns, and it would be better if no one saw her anyway.

Ethan waited by the door to the cafeteria. He looked pale and hadn't bothered to shave. "Hey," he said quietly. He didn't notice her hair or that she was late.

"You look like you got about as much sleep as I did last night," she said.

"I'm dying," he said. "I'm so hungover."

She almost envied him. At least he'd been doing something fun, and he probably got a better night's sleep than she did. She could hear Stu and the sound of his acoustic guitar. As long as they were anywhere near him there wouldn't be a moment of peace.

"The smell of that food is making my stomach turn," Ethan said, bleary eyed.

Ava smiled at them as they went to get trays, and Cate nodded back.

Every time she moved she could feel her bangs flapping like wings. Furthermore, the entire room had been lit with candles and lanterns, and she could see her bangs standing from her forehead in the shadows. It looked as if her forehead had grown buckteeth. She wanted an immediate update on the electricity situation. If they were getting out of here any time soon, she wasn't eating.

Ava wore a hideous apron in colors that should never share the same cut of cloth. A brown background, the fabric was covered in small purple and yellow crosses. She wore red slacks and a blue and white plaid shirt. Maybe she was colorblind.

"What's going on with the power?" Cate asked.

"Well, we'll just have to make do with candles for the rest of the day, or until they turn the power back on."

"You mean we're staying?"

"Well, of course!" She chuckled. "We have so much to do today. And we're doing my favorite part this morning. Skits!"

Cate didn't mean to slam her tray on the counter. Any hope that they'd get a free pass on the Engagement Encounter Weekend faded as quickly as the lights had. There was no way this woman was going to let them go when she had the power to make them all perform religious skits.

Stu sat on the edge of a table, wearing brown corduroy slacks and a sweater that was too short in the sleeves. His black arm hair crept over his wrists like fur. He was slaughtering another church song. It was one she actually liked, "Ave Regina." A lively tune, she recalled clapping her hands to it at Mass. Something about the gothic lighting and scent of bad breakfast food killed the mood.

The heat lamps had failed due to the power outage, so what remained was some cold sloppy oatmeal and a few icy strips of extremely greasy bacon. After what they'd consumed at dinner the night before, she hadn't expected anything better. Actually, she still wasn't clear on what they'd even eaten the night before. Ethan had insisted it was chicken, but she thought for sure it was beef.

In his dehydrated state, Ethan took the rest of the salty bacon. She helped herself to oatmeal, reasoning it probably wouldn't be that bad with some honey or maple syrup. She grabbed a bottle of honey while Ethan looked for a table. Mostly all the women in the room had wet heads and looked as if they were slowly coming out of comas. They sat with two other couples that seemed close to their age. After Cate set down her tray she tried to push her bangs back down so they wouldn't notice. But she could still feel them flapping on her head.

"Oh you got the eggs too?" one of the grooms at their table said.

"Eggs?" She glanced at her bowl. "I think its oatmeal."

"No. Those are eggs. Trust me."

Eggs that she'd just doused in honey. She ended up eating a piece of Wonder bread with strawberry jam over the top.

The food was horrible, but the conversation at the table turned out to be pretty good. The groom who'd pointed out the eggs and his fiancée were the same age as Ethan and Cate. Their names were Mike and Gillian, and they had a lot more in common with Cate and Ethan than being engaged. She was also an elementary school teacher, and they'd both grown up in San Diego. It was nice visiting with them and joking about Ava and Stu.

The other couple at the table was a little bit different. Their names were Matthew and Angie. Cate had remembered seeing him the night before and wondering who the lucky girl was who'd snagged him. Tall and muscular, he had a handsome, timeless face. He was dressed nicely in expensive jeans and a turtleneck sweater with a sleek leather jacket. Angie, on the other hand, was short and plump and wore very average, unremarkable clothing.

Matthew seemed preoccupied and never smiled or added anything to the conversation. Cate wondered if he was just in a bad mood because he was bored and frustrated with the whole weekend. He'd probably been dragged here, like Ethan, and was being a poor sport.

"So are you both Catholic?" Angie asked.

"No. Just her." Ethan pointed to Cate.

"I'm not Catholic either," she said. "I'm just here for Matthew."

When they looked at Matthew, he was staring off into space. An awkward moment of silence passed before he realized they'd been talking about him. "Oh, huh? Were you talking to me?" he asked.

"I was just telling Cate and Ethan, here, that we came this weekend because you're Catholic." She smiled and looked back at them. "I don't mind though. I really want to embrace his religion, and I know it means a lot to his family." That was sweet of her. She thought it strange that Matthew didn't even seem to appreciate it though. They never touched, and the only time she seemed really thrilled was when they discussed all the details of their wedding. "We're having our programs made from French parchment in Paris, and each member of the wedding party will have their own portrait sketched by a French artist next to their name on the program." The girl was wedding obsessed. Cate wondered if that was why Matthew was so distant. He was probably sick and tired of hearing about French parchment paper. She wasn't holding her breath, but hopefully the weekend would help them.

After breakfast they were all led back to the activity room. "All right," Ava said. "Find a seat. There are plenty here in the front."

The back corner had now become a coveted spot. In fact, the entire back rows had become hot commodities, and the rest of the group had beaten Cate and Ethan to their former area. They were forced to sit front row, dead center.

"Okay, first I'd like to start with an opening prayer, so everyone bow your heads and picture yourself in a nice peaceful place."

At this point, standing outside in the rain seemed nice.

"Dear Father, please help us to get through this weekend . . ."

Amen to that.

". . . with understanding and love. And please, Father, bless these engaged couples on their journey. Help them to learn more about each other and their faith and love in God together." It was the only time she'd spoken in a soft tone. "Amen."

The room followed with a chorus of amens, and she even heard

Ethan's voice in the mix too. They did some really corny skits on talking to your partner about issues you might feel uncomfortable about. Cate volunteered for the lead role in one skit just so she would have something to do. The second she'd volunteered she'd regretted it. She'd forgotten about her bangs, and now she had to stand in front of the audience with buck bang head.

"But I want to use my credit card to by those shoes at the mall." She read her wooden line from a tattered script.

"But I don't want you to use the credit card," Dawson said back. He had the lead male role, and was her fiancé in their acting debut together. Thankfully there were no love scenes. "We never talked about money before we got married."

"And now we're in deep trouble." When she looked back up from her lines she noticed that half the front row was sleeping.

After the skits, it became obvious that there was a big theme running through the whole Engagement Encounter Weekend—discussing issues and concerns *before* marriage. She'd heard Ava say it a million times. "Now is the time to come to your partner with any concerns."

The only concern she could think of was Janet. Was Janet going to drop in with expensive gifts forever? The weekend didn't really seem centered around addressing issues with ex-girlfriends. The concerns that Ava mentioned involved how they would discipline the kids, manage their finances, and practice their faith.

Ava would ask a question such as, "Have you discussed how you will discipline your children?" Then each couple would break up for a short time. One person would go back to a dorm room, and the other person would stay in the activity room, so they could write down their answers without being influenced by the other party. After ten minutes, they would meet up again to discuss their answers with their partners.

Cate and Ethan had already discussed a lot of the issues that Ava brought up. They both wanted two, maybe three children. They'd created a budget when they'd moved in together, and both had agreed to

avoid using credit cards. Oscar had provided more than enough opportunities to discuss discipline.

It was interesting to see how many couples hadn't discussed stuff.
It was hard not to overhear some of the conversations in the room.
Dawson and Summer hadn't even discussed how many kids they
wanted, and it came as a huge surprise to Angie that Matthew didn't
even want kids. For the first time, she actually thought the weekend
might be beneficial. A lot of people needed the opportunity to discuss
their future.

"Remember," Ava said over the buzz of voices. "There are no right
or wrong answers here. Every answer is *okay*. It's just important that
you discuss these things before saying your vows." She'd said it twenty-
five times.

After hours of the same drill, Ava announced that they were going to
play a game. One would've thought the dim lighting would've deterred
the woman. They all stood around while she and Stu unrolled a giant
tarp. It was covered with large rows of squares made from masking
tape. "Okay," she said clapping her hands. "This is my favorite game.
Now I want each couple to stand on a square in the first row. Okay,
everyone take their places." Cate and Ethan took a square next to Dawson and Summer. "Now, I'm going to ask questions, and then for everyone who answers yes, you can move forward a square. Those of you
who answer no stay behind." She read the questions from a pad of paper. "Do you have a monthly or weekly budget plan?"

Along with two other couples, Cate and Ethan took a step forward.
Summer and Dawson, Angie and Matthew, and even the nice couple
they'd shared breakfast with all stayed behind.

"Remember, it's okay to say no," Ava said. "The important thing is
that you discuss it. Okay, next question. Do you have plans for who will
handle each household chore?"

Cate and Ethan joined two other couples in moving forward. Since
Ethan was a much better cook, he'd prepare most meals, and Cate

would do the dishes. He had trash duty and mowing the lawn, and she had vacuuming, laundry, and dusting.

Several questions later they were tied with three other couples. She looked over her shoulder and noticed Summer and Dawson still hovering around the first row, and Matthew and Angie were barely noticeable in the dark. They were still on square one.

"All right, next question. Have you discussed how you will handle family holidays?" It was the only question Cate and Ethan really hadn't discussed. It was something she really didn't want to think about. The thought of not having her parents around on Christmas or Thanksgiving made her heart break a little bit. Worse, the thought of sharing Yorkshire pudding and turkey with Denise every year for the rest of her life made her heart ache even more. They stayed behind.

"Have you discussed—"

"No we haven't!" A frustrated voice echoed from the back of the room.

Ava looked startled, and everyone spun around to see who'd interrupted.

Matthew wiped sweat from his brow with the back of his hand. "We haven't discussed anything!"

"Matthew," Angie whispered as she touched his arm. "Calm down. It's okay."

"No. I can't calm down! I can't calm down because I suddenly realized we haven't discussed anything. And I mean *anything*. There's a lot you don't know about me, Angie. I . . . I . . . I finally realized—I'm gay!"

Dawson took a few steps away from him. The only sound in the room was the the rain hitting the rooftop outside.

"I thought so," Stu said quietly.

"Well, that's okay," Ava said. "There are no right or wrong answers here. It's okay to answer this way. As long as you discuss it *before*—"

He began to laugh, joyously. "Oh that felt so wonderful! I've finally said it! I'm gay! I'm gay! I'm gay! I'm gay!" He was practically dancing. Angie looked as if she'd just had a bucket of ice water thrown over her head.

"Angie, I love you." He grabbed her shoulders. "And I always will, but I can't do this! I can't. Oh what a release! I've finally said it!"

Angie pushed his arms off her shoulders. "And you're telling me now? In front of twenty-five Catholics? I can't believe you! How could you do this to me?" She pounded his arm with her fists. "You fucking bastard!"

He took her arm and pulled her from the room without saying good-bye.

"That is the perfect example of why you should discuss things—"

"Before you get married," the entire room said in unison.

"That's right!" Ava said.

Needless to say, the game was not the same afterward. Everyone was still reeling with the excitement and shock of watching Matthew come out of the closet. Cate was willing to bet none of her girlfriends had witnessed anything like this at their Pre-Cana weekend. They didn't see Angie and Matthew again, and Cate could only imagine what poor Angie must be feeling. It was hard to believe that she didn't have a clue that her fiancé was homosexual. It was horrible, but the whole scene had kind of added a spark to the day, and the game wasn't as boring after that.

They ate dinner with several other couples while Stu played "One Bread, One Body" on his guitar. The topic of conversation at every table was Matthew and Angie, and most people wondered how she could've been so clueless.

Ethan leaned over and whispered in her ear, "When you're finished eating, say you have to go to the bathroom and meet me at my car."

"What?" she whispered back. "We can't leave."

"We're not going to. I just want some fresh air and some time away for a little while."

"All right. Sounds like a plan."

They ate iceberg lettuce with thick ranch dressing and sandwiches with white bread and slices of orange American cheese. As soon as she was finished eating she felt Ethan's elbow in her ribs. "You go first," he whispered.

She slipped away to "the bathroom" and right before entering, she made a sharp left and headed for the door. She felt mischievous as she slipped out the front door of the convent.

Rain poured over the parking lot, and she ran to Ethan's car. It was very poor planning on their part. He should've given her his keys. She pulled her sweater off and held it over her head while she waited. Luckily it was only a couple seconds before she heard the sound of his alarm deactivating. A couple seconds later they were sitting in the car with wet heads.

"I just had to get out of there," he said.

"I know what you mean."

"I just couldn't take the darkness and the dank odor any longer. I thought we could just use a little escape, sitting in the car listening to music." It sounded like the best thing she'd heard in ages. He popped in the latest Coldplay CD, and they held hands over the center console. According to the schedule they wouldn't start their next activity for twenty minutes. They had twenty minutes of freedom. They left the car windows cracked just so they could breathe in fresh air.

"I'm sorry," she said. "I'm sorry I dragged you into this."

He shrugged. "It's no big deal. Really. I mean, don't get me wrong. I could think of about eighty million other things I'd rather be doing, but I knew it was going to be like this. It'll be over soon enough."

She squeezed his hand.

"If Stu has copies of his CD for sale I think I'm going to buy one," he said.

She laughed. "Maybe he can play at our wedding." She told him the story about how she'd mistaken the words to "Oh Lamb of God" as "Oh Canada" for most of her childhood. Listening to his laughter put her in a much better mood.

"I wonder how poor Angie is doing," she said.

"No kidding. But it's better that she found out now."

"I know. This weekend is really good for some people."

Twenty minutes went by quickly, and before they knew it, they had to go back. Before leaving, they kissed over the center console.

"Next break. Meet me back out here," he said.

"Will do."

Before bedtime, they managed to sneak off to his car again. This time, they actually became more brazen and drove to a McDonald's around the corner where they ordered soft-serves. It was dark so they figured it was safe to walk back to the building together. The air smelled crisp and clean from the rain. As they held hands, she was sort of glad they'd attended the retreat. It had been sort of fun sneaking around, and after Matthew and Angie, she realized how lucky they were to have each other.

·28·

A New Leader

The lights came on in the middle of the night. Summer moaned and covered her head with a pillow, so Cate got up and turned off their light switch. She slept horribly after that. Just as she'd drifted into a dream, a knock sounded on the door. "Time to get up, ladies and gents!" The voice was male and sounded Irish. She wondered what had happened to Ava.

After a hot shower and a blow-dry, her bangs were back to normal. She headed downstairs and expected to find Ava waiting by the cafeteria entrance with her hideous apron, but neither Ava nor Stu were around. In their place was a tall, white-haired priest with a ruddy complexion and a million broken blood vessels on his nose.

"Good morning to ya," he said to Cate. "We're goin' to have Mass this mornin', so please go into the activity room."

"Where are Ava and Stu?" Her curiosity was overwhelming.

"One of them got the food poisoning last night, and they won't be coming back."

"Really?" Her prayers had been answered. "They're not coming back?"

"I'm afraid not."

It was all she could do to keep herself from shouting *yes!* at the top of her lungs.

Mass went by quickly. The priest introduced himself as Father Flannagan. "Everyone just mostly calls me Father Nick though," he said. "I bet you never imagined you'd get marriage advice from a priest. I know it seems strange, but in many ways my relationship with God is like a marriage. I usually come to give Mass and answer questions, but since your leaders got sick, it looks like we'll do an activity. Then I'll let you guys go home a little early."

She loved Father Nick, and judging by the blissful expressions of all her classmates she sensed that they did too. He was friendly and cheerful and normal, unlike the two phenoms who'd previously been in charge.

"So I'd like to start off the mornin' with . . ." He reached for the hat, and she felt her palms grow sweaty when she remembered Ethan's question. ". . . the questions you guys asked yesterday. Don't worry. It's completely anonymous."

He pulled a tight, hard, square of paper from the hat. It had been folded a million times. It took him several minutes just to unravel it. He slid a pair of reading glasses over the tip of his nose. "Ah huh. Ah yes." A spark of wisdom flashed across his eyes. "Now I know many of you might face this sometime in your marriage. The question is, 'My fiancé wants to borrow money from his parents, but I don't want to. I feel that it might put a strain on our relationship with them.'"

He placed the paper on a chair next to him before addressing the group. "I always tell everyone who comes to me before marriage to avoid borrowing money from family members at all costs. As you go into marriage together you become your own family, and if you still rely on your parents for anything, it might create a certain amount of pressure or expectations that could make for very uncomfortable situations." He said a lot of the same things Al had said when they'd discussed her mother.

Father Nick went through several questions, and Cate was impressed with some of the things that people had come up with. There were questions about interfaith marriages and dividing family holidays.

He was about halfway through when he unfolded a slip of paper and an obvious frown fell over his face. She knew which one it was and tried to avoid eye contact with Ethan, or anyone for that matter. He looked at the group sternly. "Now, let us talk for a minute about domestic violence." Everyone eyed each other suspiciously, wondering who had asked a question that had caused this jolly old man's face to turn to stone. "Domestic violence is never okay. In any situation."

They spent an hour on the topic, and she couldn't help but notice that throughout the lecture the priest didn't look at them as she'd expected him to. For some reason she'd expected him to just know it was Ethan. However, he kept looking at Dawson, and the light bruise above his eye. She felt terrible.

They spent the rest of the morning going over the questions. When he was finished he told them that Ava had left a description of the last activity for the weekend. Each couple was supposed to split up again. This time they had to write a letter to their significant other. A letter that said what they loved most about them, and what they were most proud of—all the things they looked forward to in the future.

She could've sworn she heard all the men in room groan. She headed back to her room with Summer and began her letter.

It was nice to be able to tell Ethan how much she loved him. It wasn't every day that people told one another how much they appreciated each other, or all the special things about them. She told him that he was her best friend, and that every time she thought about him she smiled.

When she was finished writing her letter she folded it up and caught a glimpse of Summer working on hers. She'd drawn hearts and smiley faces all around the borders. They went back downstairs, and Cate couldn't wait to see what Ethan had written to her. She sort of wished she could read it in private, and not in a room filled with twenty other people.

They sat in fold-out chairs across from one another. He smiled at her when he gave her the letter.

Dear Cate,
I have to admit, at first I hated coming to the Pre-Cana
weekend. But I decided to be a good sport and go along with it
because I love you and this is what you want. However, when
we started whispering and sneaking out to my car and
laughing at the situation, it took me back to when we were
kids. And I remembered falling in love with you for the first
time. I really remembered what that felt like. I've loved you for
as long as I can remember, and it's only growing stronger.
It's not just because of your truly kind heart or all the good
times we've experienced. Everyone has a special person in their
life who makes all their problems disappear. To me that person
is you. The sound of your voice, or the way you laugh can
always remind me that everything is going to be all right.
I've really enjoyed this weekend, and I'm looking forward to a
lifetime of love and happiness with my best friend. I love you.
Ethan

"I love you too," she said as she folded up his letter.

She felt a tear run down her cheek. This is why she wished she were in the privacy of her own home. She didn't want to be a blubbering fool in front of a bunch of strangers.

She didn't feel like much of a fool, and quickly quit crying when she noticed Dawson balwing like a baby. "I love you so much, baby."

Summer cradled his head on her boobs as he cried.

"You're the best piece of ass I've ever met," he sobbed.

The weekend had seemed to be worthwhile for everyone.

·29·

Let Go Already

Halloween was always her favorite day of school. All the children came dressed in costume. They had a big parade at school, and each grade level got to participate. She loved watching all the kids in their costumes. A lot of parents came to help, and several mothers set up a party for her class afterward.

Cate and several of the other teachers at school had decided to dress up together as beauty pageant contestants. One of the fifth grade teachers, Mr. Petrowski, dressed as the MC for the pageant. Cate dug up one of her old bridesmaid dresses from her closet, a lavender one she'd worn in Cousin Val's wedding, and made a sash that read "Miss Escondido" using a glitter pen. She bought a crown and put her hair in a French twist the day of school. Simone had found an old prom dress at a thrift store and wore a "Miss Pacific Beach" sash across her chest. Mr. Petrowski wore a cheesy toupee and rouge on his cheeks, and carried a fake microphone around with him all day.

Her students were by far the cutest things she'd seen in a long time.

George came dressed in solid green. His entire face, including his lips, were covered in green face paint and he wore a gigantic green afro on his head. Cate didn't want to ask him what he was for fear of hurting his feelings. She was relieved when little Priscilla Rowlands asked. She was dressed as a black cat. "What are you?" she asked.

"I'm a piece of broccoli."

"What a creative costume," Cate said.

His chubby hands clutched a fancy gold bag of truffles. She thought it was an odd contribution to the party. It wasn't mandatory that the kids bring something. She wondered if his mom had felt pressured to provide something at the last minute and had sent him to school with a re-gift they'd had lying around their house. "What do you have there?" she asked.

He shrugged. "Some candy."

She thought he would hand it over, but he hung on to it for dear life.

"Okay, well, why don't you go sit on the carpet with the rest of the kids? We're going to sing some songs in a little while."

He took his bag of candy with him.

She greeted a scarecrow, a black and white cow, and a rock star. Her favorite costume came from the twins in her class, Hannah and Sydney Colbert. They came dressed as telephone poles and had a wire separating the two of them. Fake pigeons sat on the wire, and a little sign reading "Joey loves Melissa" was written in black marker over Hannah's stomach. Sydney had a missing-dog flyer across her chest. They were adorable.

A few hours later, she noticed George still holding the bag of chocolates. In fact, he didn't even put it down to eat a sprinkled sugar cookie. He simply moved it to his left hand while he ate with his right.

"So George, what's the bag for?" she asked.

Instead of answering, he untied the fancy string that held it closed, reached a grubby little hand inside, then handed Cate a gourmet dark chocolate truffle with white chocolate drizzled over the top. It was a strange contribution to a kindergarten party.

"Thanks," she said. "Are they for everyone else too?"

He shook his head. Then she looked at the bag and realized it probably only held about five chocolates. There wouldn't be enough for everyone anyway.

"All right then."

She could already feel a headache from all the sugar she'd consumed, so she set the truffle on her desk for later. At two o'clock she passed out all their Halloween drawings that had been hanging on their classroom walls and sent them home with sugar highs. She noticed George's bag of chocolates dangling from his hand when he walked away.

Ethan was using his new nail gun when she got home. The blast it made was deafening when he pulled the trigger and plugged a nail into the baseboard on their floor. Oscar ran to her with a piece of silver wrapping paper dangling from his mouth. "Hello," she shouted over his gun.

"Oh, hey." He set down his gun, then pulled goggles away from his face.

She pulled the paper from between Oscar's teeth. "Did we get another wedding gift?" she asked.

"Yeah."

She thought it was kind of strange that he'd opened it without her. "Who was it from?"

He paused before answering and pulled his goggles back over his eyes. "Janet."

"What? She was here?" She pointed to the floor. "She stopped by here today?" A million thoughts raced through her mind, and she wanted answers. However, the phone rang. She almost didn't answer, but she remembered that she was waiting to hear from Peg Migillicuddy about wedding plans.

"Hello." Her voice was sharp with irritation.

"Oh um, is this Miss Padgett?"

Only two kinds of people referred to her as Miss Padgett. Her students, and her students' parents. "Uh, yes," she said, trying to sound chipper. "This is Cate. I mean, er, Miss Padgett."

"Oh hi, Miss Padgett. This is Jane Franklin. George Franklin's mom?"

"Oh! Hi, Jane. Yes, yes. How are you?" Why was George's mom calling? The only time parents ever called was if they had some gripe about how their genius child wasn't getting enough stimulation or attention. Translated, *My child is completely spoiled and should feel like the center of the universe all the time, including in your classroom—even when you have nineteen other kids to deal with.*

"Anyway, I'm calling because there was a little misunderstanding . . ."

Oh here it goes. George was somehow left out, or mistreated.

". . . well, I'm actually calling to apologize."

"You are?" Cate asked, trying to conceal her surprise.

"George was a little confused. You see, I sent a bag of chocolates with him."

"Uh-huh?" Cate quickly remembered the bag, the way his sweaty little hand had crinkled the wrap.

"Anyway, he was supposed to give you the whole bag, as a Halloween gift for being his teacher. And instead, he just gave you one. I found the rest of the bag in his lunch bag."

"Oh. Well, that's okay." Despite her mood, she managed to laugh.

"Anyway, I just wanted to tell you so you know when he brings it back on Monday."

"That's so nice of you. I rarely get Halloween gifts."

"George just loves you. My husband and I think he has a crush on you."

"Oh, that's very sweet." She would've never guessed, and she wanted to melt.

She chatted with Mrs. Franklin for a few more minutes before saying good-bye. Ethan was measuring a baseboard when she returned.

"So what did she get us?" Cate asked.

"A table saw."

"We didn't register for a table saw, Ethan. We didn't even register at Home Depot." And what the hell was Cate going to do with a table saw?

The gift wasn't for them. It was for him, and clearly another attempt to get his attention.

"Ethan, she's not even invited to the wedding."

He was silent, before looking at his feet.

"Ethan? Did you invite her to the wedding?"

"No . . . not really. It's just . . . I mean . . . she came over here with the gift, and what was I going to do? I had to give her the option. I didn't really invite her. I just said she's welcome to come."

She couldn't help but laugh at what he'd just said. "What's the difference?"

"Well, it's not like I formally gave her an invitation. I just made it really casual."

"Ethan, she is so manipulative. Don't you see that it's her last-minute desperate attempt to schmooze you before you tie the knot? She can't let go of you. You guys broke up years ago, and now she just pops back into your life bearing expensive gifts."

"Listen to yourself," he said. "She gave *us* a gift for *our wedding*."

"That gift's not for us. What the hell am I going to do with a table saw?"

For this, he had no answer. "Well what the hell was I supposed to do when she came over with a two-hundred-dollar gift out of the blue?"

"Tell her that you can't take it. Thank her for the generosity, but send her home with the table saw."

His face was long. "Look, I'm sorry. What do you want me to do?"

"I don't know. I really don't know, Ethan. But you better figure out a way to give that saw back."

"I already used it to cut the baseboards."

She walked to her bedroom and slammed the door.

Caught Red-Handed

Vacation was a funny word to use for the two weeks of work she was taking off. She needed the week before the wedding to tie up all the loose ends, and of course she'd be taking a week off after the wedding for their honeymoon in Kauai. The list of things she had to do before the wedding was long and endless, and time away from work hardly seemed like a vacation. Her first day off was the Friday before her bachelorette weekend, and she spent the first portion of the morning at the mall, picking out her bridesmaids gifts. She was going to give them all pashminas, a different color to fit each of her friends.

After she returned she began packing for her bachelorette party. Her bridesmaids had booked a hotel room at the Marriott in the Gaslamp Quarter. They were scheduled to check in the following morning so they could head downtown and have the whole day to relax by the sprawling pool before going to dinner and barhopping. The Santa Ana weather had made the November air warm and dry, and they had to take advantage of getting a tan when they had the chance.

Also in the Gaslamp Quarter, Ethan would be staying at the St. James with his friends. They'd be ordering pizzas and playing poker all weekend. Chuck had been dumped by Tatiana as soon as she met a guy who cast her as an extra in a Snoop Dogg video. He'd been depressed ever since the breakup, and Cate wondered if he would hire strippers. A raunchy bachelor party wasn't Ethan's style though, and she hoped Chuck figured this out before he went to all the effort.

The whole issue of Janet had been a gray area ever since their fight. He'd already unpacked and used the saw, so he couldn't give it back to her. Though it had been discussed, he'd never been clear on exactly how he was going to disinvite her to the wedding. Part of Cate wanted to save him the embarrassment and just have Janet come to the wedding. The other part of her shuddered every time she thought of seeing her annoying face on their wedding day. Every time Cate thought about her stopping by when she knew Cate was at work, and delivering gifts after several years of not speaking to him, she felt her blood boil.

While packing for the weekend she realized she was out of film and sunscreen, and decided a trip to Wal-Mart was in order. Right before she left she remembered that she still hadn't developed the film from their trip to Playa del Carmen. It seemed like decades ago that they'd been in Mexico. It wasn't that she'd forgotten about the film. It was just that every time she thought about getting the pictures developed a wedding task had taken priority over it. She grabbed the three rolls of film and decided to drop them off while she shopped.

She bought a couple tubes of sunscreen and some travel-sized shampoo and conditioner. She decided to stock up for her trip to Kauai and added a mini deodorant and toothpaste to her stash. After she was finished shopping, she picked up the photos and tried to quickly flip through them while waiting for her receipt. She'd give them a thorough look later when she could sit down.

When she returned home Oscar had somehow managed to pull their bed skirt into his crate and had ripped the entire left half of the ruffle into a million pieces. He almost knocked her over when she let him out.

The dog was a beast, only he didn't realize this. In his mind, he was still the tiny little pup who'd slept in Grease's cage. He had the legs of a Great Dane and plowed into people and furniture as if they didn't exist. Beth called while she was cleaning up the dust ruffle.

"Are you excited?" She asked. "It's going to be so fun! We have so much stuff planned for the weekend."

"Just please don't make me wear anything *too* embarrassing."

"Oh we will." Her laugh was slightly evil. "Anyway, I'm calling because I wanted to know if you've heard from Denise. I'm just trying to figure out the final head count for my car. Parking is so expensive down there so I sent out an e-mail to all the girls saying that they could ride with me. I don't know if I should take my car or Ike's Suburban."

"She never e-mailed you back?" Cate remembered the e-mail going out over a week ago.

"No. Haven't heard a word from her."

"Well, I think she mentioned something about driving herself because she had to leave later than everyone else. I wouldn't count on her. Sorry, she's been so flaky." Cate felt a little embarrassed that Denise had been so unreliable throughout all the planning. According to Emily and Beth, who were heading up the bachelorette committee, she'd been terrible about RSVPing, and returning e-mails. She was the only one who hadn't offered any help whatsoever. "I know what it's like when you're trying to plan something and you can't get a simple answer or commitment from people. I'm so sorry she's acting that way."

"Oh, it's not your fault. Don't even worry."

They chatted for several more minutes about the weekend before they said good-bye. After she hung up she realized it had been a long time since she'd seen Oscar. Leaving him alone was like leaving a glass casserole dish on top of a hot burner. It would only take minutes for it to explode. She ran around the house and found him in the office, a lavender pashmina dangling from his mouth.

The obscenities that flew from her mouth would've made hardened criminals blush. She looked at the Nordstrom bag, ripped in two, and the pile of shawls resting next to Ethan's desk. Thank God he hadn't gotten his teeth on all of them. However, a hundred dollars' worth of fine cashmere hung from between his teeth. She lunged toward him, but he bolted, taking a trail of lavender with him.

"Oscar! Get back here!" She chased him into a corner. She pulled the pashmina from his mouth. He may as well have taken a hundred-dollar bill and ripped it to shreds.

Ethan had left a night early for his bachelor weekend. He took Oscar with him so he could drop him off at his parents' house on the way to the Gaslamp. She had the house to herself. She spent the evening wrapping the remaining bridesmaids' gifts and writing cards to each individual friend, thanking them for being in the wedding and throwing her shower and bachelorette party. When it came time to write Denise's card she imagined writing, *Dear Denise, I don't know what to say. You've been an asshole ever since I got engaged. Sincerely, Cate.*

She ended up writing something polite and generic. She took a hot bath and sipped on a glass of Pinot Grigio before enjoying a sound night of Oscar-free sleep. In the morning she drove to Beth's in Pacific Beach to meet the rest of the girls.

"Does anyone have a mint?" Jill asked when they were in the Suburban.

"I think I do." Cate opened her purse. "Oh, I have pictures. I forgot all about them." She still hadn't even had a chance to look them over. She handed them to Jill. "Here, you can look at these while I dig in my purse. They're our trip to Playa Del Carmen."

"Cool," Jill said. She flipped through the photos, occasionally asking questions, while Cate searched for a mint in the disaster zone known as her handbag.

"Who's this?" She held out a photo.

"That's the bride's parents. They were so funny." She'd practically forgotten about Cash and Honey.

"Look how pretty the ocean is," she said, passing a photo to Val. "It was just right off the pool like that?"

"It was. I tried to capture the view from the pool."

"Is that Janet?" Val asked.

"Where?" Cate wanted to know. She didn't remember taking any pictures of her. "Right over there, next to that tree by the pool bar? And who's that freakish creature she's talking to?"

"Let me see." Cate took the photo. She had to look closely, but there, in the middle of scattered lounge chairs and tourists, stood Janet, talking to Leotard Creature Man. The same guy who'd sent her running into Ethan's arms. "What the . . ." Cate said as she held it closer to her eyes. "It is her. Pull over," she said.

"What?" Beth asked.

"I can't believe this!" Cate said. "She's handing him something."

"Handing who what?" Jill asked. "Let me see."

Emily turned around in the passenger seat. "What *is* going on?"

"Oh my God! I think Janet may have slipped Leotard Man money! I have to get this picture cropped. We need to go to a photo lab—now!"

They all looked at her like she was insane. She told them the story about the creature man by the pool sneaking up on Janet and how she'd jumped into Ethan's arms and kissed him on the cheek. "I never thought anything of it, except that she was a brazen whore for kissing my boyfriend, but now I seriously think she paid the guy to sneak up on her. I think she's giving him money in the picture." She pointed to the picture. "She wanted to look like a victim in front of Ethan. I'm not kidding. She is crazy." She laughed. "And I'm not. All this time I wondered if I was overreacting, but I wasn't. She *is* after him!"

"Let me see that," Jill yanked the picture from her hand. She held the picture up to her face. "It *does* look like she's handing him something. But it's hard to tell what it is. She's so small. I wouldn't have even noticed *them* in the picture."

"I can have the picture enlarged and cropped to zoom in on them. We have to find out."

Emily gave Cate the same expression her mother would've used if Cate had said she was going drinking until two a.m. "Cate, do you really want to do that? It's your bachelorette party. I don't think you should waste one minute thinking about her. You should be having *fun*. Why do you want to run around with a magnifying glass, looking for a photo lab to do detective work for you?"

Everyone was quiet, and for a moment Cate thought they all agreed with her. Maybe she should just wait until the weekend was over. They'd gone to a lot of trouble to plan everything, and her sister was probably right. Janet was just interfering with her last opportunity to drink fruity cocktails by the pool before the wedding. But if she didn't find out, she'd be wondering about the photo all weekend.

Leslie reached for her purse. "I have a magnifying glass."

Of course she had a magnifying glass. Cate remembered the way she'd studied her ring at the engagement party.

"I would want to know," Beth said.

"If she is handing that freak money, I would go find her and stuff that photo down her throat," Val added.

"Let's just stop real quick at a photo lab downtown, and see if they can crop it while we wait," Jill suggested.

Emily shrugged. "If that's what Cate really wants."

Cate raised the magnifying glass to her eye and studied the photo. "It definitely looks like money to me."

They passed the photo and Leslie's magnifying glass around, and all agreed it looked like she was paying Leotard Man. Cate wanted to race over to the St. James Hotel and show the photo to Ethan. She wanted him to know what a nutcase Janet was. It hadn't all been Cate's imagination. Then she realized that she couldn't interrupt his party to show him this. She couldn't show up with a magnifying glass and the photo in the middle of his poker game. It would wreck all his fun and she would look like the psycho. She'd have to wait until the weekend was over.

"What are you going to do?" Sarah asked.

Cate shook her head. "What can I do now? Probably nothing for the time being. I don't want to show this to Ethan while he's at his bachelor party, and I don't think I'll bother getting the photo cropped. It's pretty obvious if you study it." Jill passed the photo back to her. "Whatever you guys do, don't mention anything to Denise. If she or Janet found out about it, they'd probably both burn the photo and negatives."

"Do you think Denise knew about this?" Emily asked.

Cate thought about it. "No. I just can't imagine that *anyone* would continue being friends with someone so crazy. I think she's just caught in Janet's web."

Cate looked at the picture again. Only a complete lunatic would've paid Leotard Man. It was sort of scary to think what she was capable of. She would keep the photos safely tucked inside her purse until the end of the weekend, and then there was going to be a reckoning with Janet. Whether it was Ethan or Cate who confronted her, she'd finally be out of their lives for good.

·31·
Cold Feet

$\mathcal{S}$he'd thought it would be impossible to relax after learning about Janet and the Leotard Man. Her nerves were on fire, yet at the same time she felt a sense of exhilaration. She could finally prove what she'd thought all along: Janet was evil. It bothered her a little bit that she'd had to find concrete proof to show Ethan what a psycho she was. Couldn't he have figured it out on his own?

Once she settled into her lounge chair at the Marriott a sense of peace came over her. Fall and winter months were schizophrenic in San Diego. One week it could be raining and everyone would be covered in heavy sweaters and long pants. The next week could be warm and dry, and she could actually get a tan. It wasn't the same kind of heat as the summer. It would get chilly at night, but it was definitely vacation weather. Whoever suggested they spend her bachelorette here was a genius.

She settled onto a lounge chair and felt the dry warmth envelop her body. She reached for the rum and Coke she'd ordered. The rest of the girls were still in the suite they shared, changing into their bikinis. She was just starting to feel every muscle in her body soften when she heard Cousin Val's heels clicking toward her. She wore a peach sarong and open-toed heels with little jewels on the front of them. She was the only person Cate knew who could pull off wearing jeweled heels by the pool. If Cate wore anything other than shorts and flip-flops she would look like a jackass. It must be fun to dress like Ivana Trump every once in a while. She was just about to tell her to grab a cocktail when she noticed the alarmed expression on her face.

"What's wrong?"

"I'm going to throttle Denise." She sat on the edge of a lounge chair next to Cate.

"What did she do now?"

"Well, I wanted to be the one to tell you this before she came down here. The other girls are getting ready, and they're just as livid as I am."

"What did she do?" Cate took a sip of her rum and Coke and leaned back onto her chair. She'd already decided that no matter what happened, Denise was not going to ruin her weekend. It was her bachelorette party. She'd already left small scars on the shower and engagement party, and Cate simply wasn't going to let her ruin this. She'd listen to Val's story while calmly sipping her cocktail. Then she'd force herself to forget about what a nuisance she was within a few minutes.

"Well," Val crossed her legs. Her sarong was short, and Cate could see a muscular line up the side of her thigh. "She strolls into the hotel room, wheeling this hideous brown corduroy suitcase behind her. I mean, it seriously looked like something a stewardess for TWA would've dragged around in 1981. I'm no friend of corduroy to begin with. And anyone who carries luggage made from it should try out for *The Price Is Right* so they can win a free set of luggage on the Showcase Showdown."

Wouldn't it just be easier to buy a new suitcase? Cate thought.

Val's voice turned grave. "Anyway, Leslie asked if overnight parking was expensive, and Denise nonchalantly says, 'Oh it was fine. I didn't drive.' Then Sarah chimes in, 'Oh. How did you get here?' and she says,

'Janet drove me. She dropped me off and then headed to the St. James. She's joining the boys for the weekend. Ryan invited her.'"

Rum and Coke spewed from Cate's mouth. "What?" She sat up and wiped her chin. "You're kidding? Please tell me you're kidding! Janet is here? In the Gaslamp? With Ethan?"

Val nodded. "I wish I was kidding, but I swear to you that is what she said. And I am not kidding, Cate, you could hear a pin drop after she said it."

"I'm going to kill her. Them. Both of them! Who the hell do they think they are?" She began to pace around her lounge chair. "I can't believe this! What kind of a woman crashes a bachelor party?"

"A crazy one."

"I mean, *who*, in their right mind, would do something like this? They're insane. The two of them."

"Well, if it makes you feel any better, she did say that Ryan invited her. They're dating now, I guess."

"I don't believe it. Even if he did invite her, I guarantee you she manipulated him into doing it. Furthermore, *even* if he *did*, why would she even *want* to go to a bachelor party? Where's my cell phone? I'm calling Ethan. I'm telling him to get rid of her. I'm telling him about the photo and he has to kick her out. This is it! I've had it!"

"Well, listen. The reason I wanted to get to you first is because you can't let Denise see you flipping out. She'll win, Cate. Those two are dying to see you fall apart right before the wedding so they can go in for the kill. If you take the bait, they'll triumph. They want to see you insecure, make you look paranoid, as if you don't trust him."

She'd told herself the same thing a million times. "So what am I supposed to do? Just sit here and take it? Just sit here and let them piss on every party like they're dogs peeing on trees to mark their territory? I'm marching up to that room right now and telling Denise to get the hell out of here, and take her little tree-pisser with her." She envisioned barging into the suite with her bikini top on, ripping Denise's corduroy bag from her fat fingers, and hurling it from the eleventh floor of the

Marriott. She'd watch with delight as her one-piece bathing suit, curling iron, and Keds smashed against the pavement below. Then she'd turn Ray Liotta on her. If she had a gun, she'd pistol whip her. The complementary hair dryer in the hotel bathroom would have to do for this fantasy. Cate began to laugh uncontrollably.

"What's so funny?"

She caught her breath. "This. All this."

Val looked puzzled. "Well, I'm glad you're taking it all so lightly."

"I mean, it's just ridiculous. The whole thing. How did I get myself into this? I got engaged, and everyone around me changed." She began to laugh harder, and the more she laughed the more worried Val looked. "What is it about this ring that has made everyone around me crazy? My family. Ethan's family. And now I'm starting to think that Ethan's gone crazy too. My life has become an episode of *Jerry Springer*. And my fiancé—the man I'm supposed to spend the rest of my life with—doesn't even notice it. He's oblivious."

Val handed her the rum and Coke. "Here. Have a sip of this."

She drank the whole thing in two gulps. "No. There is no way I'm going over there or calling him. He can hang out with her all weekend, and if he doesn't realize how truly nutty she is, well then . . . I don't know!" She started crying. "Who goes through something like this? It's not normal. It drives me crazy that he doesn't realize that she's been trying to sink her claws into him every chance she gets."

"If it were me, I'd probably call a hit man, but that's just me," Val mumbled.

"You know what? Screw them. All of them!" She was yelling now, and a few tourists turned to watch. "I've been waiting for this damn weekend for months! I just want to have fun. That is *why* I came here, and I don't care about Janet or Denise. They can just go to hell. I'm not going to go call Ethan and tell him to get rid of her. He should want to do that on his own. He knows what the right thing to do is."

Even though the thought of that damn Janet laughing and tossing her hair in front of her fiancé made her want to scream, she promised herself that she wasn't going to say one word about Janet. Not one. Even if Denise brought it up, she would act as if she didn't care. She wasn't going to give Denise the pleasure of seeing her angry. This was an issue between Ethan and Cate now. This wasn't about Janet and Denise anymore, and she was starting to wonder if it ever had been. If Ethan had just nipped it in the bud when it had begun, none of this would be happening. She knew what she'd do if her ex, Paul, decided to crash her bachelorette party. She would tell him to leave, and Ethan should do the same thing. She just hoped he had enough sense to do so.

The rest of the girls joined them at the pool. All of them except for Denise flashed her a knowing look—looks that said, "If you want, we'll strangle her."

They draped themselves across lounge chairs, and she watched Denise remove her towel. She set it on the chair, then sprinted toward the pool. The flab on her chubby legs jiggled before she cannonballed into the water. Astonished by the bold move, Cate looked at Leslie.

"We gave her three shots of tequila in the hotel room," she whispered. "I'm hoping she'll just pass out."

"You did?" Cate never knew Denise had such a wild side.

"She wanted to do them, so we didn't try to stop her."

"Cate!" Denise called from the pool. Her wet bangs were dark and plastered to her forehead as she waved. "How are you?"

"Great," Cate called back. "How's the water?"

"Freezing."

Emily sat down next to Cate and pulled something from her pool bag. "Well, Cate, it *is* your bachelorette party, so that means you have to wear a bachelorette crown!" She revealed a plastic crown that looked a little like the one she'd worn for Halloween when she went as beauty pageant contestant.

She laughed. It finally felt like a bachelorette party. "All right," she said. "This I can handle."

She sat still while Emily positioned the crown on her head. They took a million pictures of Cate in her crown. They never let her hold an empty cocktail glass, and the feeling of liquor running through her veins made her temporarily thrilled.

Denise proceeded to get smashed that afternoon. Drunk, she'd told Sarah and Emily that she liked to sing Debbie Gibson in the buff in front of her bathroom mirror.

"That's not a visual I really want in my head," Cate said.

"She's plastered," Emily whispered back. "Her nipple was hanging out of her suit, and she didn't even notice."

Cate tried to enjoy the afternoon, sip her cocktails, and participate in all the girl talk amongst her friends. No matter how hard she tried to enjoy herself, all she could think about was Janet at the St. James, having a blast with her fiancé at his bachelor party.

A miracle occurred that evening. Denise, as red as Santa's hat, felt ill. "You must have sun poisoning." Leslie immediately diagnosed her. "You sat in the sun for too long and fried yourself, and now you're sick. It's happened to me before."

It was the alcohol, and probably nothing a few glasses of water couldn't cure, but if Leslie wanted to diagnose her with something that had poisoning in its description, Cate wasn't going to argue.

"What you need to do is rest, and tomorrow you should stay out of the sun under all circumstances," Leslie said. "The dark hotel room will probably be the best place for you."

Cate wondered if she was telling the truth, or was she deliberately trying to get rid of her? Suddenly Cate felt bad, looking at Denise, her skin as fair as a baby's butt now red and blotchy. Green circles clouded Denise's eyes, and Cate didn't want her friends ganging up on Denise for her sake. She couldn't stand her, but at the end of the day Denise *was* related to the man she loved more than anyone in the world. And if anyone could relate to being sunburned, it was her. She'd lubed her entire body in fifty, nonstop, and still had red cheeks and shoulders.

"Here," Cate said, handing her a bottled water. "Drink as much water as you can. Maybe it's just the combination of alcohol and the sun. This happens to me sometimes, and I just need to drink water and rest for a little bit. I bet you'll feel better by the time everyone is ready to go to dinner."

Denise looked worse by dinner. "I don't think I can go." She looked truly disappointed, and Cate had never seen her more vulnerable. For some reason this made Cate feel bad for her again.

"Are you sure?" Cate said. "We'll wait for you if you need some time."

She shook her head. "I just really feel like I need a nap."

"Do you want us to get you something to eat?"

"Thank you, but I'm really just not feeling well."

They left her, along with Cate's crown, at the hotel. It had started to give her a headache. The girls were understanding but acted a little like her mother had when she tried to get out of catechism due to an unidentified illness.

Everyone was dressed to the nines in their sexiest clothes. Even Emily, who never ventured from khakis and basic tees, was wearing a pair of black pants and a sparkly halter top. Her sister really was cute when she made an effort, and Cate loved the fact that she was letting her hair down and cutting loose for a change.

They had dinner at Fio's, and she couldn't believe how sweet her friends were. She really hadn't wanted a big fuss, but they all insisted on going somewhere nice for dinner, making sure that her wineglass was continuously full.

After dinner, they walked to The Bitter End. She was already pretty buzzed from all the wine, and her tipsiness was only enhanced when Cousin Val suggested they start buying shots. She was having so much fun that she almost forgot about Ethan and Janet. "I love you," she grabbed her sister's head and kissed her firmly on the cheek. "And you!" Cousin Val was next. "And you! And you! And you!" She went through them all. "You're the best group of friends ever!" She pounded her Cosmopolitan. "Let's dance!"

The Killers were playing, but for some reason she wanted to do the electric slide. She convinced everyone to join her, and they didn't just do the slide to one song, but three. She was a wedding expert, and a pro at the electric slide. She really got into it, throwing her shoulders into her turns, snapping her fingers and throwing her head back when she did the grapevine.

She was drunk, and feeling free, and surrounded by the best group of girls she'd ever known. She was spinning around when she felt someone come up behind her, lightly grab her hips and turn her. They were big hands, nearly covering each of her hip bones, and the touch was soft, gentle, as if he were handling a baby.

"What brings you here?" he said. His voice was low, but she recognized it immediately. It was the same voice who'd apologized for kicking sand on her, or dripping water over her book. It was the same voice that she'd discussed red tide with, and surf lessons. It was the voice of the devil.

"I'm uh . . ." She wanted to lie. *Ethan, Ethan, Ethan.* She was marrying Ethan. "I'm actually here for my bachelorette party." There. She'd said it.

He raised his eyebrows and smirked. A deep dimple appeared on the right side of his face. "You're getting married." It was a statement, rather than a question, and he still smiled.

She expected him to ask when and where and who the lucky guy was, but he didn't seem to care. Shock ripped through her senses when she realized how relieved she felt.

"Yeah, I am." She sounded more disappointed than he had.

"Well, let me buy you a drink. A celebratory one." This was the point when she was supposed to say, "Oh that's okay. I've probably had enough to drink. But thanks though." Then she should turn her back to him and continue dancing with her friends. Instead, she followed him to the bar. All the girls were too engrossed in their dance moves to notice that she'd left them. He leaned on his elbows on the counter. As she slid onto a stool he looked over at her. His deep eyes peered from beneath his long bangs, and the corners of his lips turned up just slightly. She could see the outline of his muscles beneath his T-shirt and remembered his perfectly chiseled chest and stomach, towering over her like a statue at the beach. For some reason Ethan's body popped into her mind, and she shoved it right back out.

"How 'bout something that will go down easy?" he said. "A lemon drop?"

"Sounds great." She wondered what he was doing in the Gaslamp. Jeans weren't allowed in most bars downtown, and it usually catered to pretty boys who drove luxury cars and listened to techno. She pictured Nate hanging out at beachside bars, where you didn't necessarily have to wear a shirt or shoes.

"What are you doing down here?" she asked.

"My mom and stepfather own a penthouse down here. It's a second home. They actually live up in the Bay Area."

"So the family is here for the weekend?"

"No. I have a key. I stay there sometimes."

So he had loaded parents and an empty penthouse to himself? The situation was getting more dangerous by the minute. He pushed a shot glass toward her. "Well, here's to . . ."

She expected him to say something wedding-related, or a wish for good luck with her marriage.

"Meeting great people."

When he set his glass on the counter she felt his arm brush against hers. It felt warm, and he didn't move it. In fact, he leaned in closer to her, and when he spoke he looked directly into her eyes. She felt her palms grow sweaty and wondered if he always felt this relaxed around people he hardly knew.

"So you guys staying in a hotel?" he asked.

She told him about the hotel and how they'd hung out around the pool all day.

"Listen, I have to take a leak, but when I get back, do you want to go to the bar upstairs with me? It's quiet up there, and there are nice couches you can sit on."

"Sure." Good God, what was she doing? She should be off with her girlfriends, not rubbing up to some hot stranger she was thoroughly tempted to kiss. He leaned in, and her heart skipped a beat. Holy shit, he was going to kiss her. For some reason she didn't budge. It was all happening so fast. But then he didn't kiss her, he lifted his thumb to her face and brushed aside a strand of her hair. "You okay?" he asked.

"Yeah, I'm fine."

"You look nervous."

"No, I'm not at all."

She watched him walk away, his tight butt beneath his jeans. She wondered if she were doing the right thing. *Getting married*. Maybe she wasn't ready. If she was ready, she wouldn't be having these thoughts. She wouldn't be sitting on this barstool next to the hottest guy she'd ever met, wondering what it would be like to kiss him. Was he a good kisser? Was he good in bed, or was he one of those guys who'd gotten so much easy sex in his gorgeous life that he'd never really learned how to please a woman?

She felt scared, trapped. After next weekend, she would never experience another moment of courtship. There would be no more first kisses or stressing over which sexy shirt to wear. There would be no more firsts—period. She knew the jittery feelings of new love faded in every relationship. Of course she was still attracted to Ethan, but she didn't get butterflies every time she saw him or smile with genuine glee when his number appeared on her cell phone. Now they looked at each other's used dental floss lying like dried water moccasins in the trash can.

Maybe she was doing the wrong thing. Wasn't she supposed to have eyes for Ethan, and Ethan only? Didn't the thought of making out with extremely hot men turn almost all brides-to-be off? A normal bride would've politely declined the drink and forgotten about the guy while basking in her bachelorette glory. And what if this was some sign from

God? What were the odds of running into Nate on her bachelorette weekend?

Did she have cold feet? Getting cold feet was normal. Wasn't it? She'd heard about it all the time. But she expected cold feet to feel like a sense of horrific pressure—something the notorious Runaway Bride would've felt. Cold feet was leaving someone standing at the altar, then feeling totally relieved by the decision.

Would she feel relieved if she called off the wedding? She thought for a moment, wondering what it would be like to call it off. No wedding. No marriage. No Ethan. She'd be single and free and able to do whatever she wanted with Nate.

Before she'd had Ethan, she hated being single. She'd hated hitting the bars and wondering if she'd ever find Mr. Right. She'd hated spending Friday nights alone while her girlfriends cuddled up with their significant others. However, being single had never seemed more appealing. Freedom. She wanted glorious freedom.

However, if she was single, she wouldn't ever be with Ethan again. She wouldn't see his adorable face in the morning or feel him pull the covers over her body when their room felt frigid. She didn't want to lose him. She loved him. She just had a classic case of prewedding jitters. She remembered Sarah and Beth saying that they'd gone through something similar before their weddings. Did this mean that Ethan was going through the same thing too? Did he have thoughts of making out with other women? She wondered if he ever thought about losing his freedom too. Then she thought of Janet. He could be sitting across from her right now, wondering if he wanted one last fling. She needed to be with him. She picked up her purse, stood up, and ran from the bar.

·32·

One Last Fling

Even though the St. James was only a few blocks away, she hopped in the first cab that drove past. She knew it was totally against the bachelor weekend rules to see one another, but she didn't care. She wanted her fiancé. She wanted to feel her face pressed against his warm chest and smell his scent. She wanted to kiss him and sleep next to him, and she suddenly felt horrified that she'd even considered letting another man touch her. Hot as Nate might be, he definitely wasn't Ethan. There was only one Ethan. She didn't even care about Janet and the stupid picture. Granted, she had it safely tucked in her purse, and if she needed to pull it out, she would.

She tipped the driver well before heading inside the hotel. She went straight to the front desk and asked for Ethan's room number. It didn't take her long to learn that none of the rooms were in his name, and she had to go through several of his friends' names before she figured out where they were. She got Chuck's room number, then headed to the elevator. It was a historical hotel, and the old elevator seemed to take eons to make its way down to the lobby.

She pulled the old-fashioned wrought-iron gate open and stepped inside. Riding to the top of the hotel felt like it took an eternity, and by the time she arrived at his floor, she wondered if she should've just taken the stairs.

She could hear their voices from several yards away and followed the laughter all the way down the hall. She was surprised that someone hadn't called security on them. She knocked on the door and listened while the room fell silent. She hoped they weren't sorely disappointed when they opened the door and realized it wasn't a stripper, but rather the bride.

Chuck opened the door. As expected, he looked surprised to see her. His face was red, and she wondered why they didn't turn on the air conditioner. "Cate? Wow! What a surprise! C'mon in, sweetie."

"Thanks. Bet you weren't expecting me." She'd sobered up a tad, and now she wondered if she'd done the right thing. They were probably having the time of their lives, and she'd interrupted the party. She stepped inside and instantly felt sorry for the hotel maid. Peanut shells covered the floor. Dirty room service plates were piled on top of the television, and a plastic knife stuck from a champagne bottle. She noticed a spilled coffee mug on top of a phone book—the brown liquid had crinkled the pages. Ethan could probably afford to remodel their kitchen with the amount of money they'd make if they recycled all the beer bottles that littered the room.

Despite the mess, the room was really nice. It had the charm of an old hotel and overlooked downtown. A spread of city lights blinked from the large windows, and the spacious setting felt more like an apartment than a hotel room.

They'd set up a card table, and her eyes immediately wandered over the guys. "Hey," Ted said, looking up from his hand. He also looked surprised. She was greeted with the same reaction from all of them. All of them except Ethan—Ethan and Janet. They weren't there.

"Ethan left a little while ago to get ice," Ryan said.

Chuck glanced at his watch. "He should've been back by now. He's been gone for like twenty minutes."

"How far is the ice machine?" she asked.

"Just right down the hall."

"Where's Janet?"

They all glanced at one another, then shrugged. "She left a little while ago too," Chuck finally said.

"With Ethan?"

"I don't think they went together," Sean said.

"Which room is Ethan staying in?" Cate asked.

"This one," Chuck said, dealing cards.

"Is everyone staying in this room?" Cate asked.

"No. Ryan and Janet are staying two doors down, and Mark and I are staying next door," Sean said.

"Okay. Thanks. I think I'll go look for Ethan."

She knew Janet had gone with him. The guys didn't seem like they were lying, but they also seemed like they hadn't been paying attention. They were too involved in their game to notice if Janet and Ethan had left together, and he'd been gone for twenty minutes? The whole situation was unfathomable. It was so un-Ethan-like. She honestly couldn't imagine him cheating on her, ever. But then she knew herself better than anyone, and she never in a million years would've imagined feelings of cold feet and lusting after another man, just days before the wedding. What if he was going through the same thing—drunk? Janet's wet dream was to have him drunk and doubtful.

She proceeded to the ice machine, turned the corner, and half expected to see Ethan and Janet standing there, filling a bucket and perhaps picking out snacks from the vending machine. The little room was empty. Where the hell were they? She went back to Ryan and Janet's room, and knocked on the door. No answer. What if all the guys knew something was up, and called him as soon as she left to warn him not to answer the door. It was *Ethan* though. He wouldn't do this to her. Or would he? All she could think about was Nate, and how tempted she'd been. What if he'd been drunker and more tempted? She stopped back at the poker room on her way out. Still no sign of Ethan or Janet.

"I think I'll wait a few minutes," she said.

"Okay," Chuck said.

Was it just her imagination, or did they all seem a little uncomfortable? Maybe it was just because they couldn't cuss freely in her presence or talk about their sexual escapades while she was around.

"You want to play a hand?" Chuck asked.

"Sure." She slid into an empty seat and thought about how interesting it would be when Ethan and Janet arrived. No matter where they were, she was willing to bet they never expected to see her sitting at the card table, acting like she belonged in a Harrah's casino commercial.

She'd played poker several times. Despite the fact that her poker face was virtually unreadable, something about the game drove her crazy. Perhaps it was the suspense. She couldn't stand the anticipation of seeing what would become of everyone's hand. And it drove her crazy that everyone had the option of keeping their hand a secret, even if they won. Half the time, she outbet everyone just so she could see who had which cards. She hated secrets and thought of how ironic this all was while she was waiting to learn the whereabouts of her fiancé and his ex-girlfriend.

She played one round and surprised herself. Due to her preoccupation with Ethan she found it easy to handle the suspense of Texas hold-'em. As she collected her ten dollars it occurred to her that her girlfriends were probably searching every corner of The Bitter End for her. They'd be frantic.

"You guys have fun." She scooted her chair away from the table. "And tell Ethan to call me as soon as you see him."

Back in a taxi, her head was spinning. It was inconceivable to think of Ethan stooping so low. She thought she knew him so well. But then she'd seen all the *Oprah*s on cheating spouses or husbands who turned out to be gay. Men "on the down low" who had fooled everyone into believing they were heterosexual throughout twenty years of marriage and women who said they'd never seen a sign of philandering, let alone homosexuality. She knew her boyfriend wasn't gay, but if these women had been so fooled, why would she be any different?

She was furious. Janet should've never been there. She should've been eliminated from their lives the night she showed up at their engagement party. Maybe she was jumping to conclusions. What if Janet had just gone to lie down and hadn't even heard her knocking, and maybe Ethan had just gone for some fresh air by himself. He'd quit smoking ages ago, but maybe he'd taken it up for his last hurrah with the boys. Then she worried. What if he'd been drunk and had wandered into oncoming traffic? She thought she would start crying if she thought about him for another second. She called her sister.

"Cate! Where the hell are you?"

"It's a long story. I'm in a cab, on my way back to the bar. I'll be there in a minute."

"What? You left the bar? Why? We have three shots sitting on the counter waiting for you."

This wasn't how her bachelorette party was supposed to be. She wasn't supposed to be hunting down her boyfriend who might be off with his ex, while her friends bought her shots. She felt a tear roll down her cheek. She'd have to go back to the bar and explain to all her friends what had just happened. Her sister, the eternal optimist, would give Ethan the benefit of the doubt. She was also sheltered and naïve and hadn't even known what ménage à trois had meant until her late twenties. Beth, also an optimist, would worry about Ethan and immediately phone hotel security to find him.

Leslie and Val would tell her he was an asshole and how dare he, and start figuring out ways to call off the wedding.

Calling off the wedding? How does one go about doing that? Would Ethan and Janet get married now? She'd be free to hook up with Nate, who suddenly seemed like a cocky, womanizing idiot. Who hangs out in nightclubs alone anyway? Only a selfish commitment-phobe.

The cab came to a halt in front of the bar, and she was so worried and sad that she handed the driver a twenty and didn't bother taking change, even though the fare was only four dollars.

She closed the door behind her and hung her head low as she headed to the bar.

"Cate! Thank God! I've been looking in every single bar up this entire strip for the past hour."

"Ethan!"

His eyes were wide, and he pulled her into his arms. "Where have you been?" she asked.

"Here. Looking for you. Where have you been?"

"At your hotel. Looking for you."

"I'm so happy I found you." He sighed. "I just had to see you. I've missed you all weekend."

"I've missed you too." She felt a flutter of butterflies in her stomach as she smelled his shampoo. She couldn't remember the last time they'd told each other they'd missed each other after being apart for only one day. "I went to the hotel to find you, and the guys told me you went to get ice, but I couldn't find you anywhere. And then they told me Janet was gone too, and I thought you were with her."

The glow that had been in his eyes faded, and his cheeks dropped. "I don't know where Janet is."

"What's wrong?"

"I asked her to leave," he said. He looked so sad. She didn't want him to be sad about asking her to leave. She wanted him to feel relieved.

"She was really out of line, Cate."

She suddenly felt as if she'd been shot in the butt with caffeine. "She was?" She could feel the cold night air against her cheeks, but she didn't want to go inside. She had to hear the rest of his story.

He nodded. "I *did* leave to get ice. While I was getting ice, she showed up. At first I thought she had just come to help. A bunch of the ice fell on the ground, and we were laughing because we both slipped, and before we got up, she . . ."

"She did what?"

"She tried to kiss me."

"Did you kiss her back?"

"No. I asked her to stop, and she burst into tears. The whole thing was such a mess."

"She burst into tears?"

He shoved his hands into his pockets. "Yeah, it was awful." He paused. "I tried to get her to stop crying, and she started telling me how she'd never been happy since we broke up, and she just couldn't handle seeing me get married."

She felt like saying, *See I told you. I told you she was after you the whole time! She and Denise, scheming! You blind, trusting fool!* But she actually just wanted to hear more about Janet crying and Ethan telling her to leave. "So this all happened by the ice machine. You guys were sitting on the floor, and she was crying and there was spilled ice everywhere?"

He nodded again. "And I told her I loved you and I was sorry for her, but it was probably best if she just left."

"What did she do?"

"It was bad, Cate." He shook his head.

"What? What did she do?"

"She clung to me. I had to pry her fingers from my arms."

The whole situation was so hard to imagine, mostly because she couldn't picture herself ever behaving the way Janet had. "Where is she now?"

"I don't know, and I don't really care."

"You really told her to leave?"

"Yeah, and I should've told her the second we saw her in Playa del Carmen." He took her hands. "I'm so sorry."

She debated telling him about the photo but was so happy to see him that she didn't feel like digging the magnifying glass out and explaining the whole story. It didn't matter anymore. She'd save it for another time.

"I want to stay with you tonight."

"Me too."

They found her friends, who looked just as stunned as his had when she'd entered their hotel room. He phoned his friends from Jill's cell phone, and they all came down to the bar. The night ended up being a blast, all their friends together; it wasn't one last hurrah before she became tied down. It was a good reason to be with all their closest friends at the same time, something that rarely occurred. She wondered why they hadn't planned it this way to begin with. When they returned to the Marriott, they got their own room. He would be her last fling before the wedding.

·33·

Rehearsal Casualties

$\mathcal{S}$he'd always imagined herself running around like a chicken with its head cut off the week before the wedding. Contradictory to what she'd believed, she was remarkably calm. She had one last fitting for her dress and a trial run for her hair. There were gift bags to stuff for the out-of-town guests staying at the Rancho Bernardo Inn, and she needed to pick out gifts for her parents and Ethan's parents for hosting the wedding and rehearsal dinner. These were all loose ends that only took a couple days.

As she loitered around the house she found it impossible to relax. She felt as if she needed to be doing *something*. She spoke with Peg Migillicuddy nearly every day and called her the Thursday before the wedding to go over some last-minute details. She also needed the number of the band they'd hired, Wayne Foster Entertainment.

"Ah yes, dear. Here it is." She read the number to Cate. "Now please don't hesitate to call me with any concerns or questions in the next couple days." Peg had been wonderful. She'd faxed a schedule over several days earlier, and Cate didn't have to worry about much except getting up and having her hair and makeup done the day of the wedding. Everything else was outlined in the schedule, and Peg would make sure it all went according to plan.

She called the band's office and spoke with a very friendly and thorough program director. They discussed who would give toasts and which songs Cate wanted played. "I also have one other request," Cate said. "My fiancé is really nervous about the first dance, and I was wondering if it would be possible to get it over with first-thing, right when we come in after the grand entrance?"

"Oh yes. Of course," she said.

"And would it be possible for you to invite everyone to join us on the dance floor shortly after we start dancing so the spotlight isn't on us for too long? He really doesn't want everyone to watch us the whole time."

"Absolutely. This is a very common request," she said. "We have a lot of nervous grooms, and we do that all the time."

This brought a load of relief, and now Ethan would be able to sleep at night. "What we'll do," the program director said. "Is invite the bridal party to join you on the dance floor. Then we'll invite the parents to join you, and then we'll invite all the guests. Because if we just start off by saying, 'Everyone join the bride and groom,' people will be reluctant."

The woman was a pro. "That's perfect," Cate said.

"And let me tell you something else. You tell him not to focus on his feet—not to even worry about how he's dancing. You tell him to focus directly on you, just to look into your eyes. And I'll tell you what, the love that's on his face will be far more interesting than any dance steps he's doing. The only thing that people will notice is the look in his eyes."

"That's great advice."

"Well, after all my experience I've always found that the ones who take the lessons and have a routine mapped-out miss all the romance. It just looks stiff."

She couldn't wait to tell Ethan this. Dropping out of dance class had been the best thing they'd ever done.

* * *

The morning of the rehearsal dinner Oscar barfed on their bed-spread. What he was doing in the bedroom by himself was something neither Ethan nor Cate could explain. She was cleaning up the pile of barf when she noticed something glistening in the pile, like a small jewel in a world of tan colored crap. She leaned in closer to look and gasped when she noticed an eye staring back at her. The eye of the Ben Bridge Bear Ethan had gotten her for Christmas a couple years earlier. His chest had zipped open, and when she'd opened it on Christmas she'd found a little sapphire necklace inside.

The death of her stuffed animal was confirmed when she found its shredded remains scattered about the bathroom. Grease stood on the edge of the tub, eyeing the tattered carcass.

Sadly, she threw away the remains of her bear, eulogizing the fan-tasies she had about giving it to their first child, explaining to their tod-dler that Daddy had given it to her on Christmas the first year they'd started dating. It was meant to be passed down for generations.

"The bear!" Ethan said from behind her.

"Yes, Oscar killed him." She stuffed his last limb into the bag. "What a . . ." His voice trailed off in exasperation as he mumbled some-thing about how out of control the dog was.

After she cleaned up, she quickly showered and dressed. She'd al-ready packed her bags for the following two nights. She'd be checking in to her parents' house until the wedding. Ethan would stay with Rita and Charles, and he was taking Oscar with him.

She was just about to head out the door when the phone rang. Denise. She almost left without answering. She could always say she was going to be late for the manicure and bridesmaid luncheon and avoid talking to her, but what if she needed directions or something? She'd have to face her at some point.

"Hi, Denise."

"Oh hey, Cate. I was wondering if I would get you before you left."

"I'm actually just running out the door." *So make it quick.* "Do you need directions to the salon?"

"No. I know where it is. Um, I was calling because I wanted to ask you if you care if I wear my magenta heels? It's just that, you know, a manicure and pedicure are going to be at least thirty dollars. And, honestly, I've already spent a over two hundred dollars with my alterations and everything on my dress. I took today off work for the wedding, and I've had to put in extra hours this week just to make sure I end up getting paid. Then I have to get my hair done on top of it. I mean, this whole wedding is costing me a lot. So . . . I know you wanted us to wear black heels, but is it that big of a deal if I don't wear them?"

There were so many things wrong with this conversation that she didn't know where to begin. She was speechless.

"Like I said, things are getting really steep with the cost, and I don't really want to spend another thirty, forty dollars on shoes. I tried my magenta shoes on with the dress, and they look great."

She almost wanted to hang up, pretend the line had gone dead, and ignore Denise for the rest of the day. "I'm sorry our wedding has been such a financial burden on you," she said, trying to control her astonishment.

"Well, it just seems like a lot just to be a bridesmaid."

Cate could feel the handle of her suitcase digging into her palm and set it down. "I'll pay for your shoes. Okay? How does that sound?" Never mind that Denise made six figures a year in commission. What was she talking about with a salary? Denise's commission alone covered Cate's yearly earnings as a teacher.

Cate was too busy to discuss Denise's shoes, and the last thing she needed was a guilt trip the day before she was supposed to walk down the aisle. Cate had spent three times the amount of money that Denise had forked over in almost every wedding she'd been in. And who the hell doesn't have a pair of black heels?

"I'm not asking you to pay for my shoes," Denise said. "I'm just asking if it's *that* big of a deal if I don't wear black ones."

"It's no big deal, Denise. You'll be the only one, but if that's what makes you comfortable I don't mind. All right?"

"Yeah, cuz I mean I know you have a lot going on and the last thing I expect you to do is pay for my shoes." *Oh really? But you certainly have no problem disrupting my day to make me feel bad.*

"Denise, I really have to go. I'll see you at French Nail Design. And if you're worried about missing work, you don't have to come. I never told anyone they had to miss work today. The whole event was optional. It's not that big of a deal. All right?"

"Oh. Well, no, I'll be there. I want to come. I have something to show you."

Whatever.

After she said good-bye, she slammed the phone down.

"What's wrong?" Ethan asked.

She knew it would probably embarrass him to hear about his cousin's bad manners, and for a moment she debated keeping it all to herself. However, she was angry and she had to get it off her chest. She told Ethan the story, repeating verbatim what Denise had said.

"Are you kidding me?" he asked. "She's like the richest bridesmaid in the wedding!"

"I know. Whatever. The whole thing is so ridiculous there aren't even words." She shook her head. "I've paid for so many updos and dyed shoes, and ugly dresses and jewelry for other people's weddings. But you know what? Even if they hadn't asked me I would've done it anyway. Because it's part of the fun, and I always wanted to look good. It's a formal event. No one ever even had to *ask* me." It was true. She was the type of bridesmaid who'd simply gone along with the program, even if it had sent her into credit-card debt and taken up all her free time. She thought she'd been nice by telling the girls they could wear any black heels. She'd always assumed black heels were a staple in every woman's wardrobe.

"I'm going to say something to her." Ethan said. "I can't believe her.

She shouldn't have committed to being in the wedding if she didn't want to spend the money."

"No, Ethan. Don't. Just forget about it. I don't even care. If she wants to be in all our pictures looking as if she's about to take a trip down the Yellow Brick Road, that's fine. I'm not going to worry about this. I have so much to do today. Really, Denise's shoes are the least of my concerns. It's just the way she made me feel so guilty that bugs me."

He kissed her on the forehead, then lifted her chin. "I'm sorry."

"It's not your fault."

By the time she reached her parents' house she had forgotten all about Denise.

She met all her bridesmaids at the nail salon, and several of her out-of-town relatives joined them. Gran came, and two of her aunts. They took up the entire salon. Having her extended family in town suddenly made her so excited for the weekend.

Twenty minutes passed, and Denise still hadn't made an appearance. She wondered if she'd even have time to get a manicure and pedicure.

She was sitting with her feet in a tub of warm, sudsy water when Val turned to her. "I didn't know Denise drove a Jaguar."

"She doesn't. She drives a Camry."

"Isn't that her?" Val pulled her hand away from the Vietnamese woman who was filing her nails, and pointed outside.

"That *is* her." Cate watched as Denise locked the front door of a sparkling gold Jaguar. "She got a new car?" And apparently new sunglasses too. She pulled a pair of pilot's glasses over her eyes before tossing her hair over her shoulder. Apparently, she needed a new attitude to go along with her chic ride. However, the shades didn't really match her outfit. She wore a plain, short-sleeved cream-colored sweater and tapered yellow pants that should've been burned in the early nineties, along with her lace-up boots.

This must've been what she was talking about when she said she needed to show Cate something.

"You got a new car!" Cate said as soon as she stepped inside.

"Yes! I just bought it yesterday. The brakes died on the Camry last week, and I figured why sink more money into that car. This one will be much better for clients."

"It's nice!" Cate said, when what she really wanted to say was, *You can't afford a measly thirty dollars for black heels, but you can afford a brand-new Jag?*

Denise decided to skip the pedicure. She only had her nails done. After they were finished pampering themselves they went to a little French café in Pacific Beach for lunch. Denise followed them to the restaurant, and Cate caught glimpses of her in the rearview mirror. She drove with her windows rolled down, and Kelly Clarkson blasted from the speakers of her new car. They could hear the music every time they stopped at a light, and Denise kept checking herself out on the side mirror in the Jag.

"She's such a weirdo," Jill said.

"I know."

All her bridesmaids took a million pictures during lunch. As they'd gotten older the opportunities for them to all spend time together had become scarce over the years. Soon they'd all start having babies, and opportunities would be very rare.

"Get used to all the photos," Sarah said as she snapped one of Cate with Val and Leslie. "You're going to have enough pictures to wallpaper a large house when this is all over with."

After lunch there was a brief amount of time to nap before the rehearsal, but she ended up talking to Al in her parents' kitchen. At thirty-five, he still looked exactly the same as he had when he was in college. The only difference was that he was graying around the temples. She told him stories about Ava and Stu, and he laughed hysterically.

"You nervous?" he asked.

"A little bit. But I'm getting excited too. Now that it's finally here."

"Well, here, have a glass of red wine," he said.

He began uncorking a bottle on her parents' kitchen counter. "Any excuse to sip a little vino should never be passed up." They sipped a glass of wine before it was time to get ready for the rehearsal dinner.

She was on her way upstairs to get ready when Gran popped her head out of the guest bedroom. Her little body looked even smaller in the tall doorway.

"Hey, honey."

"Hi, Gran. Did you have a nice nap?"

"Yes. Come here," she whispered.

Cate stepped closer, and she could smell her gardenia-scented perfume.

"How are you doing?" Gran asked.

"A little nervous, but okay."

"Well listen, don't tell your mother. But I have some Valium if you think you need one. It's a very light pill. It won't knock you out or anything."

She couldn't believe her little grandmother was offering her drugs. She was the best.

"Well . . . let me think about it. I don't know if I've really reached that point yet."

"Well, you just let me know. Don't be afraid to ask."

She'd picked out her dress months in advance and had hunted high and low in every single dress boutique in Fashion Valley for it. It was a cream-colored strapless tea-length dress with an A-line skirt and black buttons up the back. She'd also splurged on a pair of black patent Marc Jacobs peep-toe pumps with little bows on the front. She added a final accent with a black brooch shaped as a rose. It was the one time she got to dress like Reese Witherspoon before a movie premiere, so she'd set her sights high.

She was supposed to ride with Ethan's parents to the church. They were all going to meet at the Padgetts' house and caravan. There were so many relatives in town that they needed all the carpooling they could get. Denise ended up driving them in her new Jaguar. Charles rode in the front seat, and Cate sat with Rita and Ethan in the back. The smell of the new car was strong and clean, and the leather seats were gorgeous.

Denise sounded like a car salesman when she pointed out all its features, and by the time they reached the chapel Cate wanted one.

The rehearsal went quickly and smoothly, which was great because she sensed everyone was starving and antsy and not in the mood to line up like little kids all night. She walked back to the Jaguar with Rita. "This is so exciting!" She hugged Cate.

"I know. I can't believe it's finally here." The air outside was clear but a little crisp. She pulled her pashmina around her shoulders. "Doesn't it seem like just yesterday that we got engaged?"

Rita looked over her shoulder then turned back to Cate. Her voice was low when she spoke. "Denise will be getting shoes."

"What?" She'd told Ethan not to say anything about it. The last thing she wanted was a big family blowout over a pair of heels the day before the wedding. "I asked Ethan not to make a big deal out of it. I really didn't want him to say anything."

Rita shook her head. "He didn't. Denise told me what she said to you this afternoon." She paused. "You know, I rarely say anything to Denise if she's out of line. She's like my daughter in many ways, but she's a grown woman. She can make her own decisions and choices, and I usually don't get involved. However, after she told me what she said to you . . ." Her voice trailed off. "I had to tell her how awful I thought it was that she called you the day before the wedding and said all that."

"You didn't have to do that. I never wanted to cause any problems for anyone. It's not a big deal if she wants to wear her magenta shoes." Just saying those words made her feel as if she were talking about one of her students.

"Well, she's getting shoes." She pulled Cate into a hug. "I just can't tell you how happy we are to have you be a part of this family. We all love you so much."

"Thanks," she said. She really needed to hear that. She'd always wondered if Denise had an influence over Rita and Charles. "I love you guys too."

On the way back to the Blakleys' house, Denise opened the sunroof. A blast of cold air poured into the car, and Cate's hair whipped over her forehead and cheeks. Ethan put his arm around her to warm her body, but her bare shoulders still felt icy, and her body shivered.

"I have a surprise for you guys!" It was hard to hear Denise over the blasting wind.

She fiddled with the CD player until their song came blasting from the speakers. "It's your wedding song!" She yelled.

"Thanks!" Cate said, wishing she'd close the damn sunroof.

"I BOUGHT THE CD TODAY AFTER RITA TOLD ME THAT I WAS DRIVING!"

It was a thoughtful gesture, but Denise's driving was scaring her a little. She sped onto the freeway and weaved in and out of traffic all the way back to La Jolla. Twice, people honked at them. Cate sat smashed in between Rita and Ethan, and she felt Rita's body become tense every time Denise switched lanes. They pulled off the freeway, and she darted up the windy curves to their neighborhood.

"Just park in the driveway!" Rita shouted over the wind and music.

"HUH?" Denise yelled over her shoulder.

"I said, you can just park in the driveway!"

"Why don't you turn the music down?" Charles shouted.

She reached for a knob on the stereo, and as she did so, Oscar darted across the driveway. Cate's scream was louder than Marvin Gaye.

"WATCH OOOOOOUT!" Ethan shouted.

Oscar missed the car by a millimeter. The dog was one lucky bastard because when Denise went to hit the brakes, she accidentally stepped full throttle on the gas pedal and drove straight through the Blakelys' garage door. The sound of would splitting was deafening. In a blur, Cate watched as a ladder and a reindeer lawn ornament smashed onto the hood of the Jaguar.

"Holy shit!" Ethan shouted. He immediately turned to Cate. "Are you okay?"

"Yeah, I'm fine." Her heart pounded so hard she thought it might pop from her chest. "Are *you* okay?"

"Yes. I'm all right." He looked to the front of the car. "Denise?"

She was too busy pushing away her air bag to answer.

Charles had managed to open his door and was no longer smashed beneath his air bag. His hair was ruffled and cheeks red from the air bag that had deployed. He helped Rita from the backseat.

Cate looked at the wooden garage door in ten million splinters over the mangled hood of her Jaguar. A box of Christmas-tree ornaments had fallen from the rafters and spilled all over the car.

"I'm okay!" Denise called as she shoved the bag away from her face. Her face looked contorted when she noticed the mess. Not only was the front of her brand-new luxury car smashed, but she'd destroyed the Blakelys' garage door, rear-ended the back of Charles's Mercedes, and damaged half their Christmas decorations.

"My caaaaar!" she yelled.

Rita helped her from the front seat. "I'm just relieved you're okay."

"My caaaahaahaahaar!" She sobbed.

The guests started to arrive in small groups, and they all stopped to survey the damage. "Holy shit," Jill said under her breath. "What happened?"

"She hit the gas instead of the brakes."

"You guys are lucky to be alive."

Eventually Cate left the damage to head in to the reception. Her neck felt a little sore from the impact of the crash, and she prayed her whiplash wasn't severe. She envisioned herself looking like a robot as she headed down the aisle tomorrow.

Oscar had dug a hole under the Blakelys' back fence, and that's why he'd been running loose. Despite the small mountain he'd created, the Blakelys' backyard looked beautiful. Little lanterns hung from every trellis, and candles and rose petals covered all the tables. A tent covered the patio, and they'd gotten heat lamps.

Cate looked around at the two families and wondered who would be the wedding drunk tomorrow. There was always a wedding drunk and a freaky relative at every wedding. As she looked around she actually concluded the freakish relative was someone from her side of the family, her father's brother, Seymour. Clearly the black sheep, he was an Elvis impersonator in Vegas. His sideburns were as thick and hairy as a shag rug, and he'd brought a showgirl with him to the event even though he'd RSVP'd for one person.

Good Time Catering had provided all the food, and Ethan's partner, Sean, had been in charge of making sure everything ran smoothly. Each guest had their choice of salmon in Thai sesame sauce, filet mignon with gorgonzola, or chicken stuffed with sun-dried tomatoes.

She and Ethan sat with Al and all their grandparents and parents. Nana was quiet for most of the dinner and asked a few times if anyone knew how to get back to her house. Cate was actually starting to think Oma was on her best behavior too. However, she became a tad worried when Oma turned a bloodshot eye on her.

"Cate?" She sounded like a man who'd been smoking for twenty years.

"Yes?"

"What the hell is that on your chest?" She pointed.

Cate looked down at her pin. "A brooch."

"A brooch? Well, what the hell is it supposed to be?"

"It's a rose." Wasn't it kind of obvious?

"It looks like a piece of charcoal."

Ethan tried to come to the rescue. "It's the latest trend, Oma."

"The latest scam!" She yelled. "And she fell for it. Trends are just scams."

"Anyone need a refill?" Al asked, holding up a bottle of wine. She sensed he was only trying to change the subject, and Cate loved him for it.

"Sure. I could use one." She held out her glass. He began to pour. Her glass filled with an inch of white wine before the bottle was emptied.

"I'll get more," he said.

"That's okay. Let me," Cate offered.

"No." He stood up, taking the old bottle of wine with him.

"There's plenty more wine in the kitchen," Charles said. "Just make sure you don't let Oscar out when you open the back door."

Cate watched him walk to the back door in his clerics. He opened the door, and Oscar came tearing through the narrow crack. It wasn't Al's fault that the dog could run faster than the speed of light. "Come here, Oscar!" he yelled. Cate had barely stood when Oscar jumped on Al's back and slammed him and the bottle of wine against the sliding glass door.

Before he'd hit the door, he'd held his hands up to shield his face, and the big end of the wine bottle had hit him right above the eye. Thank God none of the glass had shattered, but the impact of the bottle looked painful. Ethan sprinted to the rescue and dragged Oscar by his collar back into the house.

"Al, my God—I mean gosh. Gosh. Are you okay?" Cate asked as soon as she reached him.

"Yeah, I'm fine." He tried to laugh, but Cate sensed he was only trying to be nice. His eye was swelling up like an egg.

"Does your eye hurt?"

"A little."

"Al, it looks terrible."

Connie immediately provided an ice pack. "Here, Al. This will help. Put it on there right away." She held the pack to his eye until he got hold of it. Then she turned to Cate. "Why don't guys just give Oscar to The Humane Society?" she asked as if she were suggesting they donate an unwanted couch to a thrift store.

"Mother!"

"What?"

"We can't do that."

"Why not? Someone will want him. I'm sure he'll get adopted."

"He just wanted to play with Al. He doesn't realize how strong he is."

Their dog might be a raving terrorist, but Cate didn't have the heart to send him to the pound. She apologized to Al a million more times before the night ended, and he insisted he was fine. However, he didn't look fine. She could already see blue and purple traces of a bruise.

Denise had crashed the car. Oma's insults were relentless, and now the priest that would lead their ceremony had a black eye. If this was any indication of how the wedding would unfold she was definitely going to need that Valium.

· 3 4 ·

Here Comes the Bride

Cate awoke at five a.m. the morning of the wedding, and she was pretty sure she'd only fallen asleep a few hours earlier. However, she wasn't tired, and decided to start the day.

It had been a long time since she'd taken an early-morning walk on the beach. She felt jittery and figured a little stroll in the fresh air would do her some good. She was on her way out the door when she heard the guest bedroom door creak open behind her.

"Hey," she heard Gran's whisper and spun around. "Remember what we talked about?" she said, her head peeking from the doorframe. "You want it?"

A drug deal was going on in her mother's house. Cate shrugged. "As long as it doesn't knock me out or make me like the sister in *Sixteen Candles*."

Gran shook her head. "No. It will just calm you a little. I promise. I take them every time I have to do a reading at church. I'll just give you half of one."

"Okay."

Gran disappeared back into her room then returned holding a tiny broken pill. "You might want to save it for later. It's such a small dose, it might not last that long. Don't tell your mother. Okay?"

"My lips are sealed."

She put the pill in her pocket then left for her walk. She ended up sitting on the beach for a while. She loved the beach when it was this way. She shared miles of sand and white foamy waves with only a few diehard surfers. She used to walk to the beach a lot as a little girl with Emily on Saturday mornings. She'd lie back in the sand and look at the early morning fog overhead, listening to the waves and the sound of the seagulls crying as they searched for stray potato chips. As she lay in the sand she realized that she would never be that little girl returning to the beach again. She'd be married after today, and possibly returning with her own children sometime down the road.

Life would never be the same. She expected a bittersweet feeling of angst to creep on her, a sad feeling associated with letting go. However, she only felt peace. She felt truly and completely at ease. She was ready. She pulled Gran's pill from her pocket and threw it into the water.

She felt much better when she returned. She soaked in a hot tub then left for the Rancho Bernardo Inn to meet all the girls. Her mother came with her so she could have her hair done as well. Denise was the only one who wouldn't be getting ready with them. She was having her own hairstylist do it. Cate had given her specific instructions to arrive at the Inn at ten thirty *sharp*. The limo would be leaving at eleven o'clock—with or without her.

Jill was doing Cate's hair, and she'd recruited three other stylists from her salon to handle the bridesmaids. She knew they were in good hands. When Cate entered the room they all began singing.

"Goin to the chapel, and we're gonna get maaarried!"

They only sang a few lines, and she clapped when they were finished. She hugged them all, one by one. The atmosphere in the room was relaxed while they had their hair and makeup done. Her father stopped by with bagels and orange juice, and the girls munched on food while they primped.

Cate was too nervous to be hungry, but everyone insisted she eat something, so she took small bites of a plain bagel with strawberry cream cheese. The time flew past, and before she knew it, it was time to step into her dress. "Let me just pee one more time before I get dressed," she said.

"Cate." Connie looked disgusted. "That's not really a pretty thing for a bride to say. You sound like you weren't raised with any manners."

"Oh, excuse me." Cate imitated a horribly fake and snooty British accent. "Please allow me to take a moment in the powder room."

"That's better."

She found the bathroom in the suite occupied. She waited outside the door and thought whoever was in there certainly was taking an awfully long time. Maybe this person had gotten a snag in their panty hose. She was about to knock when she heard the faint sound of vomiting. Dear God, had they been getting drunk without telling her? If someone had a flask, she wanted a sip.

She knocked. "Hello?" Cate called. "Who's in there?"

"Cate?" It was Beth's voice, and she sounded weak. If they'd been getting drunk, they'd sure done a good job of hiding it. She would've never suspected that Beth had been drinking.

"Beth, are you okay?"

"Just a minute." Cate heard the sound of running water and gargling. When Beth opened the door her face looked green.

"Beth, are you okay?"

"Just a little queasy."

Then it occurred to her. "Oh my . . . are you pregnant?"

She nodded.

"Oh my God!" She jumped up, then hugged her. "Beth! This is so exciting! Why didn't you say something?"

She held a finger to her lips. "I'm only two months along. The doctor said it was best not to tell anyone until after twelve weeks."

"Beth, I'm so happy for you."

"I really didn't want you to find out like this. I don't want this to interfere with your day at all."

"It's not!"

A knock startled them. It was Emily. "We have to get you in your dress soon. The limos are waiting."

"Okay," she called. "Just give me a couple minutes."

"Listen," Beth said. "Don't worry about me. Okay? Just continue on like you have no idea."

When Cate returned from the bathroom the girls were waiting with her dress. She stepped inside, and Connie zipped up the back. She also helped pin and straighten her veil.

Her mother wiped a tear from her eye when she looked at Cate, and Cate found it hard to look at her. If she saw her mother cry, she'd probably start bawling too.

Her father came to walk with them to the limo, and Cate took one look at her parents together before bursting into tears. Her mother looked so beautiful in her pale pink suit, and her dad would soon give her away. She thought she'd gotten all her emotional sappiness out when she'd listened to Pachelbel's Canon, but apparently she'd been wrong.

The first words from her mouth were, "My makeup. Ahhhhhh! I'm ruining my makeup."

She was bombarded by her bridal squad with a dozen handkerchiefs and tissues. "That's good," Sarah said. "Get it all out now. *Before* you head down the aisle."

She took a deep breath and wiped away the last of the tears. Val was waiting with fresh concealer and mascara for touch-ups. "No worries," she said. "Your makeup still looks perfect."

She took a glimpse in the mirror and owed thanks to the grace of God for keeping her makeup intact. It truly was a miracle.

Emily and Sarah each carried a side of her cathedral-length veil to the limo. The day could not have been more beautiful. The air was dry and warm, and the sky a deep, clear blue.

Peg Migillicuddy waited for them with the chauffeur. "You look absolutely lovely!"

"Thanks," Cate said.

"So is this everyone, dear?"

"Yes—er, uh, no. We're missing Denise." She looked around, just to double-check that she hadn't slipped in sometime during her emotional meltdown. "She's not here. I told her to be here at ten thirty. What time is it?"

"Ten fifty."

Cate sighed. Just as she was about to ask someone to call her, the sound of screeching tires came around the driveway of the Rancho Bernardo Inn. She could see the smashed hood of the Jaguar, and the front bumper dangled from the car. "There she is."

"Oh good then. We'll be right on schedule," Peg said as she marked something on her clipboard.

Denise waved as she sped past them and into the parking lot. Cate could definitely tell that she'd gotten her hair done, although it was unclear exactly what she'd done. She'd driven by so fast that her brown hair had looked tight and smashed against her head. Perhaps she'd gone for a classic bun at the nape of her neck. Maybe there was hope for her. Cate had suspected she might show up with large barrel curls sticking from her head like cupcakes and ringlets dangling around her ears.

"Why don't you climb in the limo, dear?" Peg said. "I'll wait for Denise. I'd just hate for Ethan to arrive a few minutes early and see you, dear."

"Yes, I definitely don't want Ethan to see me."

The girls helped with her veil as she climbed inside, and she wrapped it gently to the side so it could rest on her lap.

She could hear the sound of Denise's heels clicking all the way to the limo, and then Peg's voice. "Oh my," she muttered. "Wherever did you have your hair done?"

"Electric Hair."

"Ah, okay." There was a moment of silence before Peg told her to join the other girls in the limo.

It wasn't Denise that Cate noticed first. It was actually Cousin Val's tortured expression. From where Val was sitting she had a head-on view of Denise climbing into the limo, and the look on her face suggested that Ted Bundy was about to join them.

The first thing Cate thought of when she saw Denise was the rapper Exhibit who hosted MTV's *Pimp My Ride*. She'd gotten her hair done, all right. Tight rows of braids covered her head—like Bo Derek. However, she didn't look like Bo Derek. She looked like Ice Cube in a bridesmaid dress.

"Do you guys like my hair?" One would've thought she was kidding, but the smile on her face was sincere. She was genuinely proud of herself.

Most of the girls shared the same expression as Val and seemed as if they'd been stricken mute since her arrival.

Cate spoke first. "Yeah, it's uh . . . definitely . . . not what I would've ever expected on you. Certainly creative . . . and so original."

"Yeah, well, I really wanted to do something original. I think I'm always really stuck in a box when it comes to fashion, and I just thought that now would be the time to try something new." She was excited when she spoke, and Cate had never seen her so animated. "I never get my hair done, and then yesterday when I was flipping through an old *People* magazine at the nail salon I saw a picture of Christina Aguilera with her hair like this. I thought, *That's how I want to wear my hair for the wedding!*"

And she hadn't run this by anyone? If she'd even held up the picture to one person and asked their opinion, she'd probably have a nice chignon at the nape of her neck right now. In a way, it was nice to see that Denise was coming out her square fashion box, but Cate had never imagined she'd go to such extremes. Her black shoes also made quite a statement. They were the kind of shoes that Cate imagined strippers wore. Huge, long thick heels, and straps that ran up her ankles. It was hard not to stare at her on the way to the church.

Upon arrival at Founders Chapel they were immediately whisked in to photos. When she'd taken photos during all her friends' weddings, she'd always thought the photography session had seemed like grueling, never-ending torture. However, at her own wedding, everything seemed to be on overdrive. She was afraid if she blinked she might miss something.

Right before it was time to head down the aisle, she took a deep breath and reminded herself to enjoy the moment. It was all going by so fast, and she was afraid if she didn't relax she'd miss all the important details. She took a few deep breaths as her bridesmaids headed through the double doors to the soft sound of violins.

Her father kissed her on the cheek before it was time to go. "I'm so proud of you," he said.

She'd never forget the way his eyes squinted around the edges when he spoke, or the feeling of his strong elbow when they linked arms. She noticed the way the golden afternoon sun flooded though the stained glass windows, and the way that Ethan's hands were crossed over one another while he waited for her. She'd never forget the look in his eyes. He looked at her as if she were the only person in the room. She saw the long white and gold robes that Al wore—his black eye. She'd never forgive the dog. She recognized faces of friends and family members. Some dabbed at tears, while others nodded. When she took Ethan's hands in her own she never wanted to look back down that aisle.

The ceremony went by quickly. Because Ethan wasn't Catholic, Al had advised them not to have a Catholic Mass.

A vintage Rolls-Royce waited for them in the front of Founders Chapel when they were finished, and Ethan held on to her veil as they climbed inside.

"You look absolutely beautiful," he said.

"Thank you." They kissed, and the photographer stuck his head in the window and snapped away at them.

"I'm serious," Ethan said. "I expected you to look gorgeous, but you really exceeded my expectations. You look amazing."

"You do too," she said. "Were you nervous?"

"I was dying while I was standing there waiting for you. I honestly thought my knees were gonna buckle when the bridesmaids were coming down the aisle. But as soon as I saw you . . . I don't know. I just felt calm."

They popped open a bottle of champagne, and the bubbles spilled onto the floor. They toasted then talked about the ceremony and how fast everything had flown by. They paused to wave at cars that honked.

Between the two of them, they drank the entire bottle of champagne on the way to the Rancho Bernardo Inn. Surprisingly, she didn't feel buzzed. On the contrary, her senses had never seemed more acute, and she felt as if adrenaline was still coursing through her veins.

She could see tons of friends walking into the hotel. She wanted to say hi, but they were whisked into another half hour of photos. They finished photos just before the grand entrance.

As they were waiting in line to go in, it became it extremely obvious who the title of wedding drunk belonged to. It was Oma. Usually, the drunks didn't surface until a couple hours into the reception. Judging from the way she was dancing, there could only be one excuse. She was hammered. She stood on the dance floor, solo, doing the chicken dance to Lionel Ritchie's "All Night Long." Bowlegged, she moved around the floor flapping her folded arms like wings. It took two of Ethan's friends from college to drag her away so they could start introducing the wedding party.

The band went above and beyond her expectations. They'd had backup singers and a horn section, and the pianist was amazing. They'd taken the program director's advice and only focused on one another. They hardly noticed anything else in the room. The first dance went by smoothly and without any hitches, and after the song ended they were received with a round of applause.

They decided to start making their rounds of saying hello to all the guests early. She was heading off the dance floor when Nana grabbed her elbow.

"Well hello," Nana said. For a moment Cate thought it was one of the rare occasions when Nana had a moment of clarity and actually remembered her.

"Hi, Nana." She hugged her.

"You look pretty," Nana said.

"Thank you."

"But the bride and groom really look the best."

"Who are the bride and groom?" Cate asked.

"Well don't you know? The couple dancing on the dance floor. The one right there." She pointed to Emily and her father.

Cate was tempted to point out that she was the bride, but thought it was a little obvious, considering what she was wearing. They helped Nana to her table then made rounds to some of the tables.

The evening flew by as quickly as the day had, and before she knew it they were cutting the cake and getting ready for the final song by the band.

"I've had the time of my life," Ethan said as they listened to the band play "Hey, Hey Good-bye." "I honestly feel like I'm floating."

The last of the guests trickled out. It felt bittersweet as she realized it was all coming to an end. The videographer managed to corner them for some final words.

"Tell the camera how you feel about the night," he said.

"Everything has been perfect," Ethan said with the microphone in his hand. "I have never been happier. In all my dreams I would've never expected anything like this."

Cate sort of felt like they were on a cheesy episode of *The Wedding Story* and wasn't as comfortable expressing herself with a microphone and a bright light shining in her eyes. "There is a bright light shining in my face, but it's not as bright as the love I feel for this guy right here." She elbowed Ethan in the ribs. He leaned down to kiss her.

"Great," the videographer said. The camera was still running. "Plans for the future?"

They thought for a moment.

"Do you think you'll have kids any time soon?" Connie chimed in from the background.

Ethan and Cate exchanged glances then turned back to the camera. "That's a secret."

They smiled into the camera then walked from the wedding, hand in hand, toward their new life together. The future was bright.

LYLES

Lyles, Whitney.
Here comes the bride

$ 13.00